T0367958

Briefly Borrowed

Also by Loryn Kramer Staley

The Righteous Enemy
1230 North Garfield
Thunder's Glory

Briefly Borrowed

LORYN KRAMER STALEY

ARCHWAY
PUBLISHING

Archway Publishing books may be ordered through booksellers or by contacting:

Archway Publishing
1663 Liberty Drive
Bloomington, IN 47403
www.archwaypublishing.com
844-669-3957

ISBN: 978-1-6657-1628-4 (sc)
ISBN: 978-1-6657-1629-1 (e)

Library of Congress Control Number: 2022900956

Print information available on the last page.

Archway Publishing rev. date: 01/19/2022

Dedicated
to
My Cowboy

CHAPTER 1

An older-model SUV cruises the park's graveled lot. With each turn, the four-door draws the attention of new mothers pushing trendy strollers and hikers setting out to enjoy the park's many trails. Tank DeLoach, the car's driver, waits in the shadows for a station wagon to make its exit from a spot under the feathery branches of a weeping willow before claiming the narrow space. Displaying the confidence of a seasoned athlete, he grabs a running shoe from the back seat. Unable to reach its partner, he steps from the car, where he plucks cockleburs from his socks.

Holding both shoes, he breaks free the caked-on mud a previous run left behind. A marathon runner with many trophies under his belt, he secures the laces with a knot he learned to appreciate during a brief stint in the navy. Giving a necessary stretch, he throws lean arms over his head and raises tight legs to his chest. By happenstance, he exchanges a timely nod with a lanky runner whose eyes are hidden behind aviator sunglasses.

"Have a good one," he offers as the runner passes by.

A glance at his wrist sends him back to the SUV. Observing the park's patrons, he places his watch under the driver's seat before returning to the shade the willow offers. Positioned behind the tree's slim girth, he watches a black sedan circle the lot.

Rounding the corner, Clay Lambert invites a smile to cross his face. His target in sight, he lets up on the accelerator before coming to a stop near the park's water fountain.

As if catching a taxi, Tank crosses over the sidewalk, jogs down the street, and picks up his pace as he rounds the corner onto Whiskey Hill Lane. When the sedan pulls up to the street's edge, he slides into the passenger seat.

"How are you doing?"

"Don't ask. It's better you don't know. I was up before the paperboy," Clay offers.

"Riding shotgun feels appropriate."

"Looking good, my man."

"It was a short run. I didn't have a chance to break a sweat."

The next turn, another right, places them on Old Lighthouse Road, a two-lane street in a working-class neighborhood lined with modest homes and a bike path meant to protect those willing to share the road. Driving alongside cars he knows all too well, Clay eases up on the gas. With the passing of each house, his heart quickens. These people are his neighbors. Many are friends. Several have been in his home and know his son. When schedules allow, they often break bread together.

He continues to wonder who called his office out of concern. The message was brief and to the point: *Your wife is having an affair.* Months later, he continues to question which left the darkest bruise— the message or the knowing smirk on his assistant's face when she slapped the folded note into his hand.

When they reach his split-level house, he lets off the gas, rolls to a stop, and, giving a dramatic sigh, parks his tires. "Something tells me if this were a novel, I'd be wise to leave out the remaining chapters."

"You've lost me."

"A mystery—possibly one involving murder. That said, don't expect a fairy-tale ending."

"What are we looking for?"

"Skip over the grass to the big window."

"The one with blackout curtains?"

"Yep. The drapes are pulled. That's the signal. Same time every Tuesday and Thursday. Just like clockwork. I'll give her this: she's consistent."

Tank gives the house the once-over. Pulling sunglasses from his face, he eyes the climbing wisteria and the roof's fallen gutters. His wife often closes the drapes at the approach of the afternoon sun, especially when it beats down on their ranch's living room. He has never considered a pulled shade a signal until now.

Weeks earlier, when Clay asked him to be his wingman, Tank readily accepted. Now he worries they may be in danger. If anything should go wrong, it is possible they might be forced to reflect on their actions while sharing a two-cot cell.

"I'm hoping weeks of active surveillance pay off. I know firsthand this isn't her first heist." Unblinking, Clay stares straight ahead. "You OK, buddy?"

"I should be asking you. I have the easy part," Tank says, talking a big game. "We are friends, and friends never bail."

"Right back at you. These last few months have been a doozy. I've spent many sleepless nights dreading this moment. I'm tired of sleeping in the recliner. The cramp in my neck has moved down my back. It's taken a while, but I've come to accept that this wife of mine is always up to no good. Most of the time, she comes across like an angry woman who lost her husband to their housekeeper. When she comes off cruise control, she becomes a stranger to me."

"You can still change your mind. We haven't committed any crimes."

Clay follows a low laugh with a slap to his thigh. "That's what I've been doing for far too long. If I hadn't, I would have a dead body on my hands. Possibly two."

Turning away, he looks out to the street. "You don't know the half of it. Believe me when I say the time to act is now. My marriage is suffering a hijacking. Molly's a wild child without direction. Our history shows she doesn't have the tools to build a solid relationship. She's always ready to hop on the road to riches. Something tells me jail time is in her future. That girl aims high and knows no boundaries. She's always on a mission to slide into a relationship she's not part of. She flirts easily, and her lovers are briefly borrowed. By that, I mean married. She's always ready to move out of her lane and skirt into another's. Some might find her a drama queen. She spits a word or two, and suddenly, she thinks she matters. There's an old saying, something about a chicken never laying the same egg twice. Molly's a mean-ass mother-clucker who will continue to hatch a few just to prove the adage wrong."

"I call it the Humpty-Dumpty syndrome," Tank throws out.

"The what?"

"A broken egg waiting for someone to fix her."

"While that may be true, I can't live like this any longer. Some days, I miss the old Molly. Other days, I slam my hand in the door, bite the skin off my lip, and, while running in circles, forget if I'm coming or going. I'm left fearing her heightening sense of awareness is leading me to schizophrenia. She's jacked me around long enough. I swear she is the reason behind my night terrors. I've lost sleep and my spare tire."

He throws a hand to his stomach and gives it a pat. "This can't continue. It's time to play the last straw. She has me going this way, that way, and, at the end of the day, running about like a headless chicken. When she graduates me to a quick course in basket-weaving, I'll be left dragging through an afternoon throwing together floral arrangements. Next thing you know, I'll be forced to join a cult where I'm left shackled in leg irons while drinking a Moscow mule out of a paper cup. God help me if she sends me to the Russian Front. Don't get me started on cartwheels and sheets of aluminum foil." Rotating his watch, he checks the time. "Are you ready?"

"Ready as I'll ever be." A pinch of panic sticks in Tank's throat and a pull at his chest warns of danger, but if he is anything, he is a man who keeps his word. "I know we talked it over, but are you sure I shouldn't go in through the front door?"

"Has to be the garage. The front door is always locked." Again,

Clay turns away. "I've been watching." Although Molly's affair puts a bullet in his manhood, he understands his actions can cost him his medical license and land him behind bars for a lifetime. "Molly might not be a Rhodes scholar, but she's street-smart. Listen, I owe you, big time."

"You don't owe me anything. If the cops come calling, I wasn't here. I'm just a guy in running shoes trying to better my time."

"That reminds me. There is a shirt under your seat. It might throw off a witness if your whereabouts are called into question. When you leave, toss it into the back seat."

"You're sure this guy won't come charging at me?" Embarrassed by the possibility, Tank looks away. Displaying weakness is something he tries to avoid. "It's not that I'm afraid. I'm a big guy and, given my training, physically fit. Not to toot my own horn, but I believe I can outrun any clown who tries to threaten me. However, I'm not Superman. Given my trick knee and the floating bone in my foot, something tells me I can't outrun a bullet."

"I'm a stickler when it comes to details," Clay assures him. "When the time is right, I want to hear about that floating bone. As for Richard, my gut feeling is he will do just as I suspect." Growing quiet, Clay plays out the scene in his head. "The gun is clean and unloaded. Hand it over, towel and all," he says, pulling the rolled-up towel from under the seat.

Tank's eyes fill with questions he knows better than to ask. In recent weeks, he has listened to Clay work through his troubles over a cold beer and gut-bomb nachos. He has come to understand it is not advice that is needed but an ear.

"The less you know, the better," Clay tells him. "Now remember, when you get back to the park, ask someone for the time. The encounter could possibly be the alibi you might later need. Go in just like we discussed. Have I told you she's been securing the gate to the backyard with zip ties?"

"She should know that wouldn't stop you." Although they've spent hours planning the attack, Tank fears the unknown factors. It might just be he is not the only one who is armed and dangerous. "Be careful, Clay."

"It's been said *careful* is my middle name. Are you ready?"

"Yep."

"Let's do it."

Before parting, they exchange a fist bump, press their palms together, and extending two fingers, share their fraternity's secret handshake.

While Clay pulls the car into the home's wide driveway, Tank steps up to the sidewalk. Several test trials have confirmed that the home's stereo speakers and its soft music drown out street sounds and car engines. Grabbing a gun from under his seat, Clay stares at the Smith & Wesson revolver, a concealed carry with rapid shooting and agility he purchased months earlier when he first got wind of his wife's cheating ways.

Navigating the property, Tank assumes his position at the garage door, where he gives Clay a thumbs-up before pressing the remote.

Once the old aluminum door lifts off the concrete, Clay hustles his way along a narrow path leading to the home's backyard.

Molly is one gasp shy of reaching her third crescendo when she hears the garage door. "Holy crap. Clay's home," she warns, sliding over the warm sheets.

Tumbling out of bed, her lover sweeps up his jeans.

"Richard, you don't have time to get dressed. Go out the back, and for crying out loud, make a run for it."

"My car's down the street."

"I don't care if it's parked on Pluto. I'd rather he catches you out-side than in here. If pressed, I'll tell him you came by to say hello."

"Look at me. I'm naked. He's not going to buy that."

"Let me worry about what he'll buy," she says, sounding off like a dead battery. Wrapped in the bedsheet, she throws open the patio door.

"Hello, Molly, Richard," Clay says, aiming the Smith & Wesson at the man he once considered not only a friend but also a trusted confidant. "That seems a bit formal. I think Dick better describes you. I can't say I'm surprised that you haven't changed since college." Holding his aim, he turns toward Molly. "He's been snaking dates since high school."

"Put the gun down, Clay. It's not what it looks like." Although her heart is racing, now is not the time to show fear or concern.

"Are you running a brothel or are you going to tell me he gives massages on the side?"

"If that's what it will take for you to put away your gun."

"In due time," he says, stepping back.

"Why are you backing away?"

"I'm afraid your pants will catch on fire."

"I'm not wearing pants."

"So I've noticed."

The look of worry on Richard's face hints he might lose control of his bladder. Feeling a cramp in his stomach, he prays a blowout is not around the corner. A wave of uneasy growls suggests the chili relleno he enjoyed at lunch comes with a price he is not prepared to pay. Embarrassed to be caught naked, he throws his shirt over his privates. When he moves to take cover behind a chaise lounge, Clay waves the gun in his face.

"Hold it right there, partner. You need to step back inside."

"Listen, man, I'm outta here. I won't see her again, I swear. She's a vagabond."

"I don't understand."

"Always on the move. I no longer want what she's spreading. I've come to understand it is revenge she seeks. I can't swear to her level of education, but I'm damn sure she's the master of manipulation. I'm betting you will agree she's always on the hunt for a street fight. I'm guessing she didn't grow up on Angel Street," he says, referencing a street known for its many churches. "She's pure madness. She's always set to slap on a Band-Aid only to rip it away. For what it's worth, there is nothing worse than a hothead with a short fuse. Half the time, I'm worried I'll make her mad."

"Why would you say that?" Molly asks, whopping him alongside the head.

"Because I don't need what you're offering. I'm convinced you know only to hold a grudge. It's been said you're a canvas of broken pieces. When I can't put you back together, I'm in the breadbasket waiting to learn what you want next. You're only happy when you have me jumping through hoops. Next thing you know, you'll be calling me with a dog whistle. I'm betting this isn't her first rodeo," he says, shooting his eyes to Clay. "I'm guessing the law would call her an attractive nuisance—tempting to the eyes but potentially life-threatening. What's worse is she's always quick to get into my pocket."

"You've said enough," Molly says, unblinking.

"I believe you get off on creating chaos," Richard says with sorry eyes. "Well, it's true. You bitch and complain all the time—always nagging and making demands. For what it's worth, there are times you are worse than heartburn."

"Coming from someone who can't multitask."

"Oh, but I can. Although I enjoy your spirited personality, I pretend to enjoy your company while ignoring you." He shoots a look to Clay, who is wearing a smile and appears amused. "She's like mountain laurel—easy on the eyes but deadly. Other times, she's like an armadillo—easy to catch until you learn she's quick to spread leprosy. She always has something stuck in her craw, and every word she speaks comes out sounding like a threat. She questions my thoughts, and when given the chance, changes my future to match hers. There isn't a gap between action and reaction. A feeling in my gut often shouts in my ear that she might just be a ticking time bomb, and when she explodes, I'll be stuck in the crosshairs. I'm always left wishing I had a stopwatch. Is there no end to your bellyaching?" he asks, looking to Molly.

Leaning in close, she shoots a wad of spit at him. "You're not worth it."

"Hell, I'd settle for the silent treatment. If I were a betting man, I'd say she loves the man she's missing. I'm guessing her favorite game is *Cards Against Humanity.* I'm sure you've heard of the hum job. She's in favor of the gum job. She lives in a bubble."

Clay understands the man's words but holds his tongue. Although surprised to hear Richard throw Molly under the bus, he understands there will never come a time when they will share a high-five.

"She's cutthroat," Richard mutters.

"I think you mean deep throat," Clay corrects with cold eyes.

"That, too. She's crazy wild like a forgotten ranch horse. Sometimes I'm left wondering what's behind her eyes." Panic rises when the ringing of his cell phone interrupts the moment. "It's my wife," he whispers through thin lips.

"Answer it," Clay orders.

"If she learns about Molly, she'll walk out on me."

"Would you blame her?"

"I'm not leaving my wife for yours."

In the passing seconds, Clay and Molly watch in amusement as Richard bobs his head to a conversation they are not privy to.

Growing impatient, Molly jabs him with her elbow. "Get off the phone."

"I'm at the office," Richard says into the phone. He lowers his voice to a whisper, hoping Molly and Clay will not hear his words. "No, it's not a strip joint, and I'm not anywhere near Broad Street." The grief he is getting on both sides has his head spinning so fast, he feels like he is sucking air on the Flying Saucer at the state fair. "I'm stepping into the elevator. I'll call you from the car," he says, disconnecting the call. "Please, just let me go. I swear I won't see her again."

Clay does not so much as bat an eyelash: after all, he does not owe this guy anything. "You have two choices. Take a bullet to the chest, and I'll call your presence here a home invasion," he lowers his aim, "or take a shot to the knee. Since you're showing it, I'm not opposed to blasting your ass."

"You won't get away with this," Molly says, running off at the mouth.

"I'll swear by my story, and you'll go along with it. That is, if I don't get trigger-happy. Just so you know, I'll shoot him if he runs." Raising his chin, Clay throws his eyes over their shoulders. "I believe you know my witness."

"I think you mean your toady," she mumbles with a half-ass grin. "Clay, please let him go. We can talk about this when you've calmed down. I believe you'll agree he's not worth going to prison."

"Let's be honest here. He's not worth much of anything. So, Dick, what's it going to be? Chest or knee?"

Pale in the face, Richard breaks out in a sweat. He has been in some trying situations before but has never looked down the barrel of a gun. The returning cramp in his stomach reminds him he should never trust a toot. "How am I going to explain this to my wife?"

"That's the least of your problems." Again, Clay raises the gun. This time, he takes aim at Richard's chest. "Choose, or I'll choose for you. I'm not asking twice."

Tears fall from Richard's eyes, and not to be ignored, a stream trickles down his leg. Reaching the ground, it puddles at his feet. "How about a toe? It'll keep both of us out of trouble."

"I'll take your phone," Clay says, ignoring the suggestion.

Richard tries to steady his hands, but they will have no part of it. Juggling the phone, and believing his day cannot get any worse, he watches wide-eyed as it falls from his grip.

"Pick it up."

Dressed in what God gave him, Richard bends over like a convicted killer in a prison shower. In the blink of an eye, the ground beneath him circles the globe before falling out from under him. Light-headed, he collapses to his knees.

"Please let him go. He's suffered enough," Molly says, matching Clay's eye roll.

"We're just getting started. Dick, be a good boy and wipe the phone with your shirt. When you're done, toss it to me. The phone, not the shirt. I think we should capture this moment."

"You've got to be kidding me," Molly grumbles.

Like a trained photographer, Clay focuses the phone's lens in Molly and Richard's direction. "Say cheese." A quick review of the photo tells him he caught them in their birthday suits with their eyes wide open and jaws dropped. Keeping the phone, he scrolls through its recent calls. When he comes across Molly's number, he looks at her with hate in his eyes. He is not surprised when she mirrors him. Returning to the phone, he searches its incoming calls. "Who's Denise?"

"Please don't involve her. I'm begging you," Richard cries. "Don't leave me making excuses."

"She's your wife?" Not waiting for an answer, he sends the photo to Denise. "You should know it's been said all is fair in love and war."

Once again, a puddle circles Richard's feet.

"Seriously, Molly?" Clay asks. "He's the best you can get?"

"It's been said variety is the spice of life. You know what else they say? One man's ceiling is another man's floor. Besides, he was interested."

"You know, I find it fascinating that people are always interested when something is free. As for the ceiling and the floor, I tend to trust the space around me." Bucking his chin, he turns to Tank. When Tank returns a nod, Clay gives the signal. With sure eyes, he turns back to Richard. "I have a few gifts for you."

On cue, Tank hands over the towel and the contents it holds.

"What is this?"

"A Smith & Wesson Mayor and hot jewelry." Clay does not share that the gun's firing pin has been ground down, leaving the weapon worthless. "You know who this is?" he asks, admiring his own weapon. "The Governor. If this doesn't scare you, I'll whip out the Judge."

Richard's eyes nearly pop out of his head. His racing heart threatens an attack, and his bowels sit ready to fire. "I don't understand. You want a shoot-out?"

Again, Clay looks to Molly. "When it comes to cheating, you might consider upping your game." Turning back to Richard, his eyes turn serious. "Are you familiar with the Castle Doctrine?" He points the gun's barrel toward the heap of sparkling gemstones. "Don't bother with an answer. In the eyes of the law, it is much like justifiable homicide. When it involves wrongful death, it lowers the burden of proof. The law allows me to protect my home, the one you are terrorizing. It also allows me to stand my ground and defend my property. I've been told Mississippi law permits me to use excessive force. The police will believe you committed a burglary. Cut and dry. I had no choice but to shoot. Like any loving husband, I feared my wife's life was in danger."

"You're acting crazy, Clay," Molly interrupts. "Have you been drinking?"

"Tequila does that sometimes, but I arrived here on my own."

"Put down the gun or I swear I'll see to it you never see your son again."

"You played me once, and you can be damn sure I won't allow it to happen again." Lifting the Governor, he aims the double-action weapon in her direction. "I suggest you pay close attention. I'm cleaning house here, one crisis at a time."

"Are you saying I'm a crisis?"

"You've been called far worse."

"Your actions might leave your son without a father," she says, refusing to take the bait for an argument he is sure to win. "We can talk this over like adults."

"Good luck with that," he mocks. "I have a better idea. Get dressed. Tank, you go with her, and don't let her out of your sight. When she looks decent, escort her to the kitchen." Turning, he steadies his eyes on Molly. "Put on a can of soup. You're making lunch."

"Lunch? For us? What about Richard?"

"What about him? For all I care, he can forage for food. Hey, if you don't like what's happening here, I'll tell your lover boy to put a bullet in you. He sure as hell can't shoot me. I'm on my property and he's inside my home, and let's not forget about Tank. Nothing like an eyewitness. Now, get moving. I'm hungry. As for you," he turns to Richard, "get the hell off my property. If I find you here again, I'll riddle your body with so many bullets, they'll have to give you an indigent's funeral and bury you in potter's field."

"What about the gun? My prints are all over it. And what am I supposed to do with the jewelry?"

A winning smile crosses Clay's face. This is not the first time he's celebrated a victory, but his cheek-to-cheek smile welcomes an outcome unlike any other. "You best be careful. I'd avoid Graham Street if I were you. DelFoit, too. Police were setting up roadblocks about twenty minutes ago. An officer told me one of my neighbors was robbed of the jewelry you're holding."

"You're crazy."

"You sure about that? Take a look around. I'm not the one standing naked in another man's home."

"Listen here, you son of a bitch. You set me up for a crime I didn't commit."

"Come on, Dicky, are we going to revisit where you'll take a bullet?" Inching forward, Clay waves the Governor in the air. "Grow a set already." Turning away, he looks to the sky. "This must be your lucky day. Are you a Leo?"

"Gemini."

"In that case, there's never a day in your favor. Still," he places his thumb on the gun's trigger, "something in that growing cumulus to the east tells me this is not your day to die. Just so you know, tomorrow's not looking so good."

"What are you saying? That puffy cloud says I'm screwed?"

"I believe we'd agree that term applies to my wife."

"We both know Graham and DelFoit are the only streets out of here."

"Do you believe in karma?"

"Hell no."

"You best watch your back. Pucker up, buttercup. You're old enough to know karma's a bitch."

CHAPTER 2

"Molly is a purveyor of lies. I'm guessing she's burdened with grief and a road map of scars. Her actions show she's not plugged into life. If forced, I would say she's always ready to stick it to the person who did her wrong. I'd like to know her backstory."

"How do you know her?" Preston Fayne asks, turning to Trude DelCamp, the most unfortunate woman he has ever laid eyes on.

"She has no manners, and she's terribly ugly. In case you haven't noticed, she has too many punches in her discipline card. I'm guessing she knows only to travel dead-end roads. It's rumored she might just be the missing link."

"I'll agree that's funny, but it's not true. She just needs tweaking."

"Widespread rumors confirm she has had her fair share of tweaks. Gossip spoken in low voices in dark alleys compares her to a puppy."

"For me to understand, you're going to have to take me off-leash."

"Always inviting the big dogs to explore her bottom. What I wouldn't give to read her diary." Feeling his eyes on her, Trude scoots over the bed to the table. Grabbing the frame, she flips the photo on its face. "She's batshit crazy, and you're impossible. Sometimes I find you're not worth the tears I've cried."

If she had known the five-by-seven photo would cause such a stir, she would have burned it, along with the memory, a long time ago.

Forced to face the music, she scissor-kicks the sheets and pokes an angry finger against the slim frame's backside. "Before the blow-dryer hits her hair, she looks like a Great Pyrenees in its adolescent years."

"Help me paint the picture."

"Mangy and confused. She's worse than that long-haired freak that hangs out in Zig's parking lot." Although of legal age, she rarely frequents the liquor store on South Third Street. It was only last week the newspaper's Sunday edition warned of the misdeeds the sketchy lot threatens, especially after the midnight hour.

"It appears I've struck a nerve," Preston observes. "I don't understand why you're getting all worked up. All I did was ask how you know her." He turns the photo upright on its easel and stares at the petite blonde longer than common sense suggests. Mesmerized by her natural and flawless beauty, he cannot bring himself to turn away from her dimpled cheeks and dark, alluring eyes. The string bikini's strapless top has him breathless. Full lips frame the whitest teeth he has ever seen, and her come-hither smile has him believing she posed just for him.

Focusing on the photo, he forgets he is under the microscope of another woman. "She sets the wow factor way above the bar, and she has a nice set of ..."

"Again, I'm reminded you can be an ass at times." Moving over the floor, Trude throws an arch in her back like an alley cat. "If you haven't noticed, I'm still here, and I can hear you. For what it's worth, she's flat as a pancake. All talk and no game."

"Hey, Amelia Earhart, cool your jets. I was going to say *teeth*. For what it's worth, I believe breasts are overrated." He is not a breast man, but if there is truth in the photo, Molly delivers there, too.

"She has more teeth than Horsetooth Mountain."

"Colorado?"

"Fort Collins. It's possible she's from Alligator."

"The town?"

"Yep."

"You have to admit she's hot. Oh, and that long-haired freak is

Ivan. He's the best mechanic south of the Mason-Dixon Line. Smart, too. Amongst other things, he picks up a lot of business at Zig's."

"By *other things*, surely you don't mean educated women. That slim mustache of his gives me the creeps."

"To be honest with you, I've not noticed his mustache."

"Thin line above a slim lip. I trust a fuller stash. Have you looked at his hands? Dirt spills out from under his nails, and he smells like the underside of a barn, and no, she's not hot. I'll admit she has great hair and she's bone thin. She either has a tapeworm or her pact with the devil is eating away at her soul."

"It's possible she knew her friends were talking behind her back."

"She should be stepped on like a cockroach. She wears way too much makeup, and her greasy, dollar-store lip-gloss is a throwback to the eighties. Don't even get me started on her eyebrows. They'd meet up in Kearney if she didn't pluck them."

"Kearney?"

"Nebraska. Smack-dab in the middle of the United States." She slaps her hands together like brass cymbals in a marching band. "Where east meets west." Leaving the bed, she moves about the apartment, gathering her clothes while hoping regret will not catch up with her. "She's always chasing after sunsets and better tomorrows. I'm telling you, she's bad news. Like serial-killer bad."

"Nothing wrong with chasing sunsets, but tagging her as a serial killer is a stretch."

"Each time she broke up with a boyfriend, she told us he died."

"*Each time*? Are you saying more than once?"

"Every single time. After a while, she couldn't get a date."

"Why is that?"

"She's cursed. No guy wants to be the next to keel over."

"That's ridiculous."

"She started it. How did you come to know her?"

"Some friends threw a pageant party. They weren't competing but betting on the winner. Next thing you know, everyone paired off. By the end of the night, it could be said we were all winners." Reliving the memory puts a smile on his face. "I went out with her a couple of times. It was a long time ago. If memory serves, I believe it was before medical school. If forced to describe her, I'd say she was adventurous."

"Was she married at the time?"

"Can't say."

"You?"

"I plead the Fifth."

"You see her in a different light. She pops pills like she is about to do time. She knows the streets. I'm betting she can't find her way out of Harrison County." Although smitten with his good looks, she is finding him less attractive. With each word he speaks, her interest in him continues to wane. Afraid he will drool on the picture, she snags it from his hand. "We attended the same high school and ran in the same circle of friends, but I didn't really get to know her. She blew into town under the radar. Whispered voices hinted she left a newborn behind. I met her at a sock hop."

"What might that be?" he asks, skipping over the rumor.

"For real? You don't know what a sock hop is?"

"My question should be proof enough."

"It's a dance in the school gym. No shoes allowed. When she was asked where she was from, she mumbled something about the Bible Belt." The memories are clear as a bell and still painful, but it is not for him to know she lost more than one boyfriend to the girl in the picture. "Sometime during the dance, she was caught boinking the football coach in the parking lot. Coach got fired, and she earned a reputation."

"Is *boinking* anything akin to making out?" he asks, knowing.

"To think, all this time, I thought you went to medical school."

"I don't recall a lesson in boinking."

"Not even after dark?"

"I'm stumped."

"Look it up when you get home. She blamed her actions on her mother, who took a beating in a gray divorce."

"Again, you've lost me."

"Father bailed when her mother turned fifty."

"I'm sure her mother's position in life took a fast turn."

"It's rumored her brother is doing fifty years in the slammer. I can't swear to the crime, but the lengthy sentence suggests cold-blooded murder. For what it's worth, I praise the Lord we're not related."

"So, what's up with the picture? Why frame it?"

Sipping the soda she'd poured before his arrival, and believing her uneasiness has gone unnoticed, she ignores the question until a proper response, one she has little doubt he will believe, comes to her. "The same reason every girl frames a photo. My tan was perfect, my weight was spot-on, and if you can't tell, I was having a great hair day."

"I'll accept that."

"For what it's worth, I had the feeling Molly lied about her mother and where she hailed from. It was rumored she was from Sugar Ditch Alley and her parents passed away when she was a young girl. I wouldn't be surprised to learn she jumped rope on Porta Potty Lane."

"Help me here."

"A neighborhood without plumbing. Mobile toilets are rooted on every corner. I'm convinced she escaped the red-light district."

"For what it's worth, those toilets have to go somewhere. As for her mother, why the lie?"

"I can't answer that, but one would think she would know her place."

"What place would that be?"

"Anywhere but here. When I see her coming, I cross the street. She's as dumb as a box of rocks. I wouldn't be surprised if she sports bloodied horns under those big floppy hats she wears. Having witnessed her shenanigans, I'm convinced her broom travels one direction—dead south." Lowering her head, she performs the sign of the cross and folds her hands in prayer. "She'll have you under her spell so fast, you'll wonder where the yellow went. Then, when she moves on to someone else, she'll sell you down the river. She has no scruples."

As the words roll off her tongue, she questions the toothpaste commercial her mother, a functioning alcoholic with a liking for vodka, often quoted when reining in her stepbrothers—a duo of misfits lacking basic know-how, simple table manners, and what she calls *niceabilities*. Looking back, it is no wonder their favorite pastime was a game of "pull my finger."

There are times she wants to pull up stakes and move to a place that offers more than the mundane routine she worries she will fall into. Memphis, some ninety miles away, is on her radar. She has watched reruns of *The Tonight Show* enough times to know she could herd a few ducks along a short carpet to a water fountain. All she needs is a job at the Peabody Hotel, a duck whisperer, and a handful of wild grain.

Frustrated by Preston's ignorance and indifference, she punts the air with her foot. Forgetting the lazy waves outside the window, she bares her teeth and pokes a plastic comb into his flesh. "Careful what you tangle with. It's been said there is a method to her madness."

"I can't disagree more, but I hope we can agree you're being a bit harsh." He reaches for the picture, but her hand is quicker, and her cold eyes invite a challenge.

"Better to be harsh than foolish. She's like a hitchhiker without a thumb—going nowhere. If asked, I would say she lacks insight. Say what you will, but from where I come from, that's a red flag. She doesn't have an ounce of fat on her or the truth in her. This is where you decide if she's worth cozying up with."

"We've all made poor choices and often regret our actions, but it's not our place to throw guilt on her. Given my brief time with her, I'm agreeing with you that she's a bit salty, but once you get to know her," he cocks his head in thought, "I'm betting she will grow on you."

"My dear Preston. I'm just going to sit here and pretend I don't hear you. I will not be blinded by her actions, and getting to know her is not in my future. As for growing on me, ticks belong on deer."

"Maybe, but you should give her a chance. I'm betting you'll invite her to your next party."

"Only if it's a séance. Hear it here first: I don't want to get close to her. I'm afraid lightning will bounce off her and strike me." Images of a Ouija board, a room filled with burning candles dripping with hot wax, and a tree branch scraping against an attic window send a shiver down her spine. "She'll likely summon the devil. She's a heathen. I hear she's into black magic and witchcraft. I've been told the trunk of her car is filled with voodoo dolls and sharp pins." Raising a fisted hand, she stabs at the air between them. "On top of all her other bad qualities, she's a freeloader. When she's through with you, you will have lost more than you've given."

"Are you referring to regret?"

"Screw regret. When it comes to Molly, you're not only flirting with karma but also skirting danger."

"I think you will agree you're being a bit dramatic."

"If you invite her into your life, she's your risk, not mine. I'm betting you'll find her halo buried under her bed."

"Once again, you've lost me."

"To ward off evil spirits and forgive her sins. You want my advice? Leave her where you found her. When the crows are through with her, the ants will take care of the rest. I'm sure you've heard it said, people like her return to their own vomit."

Blessed with assets in keeping with *Sports Illustrated* swimsuit models, T-Rude, as she is known to the young patrons she serves at Lil' Moe's fish-and-chips shack, throws down her foot and gives the floor a hard stomp. Her temperature rising, she snags a lacy bra from an overturned lamp. "She's been compared to flypaper—pulling people close only to hold them hostage until a slow and painful death takes them. It's rumored she has the IQ of dust."

"Are we talking about the same Molly?"

"The one and only."

"She's a survivor."

"Of what? Bad choices? She kisses the wrong person while declaring her love for another. I can only imagine the pain she has put on those with pecker problems."

Left scratching his head, Preston reclines against the bed's headboard. When his thoughts return to their interlude, he reaches under the rumpled pillow. Wearing only a smile, he swirls a pink thong around his index finger. "Is this what they call cat's cradle?"

Balancing on bare feet, she hobbles across the carpeted floor. In one fell swoop, she rescues the lace panty from his playful grip.

"Hey, I was hoping to keep it as a souvenir."

"I'm sure your wife would appreciate that."

In their silence, neither will admit they do not have better things to do, nor would they share that their interest in the other is quickly fading.

"I'm finding that I don't want to see you again," she finally admits. "Not like this. I'm ready to move on and meet someone to call mine."

"I understand." Tired of the banter, he takes a deep breath and studies a rugged flap of loose skin around a torn cuticle.

"Which reminds me, she bites her nails and chews on her hair." Trude is tempted to remind him his new love interest has shared a bed with more guys than the university's male dormitory, but she knows he will respond with an insult she will later cry over.

"A lot of women bite their nails."

The finger she waves in his face displays a long, manicured nail. "You can dress her up and take her out, but she'll always spew poison. It's in her blood like …"

"Serum?"

"I was going to say Lyme disease."

Trude's yammering is beginning to wear on his nerves and test his patience. It is no wonder she is always available at a moment's notice. No one else will tolerate her nonsense. On cue, another thought rushes at him. "Well, son of a gun. I didn't peg you for the jealous type."

"Jealous? Don't be ridiculous." She pushes the sheet aside, grabs worn sandals, and plops down on the bed. "I'm serious about moving on. I've never cared for heartbreakers, and players aren't my type."

"But married men are?" He is certain her words are meant to insult him, but his wide grin lets her know he appreciates the compliment. It comes as a surprise when he finds her tousled hair and spirited hissy fit arousing. In the months he has been bedding her, he has never witnessed such a fiery display.

Folding his hands behind his head, he ponders the breakup. Although sex with her is like watching paint dry, it gets the wall painted. "I'm not sure if we have some of the best sex in the world, but it's right up there."

"Are you for real?"

"If you disagree, prove it."

A pinch to her bottom catches her by surprise, and his low whistle has her returning to him like one of Pavlov's dogs. A glance at his watch reminds him he has thirty minutes before he is expected at the marina. As the boat's captain, the crew will not set sail without him, but it will not keep them from ribbing him should they learn the reason for his late arrival.

Teasing with his eyes, he wiggles out from under the sheet. He encounters little resistance when he pulls her on top of him and lifts the cool sheet over them. "I say we forget this little spat ever happened. If memory serves, I heard she married a doctor."

"An obstetrician, just like you. I will say this: if she hasn't changed her wily ways, she'll be known as Jane Doe. I've heard it said all she knows is to beg and borrow." A glance at her watch has her tearing free of his embrace and jumping from the bed. "I have to get ready for work. If I'm late one more time, I'll be unemployed and kicked out of school."

"Old man Grabby won't fire you. You're his favorite waitress. Every time I'm there, I catch him checking out your backside."

"Don't be fooled by roving eyes. He sees all, knows all, and is not afraid to let go a threatening bark. Are you stopping by Moe's? The special today is fish tacos."

"Had tacos for lunch yesterday, and the biscuits and gravy I had for breakfast are still with me."

"I have to get ready. Let yourself out. Just be sure to turn the lock. By the way, I have an appointment with you on Friday."

"I recall seeing your name on the schedule. Anything serious?"

"Just checking to make sure you haven't given me anything, you know, like chlamydia, syphilis, or the Clap," she says, stepping into the bathroom.

Keeping a watchful eye on the door, he shoves the coveted photograph under his shirt and hightails it out of there.

CHAPTER 3

"Do you remember Clay Lambert? He's the bearded guy who escaped the Lone Star State soon after college. I got a call from him yesterday. He's looking to make a move to Casino Beach," Gordy Harris, a colleague and crewmember, shares with Preston.

"Why?" Preston asks, wiping sauce from his chin. He knows Clay. They shared late-night hours together during medical school. He also knows Clay's wife. They, too, spent time together—hours he visits in his sleep but dares not discuss.

"He didn't go into details, and I didn't press, but I got the feeling he and his wife need a fresh start." Rumors of an affair have been kept under wraps, and it is not his place to share idle gossip. "I think he would be a good fit in your practice."

"Is he serious?" Preston questions how far he can go without sounding sirens. "Is he still married to his second wife? Oh, what's her name? Annie? Millie?"

"Molly. I have no reason to believe otherwise. He's a bit weak under the belt, but once he matures, I'd bet my bottom dollar he'd be an asset to your practice. He has already given notice to his landlord that they will be out of their rental at the end of the month."

Preston tucks the napkin into his shirt collar, throws back a local brew, and pushing his sleeve up his arm, pulls another rib from the rack. Fearing the look on his face will give him away, he looks out over the bay. "Do you have his number?"

Gordy pulls an old flip-phone from his shirt pocket and, with burnt-orange fingers, scrolls through his contacts. "I'm sending his contact info to you."

Licking the drippings from his fingers, Preston revisits earlier years and the moments he shared with Molly. "I'll give him a call this afternoon."

CHAPTER 4

The twenty-minute drive to the house on Reyfort Street gives Preston time to prepare for another one of those days he has come to expect—and, later, when words are exchanged, regret. If there is ever a time he needs his father lucid and on top of his game, this is it.

A beat-up Oldsmobile catches his eye as he enters the unmarked entrance to his father's four-acre estate—a place he once called home. His family's wealth, along with that of the neighbors, reminds him the dented car parked across the road belongs to the neighbor's yard man, a gritty guy who believes dinks and dents add character to the car's side doors and rear bumper. Before the day is over, he will call the president of the neighborhood association and, tossing his family's name about, demand the eyesore be tucked behind a row of trees.

Cruising at a speed the vintage Jeep appreciates, he rounds an unkempt hedge of mature boxwoods and a gathering of old oak trees draped in Spanish moss. Approaching the homestead's ornamental gates, he lifts his foot off the Jeep's temperamental pedal. A grinding screech holds on until he parks the oversized tires and cuts the Woody's flathead engine.

"Dang it, Ivan," he curses under his breath. After three months in the mechanic's garage, the rare and pricey vintage should run like a racehorse. Exiting the wagon, he closes the door with the tenderness the old classic deserves.

The home's crumbling brick-and-mortar walkway is scattered with bits of broken beach pebbles and large stones blanketed with velvety green moss. King palms planted when the house was first framed provide shade to a bank of windows meant to cool the home's dining room. A closer look gives watch to a chirping bird wandering along the winding path. An overgrown koi pond held hostage by foxtail and bluestem grasses flanks its border. The only pieces missing are a gazing ball and a concrete lawn jockey his father purchased during a drunken stupor and his mother demanded be moved to a dark corner of the home's two-car garage.

Though it was once a stately home, the Georgian classic's flat roof now gives in the middle, leaving a slope of moguls to carry the burden. Barrel tiles that gave way when Hurricane Camille ripped through the coast in 1969 are still MIA. Parapets that fell victim to the hurricane's 175-mile winds now point inland, always on watch for the next big one. When Katrina hit in 2005, fast-moving water left behind hairline cracks in the home's stucco and a mess of knotted debris. The stucco has since been patched, but dying foliage continues to mourn the storm's damage.

Out back, just off the kitchen and visible from the home's circular drive, a retractable roof offers shade to a tiled veranda. Decades have passed since the old gas grill was fired up and the weathered picnic table hosted a party. In a damp corner, a low-lying shallow place where fragrant wisteria used to grow, weathered logs offer refuge to sun-seeking lizards, small rodents, mostly river rats: and a mean bunch of fire ants that fled the Natchez Trace during its last pilgrimage tour. Window boxes that once brought life to the home's exterior at the onset of spring now sit vacant.

Broken bulbs in the old lanterns framing the door continue to escape the cleaning woman's eye. Hired soon after his mother's passing, she is built like a fire hydrant and shoots off her mouth like a loaded cannon. Although she has been with the family for ages, he wonders if perhaps the time has come to give her the pink slip. With her temperament, there is little hope she will part ways without putting up a fight.

The home faced challenges months earlier, soon after his father became wheelchair-bound. Shouting expletives, he fought the ramp, a path designed to connect the home's garage to the kitchen's wide door.

"I may be an old man, but I'm not an invalid," Duncan Fayne shouts each time the subject rears its ugly head. It is not the ideal entrance, especially when hurricane winds and rough water threaten the coast, but for a man who spends hours watching time fly, struggling with solid foods, and sipping through a paper straw, it beats surrendering his home to a coast he hopes to pass in.

Hand-hewn hickory beams salvaged from an abandoned barn in Pennsylvania's farm country and a rich coffered ceiling provide a stylish design feature to the home's generous foyer. A collection of hand-woven Indian blankets and Native American art decorate a space opposite the vestibule's wide doors. An expansive wall of narrow, multipaned French encasement windows offers a million-dollar view of the gulf—the reason the house was built on the property soon after the turn of the century.

Although faint, the beep of an alarm clock interrupts the eerie silence. Resigned, Preston gives a disbelieving nod. In recent months, and now at every visit, he unplugs his father's bedside clock. Much like today, each visit reminds that his father is onto him.

Down the hall, Rachmaninoff's Second Piano Concerto escapes rich, mahogany walls. An intense woody scent follows close behind. As he approaches the dining room, a pinch grabs at Preston's heart. The glass table, a pricey piece his mother swept up on a visit to New York, sits waiting for the next big shindig. Rosenthal plates rest alongside fine linens she just had to have when she visited Barcelona. This was before cancer laid a claim to what later would become her vulnerable frame.

A meal has never been shared at the table, and the linens remain folded in the clear plastic they shipped in. Forced to live in darkness, the china gathers dust along with the remains of curious insects that made the fatal mistake of turning toward the light.

Although decades have passed, the weeks leading up to his mother's passing remain vivid in Preston's memory. A young man, he wanted to experience his final years of high school at DeViney Pines, a boarding school in Virginia's Blue Ridge Mountains. Each time he called home, he promised to visit when time allowed. On the day of his mother's passing, he shared lunch in the cafeteria with his circle of buddies. Before dessert was served, weekend activities were planned, dates were made, and a dark corner at the local drive-in theater—rows away from the large screen and the lingering odors the snack shack coughed up—was reserved. Later, curfew sent the posse back to the dorm.

He took the red-eye out of Dulles International and was back on campus in time for dinner and Friday night poker.

The week following the funeral, his father missed opening remarks at a murder trial where he was expected to deliver convincing arguments while defending a young man on trial for killing his wife, a teacher in the city's school system. His absence was not only a turning point in his career but an end to a stellar reputation.

Now, as Preston rounds the corner, the stench of burnt hazelnut warns the coffeepot has been left on the stove again. Growing frustrated, he makes a mental note to replace the old percolator with a coffee maker with a timer.

"Dad? Where are you?"

"Where you always find me when you step away from your busy social life," a thick voice replies.

"In the bathroom?"

"In the library, you ignoramus," Duncan Fayne shouts through a coughing fit and gnarly bark. "Sometimes I worry you can't find your way out of a broom closet."

The library reminds Preston of a skit he once watched on late-night comedy poking fun at Margaret Mitchell's epic novel *Gone with the Wind* and Miss Scarlett and her Tara Plantation—that is, until his eyes fall on a watercolor. It has looked out of place since the day his father put a nail to it.

Crosshatch windows are lost behind heavy, richly hued drapes, loosely tied with braided gold tassels. Inches shy of an outlet, a highway of extension cords travels over the room's parquet floor. Bird's-eye paneling displays a collection of pictures of old people Preston hopes are not ancestors.

Although he has visited the room countless times, it is only now his eyes fall on the portrait above the room's river-rock fireplace. If memory serves, the fair-skinned man is his great-grandfather, a general practitioner who, in his spare time, fished the shallow waters of the Carolinas. It is rumored he shared his life with eight wives, each younger than the bride before her. Preston often wonders how a man short on looks managed to score with so many women. When time allows, he just might request a blood test.

A small frame, tucked away in the corner, holds a black and white photo of a young couple he believes are his grandparents on his mother's side. He reaches for it, but feeling his father's eyes on him, pulls back his hand. Looking at his father, he prays he will never be like him or the men in his family before him. A man of good looks and honed charisma, Preston finds their shortcomings too ugly to carry.

"Close the damn door. It's hotter than Dante's third circle in here," Duncan barks, rubbing at a map of varicose veins traveling his body.

Once a champion sailor and respected lawyer, Duncan now sits hunched over in a chair held together by metal screws, electronic gadgets, and caster tires. When pressed, he blames gin mixes and a life of wild nights for his blurred vision and failing memory.

In recent months, he has come to look years beyond his age. He wears patches of dry skin, deep wrinkles, and jutting bones. At first glance, one might be easily convinced he came over on the Mayflower. A second hip replacement makes little difference in his frail frame. After years of fighting old age and poor health, he now surrenders to constant battles with emphysema and stubborn infections.

Accepting he is on borrowed time, he quit living long ago. Friends are long gone, taking with them many of his memories. He no longer gives thanks for another day, instead cursing the morning sun—a reminder he will live to suffer and, like the prized plates, collect a fresh layer of dust.

Overhead, a cyclone of cinders and grit drifts from recessed skylights, giving way to a slim ray of sunlight pouring through faded acrylic. A window unit installed decades earlier, when temperatures remained in triple digits, fails to cool the air. Now, the low hum of the hard-working motor eats at Duncan's troubled soul.

"Where's Sergio?" Preston asks.

"Who the hell is Sergio?" Duncan asks with a catch in his throat.

Their question-and-answer games have become more frequent in recent weeks. Last February, in the early morning hours on Valentine's Day, when Preston learned the scope of his father's ill fate, he suggested a visit to an assisted-living facility. His father wanted no part of it. His slurred words were a jumbled mess, but the message implied that growing old was best done at home—a place where pride not only steps aside but goes into hiding.

"Sergio is the short guy from Argentina." He searches his father's face for the slightest hint of recognition, but experience reminds that what little information reaches his father's brain often remains idle. "The handyman. He usually parks the cars."

Duncan wipes a thick tongue over dry, cracked lips. A wide yawn exposes an empty space where a molar was once rooted. Although the divot is almost always infected and prevents him from noshing on salted cashews and sunflower seeds, he gave up visiting the dentist soon after joining the widower's club. "I know what he does. What are you? Ten? You should be able to park your own damn car by now," he says, combing the air with bent fingers. "You let a fly in."

"What's happening with the pool? I noticed a cement mixer near the deck."

"I'm filling it in. Damn thing does nothing but collect water."

Although Preston has design ideas to save the pool and its deck, he remains silent. History warns that anything he says will lead to nothing more than an argument that is sure to continue until his father claims the win with a greasy smile.

Crossing over the floor, Preston takes the morning's paper from the trash. The fly has since moved on, but he will be ready to take an Astro's swing should it dare cross his path again.

Content with his attempt, he takes a seat on a wounded chair his father adamantly refuses to part with. It meets the floor with three legs and a warning it could pancake in the blink of an eye. Its frayed fabric and fallen seat have him believing it holds memories of better days.

"I've been meaning to talk with you about Veta."

"Who's Veta?"

"The housekeeper. Come on, Dad. She's been with us since the earth formed."

"Aw, hell. I've been calling her Ruth."

"Is she answering to it?"

"Who cares? For what it's worth, my dog and the housekeeper are wearing the same diaper. Something tells me they have the same underlying agenda. What are you drinking these days?" Duncan asks, changing the subject. "Cowboy whiskey?"

"Although I'm tempted to join you in a pour, I'm cutting back. Is now a good time to mention you don't have a dog? And what's with the air conditioner? Sounds like it's on its last leg."

"You mean the egg-conditioner. It puts out an odor I liken to a hen-house. When it runs too long, the darn thing spits feathers," Duncan says, waving the air with a hand shaped like a knotty pinecone.

"Has Sergio taken a look at it?"

"Nah. Gives me something to bark about."

"Besides barking, what have you been doing?"

Duncan shifts about, pretending not to hear, a habit that never works in his favor.

"I asked what you've been doing," Preston repeats, lifting his voice.

"Most days, I believe I'm living the best life, and then three o'clock rolls in. Before the first commercial crosses over the screen,

Judge Judy puts me in my place. That woman scares the bejesus out of me. To quote her, I'm left promising I'll never pee on her leg, and if forced to choose, I don't want to be the windshield or the bug. I spent the earlier part of today listening to country western music. A light lunch and a cocktail left me feeling frisky, so I watched a little poor-no. Have I mentioned my knee continues to play tricks on me?"

"Yes, and it's just porn."

"Porn, poor-no, either way, it's a distant memory. Turns out that lively feeling was pent-up gas."

"What else are you doing?"

"My teeth are shifting, my nose is growing, and one of those places I was once proud of is bald as an eagle and the size of a pink eraser."

"How's it working otherwise?"

"How should I know? He's as dead as a doornail."

"Could be worse."

"I don't know about that. At least something would be happening down there. Have I mentioned my prostate is a pain in the ass? Damn doctor wants to put in a stent."

"That's not your ass."

"It's hell growing old. I eat, sleep, and sit. Next thing you know, I'll be on a leash, and if it's long enough, pissing on hydrants. Promise you'll put me down if I start sniffing rear ends and licking my own." Throwing a hand to the air, he waves away the image. "I had lunch at the club yesterday. Once small talk was over, I was made aware you've taken a mistress."

"That's quite the transition. I'm guessing you were with the usual gang."

"Kingstead and Olufsen. We're the last of a dying breed."

"How is Olufsen these days?"

"Grumpy. The last time he enjoyed a bang was in the eighties."

"You and your cronies should know an affair isn't the worst crime one commits."

"I'm willing to bet your wife has a different sentiment, and your excuses are pretty weak."

"I suppose."

"I'm no spring chicken, although there are times I'd like to ruffle a few feathers. That said, sometimes I'm an adolescent stuck in an old man's body. Other times, especially in recent weeks, I'm a cranky old goat. But enough about me. Let's talk about this woman and make it snappy. I don't want to miss *Wheel of Fortune*. I'll tell you what, that Vanna White is easy on the eyes." Displaying the tiger in him, Duncan gives a wink. "I'd give everything I own to have a night with her. If it weren't for this self-lubricated catheter attached to my you-know-what, I'd give her a spin she'll never forget. For what it's worth, there is still some puppy in this old dog."

"Given the game show's high ratings, I'm guessing you are probably not alone. I'll say this: you are in rare form today."

"I'd give darn near anything to return to a time when I lived with a menopausal woman. Hell, if she were good-looking, I'd find a way to tolerate her hot flashes. Now, about this woman, let's agree to move on. Don't say her name inside these walls. In case you haven't noticed, I'm too old to hunt down a priest and a vial of holy water she'd likely be asked to gargle."

"An exorcism? Come on, I know you mean to be funny, but that's a bit extreme."

"Don't shoot the messenger."

Turning away, Preston waves a hand through the air. "Give me the skinny."

"The what?"

"I've counted five already. God only knows how many got by me."

"Five what?"

"You know."

"Son, you are talking nonsense."

"You need something for your stomach. Have you been eating five-bean salad again?"

"I'm a grown man, and I'll eat what I want to eat." Looking away,

Duncan raises his bottom from the chair. "Excuse the gas. Damn thing keeps me awake at night. Forget the bean salad. I'm blaming the mozzarella. I expected changes in my later years, but lactose intolerance wasn't on my short list. When the housekeeper is here, I retreat to the far end of my closet. It's never pleasant, but I'd rather suffer alone than give her reason to quit. Now, let's get back to the subject at hand."

"If you don't mind, I'd rather we start a new tradition, one where father and son enjoy happy hour. How do you feel about a martini?"

"Who do you think you are? James Bond?"

"Only when I want my cocktail shaken."

"Stirred or not at all. Let's keep on point."

"How about a cognac?"

"Only if you're taking me to the South of France. Also, I'd prefer a scotch and soda."

"Consider it done. Let's get back to Veta."

"What's there to discuss? She stays until I go. Now, where was I? Oh yes, your mistress. I know firsthand her name has been mentioned in lesser circles. She's not the woman for you. Never has been. Never will be. She can't hold a candle to Peggy. I suggest you throw spit on your flame. If she isn't self-sufficient, it's likely she has dreams of marrying well. This mistress of yours knows how to work the system. If pushed into a corner, you'll learn her actions are all about the dollar sign. I'd be willing to bet she has spent her life wanting what those around her have. My dear Preston, you are not only a victim but also a target."

Clenching his jaw, Preston bites at his lip. Throughout Mississippi and its neighboring states, his father is known as a fair and honest man, always going to bat for the underdog. He would spit on the ACLU before selling out a decent man with good intentions. Preston cannot help but question why the same enthusiasm and loyalty do not apply to him. "How can you possibly say these things without knowing her? Besides, our relationship is an affair, not a walk to the altar."

"I know her type. It appears you have trouble separating reality and fantasy, or perhaps you treasure your ignorance. You must be living in *The Twilight Zone*. Any chance you know Rod Serling?"

"That's almost funny."

"I didn't mean it to be. For the love of all that is holy, please consider how your actions will forever change Peggy. Something tells me you will be throwing her heart for a loop." Resigned, Duncan narrows his cloudy eyes. "On both sides of the gene pool, you were born to swim in gravy. If you're renting this woman, you can bet she's been rented before."

A man defined by age and a crippled body, whose life warranty threatens to expire before his next breath, Duncan allows his son to imagine the other men who have been entertained by his paramour. "I've heard it said she lives fast and loose. She's been compared to a lost penny—easy to find. Don't ask me to explain. Some might say she comes from the wrong side of the bay."

Preston's struggles with his father continue to weigh on him. It was not that long ago his father was chasing miniskirts and furnishing cheap rentals with pricey furniture and circling delicate wrists and necklines with expensive baubles. "I believe the expression is *wrong side of the tracks*," he quickly corrects.

"Those, too." Shifting about, Duncan taps at the chair's gears. "You can beat around the bush when it comes to this girl who has set her eyes, and possibly her future, on you, but make no mistake: your circle of life should never overlap hers. One should bring something to the table." He turns away, his old eyes cold and distant. "The giving plate she offers is empty."

A timely ring from Preston's cell phone interrupts the lecture. Before accepting the call, he looks to his father, not for permission but understanding.

"Is that her?"

He wants to lie, but his father's eyes beg the truth. "Yes."

"Don't answer it."

"She might need something."

"Of course she does. People like her always need something. In her case, it's your wallet and your last name to follow hers." Duncan pauses to wipe at his chin. "If given the opportunity, the devil's chance to destroy your marriage." He puts a match to a Cohiba cigar and, blowing a labored breath to the flame, rolls over the floor. When he reaches the lacquered piano, he throws a hand to the keys. He closes his eyes, and a knowing whistle escapes him. He hopes the tune and its notes will come to him, but it is only the tapping of the keys he hears. "Let her go," he whispers through a lengthy cough. "I don't understand why you continue to put up with her nonsense."

Preston races to dull the images his father paints. After all, Molly is not that kind of girl. In his silence, he recalls the many times he overheard his father share with his sailing crew that he once courted a woman who put a fire in his belly, and later, an arrow through his heart. Stealing words from a tennis coach who pretended to see promise in his backhand, he nicknamed her *Potential.* At the risk of losing his inheritance, Duncan was forced to settle with Joan Waring, a woman of great wealth, beauty, and a proper education. When asked about their marriage, he always ends the conversation with the same sentiment: "Joan was first in her class at finishing school."

"Am I to believe your father, the great Early Lloyd Fayne, carpenter extraordinaire, approved of my mother?"

"Son, your mother was the pick of the litter."

"But was she your pick?"

"At the time I was to choose, hers was the only litter." Turning away, Duncan flicks ashes into the air.

A believing laugh escapes Preston's lips. Duncan talks a big game, but friends, those his father held onto after law school, knew he adored Preston's mother. Although Preston questions the gossip, it is rumored his mother was the one to settle when she agreed to meet Duncan at the altar. "While that may be true, I believe you're stretching the truth a bit. Mother came from an admirable family."

"That has nothing to do with the price of cotton." Removing his eyeglasses, Duncan places them on his lap. It is not often he regrets his words, but this is one time he wishes he could take back the ones he uses to paint a lesser picture of the only woman he ever loved. Joan was a fine woman. He was surprised all those years ago that she found him interesting and, later, worthy of marriage. At the time, his own giving plate offered only crumbs and empty promises.

Forced to help his father, Duncan was schooled in carpenter ants and termites, industrial pests that put money in the bank and food on the table. A distant relative caught his bored and disinterested expression, made a few calls, and after a college diploma was placed in his hand, a lesser law school came knocking at his door.

"Your point is fair and well-taken," he says now. "Someone once said—as with most names of late, his escapes me, but if memory serves, I believe it was a psychology professor I met by happenstance: 'There is a marked difference between heredity and environment. Heredity is when you look like your parents. Environment is when you look like your neighbor's parents.' However, this charlatan of yours falls short on both."

"Charlatan? Really?"

"She's a fraud, Preston. She's like loose change—always looking for a pocket."

"Excuse me for disagreeing."

"Tell me, why are you so hell-bent on defending her?"

"Someone has to. What do you want me to do?"

"Be the man you were born to be."

"That's it?"

"Perhaps seek an intervention."

"You're losing me."

"Are you abusing drugs?"

"For the love of God, you should know better than to ask. For what it's worth, I'm a doctor, not a pop musician."

"In recent weeks, I'm finding I don't always know what I should know."

"Age will do that to a man."

"Well, would you look at that? We finally agree on something.

There was a beautiful woman who caught my eye. Her name was Rose. A rose by any other name is, well, you know the saying."

"You've never mentioned her. Where did you meet her?"

"In a small community near Lula. She had a younger sister named Lily. She had perky breasts and legs that went on for a country mile. One look at her had me pitching a two-man tent."

"Hell, don't make me paint that picture. Why did you choose Rose over Lily?"

"Lily was too young to be plucked from the garden. Don't get me wrong about Rose. She was a good kind of crazy until evil took her under its wing."

"Drugs?"

"Everything illegal." Duncan pauses to glance at a trophy in the far corner of the room. Like his memory, the trophy continues to fade with the passing of time. "Had I held my ground, we would have muddled through a difficult life. For me, law school would have been a place where my friends prepared for their future."

Again, he pauses, this time to sip the scotch and soda he is convinced will rid him of the constant tremble in his hands and tender memories he wishes to forget. In a quiet moment, he revisits flashbacks he cannot shake. Memories of his days with Rose return a smile to his aging face. Years of child support had put a pinch in his wallet, and although Joan never let on, her sad face told him she knew about the affair and the daughter he left behind. "As for you, your future depends upon the respect of the community."

From a young age, Preston knew that one day he would be the most talked about doctor in all of Mississippi. Greater still, he would be a legend all along the gulf coast. In the idle moment, he is caught by surprise when, once again, his thoughts drift to DeViney Pines. High marks following his third form year guaranteed a future in medicine, a career he had set his sights on before he learned to read.

"Some of my fondest memories took place in my learning years, during a time I didn't expect my actions would later come to haunt me," Duncan continues. "Soon after law school, my job in the Delta had me traveling Mississippi's back roads. It was a time to remember. I enjoyed fried dills at a lively place in Hollywood—a dot on the map some twenty miles south of Memphis. Later, I rested against a cracked windshield at a blues festival in knee-deep cotton outside Greenwood's city limits with a blanket so worn, I was convinced it lost its mate when it went afloat with Brother Noah. Now is not the time to ask how the idiom *we're in tall cotton* came about. Trust me when I say, it's best to let that sleeping dog lie."

Hearing his father's words, Preston listens with renewed admiration. He has heard the stories many times, but there is something in his father's inflection that holds his interest.

"When I was hungry, I ate corn tamales offered at a kiosk in Greenville. The vendor, a big guy from Tupelo with teeth the color of powdered sugar, was wise to set up shop in a grassy field alongside the river. All I recall about the young woman who took my order was her apron. Her face lit up when she told me she bought it in Birmingham. Her name escapes me, but believe me when I say she served up a million-dollar smile and a mean tamale. I've heard it said living in the Delta might dumb you down, but there is not an ounce of truth in it."

In the blink of an eye, the smile fades from his face. "Son, an affair may be a bit rebellious and put a short-lived smile on your face, but it doesn't pay the bills or secure a position in life. It can also add a baby to the payroll."

Pausing, he takes a drag off the illegal Cuban. Through weathered lips, he blows a thick gray cloud toward the beamed ceiling. "If you must have this girl, be discreet. Anything more comes with a price—one you can't afford. Perhaps it's time to use this noodle," he suggests, tapping a disjointed finger against his head, "and give the other a break."

Preston lets loose a laugh. Were they not father and son but contemporaries, something tells him they would be the best of friends. "Sometimes I think you should have been a college professor," he says.

"How so?"

"You tend to speak in fifty-minute increments and deliver points you feel necessary to further my education. I'm sure you've been told you have the gift of storytelling."

"Billable hours will do that to a man."

For the first time in a long time, father and son share a laugh and pen a moment in history. Their eyes hint that this moment, however grand, will be short-lived.

"With all due respect, I'm not going to roll over because you say I should."

Leaning forward, Duncan takes another drag off the cigar before tapping a thimble of ash into a silver tray he keeps for sentimental reasons he no longer recalls. A slim sliver in his memory hints it has something to do with a night out decades earlier with his fraternity brothers. "Son, we come from a different heyday. We most likely agree there are only seven continents, but I'm here to say we have only six types of people in this world. Those who make things happen, those who watch what happens, and those who continue to wonder what happened."

"And the other three?"

"They apply to women. I call it the dangerous category. It's a whole new ballgame. Tread carefully: they might come across as cute and cuddly and smelling like lilacs, but underneath all that sugar lies a strong woman ready to mark her place in history. They laugh at jokes they've heard us share a dozen times. You buy them a nice dinner and shower them with token jewelry, and they'll stroke exaggerated egos until the cows come home. When it comes to sexual pleasure, they know only to please." Reminiscing about a time he will never relive, he circles the ice in his glass. "We marry the other type."

"You missed a type."

"What about it?"

"You didn't elaborate on them."

"If you know what's good for you, you shouldn't either. Girls like your muse are a dime a dozen." Duncan ends a laugh with a frothy cough.

"Are you drinking enough water?"

"I don't drink water. And quit trying to distract me."

"My apologies. Would you care for orange juice?"

"Not at this hour. Have you noticed how much better it tastes with champagne? Now, about this woman: are you telling me you honestly believe you are her only lover? I'm betting her flag is planted all throughout Harrison County."

"Times are different today."

"Oh, you young folks. Always reaching for excuses. I may be as old as dirt, but I believe you will agree my advice is spot-on. It's all cake and ice cream now, but there will be hell to pay when the candles blow out."

"You know you're not as old as dirt, but I will agree you sure the heck are working on it."

"Sit back and take a good long look down the road. Is this risk worth taking? You are holding a winning hand. If you will honor my advice, let it be that it is best not to gamble what you can't afford to lose. I have a suggestion: let her be your playmate, a pinup girl, so to speak—Miss June, July, and if she's a Leo, Miss August." Finding his idea genius, Duncan raises ungroomed brows. "I'll be candid with you. Women like your mistress should be treated like timeshares. When you check out, leave the key behind."

"You might be on to something there," Preston agrees. "We are living in a time when strippers and porn stars are instant celebrities, and while your idea sounds like a plan, it's not going to happen. She demands more from me."

"Do you hear yourself? Grow up. Be a man. You might think of me as a feeble old coot removed from the ability to think clearly, but I still have some of my wits about me. It does not work in your favor to dismiss me. This woman will ruin you, tarnish your reputation, and divide you from all you know, love, and enjoy, Peggy included. If you honor one last request, let it be that your interest in her dies here. I worry if you carry on with her, it will be your undoing. Simply put, it will be you who pays the ultimate price." Pressing against the chair's headrest, Duncan raises a hand to his chin. "Is it too much to ask that you make me proud of you?"

"You are attempting to argue what you want my position to be and not what it is. Please stop."

Unmoved by his son's blatant display of disrespect, Duncan stares into the young man's unyielding eyes. "You've heard it said, *Women like her will grab onto whoever has the bologna in his pocket.*" Releasing the chair's brake, he rolls over the rug like a lifeless sloth. "She's a scam artist, always ready to game the system. Son, if you don't defend your values, you'll lose them. Need I remind you, one falls faster than one rises?"

CHAPTER 5

"You're going to need a different car. One that doesn't tie you to me," Preston says, tossing a stack of bills on the bed. "If you're worried about cash, there's more where that came from."

"I'm not sure about this. How am I supposed to buy a car, let alone hide one? I can't park it at my house." Coming unglued, Molly recalls the dreadful day Clay caught her red-handed with Richard. The memory has her chewing her nails down to the quick and pacing the floor. A sixth sense warns she will not be as lucky next time.

"Go by Imperial Motors," Preston tells her.

"I don't know where that is."

"Used to be Ike's. Same owner, different name. Tell the salesman you're looking for a reliable car. Flirt if you must—it seems to work in your favor—but stay focused. You don't need a car with all the bells and whistles. If they have something they believe will run another couple of years, run it by Ivan."

"Who is Ivan?"

"My mechanic. His garage is on Driftwood, across from the Exxon station. Have him look it over—check the engine, kick the tires, note the mileage. He'll know what to do."

"I'm thinking we should purchase a new car—one with warranties."

"We are not *we*, and I can't move that much money without raising a red flag. Pay cash and have it registered in your name."

"My name? Are you sure? This is insane."

"Absolutely. We need to keep a low profile. Whatever you do, do not leave a paper trail. My wife can't get wind of this. Don't bother asking why."

Wife. She knows he has one, but given his words and actions, especially in recent weeks, she's let herself believe a divorce is imminent and on the horizon.

"I pegged you to marry someone with a French name. Something pretty, like Anna or Tatiana. Maybe Camelia."

"Those are not common French names," he says, laughing.

Although laughing along, she questions his protection of the woman whose bed he shares, but whose heart he has no problem betraying. "I'm not sure about this."

"What's there to be unsure about?"

"What about Clay?"

"What about him? I don't understand the question."

"What if he catches me driving a different car?"

"Wear a big hat, maybe sunglasses. Do what you can to change your appearance."

Hundreds of questions wait on her tongue, but knowing an argument will follow, she lets them slide. "What about insurance?"

"I'll pay for it. Have the statements sent to my office."

"What if they fall into Clay's hands?"

"Won't happen," he says, pulling her close. "Don't stress this." Offering reassurance, he plants a gentle kiss on her cheek. "Another thing. You're going to need a storage unit."

"Oh, Preston, how am I going to explain the cost?"

"You can't be seen driving your car here. Although it may take weeks for someone to notice, we can't risk anyone knowing about the new car." He rubs the back of his neck with an easiness to be admired. "When you're not meeting me, the car stays in storage." Opening his wallet, he forks over another stack of cash.

"Are you going to slam me with a 1099?" she asks indignantly.

"The tax form?"

"The one and only."

"This is a gift. Pay in advance. Twelve months, if they'll do it. Keep the receipts in the glove box."

"When should I do this?"

"No time like the present," he says casually. "Can you go by Imperial this afternoon?"

"I'll try. I have to be at the office in an hour."

"What's happening at the office?"

"I told Clay I'd help him with new patient charts and consultations. He also has an interview with a physician's assistant."

Months earlier, when he'd interviewed Clay, Preston was not impressed with his dossier, but learning he was still married to Molly, he hurried to add him to the payroll. Having Clay under his thumb allows Preston to know his schedule—and, when he needs to work it to his advantage, prepare it.

"Take care of it before the end of the week. When time allows, get a burner phone."

"Am I dealing drugs now, too?"

"It's cheap, prepaid, and disposable," says Preston calmly, ignoring her sarcasm. "Look for one without a contract. If Clay gets his hands on your cell phone, it wouldn't look good if we are exchanging calls."

"Where do I find one?"

"Wherever you see illegal activity, but start with a reputable phone store."

CHAPTER 6

A flashing billboard at the corner of Pelican Road and Port Sunrise announces that the temperature has climbed to ninety degrees and checking is free to new and returning customers.

Always eager to spend another's dollar when she has only pennies in her pocket, Molly wonders if she should change banks. A struggle with the lace wig the salesclerk guaranteed would hold a snug fit keeps her on focus. Each time she positions the cascade of chestnut brown locks east to west, the hairpiece heads south. Weighty bangs rest above her nose, leaving a mess of long locks flying at her face and clinging to her lipstick. An untimely glance in the mirror has her believing she looks like Abraham Lincoln.

The car's open windows must stay that way, and an oppressive easterly wind is not helping. It is only now she understands why the cab driver waited until they left the curb to inform her the car's air-conditioner is on the blink.

"If I had known I was stepping into an oven, I would have thrown you in headfirst and slammed the door," she snarls.

"You want out?" the driver asks, addressing her in the rearview mirror.

"I want my money's worth."

The driver, a morbidly obese man bald as an onion, shoves a

sweating big-sip cup into the space between them. "Wanna drink? It's cold."

"Ew."

"Yeah, I probably shouldn't drink after you. I might catch something."

One mile into the drive to Imperial Motors, she yanks the wig from her head and shoves it into her handbag. Given the car's stale air, sweat continues to roll. Using the sleeve of her blouse, she wipes her forehead. She is tempted to call Preston and demand he take care of the car situation, but a glance at the rearview mirror warns that the cabby is keeping her in his sights. It is unlikely, especially with his deep Jersey accent, that he knows Preston, but the risk is not worth taking.

"What's the address again?" he asks.

"I don't know the address. It's Imperial Motors. It's up ahead on the right. I believe I see the sign."

Hoping to make a few extra bucks, the driver speeds up. Passing the entrance, he allows a grin to own his face.

"You just missed it."

"You want me to pull over?"

"Circle the block, you idiot. It's too hot to walk, especially in high heels and this stupid wig."

The cabby slows his speed, crawls to the corner, and turns a blind eye to the posted sign allowing him to make a right turn on red. Four stoplights later, he takes a fast turn into the dealership, eases up on the gas, and rolls to a stop.

"Fourteen sixty-five," he says, throwing out a weathered palm.

Reeling from the extra mile, Molly counts out fourteen one-dollar bills. Feeling his eyes on her, she fishes the bottom of her purse for loose change. "You owe me a dime."

"Of course," he responds, giving her a handful of dirty pennies.

Hustling from the car, she skips over the lot to an orange station wagon, but stops short when a green Jaguar outfitted with a rainbow of colorful balloons flirts with her. Parked side-by-side, the cars remind her of the pumpkins she used to snatch from her neighbors' porches back in Sugar Ditch Alley, an impoverished neighborhood once known for its open sewer, slumlords, washboard roads, fields of cotton, and Darrell Getoe. Each time she passed by his house, a beastly man unknown to her offered a sleazy smile through a weathered screen door. Darrell had eyes on her since third grade—and when liberties were taken, thick dry hands reached out for her.

Years later, when puberty boosted his confidence, young Darrell came at her in a wife-beater, ducktail hair, and a pack of Marlboros tucked into the pocket of jeans so tight they left nothing to the imagination. Each time he tried to cop a feel, he was met with a slap to his face. An online search of the local paper hinted he left town in search of greener pastures after Sunday morning church service, taking with him a pipe dream, a pit-bull rescue, and a four-by-eight U-Haul trailer.

What little she remembers of the town includes boarded-up windows and doors, packs of gnarly stray dogs, abandoned gas stations along US 61, and a church across the street from Mexie's Market. As a wild child raised without direction, a house of worship and false promises never appealed to her.

Returning her thoughts to the dealership, she canvasses the lot with hungry eyes until a black Mercedes with spoke wheels and a panorama sunroof draws her in. She is pressed against the window when she hears footsteps closing in behind her. Brushing her locks aside, she turns to find a middle-aged man wearing an older man's skin.

"Hello, young lady. I'm Rex Kennedy." Extending a hand, the salesman gives a low whistle. "This is a fine car. Let me grab the key, and we'll take it for a drive."

"Hold your horses, sunshine. I have two questions. Does it have all the bells and whistles?"

"It's beyond loaded."

"How is that possible? *Beyond loaded*, I mean. It's either loaded or not loaded."

"This year's model has a mini fridge in the trunk. It's the envy of every customer who shops fresh. Have I mentioned the engine purrs like a kitten?"

"I like frozen foods with additives. Keeps me guessing about my health," she says with a cheeky grin. "I don't care for trunks. Women get thrown into them never to be seen again. Did I mention I'm allergic to cats?"

Unable to read her, the salesman shifts his weight about. "This beauty comes with cooling vents built into reclining bucket seats. Tucked inside the car's generous trunk is a keyless safe meant to protect your valuables should you feel the need. The passenger visor has a forty-watt makeup mirror for those last minute touch-ups before the theatre or opera—mascara, lipstick, and a touch of rouge. I'm sure a gorgeous woman like yourself knows the drill."

"Next you're going to tell me it comes with a water park for the kiddos."

"That's in the design phase for next year," he parries. "The extended model, of course."

"Listen up, car boy, I can't do all the bells and whistles, and I'm not interested in your spiel," Molly snaps, unamused. "Do us both a favor and save your pitch for someone who cares. By the way, nice jacket."

"Thanks." Believing he is the victim of a prank, he scans the lot for hidden cameras. "Well, the car is not driverless, and perhaps we can take out the spare tire."

"Next question—I told you upfront I have two. Do you have anything in the five-thousand-dollar range?" Turning her back to him, she scans the lot.

Left confused, the salesman withholds a laugh. "See that row of flags?" Raising a finger, he points to a lot behind the showroom. "You might find something back there."

Moments pass, and the silence they share is awkward and uncomfortable, leaving them short on words.

"Are we going over there?" Molly asks.

"I'm stationed in this section. We have several salespeople out back who can match you to the perfect car." Turning on his heel, he races across the lot toward a young couple admiring a sleek convertible with a five-figure price tag.

Wiping at beads of sweat, Molly staggers toward the flags and peeks into several cars. She is feeling the onset of dehydration when a salesman approaches.

"I'm Danny Bird. Rex told me you're looking for a car." Shifting about, he offers his card and a bottle of water.

"Did Rex mention my budget?" Taking the bottle, she throws the cold plastic to her neck. Never one to seek approval from the masses—and that includes Danny Bird—she cares about two things and two things only: herself and money.

"He did indeed," Danny replies.

"That's brilliant, given I'm sweating bullets walking around your dealership."

"Please accept my apology. Here at Imperial, we always say customers are our business."

"I think you mean cars. Cars are your business."

"Touché. I understand you don't want all the bells and whistles." Like Rex, he fails to stifle his amusement. "I have the perfect car for you." Adjusting dark frames and standing tall in a lightweight jacket and khakis, he leads her across the lot to a silver four-door. "This beauty has a few bells, but not all the whistles. I challenge you to find another car that will stop on a dime." Opening the driver's door, he invites her to have a look inside. "At forty-nine hundred, it's right under your budget. I believe you'll agree the low mileage is a bonus."

"Please tell me it has air-conditioning."

"It does indeed."

"With coolant?"

"A feature we in the business call a *whistle*."

She wants to tell him she does not appreciate his humor, but hoping to negotiate the price, she lets it slide. "I need to run it by my mechanic."

"Of course. Let me get the key. I will need a copy of your driver's license. Would you like me to ride along with you?"

"Not now, not ever, and never in my wildest dreams."

Minutes later, she is in the driver's seat wondering if the new-car smell is the real deal or the scent from the tree ornament hanging from the rearview mirror. Three city blocks later, she wipes at the beads of sweat forming behind her ears.

The traffic light up ahead is turning yellow when she catches sight of the front end of the car next to her. When she looks back at the light, she finds it is now red. The slam to the brakes throws her purse to the floorboard. Reaching for her belongings, her eyes fall on the car next to her.

Dana, a young woman she recognizes from Clay's office, offers a wide smile while lowering the driver's window. Cranking the air with her hand, she invites Molly to do the same.

"Hey, Mrs. Lambert, did you get a new car?"

"I wish. Mine is in the shop. Nothing major, just a flat tire. This is a loaner until mine is repaired." The honking of the horn from an impatient driver lets her know the light has changed and she is to get a move on. "Gotta go," she says, peeling out.

In the passing minutes, she curses her bad luck and poor timing. Reliving the encounter, she presses the accelerator to the floor. "Forget Ivan. Now I need a different car." A red light holds her at the next corner, giving her a chance to admire the dashboard's sleek and sexy gadgets—that is, until her eyes fall on the car's odometer. "Low mileage, my ass," she snaps.

The second the light changes, she circles back toward the dealership. Just when she accelerates, a cyclist racing through traffic cuts in front of her, nearly causing an accident.

"Get your murdercycle out of my way," she yells while idling next to him at the stoplight. "If you don't want to be a donor cyclist, wear a frickin' helmet."

Ignoring her rage, the biker responds with an upturned finger.

Not to be outdone, she flings the water bottle at his head. Should fingers come pointing, she will fess up to the crime, while adding he has manners to learn. Minutes later, when she turns into Imperial Motors, Danny hurries to greet her.

"That was fast."

"Once I saw the 'low mileage,'" she sounds off, "I turned back around. I need a less-traveled car."

Lifting his sunglasses, he leans through the driver's window. "Must be a typo. I'll have it corrected. I do, however, have another car, an Audi, you might be interested in. It has a souped-up engine, leather seats, and new tires."

"Any surprises I should know about?"

"It's a 2002, with air-conditioning and coolant." He climbs behind the wheel and turns over the engine. "It has just under a hundred thousand miles. If you're planning to finance, we can't do it here when the engine has over seventy-five thousand miles on it."

"That's not a problem. I'll be paying with cash."

"Great. Do you want to run it by your mechanic?"

"I don't have time. Can you hurry the paperwork? I'm trying to wrap this up during my lunch hour." It is not for him to know she has all the time in the world but cannot risk running into someone who could later place her in the car.

"In that case, I'll make you a sweet deal. Something I call the Triple D."

"It kills me to ask what that stands for."

"Danny's Deal of the Day. By the way, the Razorback bumper sticker and the hula dancer are on the house."

"Actually, one is on the bumper and the other is on the dashboard. For what it's worth, I was hoping for a coffee mug," she responds with her usual sarcasm.

CHAPTER 7

The drive-out tag has been attached to the Audi's rear bumper for only a handful of days when the car's hacking cough and thick gray fumes escaping the tailpipe have Molly cursing the salesman who suckered her into buying the junker. The interior smells like a litter box, and the shoulder strap works double-time as a straitjacket. The brake pad responds with a lingering bark each time she gives it the boot. A near collision at a four-way intersection near the marina's entrance leaves her wondering if a crash helmet is in her future. When time permits, she will file a complaint with Ike, the owner of Imperial Motors, and Danny Bird, who lives up to the industry's reputation.

The plastic hula dancer rocks the car's dashboard while she, still in a stranglehold, rakes slim fingers through a flame of fiery red hair. A nod of approval from the sedan's rearview mirror puts a mischievous smile on her face.

Exiting the car, she fumbles with a ring of patchwork keys. Finding the coast clear, she meanders the marina's parking lot, giving herself time to find the words to explain to Preston that the rental unit's statements will be sent to Celeste, a trusted confidante. Earlier in the day, when she asked the woman at the storage facility to place the receipts in the car's glove box, she was given a look that said not only no but *hell no*: "That would require us to enter your unit, and we aren't doing that without a court order and a deputy sheriff."

Onboard the boat, Preston runs his tongue over hungry lips. Careful to remain out of sight, he gives the door a gentle kick, allowing Molly safe passage.

Once inside, she turns the lock, and with a titillating sway she knows he cannot resist, beckons him to her side.

"Hot damn, Molly." Taking her in his arms, he explores the small of her back. Holding her with a kiss, he moves on to the curve of her neck. Horned up, he lifts her narrow hips to his, and with passionate finesse certain to drive her wild, nibbles at her lip.

Molly's gentle sigh encourages him to linger a little longer. Pleasing her excites him, and knowing she will soon return the favor sends him over the edge.

A gentle pull at her dress offers a teasing glimpse of a black leather bustier and scant apron he doubts would ever pass muster in a chef's kitchen.

In the coming minutes, silk panties fall from her hips. A practiced shimmy has the dress pooling at her feet. She displays the grace of a trained ballerina as a tantalizing sway of her hips knocks her striptease out of the park. Feeling Preston's eyes on her, she reaches for her bag. A lingering search for the pink feather duster gives him a peek at her backside.

"*Oui, oui, monsieur*," she says, acting playfully coy.

"What is mademoiselle's job today?"

"What is it you wish of me?"

"You can be sure it isn't housekeeping."

Taking his hand, she guides him through the boat's salon toward the aft cabin. Along the way, the apron slips from her hips while the feather duster brushes along the floor, sweeping away their sins.

Standing tall behind the cabin's door, Preston attempts a provocative striptease he learned watching late-night television. Holding her with his eyes, he tosses his shirt to the cabin's far corner. Linen slacks soon follow.

Moving over to the bed, she tosses the pillows to the floor. She reaches for her wig, but Preston is quick on the draw.

"Leave it on. It's working for me. Grab the feather duster. I say it's time we have a little fun."

CHAPTER 8

It is the first day of June, and the fog is lifting over Casino Beach. Near the mudflats, in the mucky shallows, a washed-out metal buoy bobs in rhythm with slow-rolling waves. South of the bay, along the Low Mile, food trucks serve up oyster po'boys and the gulf's daily catch.

Amateur photographers, tripods in hand and cameras swinging at their sides, hurry to catch a snowy egret basking in the dog days of summer. Their need to rush ends when a flying fish catches the egret's eye.

In the shallow waters, a safe distance from the deepwater port, day sailors onboard catboats and Flying Scots repeat drills they hope will later earn the much-desired Skipper Award. Shouts are heard and fingers point when a cigarette boat parts their water, leaving their two-man scooters in its wake.

Outside the channel, where the water's depth reaches ninety-plus feet on the outskirts near the markers, a fishing boat pulls trawl netting through the dark water, hoping to ensnare a generous catch of unsuspecting shrimp, fresh oysters, and the occasional speckled trout.

Positioned against a wooden boom, Preston watches a Twin Otter seaplane prepare for landing. Squaring broad shoulders darkened in recent days by the warm sun, he lets go a deep sigh while stretching tired arms. His last hours were spent scrubbing salt water from the boat's windows and teak deck, and although his back was feeling the pain, attacking barnacles near the boat's underbelly. A hand through damp hair and over his forehead warns he is sporting the scent of hard work.

Adrift, a blue-water cruiser he claimed when his father gave up sailing, is outfitted with a week's worth of provisions and essentials. A circular life preserver displays the boat's name in a swirl of whimsical letters. Foul-weather gear and waterproof flashlights wait under lime-green vinyl cushions—not his color of choice, but one he will live with until pressed to make a change. Although his father no longer joins him on the boat, Duncan's tackle for deep-sea fishing remains stored in a bin near the boat's dive platform.

A list of man-overboard drills hangs from a bronze hook near the helm. Inches away, in a frame made of teak his father salvaged from a boatyard when he traded a sailboat for the cruiser, is a generous menu of bar drinks. It includes the Quarter Deck and the Poop Deck, spritz cocktails his father perfected over the years. Lately, Preston has come to enjoy the vodka aperitifs, too.

Out of the corner of his eye, Preston watches a blonde beauty like none he has ever seen approach the pier. When Peggy turns in his direction, he admires her smile. White capris kiss her slim ankles, and a boatneck sweater the color of mango sorbet matches a narrow strip on the tongue of her leather topsiders. A diamond pendant he gifted her for reasons he no longer recalls sits nestled in the curve of her neck. Each step is perfectly planted, and the gentle breeze moving through her hair attracts the eye of every sea captain, first mate, and deckhand south of Hattiesburg.

"There's my little skipperette," he says, blowing a kiss off his hand. "Fluffy white clouds and a blue sky taking us out to sea can't hold a candle to you."

"Among your many other wonderful attributes, you're also poetic. Another reason why I love you."

"Welcome, my lovely lady," he says, pulling her into an air hug.

"If you'll excuse me, I have to jump in the shower. Our guests will be here any minute."

Convinced he is the most handsome man in all of Casino Beach, and possibly throughout each and every nook and cranny along Mississippi's Gulf Coast, Peggy matches his wide smile.

"Don't rush. I promise to greet them with open arms. By the way, I'm sorry I'm late. Traffic on the boulevard was bumper-to-bumper."

"Don't give it a second thought. All that matters is that you are here with me."

CHAPTER 9

"Welcome aboard. I hope you didn't have any trouble finding us," Preston says, greeting Clay with a pat to his shoulder.

"Your directions were spot-on. It's impossible to miss the gargantuan anchor lodged in the sand. The dandelions are beautiful this time of year."

"City can't bring itself to get rid of them. You must be Molly," Preston says, turning to the petite blonde at Clay's side. Hoping his wide grin is not obvious, he cups her small hand in his. Keeping her hand longer than manners allow, he massages her slender fingers. "I've heard so much about you, I feel like I've known you all my life."

"Clay's had so many nice things to say about you. Something tells me you two will work well together."

"I have to agree. The time to take on another physician is in the here and now. I'm thrilled the practice is growing by leaps and bounds, but a sudden growth in new patients is cutting into my free time. I'm already spread too thin as it is. As for your husband, he's an asset, not only to the practice but also to the community."

Although Molly nods in agreement, her expression speaks a different truth. Earlier in the day, just minutes before Clay hurried off to the office, she caught a glimpse of his schedule. He has too much free time on his hands, which she worries will cut into hers.

Holding her with his eyes, Preston gives her delicate hand a gentle squeeze. "Dana tells me Clay's appointment calendar is filled through October."

Left standing on the sideline, Clay blushes a little. A natural achiever, he is not one to seek recognition. "Dana works primarily with Preston, but she's balancing my schedule until I find an assistant," he hurries to explain.

Aware eyes are on her, Molly slips her hand from Preston's grip and places it on Clay's back. "As you can see, my husband is very modest."

"An honorable characteristic. Clay tells me you have a son."

"Stepson. I'm Clay's second wife." She turns in Clay's direction. "Or am I your third? Given your alimony and child-support obligations, I've lost count."

Startled and slightly embarrassed, Clay swivels in Molly's direction. Until now, she has always referred to his eight-year-old son as theirs. Although there is some bitterness and consternation regarding his previous marriage, it is not like her to mention it or lessen her relationship with his son. She knows all too well his marriage to her is his second, after all: she was the mistress who shared fault in breaking up his family. The telephone call she placed to his wife in the minutes following a fallout where he begged to end their affair cost him his marriage. It is only in recent months that she has continued to remind him that he suffered a haircut in the divorce. Looking at her now, he takes her derisive smile as a challenge and has little doubt he will later hear what is eating at her.

"Whitt lives with his mother in New Orleans," Clay shares, as Peggy's timely appearance interrupts the conversation.

"Welcome to the Poor Man's Riviera. I'm Peggy Fayne."

"I'm Molly. Molly Lambert." While greetings are exchanged, she gives Peggy the once-over. She is quick to notice that the woman's tiny frame appears solid, and although unpainted, Peggy's nails have recently been treated to a manicure. As much as she hates to admit it, the boatneck sweater emphasizes her rival's delicate collarbone while drawing attention to a large diamond pendant.

"Welcome to the widowmaker," Peggy greets, displaying a genuine smile.

"Is that the boat's name?" Molly asks.

"Not exactly, but this boat has a habit of luring my husband into rough water."

"This boat is as seaworthy as they come," Preston argues, brushing her off with a gentle wave of his hand.

"Of course it is." In fun, Peggy turns back to Molly. "That's why we recite the old Fair Winds and Following Seas before each voyage."

"I'm not sure I know what that is," Molly replies.

"It's a blessing often given at the time of retirement or a farewell ceremony," Clay offers.

"It's also spoken when there is a change of command," Preston adds with a hint of authority.

Molly's eyes light up and an upturned smile owns her face. *There is going to be a change all right. Just you wait and see.*

Always the perfect hostess, Peggy shifts the conversation to something more pleasant. "I've made my famous Peggy-ritas."

"Is it a margarita?" Molly asks.

"It's my own concoction. I hope you'll give it a try and let me know what you think."

"Of course. That's what friends are for, especially new ones."

The savory scent of seasoned crawfish and Old Bay drifts along the deck and between them, cutting their conversation short.

"Preston is convinced everyone loves Cajun food as much as he does."

"I feel terrible," Molly apologizes. "I didn't think to bring something."

"Don't be silly. You're our guests."

"Which reminds me. Guests of guests cannot invite guests," Preston says, placing his hands at the helm. As always, the old saying delivers a laugh.

Tickled by the words she has heard a hundred times, Peggy raises a glass pitcher into the air. "Show of hands if you want salt on the rim."

After throwing a hand in the air, Clay turns back to Preston. "My first boat was a thirty-six-foot Catalina," he begins. "I bought it for a song and dance in Kemah, a city southeast of Houston. I'm sure you know it. An old friend who lives in Nassau Bay told me about it. The owner was facing a divorce, and the boat was the sacrificial lamb. In parts of Texas, where I first learned to maneuver the water, we day-sailed on freshwater lakes. The mosquitos were the size of teething toddlers and just as annoying." Clay wishes he could erase the image of the day he took the boat out for a test run. He and his crew nearly drowned in waist-high water when a fast-moving cutter sent a wall of water their direction. "How long have you been sailing *Adrift*?"

"Since the day I took my first step. She belonged to my father. Given his age, it takes all I have to get him out on the water. She is a solid vessel. Canadians did an outstanding job when they designed this machine. It tracks well and is great for racing." Displaying perfect teeth, Preston gives a proud smile. "As with most boat owners, I always say she is my little thimble in the ocean."

"Back in the days when my summers were free, I sailed the Carolinas' Outer Banks," Clay shares. "Outside of hurricane season, it was nothing less than perfect. I upgraded to a Morgan when I received my first paycheck. When I was a kid growing up in New York City, my parents rented an apartment on the eighteenth floor in an old building with floor-to-ceiling windows looking out over the Hudson River at New Jersey." He pauses to enjoy a hearty laugh and relive memories so vivid, he feels like a curious kid again. "I grew up believing New Jersey farmed our fruits and vegetables."

"I've sailed those waters a few times. Mag Pie and I sailed a Morgan through the Grenadines."

Although she laughs along, Peggy shakes a no-nonsense finger. "Oh, Preston, they don't want to hear about our honeymoon or that you call me Mag Pie."

"Oh, but we do, Mag Pie," Molly says, kicking off strappy sandals and tucking tanned legs at her side. "I want to hear all about your honeymoon and that gorgeous ring," she says, pointing to the jewel on Peggy's finger.

"It belonged to her mother ... Harry Winston, I believe," Preston explains.

Unfamiliar with Harry Winston, Molly points to her own ring. "Allow me to introduce Itty-Bitty Betty. Given our finances, I worry it's either diamond dust or cubic zirconia."

"That diamond dust, as you call it, set me back a pretty penny," Clay reminds.

"We were undecided on where we wanted to go for our honeymoon," Preston throws out. "I grew up here, so I was always out on the water. Peggy's idea of being on the water is sunbathing poolside or walking the beach, where she snaps pictures of those worthless weeds shooting up along the coastline."

"As it should be," Peggy chimes. "I adore the golden dandelions. They may be weeds to you, but there is something about their angelic petals I can't help but love."

"Same here," Molly interrupts. "Not the dandelions—they make me sneeze—but sitting poolside. If I can't relax on the water, I want a cold drink in my hand and the waves lulling me off to sleep. There's something comforting about the afternoon sun on my face and feeling warm sand between my toes. If it's allowed, and even if it isn't, I'm going topless. There is nothing worse than uneven tan lines."

Peggy cringes at the thought of exposing not only her skin to the sun's rays but parts of her body she keeps private and shares only with Preston. "Preston spends most of his free days visiting islands he's explored a dozen times. I decided we needed to explore something different. Something outside the life of luxury."

"While I concurred," Preston added, "I agreed not for long. A week at best. I suggested visiting national parks, rafting the Rio Grande, or windsurfing over San Diego's Torrey Pines." Revisiting the memory puts a grin on his face. "Peggy wanted to honeymoon in Italy. She spent a year in Florence at the Palazzo Pitti where she studied the rooms of Palatine Gallery." He gives her a wink he knows she will appreciate. "Tell them about your favorite room."

"They were all masterpieces, but my heart fell for the Room of Jupiter. It displays the Veiled Lady, the woman loved by its creator, Raphael, a sixteenth-century artist." Pausing, she places a hand over her heart. "It was magical."

Always careful to hide her inner thoughts, Molly sits in envy. She has never been given the opportunity to travel abroad or explore places she has only read about in magazines stolen from waiting rooms and the neighbor's mailbox. "Given Clay's financial obligations, I'm lucky to explore Casino Beach." Her anger building, she shoots dark eyes to Clay before returning to Peggy and Preston. "How did you lovebirds meet?"

"We were introduced through a mutual friend," Preston explains. "A warming sensation in her heart told her we'd be perfect for each other. When she thought I wasn't listening, she mentioned something about line dancing. Over the next several days, she sent us candid photos she thought we'd enjoy. The first picture I received showed Peggy perched on a rock overlooking the Grand Canyon."

"I received a picture capturing Preston resting against a wine barrel in France."

"She was wearing a turtleneck sweater," Preston adds.

"He sported ugly shoes. For what it's worth, I dodge line dancing."

"I wanted to see more skin."

"I hoped he was open to new shoes."

"I don't care for turtlenecks. I feel like I'm choking to death," Molly interjects. "I go to great lengths to dodge museums. The artists I know are a bit off-center. I wouldn't trust them to water my lawn. I've never been to Italy. Come to think of it, I haven't been out of Mississippi."

Rambling a bit, she leans in. "As a young girl, when I pictured my wedding, I dreamed of wearing a lace gown, a veil so long it would sweep the aisle, and the church choir singing from the balcony. I wanted to be the envy of every woman who gathered to celebrate my special day. As it turned out, we were not given a lavish wedding in a historical cathedral known for its stained-glass windows. We didn't register for gifts, decorate a hall, or design a red-velvet cake with a slice left over to enjoy on our first anniversary. When our wedding day arrived, we stood side-by-side in a civil ceremony, nodding to a lowly official in juvenile court whose sad face let on he was counting the days until he would meet up with us in divorce court. I wore a white dress with bell sleeves that flared just below my elbows, and Clay wore a button-down shirt I ironed just before leaving the house. There wasn't a bouquet to toss, a shower of rice to run under, or a cork to pop."

"Oh!" Peggy lets slip.

"It was nothing like what you must be thinking," Molly adds. "The city court clerk had a full schedule, and neither of us has family to speak of. Given Clay's commitments, money was tight. We honeymooned in Jackson."

"We stayed at the Magnolia Inn," Clay adds.

"I spent the first day sprawled out on the hotel's rooftop garden like a desert lizard. I ended up with a painful sunburn from my forehead all the way down to the soles of my feet. The rest of the trip was awful."

"It wasn't much fun for me either," Clay snickers.

Preston laughs along until Peggy shakes a finger at him.

"We've stayed there. It's a nice place. I recall the room service is award-winning," Peggy says with a smile.

Clay uncrosses his legs and shrugs his shoulders. "I was doing my residency. Money and time were commodities I had yet to enjoy."

"We were so poor, I couldn't afford to window-shop," Molly adds.

"You're making it sound like we were living on skid row," Clay defends.

"Darn near. I painted my nails with polish I purchased at flea markets. Later, when I learned the FDA had pulled them off the market, I worried I'd wake up one morning with nails thin as paper."

Interrupting, Preston invites Molly to look out over the water.

"See that flat coast behind you? It's what the locals call the Low Mile, but trust me, that's the great state of Mississippi. As of right about now, give or take a mile, we are in international waters. You, my friend, are out of Mississippi."

Looking back at the coast, Molly's face lights up. "Oh, Preston, I will remember this day forever."

"My wife is from a town of not many," Clay throws out in a whisper.

"This calls for a celebration," Peggy says, breaking the awkward moment with the clap of her hands.

"I want to hear about your honeymoon," Molly says, inching forward in her chair.

"I read an article about an offshore sailing course," Preston begins. "Before talking it over with Peggy, I called the school. An hour later, we were booked on a fourteen-day excursion. After I hung up the phone, I called Peggy. I gave her the details, but I have to admit, I may have embellished a little. In the long run, she was thrilled."

"A little? I was falsely led to believe we would sail the waters on a crewed yacht, which I might add included a chef."

"I failed to disclose we would be the ones wearing aprons." He turns to Clay, who, besides giving up a grin, offers little support. "She arrived with three bags."

"Three bags for a sailing vacation?" Clay asks, roaring.

"I always overpack. There is nothing worse than not having something to wear," Peggy throws out with a smile.

"That's never been a problem for me. She, on the other hand, packs like she's staying for a lifetime," Preston teases.

"That's simply not true."

"Tell them how many swimsuits you packed."

"Let's agree it was more than ten."

"We took the red-eye out of Miami. Turbulence held onto our coattails all the way to Saint Lucia. I felt sorry for Peggy. When she wasn't bouncing around in her seat, she was eyeing the long line to the plane's lavatory. She never put down the barf bag. I've traveled a great deal, but I'll agree that was one rough flight. When we finally arrived on the island, it was after midnight, and we were beyond exhausted. We couldn't see the moon for the dense rain forest. Never saw another set of headlights or a streetlamp."

"When we checked in at the resort, a woman at the desk handed us an envelope with sailing info and these little plastic cups," Peggy says, holding her fingers inches apart. "I swear they were filled with antiseptics and germicide. One sip had my intestines in a knot." The face she makes mirrors the one she gave that night years earlier.

"We dropped off our bags, which included diving gear, and followed the signs to the resort's tiki bar. It was laid out like a gazebo—open on all sides with several hammocks overlooking the bay." Preston speaks slowly, as though reliving the island's warm sand under his feet and a gentle breeze at his back. "I wanted to read through the material, but Peggy insisted we relax and enjoy a cocktail. Once she let her guard down, no doubt brought on by what we hoped was rum, I studied the material while she studied the guests at the bar."

"I was curious if our captain and crew had arrived," Peggy explains. "We were celebrating at the bar, not so much the wedding but having survived the life-threatening drive through the mountainous terrain to the resort. I swear we were on a bus held together by staples and Elmer's glue. Our driver, who drove like Steve McQueen, felt it his duty to point out the cars and buses that weren't as fortunate. Preston, do you remember his broken English?"

"Botched and mutilated."

"After our second drink, we wagered who could spot our captain. I just knew I could pick him out of a crowd."

"And she did. She poked me in the ribs and pointed to a tall, gnarly guy with a deep tan and bleached hair. Well, sure enough, he takes the stool next to her. It took only a second for her to ask if he was with Island Sailing."

The memory puts an easy smile on Peggy's face. "Our captain was a trust fund baby with a free spirit. His name was Hamm. If I'm not mistaken, I believe he told us it was a family name. I recall hearing he was named after his great-grandfather."

"I've never sailed with them, but I understand they have a decent sailing school," Clay adds.

"You have no idea," Peggy says with an easy laugh.

Warmed by the midday sun and the memory, Preston laughs along. "The following morning, we met up in the hotel lobby. Hamm was there …"

"Along with eight sailors I thought were the crew," Peggy adds.

"We were shuffled into a conference room where Hamm set up easels displaying navigation charts and diagrams, man-overboard drills, distress signals—all sorts of how-to-survive-on-the-water presentation boards. When we were asked to take a seat," Preston says, turning apologetic eyes to Peggy, "all hell broke loose."

"I thought there had been a mistake," she says. "We weren't there to learn to sail and chart courses, but to celebrate our marriage and enjoy our honeymoon."

"So what did you do?" Clay asks, inching forward in his chair.

"I can't speak for what most would do, but I immediately resigned from the course."

"Peggy was madder than Lewis Carroll's hatter."

"The instructor called me Alice for the duration of our honeymoon, and those other people we thought were the crew were also enrolled in the course."

"Are you saying you shared your honeymoon with strangers?" Molly asks, scrunching her nose. Although she shudders at the thought, she would have welcomed such an adventure.

"Darn near, and we didn't have time to dive. Preston, tell them about the couple from Ann Arbor."

A man who enjoys the spotlight, Preston jumps at the opportunity. "They were seasoned sailors. Judy and … I can't recall his name."

"Doug. Surely you remember it was short for Doug."

"That's right. How stupid of me to forget. When we learned we were sharing a boat, they casually called the aft cabin."

"That's usually the larger cabin," Clay explains to Molly.

"Thanks, Einstein," she spouts, tongue-in-cheek. "He forgets I've been on a boat before."

"Peggy suggested we flip a coin. Heads picked first. She tossed the quarter into the air, and like children waiting to hear who their teacher will be in the coming school year, we watched in anticipation while the coin circled the air before taking a hard landing on the dock." Recalling the moment and the high-five they exchanged, he gives a tender smile. "She may not know it, but Peggy is always at the helm. I show her the map and line up the coordinates, but she charts the course to her own destination."

"Our destination," she corrects, lovingly.

"I have to admit, there is some satisfaction knowing someone had a honeymoon worse than mine," Molly says, licking the salt from the rim of her glass.

CHAPTER 10

"Hey, big guy, I'm lucky," Molly says, pulling at the front of her blouse. The snaps pop open, exposing sun-kissed cleavage and a comical tattoo of a miniature poodle she drew on earlier in the day with a marker. "And now, so are you."

Preston cannot hide his disappointment. What is more frustrating are the hours he wasted rescheduling his appointments so he could sneak away. "While that remains to be seen, what's with the hair? You look like a cotton ball."

The lack of expression on her face tells him his observation, along with his humor, is lost.

"Lose the gum. While it may work for some, all I see is a mass of toothpaste rolling over your tongue."

"That's a problem all of a sudden?"

"Not all of a sudden, but always."

While he undresses, she presses a small mirror to her face. Taken by her beauty, he watches as she runs slim fingers through platinum blonde hair. His interest soon spills over onto a web of spider-leg lashes, vampy brows, blood-red lips, and purple eyes.

"Careful with the lipstick. Even the smallest smudge can get me into trouble."

Although she laughs, once again she is reminded of his concern for his wife. He does not mention Peggy by name, still, she hates when he allows his thoughts to turn to her. After all, this is her time with him.

"Perhaps I should wear a color closer to the pasty red Peggy wears."

A foghorn sounds out over the water, reminding him that he should tread carefully. They have been reunited for only a short time, and he is not sure he can trust her. A walk down memory lane reminds there may never come a time he can fully trust her actions. "What's with the purple eyes?"

"They match my blouse."

"As good a reason as any to harm your vision. Colored contact lenses can cause damage, including blindness. I hope you were fitted through an ophthalmologist."

"Given the cost of health care, I can't afford the appointment. I was forced to buy them from a renegade carney at a three-day carnival outside Biloxi," she says, staring him down like a suited-up sheriff in a Jimmy Stewart western. "I was there to see the bearded lady. Now that I think about it, she looked a bit like Peggy. You know what I'm talking about." Pausing, she swipes a finger over her lip. "That fine white fuzz that appears above her lip when she's had too much fun in the sun."

"Although I'm entertained with your getups, will there ever come a time when you'll arrive in basic black?" he asks, skipping over the insult thrown at his wife.

"Basic black often comes with orange lipstick."

"Is this a good time to explore our differences?"

"Only if you want to rendezvous alone."

Shifting gears, he pulls her close. The scent of her perfume sends him over the edge. Their lingering kiss is long, hard, and full of promise. Hunger has him grabbing onto the waistband of her jeans. The longing in her eyes lets him know she wants him, too. He traces her neck with his tongue, and when he moves on to her hot spots, sparks begin to fly. "I'm going to enjoy you from stem to stern."

"You're not hearing any resistance from me," she says, displaying a seductive smile. "Have I told you I love that you are a man of your word?"

"More than once, baby. More than once."

CHAPTER 11

A spicy bouquet of seasoned crab and Andouille sausage follows Peggy to the front door. Exchanging a hug, she escorts Molly toward the terrace. "I'm so glad you are able to join us. When Clay mentioned you had another commitment, I was sorry we wouldn't be together."

"I wouldn't miss this evening for the world. I'm just sorry Clay arrived without me."

"Don't give it another thought."

They are several steps into the living room when a fat cat brushes Molly's ankle with its long, thick tail. In a quick turnabout, the feline scurries off, but not before vomiting at her feet.

"What the hell was that?"

"That's Jupiter. You'll have to excuse her. She's a little sneakster with a sensitive stomach."

Molly wants to sweep up the little monster and drop-kick it through a window, but feeling Peggy's eyes on her, she shrugs off the idea. One thing is certain, though. Jupiter will not be so lucky next time.

"Great name," Molly says, recalling the afternoon on the boat when she learned Peggy studied in Italy. "Did you name her after your favorite room in the, I'm sorry, I don't recall the name of the gallery where you studied."

"The Palatine. Actually, she's named after the planet." Peggy rushes a hand to her mouth as if to share a secret. "She's always gassy."

"She's not alone, but we'll save that conversation for another time. I had a cat once. Silver. Not the color, but her name. I think she was part crow. She was attracted to all things sparkly. I had to give her away when Clay and I married. He swears he's allergic to cats and dogs. Every time we picnic at the park, I catch myself reminding him it's a good thing he's not a veterinarian."

"Well, Jupiter can be a handful at times, but I can't imagine parting with her. We rescued her right after we married."

Forgetting the cat and her desire to take its ninth life, Molly eyes the living room's decor. The Faynes' home is nothing like the cramped rental she shares with Clay—a place held together by paneled walls and floral wallpaper slapped on before electricity was invented. While Peggy's home offers generous views of the bay, the rental's narrow windows offer little to see but asbestos siding and untamed weeds sprouting up from the cracks veining the concrete driveway. Clay promised the arrangement was temporary when he sweet-talked her into signing the lease, but she is not holding her breath.

"What is that?" Molly asks, pointing to a small gown displayed in a lavish frame above the room's brick fireplace.

"A wedding dress. It was a gift from my great-grandmother. She grew up in a fishing village near Ronne, in Koge, a village south of Copenhagen."

"It's a bit small, would you agree?"

"When it came to their weight, the women in her part of the world tended to overestimate their poundage. Their miscalculations kept them thin and always hungry, and although I can't swear to it, probably grumpy as well."

"In my part of the world, we eat a lot of fried foods," says Molly. With a hint of envy she hopes to hide, she admires the room's white sofa. Its tufted leather begs her to take a seat, kick off her shoes, and rest for a spell. Images of the sofa bed and the galley kitchen Clay swore one day soon would be a distant memory, along with their bathroom that offers a cracked sink with a steady drip, seep into her thoughts.

A sweep of the room has her admiring a pair of gold candlestick lamps and the soft light they cast against the room's papered walls. She doubts she will ever have matching lamps. The rental's montage of mismatched fixtures, adorned with torn shades one would expect to find in a college dormitory, leaves her begging for more. Although Clay's ex-wife did not deserve it, she was awarded the house and its furnishings, along with a six-digit settlement and twelve years of alimony when the judge, a recent divorcee with a thorn in her side and three kids strapped to her leg, identified with her pain and suffering.

The room's wet bar displays crystal stems of every shape and size. Beaded throw pillows decorate a window seat overlooking the bay. A closer look has her believing they are expensive, unlike the dull, tattered cushions she tucks under her feet during late-night television. Although her knowledge of art is limited, she recognizes a New Mexico landscape by Georgia O'Keefe.

"I took a few art classes at Mississippi State," Molly chuckles. "It's been said I have a lot of Mississippi in me. To avoid learning a second language, I took a two-credit course where we beaded jewelry. It kills knowing I'll never get those hours back. When I was a young girl, I went frog digging and chased dirt devils in plowed cotton fields with my friends." Although laughing, she has fond memories of racing into the center of dirt tornadoes twice her size. "We spent our days roaming ditches and drinking warm water from a garden hose. After a rain shower, we ran through otter puddles. In the summer, when the days were long and hot, we sat on the stoop playing El Camino, no return. It was a game similar to 'slug bug, no punch-backs'—both always ended with a fist bump."

"I'm not familiar with it, but I'm sure it was fun. Is Mississippi State in Starkville? I always confuse it with Delta State."

"Starkville. I wanted to stay close to home."

"*Home is the nicest word there is,* I've heard it said. Laura Ingalls Wilder nailed it. Where is home for you?"

"I've spent years pondering that question. When I was a young girl, I overheard my grandfather whisper to his friends that most of the kids in our neighborhood were conceived on torn vinyl in the back seat of a car in the late-night hours after tequila was enjoyed."

"I'm sorry."

"Don't be, and please forget what I said about my grandfather. He never drank too much or consumed too little. I'm from Leland," Molly says, not caring about the lie. "My stepfather was a drunk-ass deadbeat, always begging for a handout he was convinced would turn his life around. As it turned out, Lady Luck was never in his corner." An uneasy feeling reminds she will never go back to the place she hurried to flee. "After years of watching my stepfather fall into a place I never wanted to visit, I sought out an escape route."

"Is Leland home to the creator of *The Muppets*?" Peggy asks, changing the subject.

"The town honors Jim Henson every October with Frog Fest," Molly says. "Miss Piggy was my favorite, but because I was a shy child, Wonder Woman became my hero. As we speak, Leland is hoping to turn the town around through a takeover project."

Turning away, she steps over the floor to the large saltwater tank against the room's far wall. She gives the glass a gentle tap, and a smile comes to her when a lionfish darts toward her finger. "I've always wanted an aquarium. Clay says they are too much upkeep."

"Sometimes, especially initially," Peggy admits. "It's a delicately balanced environment. I can watch the seahorses all day. Sometimes I think they are watching us. If you'll notice, their posture is always perfect." Standing on tiptoes, she sprinkles orange flakes into the tank. "I had to twist Preston's arm to have this custom-made piece. He would be content with a glass bowl and a pair of goldfish."

"I'd settle for that." Spinning on her heels, Molly lets her eyes scan the room. "Your TV trays are pretty. Growing up, we had only one.

We took turns eating in front of the television. By the time it was my turn at the tray, my dinner was either cold or tough. Sometimes both."

"These are nesting tables," Peggy corrects. "I imagine they could serve the same purpose, allowing the family to gather in front of the television, but they are tables that graduate in size. They are more decorative than functional."

Moving over the floor, Molly points to a trio of black-and-white photos near the entry hall. "I love the sketches."

"These are ledger drawings penciled by Native Americans."

"You excel in decorating. A realm I have yet to master." Although Molly shrugs a little, she is quickly drawn to a thick white rug. "Is this angora?" Bending on one knee, she sweeps an open hand over the luxurious plush wool. "I just want to strip down and curl up in it."

"It's Australian sheepskin. It was a gift from Preston for my birthday. That's why we're entertaining poolside. I would hate to spill red wine on it. Preston keeps reminding me it cost a small fortune."

"Your birthday? Was it recent?"

"Last week."

"I'm sorry we missed it. I'm sure Preston showered you with a wonderful evening of celebration." A skip in her heart reminds that she will ask him about it later.

"He always says it's important to celebrate the little things. He came home at lunch with an arrangement of white hydrangeas similar to the ones I carried in my wedding bouquet. Later, we wined and dined at the Lighthouse. As always, he requested our table near the window. When we returned home, he surprised me with the most beautiful silk camisole from my favorite boutique in New Orleans," she shares in a low voice. "Before the night ended, we sang our song."

"You have a song?"

"Sonny and Cher's *I Got You Babe*. It's our go-to karaoke duet. It's not my favorite song, but Preston knows all the words. Please don't let on I told you. He doesn't like to show it, but he is such a romantic."

"You are one lucky lady. I'm surprised when Clay remembers a card."

"You'll just have to train him."

"Like a dog?"

"Into the husband you know he can be. Speaking of husbands, we should join ours," she says, making her way out to the terrace.

"Hello, ladies. Molly, I'm glad you are joining us," Preston says, greeting the twosome with his signature smile.

In this moment, Peggy finds him far more handsome than ever before, even though he does not look any different than he does every day. When she glances at Molly, she is surprised to find her eyes fixed on him, too. Feeling something is not right, she fails to hear Preston call out her name.

"Hello? Peggy?" Preston repeats. "Come back to Earth."

Startled, she turns her wrist and spills her drink. Although all eyes are on her, she hopes her concern is not obvious. "I'm sorry, Preston. What were you saying?"

"I was asking if you want me to freshen your drink, but it appears you need a new one."

"Make it a double."

He raises his brows, but the look she gives suggests he move along.

"Miss Molly, what can I get for you?"

"Hey, gorgeous," Clay greets, blowing a kiss Molly's direction.

She returns an air kiss before turning to Preston. "You look so angelic, I'd hate for you to move a muscle, or two. That said, I'll have what you're having."

"This, my friend, is my famous Quarter Deck cocktail. Along with my secret ingredients, it's made with imported rum and fresh limes. None of that bottled stuff."

"Although tempted, I think I'll stick with my usual—red wine, if you have a bottle open."

"Of course. Coming right up. Just promise you'll give the Quarter Deck a fighting chance sometime."

"You have my word," she says, throwing out her pinky finger.

Once again, Peggy is taken aback. She does not want to believe

Molly is flirting with Preston or has already forgotten about the rug and her concerns, but an uneasy feeling tells her she should trust her intuition. Although Preston adamantly denies stepping out of their marriage, she has been given reason to believe he has cheated. When she turns to catch a glimpse of Molly, she is startled to find her staring in her direction. When Molly's interest turns back to Preston, she cannot help but feel Molly is friendly toward her for a reason. She is tempted to shout *down in front*, but quickly realizes Molly is not the only person standing in her way.

"I'll grab the appetizers," she says, escaping into the house.

Bored with Clay and Preston's exchange of medical jargon, Molly makes her way to the patio's wet bar. She is topping off her drink when she eyes the sheepskin rug.

Moving inside, she calls out Peggy's name. Not hearing a response, she looks to find Dana, Preston's assistant, standing at the front door.

"Hello, Mrs. Lambert. I'm sorry for the interruption. Dr. Fayne asked me to drop off these papers."

"Come on in. Preston and Clay are out on the patio."

Just as Molly rounds the corner, the heel of her shoe catches on the rug's thick whiskers. Stumbling forward and unable to catch her balance, she lets the glass slip from her hand. She watches in horror as the slow-moving sea of red sails through the air before taking a crash-landing on Peggy's prized rug.

"Oh, Molly! Are you hurt?" Peggy asks, racing in from the kitchen.

"I'm so sorry, Peggy. My shoe got tangled up in the rug. I know how much it means to you. I'll have it cleaned right away."

"Don't give it a second thought," she says, expecting a pinky promise.

Hearing the commotion, Preston runs inside like he is stealing home base. Wide-eyed, he is drawn to the spill and the spray of shattered glass.

"Is anyone hurt?"

"I'm sorry, Preston," Molly says, displaying fake tears.

"It's no big deal. I'm sure the stain will come out." Moving to Peggy, he cups her chin in his hand. "If we have to replace it, we will. It's not the end of the world."

"It was an accident. Molly, promise you won't give it another thought," Peggy says.

"I feel awful. Please, let me have it cleaned," Molly again offers.

"Try club soda," Dana suggests.

"Dana, what are you doing here?" Preston asks, surprised to find her at the door.

"You asked for these files to be delivered."

"Thank you. I forgot all about it."

"Preston," Peggy cries out.

"You've cut your finger!" he exclaims.

"It's nothing, really."

Although the cut is superficial, Molly watches Preston tend to it like the skilled surgeon he is. "One would think she severed a limb," she mutters under her breath.

CHAPTER 12

Although Peggy sleeps through the ringing phone, Preston is not taking any chances. Phone in hand, he crawls out of bed and tiptoes down the hall toward the kitchen.

"This is Dr. Fayne," he whispers, rounding the corner.

"I need to see you," Molly says in a low voice. "I'm craving you. Head to toe and everything in between."

"Can we talk about this tomorrow?"

"I don't think so. You know things didn't end well the last time I saw you, and now, when I want to enjoy your knowing touch, explore your lips, and feel your body against mine, you turn me away."

His interest piqued, he ducks into the walk-in pantry. Leaving the door ajar, he allows the sliver of light from the oven's slim clock to light up the small space.

"It's late. You know I can't get away. Please describe for me what it is you're wanting. Be specific. I want to hear every detail."

"It's only two o'clock. You can always get away—that is, if you want to. If Peggy questions you, tell her you are needed at the hospital. I'm pretty sure she will buy anything you sell her. Need I remind you of the purpose of your private phone?"

"At this hour? It'll look suspicious."

"Don't be ridiculous. You're an obstetrician. Everyone knows babies come at all hours of the night." Angry that her demands do not have him on the highway, she paces the rental's floor like a caged animal. Knowing these same demands and actions worked on the men before him has her wondering if she needs to up her game. "I might just have to tell her about us. Perhaps I'll mention the mole on your hip, the lone hair on your shoulder, you know, the one that pops up out of nowhere and grows like a weed. Should I mention that little shiver you do after …"

"That won't be necessary," he interrupts. "I'm hoping you won't do this. I'm sure you know the old adage *Loose lips sink ships*. Trust me, we would both go under, and I'm willing to bet we won't be thrown a life preserver."

"Think what you will. I'm leaving tomorrow for a spa vacation. So, ta-ta until next time."

"Wait," he says, clearing his throat. "Thank you, Dana."

"This isn't Dana."

"I understand. Please let the hospital know I'll be there in twenty minutes. We'll talk about that spa vacation when I get there."

A rhythmic beep pulls Peggy from the warm sun, cool sand, and piña colada a cabana boy offers along with a wide smile. Startled, she escapes the dream and shoots up.

"Preston? Where are you?"

"I didn't mean to wake you," he says from behind the bathroom door.

"Is everything OK?"

"I have to go to the hospital."

"At this late hour?"

"Believe me, I hate it more than you do. It's nights like this I often find myself wishing I worked a nine-to-five job."

"Be safe and hurry home. I'll keep your side of the bed warm."

Knowing this is a promise she has kept throughout their marriage, a warm smile crosses over his face. Hearing her sigh, he considers returning to bed and taking her in his arms, but fearing Molly's wrath and the hell that is sure to follow, he sticks with the plan.

"Promise you won't wait up. You know what they say about new-borns: *They will get here when they get here.* I'm so tired, toothpicks might be keeping my eyes open." He crosses over the floor and, brushing her hair aside, plants a tender kiss on her forehead. "I love you, Mag Pie."

Catching a woodsy scent, her pulse quickens. Biting back tears, she rolls over onto her side. Questions rush at her, but one is the loudest: *Who is the woman pulling him from our bed?*

Hearing the garage door return to the concrete throws her mind into overdrive. Over the years, she has come to accept that nurses find him attractive, women in the neighborhood appreciate his quick wit, and young girls at the club swoon each time he engages them in small talk and idle chitchat. She wants to believe his love for her will keep him faithful, but his cologne warns of a different truth. She is relieved when a faint beeping noise interrupts her untamed imagination.

Throwing the blanket aside, she follows the low beep into Preston's closet, where she finds a cell phone tucked under hospital scrubs he wore earlier in the day. Although hesitant, she places the phone to her ear.

"This is Peggy Fayne."

"I'm sorry to disturb you. This is Kim at Mercy General."

In the seconds that follow, she is subjected to garbled words and muffled voices.

"Sorry about that," Kim apologizes. "It's another crazy night. Must be a full moon. Will you please let Dr. Fayne know he is needed in the ER?"

Doubtful of Preston's actions, the hairs on her arms stand tall. A tightening in her chest cautions something is not right.

"Preston just left for the hospital. Have you tried paging him?" In the lengthy pause, she again hears whispered voices and a shared laugh.

"I'll page him now. Again, I'm sorry for disturbing you."

"Where is your car?" Molly asks from behind the door.

"Down the street. It's best my car is not spotted in your neighborhood." Shifting about, Preston navigates the porch's crumbling concrete. "What might that be?" he asks, pointing to a metal piece tacked near the door.

"A mezuzah. Our landlord is Jewish." She takes his hand and leads him down a flight of stairs. "This is an older, established neighborhood with a synagogue on every corner. This was once a darkroom," she says, moving through a windowless room. "I've been told the original owner was a photographer for a daily paper and developed his own film down here. Now that I think about it, he may have been a taxidermist. That said, watch your step. As you can see"—she points to a row of cardboard boxes busting out with Christmas ornaments—"we use it for storage."

Fighting the urge to remind her he is not here for a tour, he acknowledges her words with a simple nod.

At the end of the hall, they step into a makeshift bedroom where a mattress rests on candy-stripe carpet. A wicker headboard and two beanbag chairs hold up the wall. A collection of sewing mannequins huddled in the far corner gives him the chills. A tower of desktop computers popular in the '90s hugs the room's cinderblock wall. Stepping over the carpet, he ducks under the low ceiling.

"I imagine this room was built for a hobbit," he says, brushing cobwebs from his hair. Scanning the small space, he eyes a six-string and a stack of sheet music. "Is that a set of kettle drums?"

"Clay collects music memorabilia."

"First I've heard of this. Remind me to give him a set of tom-toms on his next birthday." Studying the room, his eyes skip over a box of costume jewelry and stacks of yellowed newspapers before taking a hard landing in the room's dark corner. "Is that a dance pole?"

"Depends who's asking." Moving to the bed, she tosses a wire cowboy figure to the floor, pulls back the bedding, and throws a match to a large candle. "It's not the Four Seasons, but given our situation, it'll have to do."

In anticipation, he watches the slim straps of her dress fall from her shoulders. Before the dress hits the floor, he reaches for her. Pulling her onto the mattress, he kisses her breast before taking her nipple. He tongues his way up to her parted lips. When he cups her face, her eyes beg for more.

"Preston, you're driving me wild."

"You haven't seen anything yet."

"Please, just tell me you're going to leave her," she whispers in his ear.

"Sweetheart, why are you bringing this up now? We are supposed to be enjoying each other."

"I asked if you are leaving her, but all I hear are crickets."

"Call pest control."

"Please be serious. Lose the spouse and keep the house."

"You sound like you're ready for a street fight."

"Do you love me enough to leave her?"

"Hell, all you do is nag and nag and nag. Why do you choose to ruin a good moment?"

"I'm feeling stuck." She questions if she should continue, but knowing that tactic never works in her favor, she carries on. "Is Peggy the beneficiary of your estate?"

His interest waning, he rolls over onto his back. Giving a stretch, he massages tired hands. "Of course she is. She's my wife." It is not for Molly to know that if he dies before Peggy, she will receive a large payoff. If she were to pass before him, he will be set for life.

"What if she dies first? What then?"

"You sound like popcorn in a microwave oven."

"Speak English."

"All I hear is you popping off questions. I feel like I'm on a game show without any winning answers." Believing she is reading his mind has his brain dead and his stomach doing cartwheels. "Are you finished yet? I'm worried you might run out of breath."

"I'm tired of the pillow talk and feeling used. You bed me on your schedule. I'm worth more than that, and I deserve an answer."

"There isn't one." Grabbing a pillow, he inches over the mattress. "Might I remind you I'm here on *your* schedule?"

"While I agree that is true, I believe we both know what we have to do," she says, throwing her hands to her neck and pretending to suffer a strangling.

"Whoa right there, Molly. Time out. What in God's name are you suggesting? That I kill my wife?" Biting his lip, he quickly regrets the words as they roll off his tongue. If she is recording him, he hopes the inflection in his voice will keep him off death row.

"I'm suggesting nothing of the sort, and most women would question your questions, but since you brought it up, I'll make a suggestion. In the late-night hours, when she's enjoying her second bottle of wine, replace it with paint thinner. Use your charm to convince her it is fancy wine from her beloved Italy. If she wants something stronger, serve her a chlorine bleach and vinegar cocktail. If that doesn't work, it's time for you to take action."

"Chlorine bleach? That cocktail will kill her!"

"Bingo. I know the difference between happiness and distraction. If I'm wrong, now is the time to correct me. We are either in this together or the time has come for us to accept that when it comes to love, we are miles apart."

Believing their affair is quickly running its course, she turns quiet. She is tempted to mention the man she met last week at the Sand Bar. After buying her several drinks, and speaking with honey on his tongue, he tried his best to skip over her heart and into her pants. Fearing unnecessary repercussions, she decides to hold that card for another time. Until Preston is committed, he does not need to know about her frequent stops at the inner-city tavern. "I will do whatever it takes to be with you."

Understanding there are many moving parts at stake, Preston

remains silent. Over the years, he has witnessed divorces where men like him have lost half of everything—the house, their retirement account, and of course, the added expense of dollars spent in alimony.

"Divorce will ruin me. Although Peggy can opt for payments over a period of years, it's possible she will want a one-time payment."

"Why?"

"To be rid of me."

"Oh, hell, Preston. Consult a lawyer."

Given their lifestyle and his wrongdoings, it is likely he will be forced to hand over big bucks each month until his death or Peggy's remarriage. After years of listening to his father fault the legal system, he is certain the courts will see to it she is not left indigent. There is also the possibility he will lose his practice. If his patients get wind of his affair, they might take their personal business elsewhere.

"Preston, what are you asking of me?"

"Time."

"You should know by now waiting isn't my forte."

"Believe me when I say, I know your forte."

"Please be serious."

"I'm dead serious."

Taking his hand, she brushes her body against his. Leaning against him, she runs her tongue over his warm, moist lips. "Don't let me suffer another day. It's time for you to choose."

Taking her by the wrist, he pulls her under the sheet. He nibbles on her ear before moving on to her neck. When she raises her hips, he heads south.

The beeping of his pager kills the moment.

A crescent moon hangs in the rising mist, and a wave of bellowing clouds drifts in from the east, opposite the late-night traffic. Worry begins to set in when Peggy notices flashing red lights up ahead on the bridge's far-right lane. It takes only seconds for her mind to bounce about with scenarios of what-ifs. Perhaps Preston is having car trouble and, having forgotten his phone, is waiting for help to arrive—or worse, he has suffered a heart attack or stroke.

Throwing caution to the wind, she presses hard on the accelerator. When the car comes into view, she breathes a sigh of relief. A quick glance at a fresh scrape along the driver's side of the two-door sedan has her believing the car T-boned on the bridge. Eyeing the out-of-state tag, she drives on. If Preston is in trouble, her help is needed elsewhere. Exceeding the posted speed limit, she hopes her call to 911 will set her free.

While cruising the highway, snippets from the morning's paper have her on high alert. Crime is on the rise, and once again, a serial killer is on the loose. Knowing Preston will give aid to anyone in trouble, she worries he may have met up with, and fallen victim to, the man the paper dubbed the Midnight Murderer.

Diverting her eyes from the road's seamless traffic, she glances at the small digital clock on the dashboard. Although it is late, she will not rest until she knows he is safe and sound.

When the lights of Mercy General come into view, she exhales. With her destination now in sight, she navigates the traffic lane directing her to guest parking. Up ahead, a security guard patrolling the hospital's main entrance motions for her to move on. Farther down the sidewalk, an elderly man hobbles along on crutches too short for his tall frame. At a distance, she thinks his bent body resembles a question mark. A striped lane marker meant to guide traffic along the narrow lane and a flashing light let visitors know the parking garage is open for business.

A wrong turn has her at the entrance to the physicians' private lot. She wants to explore the forty-space area, but getting through the parking machine and under the access barrier poses a problem. Headlights in her rearview mirror—and a long, constant honk of a horn—forces her return to incoming traffic. It is a stroke of luck when she enters the garage and secures a space on the second level.

The dark corner spot looks out over the hospital's impressive entrance but offers little view of the physicians' lot. Searching the area for signs of life has her feeling like a private eye hoping to catch a criminal. Hours spent watching fast-talking late-night commercials reminds all she needs is BDUs, a TAC visor, and a hydra light that runs on water. She will not be surprised if Sherlock Holmes and Nancy Drew come tearing around the corner. Finding Preston, they would shoot questions at him and solve this mystery in record time.

The distance between the lot and the garage's second floor, along with the dark sky, hinders her vision. She wants to kick herself for not bringing Level 3 body-bugging devices, car trackers, binoculars, military earplugs, and flip-up night vision Tac glasses—surveillance gear she expects only the best secret agents always have on hand. A quick search of her purse tells her the low-beam light on her cell phone will have to do.

She hurries over the concrete and down the stairwell, taking two steps at a time, until she reaches the ground floor. Relieved to find the street deserted, she hustles over the concrete to the lot reserved for the dozens of doctors the hospital has on-call. While trespassing is not a law she has broken before, she is willing to take a stab at it if Preston is in danger—or, as she suspects, up to no good.

As the minutes pass, panic sets in. Questions come flying at her when a quick sweep of the space confirms his car is nowhere in sight. *What if he has gone over the side of the bridge? Is it possible he has been carjacked? Perhaps he has already returned home and, finding me missing, is beside himself with worry.* She is considering a snoop through his cell phone's incoming and outgoing calls when the purr of an engine forces her to take cover behind a late-model hatchback.

Quick to embrace the life of Columbo, Peter Falk's fictional detective, she watches Preston's car slip under the lot's orange and white barrier. Lurking in the shadows, she holds her breath when he passes by. When the lowriding car pulls into the empty space, her stomach twists and churns. Careful to remain low, she watches the door swing open and Preston swivel in his seat before exiting the car. It takes only a breath for her eyes to fall on the lab coat falling from his shoulder.

His playful whistle breaks not only the night's silence but also her heart. Rounding the hatchback, she steps into the light.

"What are you doing here?" Preston asks, jumping back.

"I was going to ask you the same thing."

"Are you OK?"

Curious if he will lie straight to her face, she closes the space between them. "I was worried about you."

"I told you I was called to the hospital. Don't you remember?"

"I've been here. Waiting and watching."

"Why would you do that? Did you have a nightmare or something?"

"Just the usual one—you know, the one that returns each time you are pulled from our bed."

"I've been here the entire time." He reaches for her, but quick on her feet, she pulls away. "Let me walk you to your car."

Ignoring his offer, she remains planted. "Why are you out here in the parking lot?"

He wants to high-five the million-dollar question, but the look on her face begs not for celebration but answers. In a fleeting moment, it occurs to him she may have followed him when he left the house, but he is quick to brush it aside. After all, there was a more telling place to confront him.

"When I first arrived, I parked in the ER lot. I slipped out now to move my car. This is my story, and come hell or high water, I'm sticking to it. You can choose to believe me or call me a liar."

"The ER called for you."

"Of course they did. That's why I'm here, Peggy."

"After you left the house."

"Sometimes that happens. Lines get crossed at the desk."

"You were gone for almost fifteen minutes. See for yourself," she says, holding out his phone.

Although hesitant, he takes it from her outstretched hand. A quick scroll confirms incoming calls, his lies, and reason for her doubt.

"Again, lines were crossed. If you believe I'm stepping outside our marriage, you might consider hiring a private investigator."

"Regarding crossed lines, you might find it interesting that I arrived at the same conclusion. Forget the investigator. My eyes need to see the truth."

"Listen, I need to get back inside. We can talk about this in the morning."

"Waiting won't change the results."

"Fine," he says, turning on his heels.

Left standing in the dark, she shuffles back to the parking garage and up the stairs she raced down earlier. Heartbroken and none the wiser, she sits behind the steering wheel for several minutes until her eyes fall on her key ring and the spare remote to Preston's car. Although she argued against having it, suggesting it was best kept at home, he insisted she place it on her ring of keys. She stares at the key until she understands its message.

Once again, she takes the stairs two at a time and races over the concrete. When she reaches Preston's car, she gives the remote a gentle press.

Nestled in the driver's seat, she ignores the scent Preston's cologne left behind. Growing giddy when the dash lights up, she falls into the life of a secret agent. Searching the parking lot, her heart settles when she finds it quiet. Worried she might change her mind, she activates the navigation's history. In a flash, a menu of addresses blows up the screen. She recognizes several destinations—a restaurant they often frequent, the shortest route to a resort in Destin they visited last year at Christmas, and Café Thirty-A, their go-to restaurant when Preston has a hankering for mussels.

Hearing voices, she again searches the lot. Careful to stay low, she grabs her cell phone. Keeping a lookout, she scrolls through the remaining addresses, snapping pictures along the way. She is almost looking forward to studying the places Preston visited, but only if the saved addresses cough up the name and whereabouts of the woman threatening their marriage.

CHAPTER 13

Peggy navigates the room's round tables and high-back chairs. A deserving smile owns her face. Always the professional, she will not let the events of the previous night interfere with her responsibilities. As president of the Auxiliary Club, she quickly observes the volunteers have gone beyond her expectations in decorating the Dinghy, the yacht club's modest event room. She cannot recall who was assigned the project but is pleased with the extension table near the entrance. Eager to greet the guests, it holds gift bags and folded programs a volunteer will later provide to members in good standing and their invited guests.

The event's only glitch occurred minutes earlier when Dana sent a text message apologizing that she has been called into work and will not be able to donate her time at the luncheon. Desperate to find a replacement to hand out gift bags, Peggy is disappointed when her call to Molly goes to voicemail. Hearing her name, she turns to find Tootie Sanders heading her direction.

"Peggy Fayne, you have outdone yourself. Tying the club's burgee to the chair back is brilliant. I only wish I had thought to do it last year for the fashion show."

"You are too kind, Tootie. Not only were your decorations the talk of the club for months, as was our lively group, but you also hit an all-time high with the fundraiser. I'm sure you are aware we now have a two-drink limit," she says, recalling the event and the endless margaritas their lively guests enjoyed. Humbled by the compliment, she admires the yacht club's turquoise and gold flags secured to the chairs. "I have to agree. The pop of color does wonders against the white linen."

Hearing a commotion, she looks toward the door. As she turns to step away, Dixie Lannigan, a longtime member of the Ladies Auxiliary, reaches for her elbow.

"I heard Preston has been elected to the board," Dixie says, clapping her hands like a young child.

"Serving as the club's vice-commodore is a feather in his cap," Peggy adds. "To celebrate the position, Preston and I are replacing the deck furniture. I believe we will all agree it's time. The pillows are not only tired but also weathered from the elements and dull in comparison to the new ones we purchased. After years of service, those old, faded pillows deserve to retire. Given its years of active duty, the teak furniture finally surrendered."

Pausing, she glances about the room. "If space allows, we want to build a snack bar with a pizza oven, refrigerator, and an icemaker—one of those fancy ones that allows us to serve snow cones. It makes more sense than running through the clubhouse to the restaurant, especially for the little ones who move about with wet feet. If donations pour in, we would like to include cornhole and pickleball. They have become popular all over the world and common in retirement communities and recreational facilities."

"Forgive me," Dixie interrupts, "but these sound like games one might play when handcuffed and forced into isolation."

"I've been told from a reliable source that pickleball is like a dog park. Fun happens even if you arrive without a dog."

"And cornhole? I fear you're going to tell me we will also be forced to play pin-the-tail-on-the-donkey."

"I believe that's in the budget for next year," Peggy says. "Perhaps we should agree to save this conversation for another time."

"I tend to follow the green banana rule: invite me to participate when the game is ripe. Until then, I'll stick with horseshoes."

"Our consultants promise these are the games of the future," Peggy assures her. "I only wish Preston's father could be here to see the changes. I bet he would raise eyebrows learning these games are coming to the club."

"Duncan Fayne is a great man," Dixie says, reminiscing about Duncan's good days. "He has never been one to know a stranger for long, but what I appreciate most about him is once he gives up the attitude, he is easy to love." Breaking out of her reverie, she moves on to more important matters. "I want to hear all about your plans for Mother's Day Brunch. I'm sure it's been quite the undertaking, especially with the regattas underway. If you're sharing any new recipes, I'd like to include them in the annual cookbook."

"Of course." Flickering lights and the tap of the microphone lets Peggy know it is time to get the show on the road. "I have to go, but let's get together soon."

"Good afternoon. I'm Peggy Fayne," she says, taking her place at the podium. "I want to welcome you here today as we celebrate our annual luncheon and welcome new members. Many of you know this is the club's kickoff event leading into the regatta season. We want to extend a warm welcome to our guests. I believe you will find the Ladies Auxiliary at Gulf Harbor gracious hosts, and when we navigate out of the marina, accomplished sailors and yacht-women."

Laughter fills the room and glasses rise for a deserving toast. Having chaired many of the club's events and familiar with the routine, she allows the customary pause.

"I want to give a gentle reminder that your Galley recipes are due at the end of the month. If you're able, Dixie is asking for photographs of the finished dishes. For our visiting guests, this is the club's annual cookbook. That said, please welcome our emcee, my good friend and former model, Tootie Sanders. When Tootie and her husband, Commodore Dell Sanders, aren't exploring the Outer Banks, she serves as captain of the Skipperettes, a program introducing our young women to the great sport of sailing."

Giving a pageant wave, Tootie makes her way to the podium.

Amidst the applause, Peggy steps away and returns to her place next to Dixie. An uncomfortable feeling washes over her when she reads Dana's text message. A sixth sense has her questioning the last-minute bail-out. Desperate to find a replacement, she studies the program. As she runs her finger down the list of names, a smile returns to her face.

"I'm expecting Molly Lambert. When she arrives, will you ask her to help with the gift bags?"

"What happened to Dana?"

"She's not going to make it. Something's come up." She hopes the uneasy feeling in her stomach does not show on her face. "I need to step out for a bit, but I'll be back in time for dessert."

Escaping the club, Peggy drives likes a speed demon out to win the Indy 500. Parking her tires at the marina, she steps out of her high heels—no need to give notice of her arrival. The plan is to take Preston and his guest by surprise.

Left unlocked, the boat's iron gate swings open with ease. Afraid to learn what waits on board, her mind swims through a sea of worry. Minutes earlier, during the drive, she was certain she could manage the truth, but now, here, in this place, worry throws its weight on her.

In the near distance, a playful laugh and a hint of lovers' music escape the boat's cabin. Believing her suspicion is confirmed, she places a hand over her heart. A woman's voice lets her know Preston is not alone. Her heart cramps and her knees buckle, leaving her unsure of her own strength. An alarm sounding in her head reminds her there will be consequences of her actions. She could lose Preston—not just in this moment, but in all those she wants in their lifetime.

Filled with angst, she doubles over. Although her heart cannot handle it, her eyes need to see what her future holds.

"Peggy's here," Preston says, looking out the cabin's open window. "Grab your clothes and hide in the shower. For the love of God, do not run the water."

"I'm not moving."

"Do it and don't make so much as a peep. When the coast is clear, let yourself out."

Throwing on trousers and buttoning his shirt, he steps into the salon just as Peggy steps up to the door.

"Hey, honey. What brings you here?"

"I'm on my way to the club. The luncheon is today. I was driving by, so I decided to pop in to say hello." Faking a smile, she searches the cabin for evidence his guest may have left behind.

"I'm glad you did. I came by to check the water pressure. It's been acting crazy. Hose came off and sprayed everywhere. You wouldn't believe the mess."

"It's good you keep extra clothes on the boat," she says, eyeing his shirt. "I'm glad I was able to see you, if only for a moment." Turning away, she bites back questions she wants answered.

"I have to get back to the office. How about we do something special tonight to celebrate the luncheon's success?" he asks.

"What do you have in mind?"

"I'll do whatever my bride desires," he says, ushering her out the door.

CHAPTER 14

The hat's wide brim shields Molly's face from curious passersby and the marina's nosy neighbors. Dark curls bounce off her slim shoulders, while low-slung hip-huggers, made popular in the 1970s when disco hit the scene, sweep debris along the sizzling concrete. Each time she meets an approaching car, she takes a long, deep drag off the cigarette pinched between slim fingers. With each breath, her lungs burn, but the disguise is a clever one. Should her whereabouts come into question, she will laugh it off. A blonde since birth, she's sure no one will believe she is the brunette seen smoking.

"Hey there, hot stuff. I'm glad you came back," Preston says, greeting Molly with a hungry kiss. "I'm guessing smoking is now part of your getup."

"I think of it as yoga. I breathe in. I breathe out. I believe you will agree I wouldn't have to arrive in disguise if we were a couple."

"We are a couple." Closing in, he places a kiss on her forehead. "I like our situation just the way it is."

Pulling away, she crosses thin arms over her chest. "I don't want to be your *situation*. I want to be your wife."

"We both know I have a wife. I'm beginning to believe you hang around for reasons I can't understand. Perhaps it's not my heart you are seeking but validation. That said, let's agree to enjoy these moments we are able to share. After all, ours is a complex relationship. By the way, how was the luncheon?"

"The food was awful and the speaker was a bore. I'm beginning to think you're not in love with me. You hide behind lies—the same falsehoods you tell your wife. Look at me, Preston. I'm done sweeping everything under the rug. You want me to believe you're wasting your time with her, but the truth is, you're wasting mine. It seems every time I turn around, you hand me another skirmish."

"You're talking nonsense."

"Am I? When it comes to the truth, I'm finding you tend to be a little iffy."

"That's not true, and you know it."

"Why are you here with me? Everyone speaks highly of Peggy. I've been told her heart is as big as the moon. From what I understand, she is the perfect hostess, the envy of every married woman, and the apple of your eye."

"What can I say? She's too good for me. I need a woman who negotiates with the devil."

"I know you mean that to be funny, but it isn't."

"Lighten up, Molls. Life is too short to be uptight."

"I'm not uptight. I'm filled with doubt."

"Don't be."

"Are you sleeping with her?"

"Who?"

"Peggy."

The tone in her voice warns he should tread carefully, especially if he does not want to hear an earful. "I've moved to the guest room."

"Really? You're not just saying this to get me off your back?"

"If I knew this is all it would take, I would have said it a long time ago."

"Quit toying with me. I'm being serious."

"Ditto."

"Do you want to know my problem? I'm always here for you. It's because I love you that my heart doesn't hear when you say stupid shit. Do you want to know your problem? You prey on my innocence."

"Your innocence? Oh, dear lord, Molly. You are either delusional or joking. I'll let you decide. Have you forgotten you're cheating on your husband? Look in the mirror. One of us needs a reality check."

"Whatever. I'm tired of pretending to see the good in you."

It has never been on his radar or his intent to leave Peggy. This is a phase he is going through, a rite of passage, so to speak. He assumes that, at the end of their fling, Molly will go her way, and he, his. The cold look she gives warns her wheels are coming off.

"Are you telling me that whatever this is between us is all it will ever be?"

The mood now fading, he buttons his shirt and reaches for his keys. "Life is a gamble. You make your bet. I make mine."

"Best not play cards that don't belong to you."

"I let the cards fall where they may. I have to get back to the office. I'm sure you're aware I have a full schedule this afternoon."

CHAPTER 15

The moon is rising, and twilight is approaching. Darting through traffic, Molly zips through a busy intersection. Driving like she was due at the storage unit yesterday, she steps on the gas, challenges flashing lights, and cuts off an aggressive driver. A change of lanes has her jumping a curb, splitting a wall of trees, and scraping paint off an unsuspecting fire hydrant. Worried her presence might draw unwanted attention, she cuts the headlights when the rear bumper clears the compound's electric gates.

A sharp left turn takes her out of sight of the property's security camera. Arriving at the last unit on the first row, she circles back around.

Remaining in the shadows, she searches her backpack for the baseball cap she lifted from Clay's gym bag. Given that he rarely has time to hit the gym, the missing cap continues to go unnoticed. Pulling her hair into a ponytail, she pulls it over the strap.

The unit's overhead door travels the metal track without a squeak. It served her to complain to the manager earlier in the week when the door made a frightening screech she likened to a catfight she was once forced to witness.

Along the back wall, in a dark corner, a narrow table displays a generous collection of styled wigs. Coiffed and sprayed, the lifeless hair sits mounted on foam heads. The longer tresses, those she prefers to wear, cascade over the table's rough edge.

Painted faces display siren-red lipstick, rouged cheeks, and arched brows drawn with chalky pencils. A nose ring and a chunky bronze necklace adorn a plastic head she snatched up at a closeout sale when the clerk stepped away to assist a paying customer.

The brunette with the bob displays a beauty mark on her left cheek. The foam head resembles a supermodel whose name escapes her, but her favorite is the untamed redhead. When the salesclerk called it a wild mess with endless possibilities, she knew right then and there she had to have it.

Flecks of black mascara, iridescent body glitter, and layers of loose powder freckle a three-panel makeup mirror brought to light by a rechargeable battery she purchased soon after learning the unit was without an electrical outlet. The whole shebang set her back a few pennies, but because she needs the mirror's lighting when getting dolled up, the added cost was money well spent.

"Come on, don't fail me now," she says, sliding over the Audi's leather seat.

Three turnovers later and a no-nonsense stomp to the accelerator, the car finally comes to life. Driving out to the street, she leaves the temperamental engine running while she backs the Lexus into the empty space. A round of expletives escapes her when she returns to find clear liquid dripping from the Audi's exhaust pipe.

Minutes later, she finds traffic on I-90 heavier than usual. Careless drivers are switching lanes without giving notice, eighteen-wheelers are hauling ass, motorcyclists ride bumpers until an opening allows safe passing, and young drivers determined to exceed the speed limit also ignore the state's texting laws.

She is turning onto the freeway ramp to the bay bridge when the windshield fogs over. Cursing the old defroster, she rolls down the window. A deep breath invites the salty scent of the bay to cleanse her lungs. Tapping her fingers against the steering wheel, she cranks up the music and softens her gaze.

"I'd sell my soul to the devil to live near the water," she says in a low voice.

Up ahead, a lightning strike threatens the bridge's flashing lights. Regretting her choice of words, she hopes the booming thunder that follows is not a message from hell's ruler.

Two miles later, she takes the roundabout to Seagrove Shores. Missing a curve, she climbs a curb, rolls over a growing sinkhole, and while searching for the brake pedal, travels the sidewalk. The engine coughs up a sneeze, and the rear bumper takes a healthy bite out of a young magnolia, leaving a fast-moving cyclone of shredded bark in her rearview mirror. A second glance in the mirror confirms the car lost a hubcap.

A roll through a dark intersection has her on a journey she may later regret, still, she proceeds. After all, it is not revenge she is seeking but knowledge. Not the dangerous kind, but information she will fine-tune and, when the time is ripe, use to her advantage. Slowing her speed, she pulls over to the street's narrow shoulder.

While waiting for courage to kick her out the door and send her on her way, she plucks lint from the catsuit she picked up at a theater auction. While the clock ticks away the minutes, she wraps a dark scarf around her forehead, trades black loafers for leather sneakers, and rubs a charcoal stick over her cheeks and across her forehead. Nights spent watching reruns of *Hogan's Heroes* tells her this is a winning disguise.

"I look like I'm waiting to make a tackle on the twenty-yard line," she says as she catches her reflection in the rearview mirror.

Up ahead, just beyond the park, sits Preston's house. Stepping from the car, she swallows nervously. Careful to stay low, she lurks among low-lying bushes and slow-growing trees as though she is on the lam. Tucked behind the neighbor's mailbox, she maps out her route. The earthy smell of wet soil threatens to foil her plans. A slip on the wet grass brings her to her knees. She curses the light shower until realizing the cool water is from the neighbor's lawn sprinkler.

She is inching along a dusty grove of pine needles when a thorny bush takes a bite out of her catsuit and nips at her thigh.

"I'll be back with clippers," she warns under her breath.

Lurking in the shadows like a hunted criminal up to no good, she takes refuge behind a fat tree. Finding the coast clear, she makes her way to the home's open window, where the sound of Marvin Gaye's *Let's Get it On* escapes the metal screen.

Remaining in the shadows, she peeks in to find Peggy and Preston nestling close together on the sheepskin rug she recognizes from a previous visit to the house. Like the room's roaring fire, her temperature rises when her eyes fall on the uncorked bottle waiting in an ice bucket within arm's reach.

She gives the ground a hard stomp when Peggy laughs at something Preston whispers. When he takes Peggy's hand and pulls her close for a kiss, she is set to explode. Clenching her jaw, she makes a fist. Cornered in the shrubs and feeling trapped, she wipes at the sweat pooling above her upper lip. When a bitter taste rushes her mouth, she spits at the ground.

If only he knew I am watching.

Seeing Preston plant a kiss on Peggy's neck has her throwing a hard kick to an innocent shrub. Regret comes at her kicking and screaming when a sharp pain in the arch of her foot shoots up her leg. Later, if asked about the injury, she will describe this moment as a near-death experience.

Returning to a bad habit, she chews on her ponytail while Preston and Peggy get all lovey-dovey. Their playfulness has her wishing she had a gun. Uncertain who would take the first bullet, she decides to let her aim choose the target.

When Preston places his hand on Peggy's thigh, she fears she might go ballistic. When a scream threatens to escape, she falls into breathing exercises she learned in a meditation class she attends twice a week at a local fitness center where she pretends to be a paying member.

Every Wednesday and Saturday, she slides in through the center's front door, and an hour later sashays out the back with rolls of toilet paper and scented bath oils buried deep in her gym bag under soiled workout clothes she knows will go unsearched if she is questioned. If God should strike her dead for the lies, deception, and theft, she promises he will hear about it, even if she has to scale heaven's pearly gates to get in front of him.

The nerve of him to cheat on me with her. He belongs to me, she tells herself, pulling a cigarette from her pocket. Shifting her weight about, she strikes the match against the book's coarse strip. Realizing her mistake, she hurries to blow out the flame.

"Preston, I think someone's out there," Peggy whispers.

"Out where?"

"Near the window."

"A Peeping Tom?"

"I saw a glowing light, and unless my eyes are playing tricks on me, I'm pretty sure I saw a moving figure."

Sliding into slippers, Preston makes his way to the open window, where he cups his eyes with his hands and presses his face to the screen.

"I don't see anything, but I smell sulfur. That light you saw," he says, sniffing the air, "might have been the strike of a match."

"Who would be burning matches outside our window?"

"No idea."

Tucked low under the window's ledge, Molly presses her back against the house. Believing the coast is clear, she darts from the safety the bushes provide. Flailing about, she dodges low-lying branches and patches of wet grass. Fumbling in the dark, she moves about aimlessly before catching her shoe on a raised brick. Searching the air for support, she loses her footing and falls hard into a raised garden. The pain in her leg has her blaming Preston and Peggy for her bad luck.

"I just heard something," Preston says in a low voice.

"What do you think it is?" Peggy asks in a voice out of tune.

"A wolf on the prowl, perhaps."

"We have wolves here?"

"They have to live somewhere. It could be a cat rustling near the bushes. Maybe it's the neighbor's dog looking for his tennis ball." Flipping on the porch light, he gives the door a gentle push. On the way out, he pulls a pitching wedge from the hall closet.

"What are you doing?"

"I figure while I'm out there, I might as well work on my chipping."

"Seriously?"

"I might have to defend myself. You stay here. I'm going to check around the house."

While Peggy looks on from the safety of the door's threshold, he probes dense bushes, thorny brambles, and a row of overgrown boxwoods. When the neighbor's cat darts out from behind a tree, he jumps out of harm's way.

Crouched on skinned and bloodied knees in the neighbor's yard, Molly lets go a breath. She is no doctor, but a throbbing pain in her hand tells her she broke her finger in the fall and shredded the skin on her arm from her wrist to her elbow. Hearing Preston and Peggy's playful laughter adds to her pain. Not to be outdone, the wheels in her head take a dangerous spin.

Listen up, Preston Fayne. You should know by now I don't get mad. I take action.

CHAPTER 16

M olly meanders the marina in a blonde wig, boyfriend jeans, and nude espadrilles. A cropped tank top fraying at the edges and a sun visor resting above dark sunglasses complete her disguise. A navy and gold boa she threw over her shoulders before leaving the house rides on the air with each step she takes toward the trawler.

Grabbing her from behind the door, Preston pulls her close. A glance over her shoulder has him eyeing the salsa-red two-door she arrived in. "What's up with the car? Given you parked over the line, something tells me parallel parking isn't your strong suit."

"I'm sorry. Are you talking to me?" Turning her back to him, she looks about the cabin.

The game has grown old, but if he wants to keep her happy, it is in his best interest to play along. "What's up with the car, sweetheart?"

"That wasn't so hard, was it? Mine is in for an oil change. Service manager called about an hour ago. Piece of junk needs new shock absorbers and brake pads. The defrost is on the blink again, but I told him I want to wait on it." Always prepared to take advantage of a situation, she uses both hands to grab this one. "Damn thing spit and sputtered and coughed up fumes all the way to the dealership. I can't believe I was suckered into paying twelve grand for the lemon. What a rip-off. Every time I get behind the wheel, I'm reminded of a motor scooter I rented in Mexico."

Preston turns toward her so fast, he fears whiplash will take his life. "Did I just hear you say Mexico? I thought you said you've never been out of Mississippi."

"You either heard me wrong or, once again, you aren't listening. I said Gulfport. I rented a bike in Gulfport." Nostrils flaring, she wants to kick herself for the mistake.

"I think you'll agree those places sound nothing alike."

"Whatever. I'm sure I'm not the only person who has told you that you need a hearing aid, but we'll save this conversation for another time when your hearing is better."

"I don't have a hearing problem."

"I understand denial is one of the many symptoms," Molly says. "I might just enroll you in one of those annoying consumer trial programs. Every time they pop up during my favorite television programs, I turn off the volume. Just recently, I've come to notice that you don't always hear thunder. I would just like to know if you have a condition so I can have more compassion. It's possible you have cotton stuck in your good ear. Now, let's agree to stay focused on the car. I have to kick-start the darn thing every time I turn the key. When there is a drop in temperature, it responds with a lingering cough, and a high-pitched bark escapes the tailpipe. I'm beginning to think a nursing home is in its future. Next time I see that salesman, I'm tossing him back into the rust pot."

"I don't understand. You're going to have to throw me back to a place where I can catch up with you."

"Fake tan."

"I'm referring to the car. Did you really pay twelve grand? I gave you ten thousand."

"I know, but at the time, it appeared the best bargain. I financed the balance," she adds like a freeloader eager to line her wallet with someone else's money.

"Why didn't you tell me?"

"You were already so generous, I didn't want to sound petty."

"Two grand is pocket change," he says, throwing open his wallet. "This should cover any added charges. Pay it off today. You don't want a finance company calling your house. If Ivan has some free time this afternoon, I'll ask him to look at it."

"I don't think that's a good idea. It'll draw attention we don't need." She wants to complain that the bills are not crisp like the others he has turned over to her, but listening to the voice of reason in her head, she holds her tongue. As for Ivan, she cannot risk him ratting her out by telling Preston he never saw the car nor gave it the all-clear—or worse, learning she milked him for more money than its purchase price. "Let me handle it. You have better things to do with your time, and first on your list is me."

Reaching for her with hunger waiting on his lips, he pulls away when she cries out.

"What's wrong?"

Revisiting the hard fall she suffered in his neighbor's unkempt flowerbed, she hurries to come up with a believable story he just might buy. A fall on the tennis court comes to mind, but he knows she has not picked up a racquet in months. She recalls hearing that a friend broke his wrist when he tangled with a garden snake, but that scene will never play out for her. A game of basketball bounces around in her head, but it takes an afternoon for her to play a simple game of HORSE. Coming to her rescue, the two-door catches her eye.

"I slammed my finger in the car door," she tosses out without guilt.

"I would expect to find torn skin and perhaps some bruising," he says, taking her hand. "What happened to your arm?"

"I fell when I finally freed my finger. I'm just glad I didn't tear my rotator cuff. I've been told a torn cuff can take up to one year to heal."

His thoughts quickly turn to the episode outside his home's window. He cannot put his finger on it but wonders if she might be hiding something. "Looks like you broke your finger."

"No need to fuss. For what it's worth, I have plenty more. I'm guessing this one will be better than new in no time."

She is relieved when the ringing of his cell phone interrupts their conversation and her medical examination. Her cold heart feels a chill when he holds a finger to his lips on his way out to the deck.

Stepping out of her clothes, she jumps into bed and pulls the sheet up to her chin. Glancing about the cabin, her eyes fall on the bedside table where she zooms in on his wedding band. Early in their affair, a time not so long ago, he made a habit of removing the ring when he was in the act of cheating on his wife. She wants to believe her constant nagging did not play a role in it.

Never one to miss an opportunity, she swipes the ring from the table. Staring at the gold band, she criticizes the inlaid diamonds she believes are fake. The band's etched inscription, *Forever and Always,* makes her temperature soar. Holding the ring close, she scoots toward the open window. Although Preston's back is to her, she hears him say 'I love you' into the phone.

Always ready to teach him a lesson, she tiptoes into the bathroom and turns the lock. Plopping down on the toilet, she forces her thoughts to decide her next move. Seconds later, when Preston calls out her name, she gives the flusher a determined push. Wearing only a smirk, she watches the ring put up a good fight before circling out of sight.

CHAPTER 17

C lad in skimpy bikinis and sipping fancy drinks topped off with tropical paper umbrellas, the women on board the *SlipNFall*, a Sea Ray Sundancer, gossip a little and laugh a lot. Behind cupped hands, they cackle like Old MacDonald's farm hens. Twice, Rick Finley, the boat's owner and captain, threatens to toss them overboard. Both times, they dare him.

Moving under engine, Rick motors the Sea Ray into the marina's covered slip. Although the midday sun calls for a squint, a smile crosses his face when he catches sight of Preston, his marina neighbor and close friend. He throws a buoy to the boat's port side and tosses the mooring line to Preston.

"Welcome home, my friend," Preston says, securing the rope to the pier's thick post.

A big guy with a square jaw, a wandering eye, and a face full of wrinkles one might expect to find on a young shar-pei, Rick is built like a grain silo. When he is not tinkering on the boat, he practices personal injury law at a two-man firm in Mobile's famed Van Antwerp Building. Since moving from Pearl, Mississippi, to Alabama, he has called a three-story late Victorian on State Street in De Tonti Square home. When the fog rolls in and the wind blows to the north, the stench of seaweed and regurgitated chum drifts through the old home's thin walls. In his free time, which he complains is never enough, he takes to the open water.

"Looks like life's treating you well," he says, giving a thumbs-up while adjusting the elastic band of black and gold slacks better suited on Liberace.

Looking at his neighbor, Preston believes the only pieces missing are a grand piano, a gold candelabra, and a diamond-studded belt.

"This is Poppy Epstein. We went to high school together," Rick says, introducing the small man over his shoulder.

Repeatedly told he smells of catnip and garlic, Poppy, a small-town dentist short on looks and petite like Sammy Davis Jr., carries the confidence of a stand-in actor in a low-budget film—pompous and unsure. It is no secret he often gets grief from his colleagues for being the consummate interrupter. He blames his patients for the bad habit. "They can't talk, so I just keep on keeping on."

"It's nice to meet you, Poppy. Any friend of Rick is a friend of mine," Preston greets with a genuine smile.

Poppy is turning to introduce Shay, his wife, when a woman in a maternity dress and neck brace calls out to Preston.

"Hey, gorgeous, come on over. I'm sure you remember meeting Rick at the Jerry Ellis Junior Regatta."

"Of course. It's nice to see you again," Molly lies.

One look at Rick sends her brain into overdrive. Their time together included exploring hands and his wet tongue making unwanted advances when he thought no one was watching. A hard stomp to his big toe sent a message he was quick to understand.

"You're looking well," Rick says, recalling the pain she put on him. Stepping to Poppy's side, he takes him by the collar. "This is Poppy Epstein. The beauty in the white dress is Shay, his most recent wife," he shares. "He has a pacemaker and lupus. Doctor wants him to stay under eight thousand feet. Once you get to know him, you'll agree he's kind of old-school. Shay is his third wife. Never met the one in the middle, but I understand she was one holding cell shy of crazy. Shay is a little high-strung and self-righteous, but you'll overlook her faults once you get to know her. His first marriage was a shotgun wedding that didn't end well."

"Shotgun? Are you having me believe they exchanged vows in the woods surrounded by deer?"

"His girlfriend got knocked up. Her daddy was an old cotton farmer with an itchy trigger finger."

"Some women have all the luck."

"I believe you've met Valerie." He gives an Oscar-winning grin as they exchange a perfunctory wave. "Please forgive me. I wasn't aware you and Preston are expecting."

Quick on her feet, Molly feigns surprise. All eyes follow as she rips the brace from her neck and pulls a small feather pillow out from under her dress.

"I must look ridiculous. I had an audition and forgot all about this getup."

"Never ridiculous," Preston says, taking her in his arms. "Keep the wig on," he adds in a low voice. "We don't know who they know."

Molly's nod is followed by a forceful nudge to his ribs. He quickly obliges with a smooch to her cheek before facing curious onlookers.

"We're heading south toward Devil's Island," he tells them. "We'd love for you to join us. Rick, I know a boat you might be interested in."

"Tell me about it in a whisper. I don't want my wallet to hear. Better still, tell me about it in an email."

"It's a forty-foot Mainship trawler with two diesel engines. I'm looking for partners. I spent a weekend on her months back when the owner made the voyage to Casino Beach for the Mayor's Cup. It's in dry dock in Stuart. I wouldn't be surprised if she's sold before the end of the month. Owner is moving to New Mexico. You should meet this guy. He's a brainiac. I listened to him talk about nuclear security, dilithium crystals, magnetic field laboratories, and weapons codes. When he described trigger devices for nuclear warheads and mac-roscale systems, I asked to change the subject to something I could understand. We talked about boats the rest of the evening."

"Hell, I'm lucky to finish the paper's crossword," Rick says, raking a hand through a mop of unruly hair. "About this trawler. What's the hull?"

"Solid fiberglass."

"Sweet. Hey, Poppy, you're a boat guy. Are you interested in a three-way?"

"What's it going to cost me?" Poppy asks, recalling a three-way that was shot down at a fraternity mixer by a woman he was dating and her sorority sister. Now, each time he coughs or makes a sudden move, a biting pain travels down his back before crash-landing where a ten-inch skewer kabobbed him.

"If you have to ask, you can't afford it," Preston says with an easy laugh.

"I've been told the second happiest day of your life is when you buy a boat. The happiest is when you sell it," Poppy says, believing he is the smartest person on the boat. "I know to tread carefully."

"While many find that to be true, myself included at times, I'm really interested in this one. It has Raymarine electronics and a Sabre Lehman engine that produces 135 horsepower. It holds enough fuel to get us to Havana and back. The staterooms are built-out to the max—king beds, double sinks, and large showers. My friend tells me she's in turnkey condition."

"Well, you'd have to get her back in the water," Poppy chimes, "and I'm not so sure I'm interested in a trip to Cuba. I've spent my sailing years navigating a Soling."

"In these parts?"

"Hilton Head."

"As for Cuba, it's all about the cigars, my friend." Lifting a finger, Preston points to the brown tube peeking out from Poppy's shirt pocket. "She has a new canvas Bimini, and the owner tells me she is always moored under cover. She'd fit right in."

"What's the asking price?" Rick asks, pretending to reach for his wallet.

"It's a fair price, but I'll see if I can talk him down a little. I have a counteroffer in mind."

"I don't know about this. I'm a sailor. I don't know if I could handle a boat that size," Poppy says with a snort.

Preston pulls aviator sunglasses from his face and, finding a smudge, uses the corner of his shirt to wipe the lens. "I'll be your captain. When you visit, I'll make myself available to get you out of the channel and back into the slip. While we're out on the water, you can practice maneuvers."

"What about upkeep?" Rick asks. "Engine care, haul-out maintenance, and off-season treatment can be time-consuming and costly."

"I'll handle it on this end and bill you for your half." He glances over at Poppy, who is picking the skin around an aging scab. "Or third, if Poppy is on board."

"I'm in," Rick says, bobbing about. "I'm hoping you'll handle all the paperwork and insurance. We're going to need a covered slip. What do you say, little buddy? Are you in?" he asks, looking to Poppy.

"Like bell bottoms in the '70s."

"I was hoping to hear *hook, line, and sinker.*"

"Those, too."

The deal now sealed, a smile comes over Preston's face. "You won't regret it. This calls for a celebration. Oh, before I forget, there is one more thing. We need a name."

Turning silent, Rick tosses several names about in his head. "What's its current name?"

"*Trade Winds*, but the owner is keeping it."

"What about *Sea Dogs*?"

Preston shakes his head. "I think I've seen that somewhere." Hearing laughter, he turns to the women onboard. "What about *Babes, Too*? Better still, how about *Trois Hommes*?"

"In French, that translates to three men. I have a wife I have to answer to. Come on, guys. This is a no brainer," Poppy says, rubbing his small hands together like a boy scout hoping to start a campfire. "A gynecologist, a lawyer, and a dentist walk into a bar ..."

CHAPTER 18

"Hey, honey, how's the boat?" Peggy asks, holding the phone close. "I hope I'm not interrupting."

"Not at all. It's great to hear your voice," Preston shouts over the roar of the boat's engine. "You should be here. The deck is beyond-crazy big. You're going to have a hard time choosing where you'll want to sunbathe. The weather is finally agreeing with us. Other than a brief shower, yesterday's forecast moved out toward the Atlantic. The guys are so excited. We are tossing a coin to determine who gets to play captain. We're out on the water now. Rick is beginning to think he's Jacques Cousteau. Get this: he's using sweet corn to snag a sailfish."

"Well, Stuart is the Sailfish Capital of the World."

"While that is true, I doubt corn, sweet or popped, is their meal of choice."

"Have you decided when you're coming home? I'd like to plan something special. Date night, perhaps. Maybe a movie and dinner at ..." Hearing a voice, she pauses. "Who am I hearing in the background?"

Preston turns toward the deck, waves an arm in the air, and pretends to slice his throat. He hopes his unruly crowd, Molly included, understands to keep quiet.

"That's Poppy. He's Rick's friend. I thought I told you he's in on the deal."

"The dentist?"

"That's right. He's not the kind we typically run with, but I doubt he'll spend much time here. I'm crossing my fingers we'll be able to buy him out before the end of the year," he shares in a low voice. "The guys are having a great time. I'm sorry, sweetheart, but I need to go. Rick has something on his line. I'll call when I know when we're coming home."

"I love you," she reminds in a faint voice.

"And I love you," he whispers, aware Molly is at his back.

As she ends the call, Peggy's mind is racing with questions. She would have sworn she heard a woman's voice. A sick feeling has her hoping it is not the woman who holds Preston's interest. Lifting the phone, she calls his office.

"This is Peggy Fayne. Is Dana available?"

"Let me take a look at the board," a voice answers.

During her wait, Peggy hears office banter in the background and several voices, all unknown to her.

"Mrs. Fayne, it looks like Dana stepped out. I'll have her call you when she returns."

"Thank you, but that won't be necessary."

CHAPTER 19

"I'm sorry, Molly, but I have to cancel," Preston apologizes.

"Cancel what?"

"Tonight. I can't get away."

"I don't understand. This is date night. It's always our night. What could be more important than our time together?"

"Peggy wants to see a movie." Standing at arm's length, he prepares for her drama. In recent weeks, he has come to understand that she accepts neither the truth nor a lie.

"Can't she go without you?"

"Once again, I'm reminded you don't have a difficult time asking hard questions. Perhaps politics is in your future." Knowing any explanation will go challenged, he sticks with the truth. "She's asking for date night."

"Tell her you have other plans."

"Are you crazy? As my wife, she expects to be first in line when it comes to sharing my free time. I'm beginning to think you can't separate right from wrong."

"Not to worry. I'm too tired to argue your song and dance, and loving you comes with a menu of empty promises." She scanned the paper's movie section earlier in the week. Tonight is the opening of Sawyer Santana's new movie. The title escapes her, but movie critics compare him to a young Rob Lowe. "Well, I suppose it's good you're going out with the old ball and chain for a change. Just don't sleep with her. If she tries to slap cuffs around your ankles, make a run for it."

"Why would I sleep with her when I have you?"

"Loss of vision, perhaps."

"Are we OK?"

"Of course. I'll find something to keep me busy."

CHAPTER 20

Preston and Peggy are settling into their seats in the theater's middle section, one row behind the wheelchair deck, when advertisements and reminders of the theater's rules light up the screen.

Keeping with the rules, Preston turns off his cell phone. If he were a gambling man, he would bet the cash in his pocket that Molly is sitting armed and ready to blow up his phone with nasty text messages and degrading voicemails. History reminds it is best to delete her texts and toss the voicemail rants to the trash.

"Thank you for tonight. It reminds me of our early years when we were first dating," Peggy says, taking his hand.

"Let's hope I don't fall asleep like I did at that chick flick we saw on our first date."

A trailer for an upcoming movie is playing on the big screen when he feels a tap on his shoulder.

"I'm sorry to disturb you. Are you Dr. Fayne?" the usher asks, keeping the flashlight's beam on the floor.

"Yes, I'm Dr. Fayne. Is there a problem?"

"You have a call from Dr. Lambert. If you will follow me, I'll show you to the house phone."

"I'll be right back," he says, turning to Peggy.

Following behind the attendant, his thoughts race with what lies ahead. A sixth sense warns Molly might be up to no good.

"Your call is waiting on line two." The attendant points to a three-line phone before stepping away.

"This is Dr. Fayne."

"Meet me outside," Molly orders.

"I can't. I'm with Peggy."

"Ask for a hall pass. Better still, tell her you're needed at the hospital."

"She knows Clay is on call."

"Make up something. Tell her he's shorthanded and needs your help."

"Oh, for Pete's sake. She's not new to this routine. She knows the hospital has its own doctors on call."

"I'm sure you don't want me to come in there. Do me a favor and hurry. I'm parked illegally." As a precaution, she activates the car's emergency flashers. "I'm in the Audi. Hop to it and do it. If I get a ticket, it's on you."

Stuck in the muck he created, he drags heavy feet through the theater. Ducking low, he falls into the seat he vacated minutes earlier.

"I have to run to the hospital. There is a situation with one of Clay's patients. I shouldn't be more than an hour. I'm sorry, Peggy."

"Don't apologize. I knew when we married this would be the life of a doctor's wife. Promise you'll hurry back. Without sharing the treats I've planned for tonight, I want you to know this will be an evening you will enjoy."

Ignoring the catch in his throat, he plants a kiss on her cheek, grabs his sweater, and races out to the waiting car.

"Have you lost your ever-loving mind? What if Peggy follows me?" he asks, sliding into the passenger seat.

"Peggy. Piggy. I don't care what you call her. Something tells me she's the type to rescue wounded squirrels. Correct me if I'm wrong, but I'm guessing ornithology is in her future. Either way, I would have driven off. Besides, she doesn't know this car, and I'm guessing the wig would throw her off."

"I'd still be seen driving off with another woman, and ornithology applies to birds. If she goes looking for my car, she will find it."

"Tell me why I care."

"I told you I couldn't see you tonight. What is this about?"

A desperate search has her reaching for his groin. "I'm in the mood for you."

"Listen, Molly, you excite the hell out of me, but sometimes I'm left questioning your actions and poor timing. I just left my wife on date night. What are you thinking?"

"That you want me enough to leave your wife on date night. I don't believe you'll be disappointed." She eases up on the pedal and gives him a look he is sure to recognize from their many liaisons. "I've booked a room at a hotel on Lee Street. Don't worry, I'll have you back at your precious movie before they run the credits—that is, unless you want to stay through the night for Chef Freddie's signature waffles." She grabs him again, this time with less force. "Breakfast in bed is often worth more than the hotel's standard rate."

"It'll have to be a quick spin."

"That's fine. Those are fun for a change and often more enjoyable than a fishing expedition."

"Where does Clay think you are off to?"

"Running my traps."

"You have traps?"

"We all have our traps. I just so happen to have more traps than I can count," she says, stepping on the gas.

CHAPTER 21

A rambunctious crowd circles the boat's generous deck. Bartenders working the trawler's open bar are busy with cocktails flavored with a jigger of rum or a shot of tequila. Crews from competing yacht teams and members of the club move about the deck waiting to witness the boat's christening. Laughter and cigar smoke drift over the marina, and island music floats on the air. Like the drinks served at the station, conversation is flowing.

Molly and Clay move about hand in hand, a display of affection she demands. When he stops to mingle with a group of old goats she finds boring, she travels about the boat in a designer dress she snatched up at an outlet store. When offered a treat from a passing tray, she nibbles at a chocolate-covered raspberry and a steamed artichoke wrapped in sun-dried tomatoes. Feeling eyes on her, she pushes back her shoulders and forces a smile.

On the far side of the deck, Dana is surrounded by a circle of elderly men unknown to her. Enjoying the attention, she shows off her youthful figure in a jumpsuit the color of virgin snow. Spandex fabric hugs developing curves, and a plunging neckline exposes cleavage some might believe was sculpted by a plastic surgeon.

She causes quite the stir among the men on board and raises eyebrows among the women, who speak in whispered voices when sharing their disapproval. Offering a wide smile, she ignores their stares. Continued glares confirm she is looking mighty fine in stilettos she purchased in the early morning hours when the corner thrift store opened its doors for business.

Parading the boat, she moves about as though she is queen of the Mardi Gras. All that remains to complete the ensemble is a fleur di lis tiara and a wraparound pageant sash. When she catches Preston's smile, she makes her way to his side.

Cooled by the little shade the boat's Bimini offers, Peggy watches the playful exchange between her husband and his young assistant. Heads turn when the space between them grows shorter, their smiles become wider, and their voices lower to a whisper. She grows envious when Dana laughs at a joke she is not privy to, and when she brushes against Preston's shoulder, an uneasy feeling rushes her veins. It is not easy watching Preston's playful affection with another woman, especially one who has so little to offer—unless innocence is a growing gift.

When Dana leans in to share a secret for only Preston to hear, a lump grows in Peggy's throat. She cannot help but wonder if Dana is the woman playing house with Preston.

Alone on the sideline, she watches as the growing crowd circling them laughs at something Preston shares. When their guests encourage Preston to act on his teasing threat to throw Dana overboard, her heart falls to a threatening pace. It does not take long for her curiosity to become an obsession. Were they the best of friends, she would have been right there with them. Given the recent changes in their friendship, she remains out of the spotlight in a lonely corner where her heart is forced to admire Dana's youthful beauty.

As with so many others on board, Dana's spirited personality makes up for her shortcomings. A curious look at her ears shows that they are not pierced. A dark place in Peggy's heart wonders if the same can be said of her virginity. She struggles to believe that Preston could find her interesting. Perhaps he is taking advantage of her innocence. Dana's young age does not allow her to speak of great adventures, appreciation of national monuments, or worldly experiences she has yet to enjoy. It is possible she has never cast a vote for a worthy politician. A tug at Peggy's heart suggests these just might be the reasons for Preston's affection.

A reporter from the local newspaper, a daily rag that in recent weeks has come to skip Tuesday's print, interrupts her thoughts when he asks for a picture. She forces a smile, knowing a photo, if not several, will grace the cover of Sunday's edition.

Across the deck, the alarm on Preston's watch signals the time has come to get the show on the road. He navigates the poop deck, pausing briefly to raise a flute and shake hands with neighboring boat captains and aging club members whose earned tenure expired decades ago.

"Here's to the man of the hour," a portly man says, lifting his glass.

"Hey, Captain, did you remember to bring a silver dollar?" Penn Rhallins asks. A member of the yacht club and an officer on the board, he recently endured this same teasing when he christened *4Jewels*, a forty-five-foot Catalina Morgan named for his third wife, a young hygienist he ripped from the arthritic hands of his aging dentist.

Preston pulls a shiny coin from his pocket and waves it overhead. "A symbol of generosity to this vessel and my commitment to tend to her every need and desire. I'm afraid I'll have to ask that you close your eyes while I hide it. The last time I hosted a function on my boat, the silverware went missing."

Peggy laughs along with those who gather around Preston. When she catches him watching, she returns a warm smile. She learned early on in their marriage that he loves the spotlight, and to his credit, he wears it well. As for her, she goes out of her way to dodge attention. As with most occasions they have celebrated of late, this, too, is his time to shine.

Tapping at his belt buckle, Shep Warden, the club's rear commodore, allows the laughter to die down before calling for Preston's attention. "What about a virgin?"

"Couldn't find one in all of Mississippi," Rick tosses out before

Preston can answer. His laugh is cut short when Valerie jabs a finger into the fleshy part of his arm.

Surrounded by landlubbers, experienced sailors, and master yachtsmen, Preston fears Rick's words will muddy the waters beneath them. He does not see a reason to explain an old sacrificial ritual asking Neptune, the God of the Sea, for his blessing. The same is asked of Poseidon, the Greek God of the Sea. To his knowledge, the blessings are centuries old, and in recent years, rarely practiced. Still, there is no need to cause waves.

A slow-moving wave gives notice of the fifty-four-foot Sea Ray motoring through the marina. When the *SeaAlice* passes by, those onboard the Mainship howl with laughter, many holding their glasses in the air. In return, the Sea Ray's captain offers a gentleman's wave.

"Must be in pharmaceuticals," Shep says, throwing out a laugh.

Preston waits for the camera flashes to pass before inviting Rick and Poppy to join him. "It's time to get this ceremony underway."

He is stepping aside to make room for his partners when he catches sight of Shay and Valerie exchanging a cheeky wave. Off to the left, near the deck's iron gate, he turns to watch Peggy welcome Molly and Clay.

The growing crowd is opening to allow Rick to pass when again, his eyes fall on Molly. Taking hold of Rick's elbow, he speaks in a whisper. "This could be a real shit show in the making. Everything is happening all at once, and none of it is good. I don't care if it takes Mother Teresa or one of Charlie's Angels, keep the women away from Peggy."

"Who is Peggy?"

"The blonde in the red maxi. Do me a favor and keep your questions to a minimum. I promise answers will come later. Whatever you do, don't put the pigeon among the cats. It will mean immediate death if Peggy speaks with Valerie and Shay. I think you'll agree, this is neither the time nor the place for a showdown."

Rick searches the deck with curious eyes until he finds Molly.

"She's becoming problematic," Preston says, following Rick's gaze. "I'll explain later. All I know is if Peggy gets wind of this, she'll raise holy hell and nail my ass to the wall."

"No need to explain, buddy. I'll make sure you dodge a bullet."

"Thanks, my man. I owe you one. Now, let's christen this boat."

Minutes later, when all eyes are on him, Preston takes a batter's swing at the boat's bow.

"What the heck, man? It's bad luck when the bottle doesn't shatter," Rick shouts. Always superstitious, he offers folded hands to the open sea and mutters a prayer.

Unlike his jittery partner, Preston pushes aside every omen, myth, and curse he knows all too well. Swinging through like Hammerin' Hank Aaron, he strikes the bottle against the boat's bow a second time. Success comes on the third attempt, encouraging him to shower under the imitation bubbly. While the crowd cheers, he tosses the scored bottle and its safety net aside. Grabbing the Bollinger, James Bond's signature champagne, he twists the wire cage from the cork.

"Here's to *Open Wide*," he says, raising the bottle into the air.

On the far side of the deck, away from all the hoopla, Shay searches the crowd. Except for Valerie and Molly, she does not expect to find a familiar face. Her eyes pass over the blonde at the bar until the young woman turns in her direction.

"Poppy, that woman over there looks like Molly. She would be a dead ringer if it weren't for her hair."

"Maybe they're sisters."

"The resemblance is uncanny," she says, taking him by the hand. "Let's introduce ourselves."

"Slow down there, Cinderella. It's nowhere near midnight, and that blonde pumpkin isn't going anywhere. I've had my eyes on the guys near the cabin. I want to know what boats they own."

"Seriously? You can ask later."

"I want to know now."

"Let it go. Let's visit the bar. I hear the bartender makes a five-star margarita." She is reaching for his hand when they bump into Valerie and Rick, who are tossing back fat gulf oysters.

"We're heading over to meet the blonde at the bar. I swear she's the spitting image of Molly." Wrapped up in the excitement, Shay turns back toward the bar. "Where did she go? She was there a minute ago. And where is Molly?"

"She's inside. Preston has her mingling with the guests." Feeling the heat, Rick hopes the lie prevents a catfight. "Let's go in. She's been asking about you. Don't make a move," he tells Valerie while nudging Shay toward the boat's salon. "I'll be right back with a plate of Blue Points."

"What about the woman Shay saw at the bar? I want to meet her, too."

"Later. I'm on a mission."

Left with an empty glass and a hankering for oysters, she questions what she is witnessing. She, too, noticed the woman at the bar and the man at her side. When the man stroked the woman's slim back, she caught sight of a ring, likely a wedding band, on his left hand. Like Shay, she found the woman familiar, right down to the way she threw her head back when she sucked the juice from the lime the bartender placed on the rim of her glass. It was hoop earrings peeking out between her tresses that left her curious. She has seen them before.

She is heading toward the cabin when Preston's boisterous voice invites a blonde in a strapless maxi to join him at his side. Curious like a cat, she cuts through the crowd, bumping elbows and stepping on toes, until she is up front and center with a bird's-eye view. Wrapped up in the excitement with old friends and new acquaintances, Preston fails to notice her presence.

"I want to thank all of you for joining us in this special celebration. I believe you know Peggy, my wife." Stepping aside, he allows the spotlight to shine on his bride.

The crowd gives a round of applause, and the photographer snaps several shots. When smiles turn forced, the photographer lowers the camera, gives a thumbs-up, and returns a plastic cap to the camera's lens.

As for Valerie, she has a growing list of questions for Rick, who just happens to sidle up. "What was that about?" she asks.

"I'm not sure what you mean. I'm a happy-go-lucky guy who wants to enjoy oysters and time away from the office."

"That was quite a circus back there. Where did you learn to juggle? Should I expect a mariachi band to circle the deck?"

"I was helping a friend. Is that a crime?"

"Depends. Are you helping or hiding?" she asks, foregoing a response. "Tell me what you know about Peggy."

"I know what you know, nothing more. I'm learning of her just as you are."

"And Molly?"

"I thought she was his wife."

CHAPTER 22

Dewey McNickle's office occupies a second-floor unit in a strip center at the corner of Veterans Boulevard and East Pass Road. Despite its low rent, the building turns over more tenants than the apartments skirting the community college's campus. Soon after Vinnie's Bait and Tackle moved into the space below his small rental, he threatened to break the lease. Built like a Bantam rooster, his short legs and a full chest carried him through the weeks he complained about the smell of scaled sardines, shad, and mackerel until his landlord agreed to cut the rent.

Dressed like sex symbol Tom Jones in an open-collared shirt and tight-fitting stretch pants, Dewey is spinning circles in his rolling chair and beating on the arms like a buzzed drummer at last summer's music fest when he hears footsteps coming down the hall. Parking his ride, he throws a straw hat over his shoulder and runs a hand over a field of hair plugs the color of ripe wheat ready for harvest. He sprays the room with rose-scented freshener and takes a match to a coconut-scented candle he received months earlier from an appreciative client. An untimely inhale burns his nostrils and brings tears to his eyes. Not to be ignored, a poorly timed tic tugs at his cheek. A quick glance in the compact mirror he keeps in a drawer alongside paper clips and a roll of antacids has him believing he looks like a newly hatched chick.

Time does not allow him to brush dead flies from the windowsill or take a broom to the triple-thread cobweb spanning the room's double windows, and—because he is the king of pencil-pushing—sweep away a week's worth of shavings. It is only now he regrets letting the cleaning service go when he refused their demand for a raise.

"Hey, Dewey," Preston says, taking a seat. A strong rush of the room's odor threatens to turn his stomach. "I hope I'm not interrupting your lunch."

"No, no, not at all," Dewey says, pointing a stubby finger to the floor. "Vinnie gets fresh bait on Thursdays."

Shifting about, Dewey cracks his knuckles before adjusting the waistband of his pants. Settling into the rolling chair the previous tenant left behind, he pulls at a fallen sock that continues to throw a cramp at his toes. He lets out a cry when the chair's coiled spring throws an unexpected poke to his tush. "What can I do for you today?"

"I'm interested in a life insurance policy."

Dewey rubs at the folds along his neck and, letting go a sigh, sinks deep into the chair's vinyl back. He wraps his hands behind his head and, feeling the scab of a recent implant, picks at his scalp. "Well, you've come to the right place. That just so happens to be what we do here." Once the words escape him, he worries Preston will inquire as to what he means by *we*. A loyal and longtime client of the agency, Preston is aware Dewey runs a one-man show.

Dewey opens a green folder and, with a cockiness one expects from a trader on Wall Street, slides the eraser end of a pencil into the electric sharpener. A puzzling grind has him rescuing the pencil from the cylinder's grip. Holding his breath and tapping at the twitch in his cheek, he throws the pencil into the trash. Words escape him, but the reddening in his face does not.

"I assume Mrs. Fayne will be named the beneficiary."

"Actually, I'm thinking we might be better served with a joint policy."

"Ah, yes. The old double scoop. Policy pays out to surviving spouse. You might consider talking to a tax lawyer, you know, estate taxes and all. How much are we talking?"

"Two million dollars."

"Whoa. That's big-time money." He has written large contracts before but is never the big man on campus when it comes to seven-figure policies.

"We live big."

"I'll have to run this by our underwriters." He spins around and glances at the calendar tacked on the wall behind his desk. "It may take several days. This is more than I'm allowed to approve."

"Listen, my man, I understand, but I know you'll make it happen. You and me, we're a lot alike. I save lives on this side of the soil. You look out for them on the other. While we are still breathing, we have to look after each other."

Dewey's fat fingers roll over the computer's worn keys. Nervous about the numbers, he prays he will not suffer another twitch. "I don't know if you know this, but I was among seventy agents considered for agent of the year."

"Did you win?"

"I tied for last place with a guy in Tupelo."

"I'm betting you'll win next year. Forgive me, but I've noticed your repetitive tics. Do you have Tourette's syndrome?"

"I'm not sure."

"I can recommend a doctor."

"Maybe next time. No offense, but I don't really care for doctors."

"Hey, do you like to sail?"

"I like the water—mostly from a distance, though. I never learned to swim."

"You get this policy worked out, and we'll go sailing. I'll arrange for swim lessons. Heck, I'll join you. It's been suggested a time or two that I might consider slowing down my breaststroke. You'll enjoy the wind in your hair and a breeze at your face," he says, eyeing the field of plugs Dewey has yet to reap. "Tell me, Dewey, how many years did you attend insurance school?"

"It's nothing like that. I was in my Cow Year at West Point when I realized a military career wasn't in my future. When I didn't advance to a squad leader position, I jumped ship. I returned home, where I attended a three-day conference at the coliseum right here in Biloxi."

"For real? Are you telling me you have control over millions of dollars after just three days? That's brilliant. That's the kind of stuff you read about in books and see in movies. You could be the next Burt Reynolds. Promise me you won't fall in love with a cocktail waitress. Trust me, I've heard that can get costly." Again, he runs his eyes over Dewey's hair. "I'm guessing, somewhere in between, we know someone who knows someone."

"You make it sound glamorous, but I'm here to tell you the instructors were boring, and the buffet was horrible. I don't recall who catered the event, but I'm here to tell you I grew up believing only Sam-I-Am and Guy-Am-I liked green eggs and ham."

Leaning forward, Preston places his elbows on the desk. "Commitment and discipline make a man. Do you want to know who I admired when I was a young boy? Other than my father, of course. A man named Sam. This man had it all figured out. I'd ride along, shotgun of course. That's what we did back in the day. I was planted in the passenger seat while my dad drove like the boss he was born to be to the filling station on South Street. That's what they called it before gas stations became known as service stations. The attendant, likely a young boy headed at month's end to Boys Town, filled the radiator with water, pumped air into the tires, and after wiping the dipstick with a rag, topped off the engine with motor oil.

"Further down the road, where rubber gripped gravel and grazing cattle swatted horseflies with matted tails, there was a two-bay station and a guy named Sam. He always looked dapper in a button-down shirt and khaki pants. He'd fill the car's old tank, never once asking my father if he wanted regular or ethyl. He just knew what the engine needed to make it purr. While the pump was pumping, he ran a squeegee over the windshield, twice sometimes in the summer months when Miller moths and hoppers held on after hurricane winds. While he waited for the tank to fill, he checked the tires. He didn't just kick our old Goodyears like those guys at other stations: he got down on his knees, air hose in hand, and treated each tire with tender loving care. I'll say this: my father never suffered a slow leak or a blowout."

"I suffered both last week," Dewey admits.

"I hope we're still talking about tires. Either way, I hate when that happens. Once, when my father's car was making a funny noise, he stopped at a filling station with a single pump and a sign letting the lost and hungry know maps, sandwiches, and bathrooms were available on down the road. This young kid with jet black hair and an anchor tattoo on his bicep came up to the car. 'I'm Jesse,' he said. Well, Jesse didn't pump gas, wash windshields, or give a flying ... I think you get the point. You, my friend, are like the Sams of this world. You care about people—not just drivers and their automobiles, but keeping them safe when bad things happen. If I could, right this very minute, I'd pin a medal on you." He points a firm finger at Dewey's chest. "You, my friend, are a Sam."

A smile travels over Dewey's face. Aside from earning the Cub Scout's Bobcat badge and singing in the church choir, he has never been told he amounted to much of anything.

"I'm stuck in doctoring," Preston continues, "but you offer the next best thing—life insurance. Plus, you didn't waste all that money on medical school. A long weekend got you where you are today, and to top it off, you have a life. Doctors have little time to enjoy the nightlife. We rarely sleep more than four hours each night and can only dream about luxurious vacations abroad with a gorgeous babe clinging to our side. Hell, we can't even hit the open road or mingle with the bar crowd at happy hour. We are always on call. I can't tell you all the nights I craved a beer. For me, a cold brew is always on my mind but never in my hand. You have it made in the shade. I'll say this: if I could do it all over, we just might be sharing a shingle. Imagine it: Fayne and McNickle."

"I think my name should go first. After all, I have my license," Dewey says, filling his sunken chest with pride.

"Of course. Forgive me. I was so wrapped up in the idea, I forgot you are Sam the man."

"You would give up doctoring to sell insurance?"

"Much like envy, I've been told regret is a horrible thing. Just knowing you are content in your career makes me proud to call you my friend. Now, let's get this policy behind us. We have some swimming to do. Please have everything sent to my office. While you're at it, be sure a copy is forwarded to Neyland Waters, my attorney."

"I know Mr. Waters. I'll give him a call to let him know it's coming."

"Be brief. When it comes to billable hours, he pretends to be hard of hearing. Cha-ching, cha-ching, cha-ching. Should you need me, I'll be out on my boat. Best to call my cell phone."

"Driving in this morning, I heard a storm is heading this direction."

"I'm sure I've weathered worse. Speaking of that, please excuse me while I call my wife. I forgot to tell her I'd be away."

Steps away from Dewey's office, he rounds a corner and comes face-to-face with a young woman he guesses is in her early twenties.

"Excuse me, do you work in this building?" he asks.

"No, but I'm familiar with it."

"I'm looking for Dewey McNickle's office."

"You just passed it."

"I guess I wasn't paying attention. I'm Dr. Fayne. Preston Fayne." Extending his hand, he offers a million-dollar smile.

"I'm Tess," she says with a twinkle in her eye.

"When we're through here, would you care to join me for a drink?"

"I'd love to, but I can't today."

"Give me a call. I'll make myself available," he says, placing his card in her hand.

CHAPTER 23

Peggy's drive through the marina reveals that a pizza parlor down the road is delivering despite threatening weather, and the fueling station is closed until further notice. Knowing Preston is out on the water, weathering a storm the meteorologist reported has hurricane potential, has her concerned for his safety. Earlier in the week, when he reminded her he would be attending a medical conference in Pensacola, she worried he was not being truthful. Thinking about it now, she is still not buying his story.

A glance in the rearview mirror returns a smile to her face. Changing lanes, she allows the car behind her to pass. Keeping a safe distance, she follows the driver to a row of slips overlooking the channel.

Unaware he is being followed, Rick parks his car in a vacant space near his slip. He is stepping up to his boat when he hears someone call out his name.

"I'm hoping you have a minute," Peggy says, rushing across the dock. "I'm Peggy Fayne, Preston's wife."

"Of course. How are you?"

"I'm hanging in there." Giving him the once-over, she pulls the sunglasses from her face. "I'm hoping you can tell me what Preston doesn't want me to know."

"I don't understand."

"I've been given reason to believe you do."

"Whatever answers you're seeking, I can't help you. When I'm not practicing law, I do mathematical equations. For what it's worth, I've been told a time or two that relationships are not my strong suit."

"Neither is math."

"Excuse me?"

"It appears you can't put two and two together."

"Listen, I need to take care of some things. Although it's nice to see you again, I suggest you take your line of questioning elsewhere."

"I know he has a mistress. I need to know if she's with him now."

"I have no idea what you're talking about. My relationship with Preston is on the up-and-up. We both enjoy boating, nothing more."

"Am I to believe you have no knowledge of his infidelity?"

"I really need to go. Perhaps you should be having this talk with him or a licensed marriage counselor."

"Great job dodging my questions and throwing out new ones," she says, turning on her heels.

CHAPTER 24

Open Wide is edging up to the eastern side of Deer Island when the wind begins to pick up. Low-lying fog follows a drop in temperature, and threatening skies circle the deck.

"Grab flashlights and throw on foul-weather gear," Preston shouts.

As the minutes pass, he checks the radar and monitors the storm's path. He grips the helm as serious headwinds and fast-moving water toss the trawler about, rolling it from side to side like the tidal wave pool at the city's water park. Years of sailing these waters tell him a wicked storm is brewing. Should it linger, the boat will run out of fuel, leaving him without an alibi Peggy will believe.

"We're on the edge of wetness," he says, borrowing a line from the late comedian and talk-show host Johnny Carson. Focused on the instrument panel, he looks to the south, the direction they are escaping. "It's coming at us. Everybody take cover."

Although skilled at telling lies, Molly moves about in worry. The whopper she told Clay will never hold up in court. "Why can't we drop anchor? There's no reason we can't wait this out."

"Look around you. Those are high seas out there. It's best that we get to shore." Just as the words escape him, the sky breaks open. "Take cover," he shouts over howling winds.

He is cursing his bad luck and poor timing when a wall of cold, dark water slams the trawler. A bolt of lightning follows close behind. Knocked about, he struggles to regain his balance.

When the boat reaches the marina, Rick is ready to guide him into an empty slip on the east side, far removed from 28W.

"Peggy's been here. She's looking for you. She asked so many questions, I thought I was the one in trouble."

"Preston, you know I can't go home. I'm supposed to be in Heber Springs with Celeste," Molly whispers in a loud voice.

"Need I remind you that I have my own problems to deal with? I can't speak for you and how you will explain this to Clay, should it even come to that, but you can be damn sure I need a solid alibi."

"What am I supposed to tell Clay? That I'm attending a reef and reptile expo?"

"Well, you've been known to drink like a fish."

"You have me confused with your wife—you know, the woman who is always in the booze and never without a drink in her hand."

"It's her hand."

"She drinks more alcohol than Betty Ford."

"For crying out loud, Molly, ease up on me. I'm not a student of history, but please keep Betty Ford and her struggles out of this. I'm sure you're aware she established the Betty Ford Center."

"Forget what I said about Betty Ford. The press was quick to let us know she had her own issues to deal with. I think you will agree Peggy drinks more alcohol than lab rats. I'm beginning to realize you don't love me enough to keep me out of harm's way."

"I may have just saved you from drowning."

"If you say so. Why are you holding back, and where do I fall short? I keep giving and giving, but it's never enough for you. I'm always here for you. Is it too much to ask the same commitment from you? Don't cower behind the truth. I'm tired of filling your life's cubicles. Go home to the missus. History shows she will put up with your nonsense."

"What do you want me to do?"

"Go home. Watch the evening news. If Peggy's hungry, take her to one of those pancake houses where she can fill up on fried eggs and hash browns. Better still, take her to Cracker Barrel. I understand she never leaves there without a doggy bag."

"What about you? What will you do?"

"I'll stay here. If you're with her, she won't come here. Just be sure to come back."

"I think we should go to a hotel."

An arm's distance way, Shay throws an ear to their conversation. There is something about Molly's body language that has her antennae up. She is about to ask about Peggy and their need to dodge her, but the look on Poppy's face suggests she do only two things: bite her tongue and hold her breath. "Something's not right here," she whispers. "I don't want to be a party to this any longer. Let's just go home."

"We'd get home at two in the morning," Poppy says, waving her aside. "Preston, I'll get rooms across the street. Meet us at the hotel. Molly, you come with us."

"Good thinking, my man," Preston says, displaying a forced smile.

"I'll park Molly's car near my slip," Rick says, winking his good eye.

CHAPTER 25

"Who is Peggy, and why are they avoiding her? I still can't believe we've been forced to share a room in this no-tell motel. This is a new low, even for us," Shay whispers under the blanket.

"Keep your voice down. They'll hear you." A creature of habit, Poppy rubs his hands together. "I'm thinking Molly might be his mistress."

"His what?"

"I don't know. Maybe he's seeing her on the side."

"Is this Peggy woman his wife?"

"Again, I don't know."

"Barry Epstein, what have you gotten us into this time?" she asks, throwing out his given name.

"Please lower your voice."

"I don't care if they hear me. I don't like her. Come on, Poppy. You surely agree it was a bit awkward when she walked out of the bathroom naked as a jaybird." Before he can answer, she responds with a kick to his knee. "Hers was the second crescent moon I've seen tonight."

She attempts a laugh, but he is quick to place his hand over her mouth. A finger pressed against her lips begs her to be quiet.

Buried under the blanket, her eyes grow wide when the neighboring bed replies with repeated squeaks. "Sounds like they are taking their first violin lesson," she says, giggling like a schoolgirl.

"I think they agree with you."

"Surely they realize we can hear everything, and by everything, I mean the lip-smacking, whispering, and the occasional moan and groan. I swear she's giving birth over there. Their activities have me feeling like a lowly prop in a low-budget porn film, and he's the Ever-Ready Bunny–keeps going and going and going. I'm betting he's packing a Duralast Gold."

"The car battery?"

"The one and only."

"Shay, please. You're killing me here."

"Are they hiding under the blankets, too?"

"How would I know?"

"Take a peek."

"I'm not going to look over there."

"You should. You got us into this mess."

"What if they are watching us?"

"I don't think you have to worry about that. We're hiding under the sheets talking about what they just might be doing above them. We're forced into shame while they're rocking the headboard. I'm tempted to jump out of this bed, flip on the light, and demand I get my money back."

"Let's just get through tonight. We can't drive home. The weather is iffy, and I'm exhausted. Besides, it would be awkward to pack and dash."

"Poppy, I'm not comfortable sharing a room with them."

"You heard the desk clerk. This is the only room available."

"What if his wife comes in shooting? You know what they say: it's all fun and games until someone is murdered."

"You're talking like we're in a Stephen King novel."

"We just might be. Murder is hurtful. This is wrong, and you know it."

"Oy vey," he murmurs into the dark.

CHAPTER 26

A heavy gray fog is moving in. Pushed by a northerly wind, it slowly blankets the Low Mile. A soft rain taps at the car's windshield. Up ahead, a streetlamp lights up the beachfront and the Mississippi Sound. The daughter of an avid sailor, Peggy knows these waters. When her father was not on call at Mercy General or expected at the yacht club, they were on board the *Weekender*, a forty-four-foot Countess that replaced a Pearson 43 when her father's stock portfolio tripled in value.

As she travels west, clouds drift in from the north, opposite the crawling traffic. Stuck at a stoplight, she pushes up a sleeve like she's going to a blood drive. Nerves have her rotating the slim bracelets stacked on her narrow wrist. The turn into the marina has her heart racing faster than Seattle Slew's when he crossed over the finish line to win the Triple Crown. Unlike the decorated steed, she is not embracing the feelings of a winner.

Fraught with worry that the truth might be more than her tender heart can handle, she eases off the gas. Although she is hoping to catch Preston red-handed, the need to hurry teeters on what she might find waiting for her.

She circles the lighthouse and inches along the concrete where Preston always parks his car. She stares at the empty space until a deep sigh returns her to the million-dollar question.

How is it possible that both his car and his boat are missing?

CHAPTER 27

A sweep of the Safe Harbour's famed dining room lets visitors know there is not a table available and the wait to be seated is a long one. Hardworking air-conditioning units keep the large space at a comfortable temperature, while vintage palladium windows welcome the afternoon sun and offer generous views of the gardens and grass tennis courts.

Instrumental music escapes hidden speakers, drinks pour nonstop at the horseshoe bar, and servers hurry to deliver chilled dishes before they turn warm and hot plates before they catch cold. Once boiled crawfish and fried shrimp platters arrive at the tables, business turns to pleasure.

Behind the kitchen's sleek stainless steel doors, the staff hurries to shuck a fresh haul of fat, salty oysters. A barmaid polishes away water spots the dishwasher leaves behind, while Satch, the hotel's legendary bartender, artistically displays a chilled bottle of Perrier-Jouët in a silver bucket filled with diamond ice.

Before the clock in the kitchen strikes straight up, a college kid working the summer at the hotel crosses over Beach Boulevard to the marina. He parks the Yamaha cart in a nearby slip, and with a skip in his step and a whistle on his tongue, saunters his way to 28W. Instructed in advance to ring the aged bronze bell next to the gate, he knocks the clapper against the bell's lip after placing the covered tray and silver bucket on the pier's concrete dock. Knowing a generous figure always appears on Dr. Fayne's receipt, he does not wait for a tip.

Hearing the bell, Preston slides out of bed and into a silk robe, a gift from Molly he dares not take home to his closet on Starlight Cove. Once a display of affection and now a demand, he blows an air kiss across the cabin.

"Tousled and mussed-up hair is a look you wear well. Don't move. I'll be right back."

Naked from the neck down, Molly returns a flirty grin. "I won't move a muscle."

Intrigued by her playfulness and smoking hot body, he returns to the bed, where he closes the space between them.

"You excite the hell out of me," he whispers, going in for a kiss.

"Ditto, but what about lunch?" Giving his hand a lover's squeeze, she runs a finger over his lips, along his chin, and through the graying hair on his chest. When she raises her hips to his, a telling sigh escapes parting lips.

"Forget the oysters. I don't need them when I'm with you."

In the following minutes, while the oysters turn warm and the champagne sets free its bubbly chill, the ringing of his cell phone interrupts their romp.

While he delivers instructions to his housekeeper regarding the spare key's hiding place, Molly steps from the bed. A smile comes to her when she hears him confirm the home's alarm system is turned off.

Turning back, he offers a pouty face she understands to mean he wants her to stay. The look she returns is filled with apologies. Ending the call, he moves his hands along her narrow shoulders to the small of her back. His body quivers and goose bumps sweep over his arms. Overwhelmed with desire, he nibbles at her neck.

"You can't leave now," he says, eyeing her bare bottom.

"Preston, you know I can't stay."

"At least join me for champagne."

"I wish I could, but I'm expected at the luncheon. My absence will raise eyebrows."

"Same time tomorrow then?"

"And every day after that, except Thursday. Can't do Thursday." Moving close, she plants a tender kiss on the tip of his nose.

Hating when she makes herself unavailable, his warm eyes turn cold.

"I'll see what I can do."

"Please do. If it works out, get a room at one of the casinos. That's our best bet."

"So now you're a comedian, too?"

"I don't mean to be funny. Ivan is coming by to look at the Jeep's engine. It's been acting up. Just yesterday morning, the damn thing cut out twice. If it hadn't been for the driver behind me, I would have been stuck on the bridge. Speaking of stuck, have you seen my wedding band? I seem to have misplaced it."

"Can't say I have."

Across town, the club's annual fashion show is preparing to take the stage. A glance at the rack of clothes outside the changing room has Peggy recalling her conversation with Dana. She was practically on her knees when she begged her to model the club's signature active wear. Although it is painful to admit, Dana has the perfect figure to show off the short tennis skirts and trendy dresses.

"Excuse me, Peggy. Have you seen Dana?" Bunni asks, having already searched the banquet hall and changing room.

"Has she signed in?" While preparing for the show, Peggy arranged for a sign-up sheet to be taped on the changing-room door. In addition to insuring each model's arrival, it also keeps tabs on the pricey clothes that often walk out the door.

"No, not yet. I'd like a walk-through before she takes the stage. If you see her, will you send her my way?"

"Of course. In the interim, I'll text Molly Lambert. She is planning to attend. Maybe I can convince her to fill in if Dana doesn't show." Pulling her cell phone from her purse, she taps away at the screen. "I'm calling Preston. It's possible Dana has lost track of the time." Hearing the receptionist's voice, she holds a finger to her lip. "Hello, this is Peggy Fayne. Is Preston available?"

The receptionist, an older woman she has yet to meet, lets her know he stepped out for lunch. "His next appointment is in forty minutes."

"Is it possible to speak with Dana?"

"She left the office around eleven."

"I'm hoping she's on her way to the club. Sorry to disturb you."

"No problem, Mrs. Fayne, but I don't believe she is coming your direction. She said she didn't want to be late for an appointment in Hattiesburg."

Before the call has time to disconnect, suspicion creeps in. Dana canceled on her once before, but she sent a text letting her know. She wants to trust her husband, but the pain in her heart reminds she should keep her eyes wide open and an ear pressed to the ground.

Grabbing her purse, she races out to her car. Skating through flashing lights, she prays a collision is not in her future. Because time does not allow for a leisurely drive, she takes the turn into the marina on two wheels. If there is ever an opportunity to catch Preston in the act, she believes this is it.

A glance up the street has her slowing her speed and rolling to a stop. The boat is in the slip, and Preston's car is nowhere in sight.

Unsure if she should be relieved or disappointed, Peggy turns the car around and returns to the yacht club. Minutes later, when she takes her position at the podium, she sees Molly rushing through the door. Not to be distracted, she continues speaking of the club's annual cookbook and requests for recipes. Out of the corner of her eye, she watches Molly roam the event's room before heading backstage.

When the lights dim and the curtain lifts off the deck, Molly steps onto the stage sporting a lace tennis dress with an open back. A tennis racquet rests against her shoulder. Working the crowd, she takes several practice swings before pretending to serve an invisible ball. Loud cheers confirm she not only owns the runway but also the event.

"She's knocking them dead. Don't even get me started with her winning smile," Bunni whispers to Peggy. "We must sign her up for next year."

"I agree." Peggy watches Molly sashay along the stage before stopping at the end of the runway to take a pirouette and hold a model's pose. "I'll say this: she has stage presence."

The women roar when Molly edges the dress up her leg, giving an intimate glimpse of tennis panties and sun-kissed thighs. With confidence to be admired, she saunters along the runway toward Peggy's table, where she blows a juicy kiss off her hand.

CHAPTER 28

Oyster shells, withered lemons, and an empty champagne bottle wait on a tray at the end of the pier. Curious to learn who enjoyed lunch on the boat, Peggy searches the stems for lipstick. A glance at the crystal flutes reveals someone has taken the time to wipe them clean.

Except for a lingering fragrance, she finds the boat's cabin in order, and the usual suspects fail to share their secrets. The sink is dry, the trash can is empty, and the salon's throw pillows are fluffed and carefully arranged along the banquette. Although hesitant, she makes her way to the aft cabin—the stateroom Preston settles into at the end of the day when he stays overnight on the boat.

Hoping to dodge an arrow to her heart, she pulls back a corner of the bed's duvet. Steeling her spine, she prepares her tender heart for any evidence that might leave her questioning Preston's love for her. Sweeping a hand over the silk bedding, she finds the sheets not only tousled but also warm. A fragrance she believes is lilac or lavender races to envelop her. It is nothing like the magnolia and gardenia scents she wears.

In a different time, when Preston's taking of a mistress was a concern she never entertained, she would have undressed, tossed the day's headaches aside, and slid under the sheets, counting the seconds until his busy schedule allowed him to join her—but not now. This is no longer her comfort to enjoy. It was not her body, one faithful to her marriage, that cozied up with Preston on these sheets.

Unable to hold back tears, she curses the bed and the woman who tangled in it. Disturbing images her mind hurries to paint have her grabbing her throat. *This must be what drowning feels like.*

Making her way to the salon, she wipes at tears she is embarrassed to cry. Struggling with the lump in her throat, she throws open the cabinet under the sink. Taking a garbage bag in one hand and a can of spray paint in the other, she returns to her husband's lair and the scandalous scent of his sins.

"How could you do this to me?" she cries, ripping the sheets from the bed and forcing them into the trash bag. Ready to throw a match to it, she hopes there will never come a time when she will be asked to explain this moment of madness in a court of law.

Driven by anger and skating on what little pride remains, she drags the bag down the narrow drive toward the marina's showers. Holding her head high, she ignores curious looks from four women seated at a table as she passes alongside the restaurant's patio. Given their coifed hair and cherry-red lips, there is little doubt they have witnessed far worse.

Inside the bathroom, she lets go a guttural cry. Filled with rage, she lifts the bag and slams it against the cold concrete wall. Hearing a cough, she turns to find a duo of old biddies applying lipstick the color of ketchup at the vanity's generous mirror. She is drawn to the shorter woman, who is wearing a ballerina slipper on her right foot and a slingback wedge on the other. Both women give a sympathetic smile while snickering behind cupped hands. She wants to tell them where to shove their pity, but catching her own reflection, she bites her tongue. There is, after all, a chance they know her.

Once the old ladies are on the opposite side of the door, she tears at the bag until the sheets give up the good fight and crumple to the floor. Again she catches a whiff of the scent she struggles to recognize.

Fueled by disappointment and a healthy dose of hatred, she gives the spray can a vigorous shake. Removing the cap and pressing the nozzle, she lets go her rage on the bedding while cursing Preston and the day they met.

CHAPTER 29

Years of working the Low Mile's many marinas and casinos has let seventy-four-year-old Eldra Medera witness many things. Months earlier, a young woman went from slip to slip seeking odd jobs for pennies on the dollar. She offered to scrub decks, walk dogs, change cat litter, and shop for groceries. On an afternoon much like this one, she gave birth in a dark stall furthest from the building's door. Unmarried and with a newborn, she became Eldra's shadow. She has since moved on, and like the building's old walls, memories of their days together are slowly fading.

In recent weeks, when a middle-aged woman learned she would be denied alimony and child support, she took a sledgehammer to her soon-to-be ex-husband's mistress: a forty-eight-foot cruiser. Police found her hiding under dirty, wet towels in Eldra's cleaning cart.

For Eldra, finding a young woman huddled in a dark corner wringing her hands is nothing new. Eyeing the bed linens, she pushes the cart aside. Tugging at rubber gloves one finger at a time, she pulls them from her hands. It is a struggle for her old knees, which buckle more often than the wide belt holding up her pants. Still, she takes a seat on the cold concrete.

"Tell me, pretty lady, what brings you to my floor?" she asks, shifting about until her old bones settle. "We both know you don't belong down here."

"My husband's roots are planted under another woman's tree," Peggy cries. "There is no pain worse than heartbreak."

"Don't let a pretty woman like yourself engage in an ugly relationship you're not part of."

"I don't know what to do. I'm feeling so alone. I thought I married a legend, but now I'm struggling to find the good in him. We've suffered the usual hiccups—roving eyes, unexplained absences, small-town gossip—but now, at the bottom of the ninth, I'm left throwing in the towel. I worry I'll live out my life tossing back wine and noshing on Pronto Pups. I'm drowning here, even if it's only in pity."

"I won't let you drown on my shift," Eldra says, reaching for her hand. "In these parts where I come from, I believe you have only one option: live your life knowing it's OK to cry. It doesn't make you weak. It shows emotion. Look around you—not here in this old bathroom, but in your everyday life. Your world isn't going anywhere until you right your ship. As for the Pronto Pups, I'll join you."

"I don't mean for you to worry about me. I'm going to be OK. I may be crying on this old floor, but I'll turn my life around." Pausing, Peggy wipes at her face with the back of her hand. "There was a time I believed I would never grow tired of watching his lips tremble just before he kisses mine or the way his neck curves when he comes in close for a hug or a peck on the cheek. I want to believe he doesn't notice, but I'm beginning to believe he does these things on purpose. Maybe he knows these are just two of the many reasons I fell for him."

"Young lady, I'm hearing both pain and love in your voice."

"I'm a mess. Just last night, I ate a bag of popcorn in bed, slept with my jewelry on, and ate my breakfast for dinner. When my alarm called out in the midmorning hours, I cursed the sunrise. In my disappointment, I called the passing hours a kumbaya moment. Today, in the here and now, something is different. Something is pulling him away from me. Something bad. I don't know what it is, but I feel it. There are times I'm left with nothing to do but wait for it to happen."

"Have you tried praying?"

"Prayers and wallowing in self-pity and nostalgia won't stop it. A dark cloud is looming overhead, and in its wake, it will leave behind something I won't be able to handle. Perhaps it's my own Armageddon. It frightens me that while my heart wants to trust him, I'm foolish to believe his life with me is the air in my lungs. Is it possible I've been preparing for this moment?" she questions, not waiting for an answer. "Maybe his cheating ways and lies are meant to end my pain." Rolling her hands, she looks up the wall to the concrete ceiling. "I spent many nights in that cabin on these same sheets he shares with her. His affair is a slap in my face."

"Everything's going to be OK," Eldra offers, giving Peggy's clenched hand a knowing pat. "My baby girl, the youngest of my four daughters, is a wild child with little means and a shipload of big dreams. In the early morning hours when the city's bicentennial parade traveled along Main Street, she marched up the stairs to the county courthouse where she divorced her husband, a doctor specializing in orthotics. Three days later, she married a mime who makes pretend box experiences outside a coffee shop in the big city known as Houston. Not to be undone, her ex-husband ran off with a stuntwoman. It's not a proud moment in my family's history, but I'm here to say women like my daughter tend to need something they really don't want. It becomes a challenge they must win. Don't ask me why, but I believe it involves a glitch in their gene pool.

"Men cheat, and so do women. It's only their reasons that differ. A woman strays when her husband ignores her or forgets to tell her she is loved and appreciated. For reasons unknown, these men often choose to forego telling the one they love that she's beautiful and important in his life. Emptiness leaves her broken heart feeling abandoned and vulnerable. As for men, they cheat because they can. They'll entertain anything with a pulse. It doesn't matter the dollars they have in the bank, the children who wait for them at the door at the end of each day, or that the greatest angel on Earth vowed to love them for a lifetime.

They need something we can't give them because we've already given them all we have to give."

Leaning close, she cups Peggy's chin. "Men are all alike. It's been said God gave them faces so we would know which one is ours. If you haven't noticed, he did the same with puppies. In time, you'll learn men are not like us. I've heard it said their realities are not our realities. Their confidence is oftentimes so defective, they cast aside all their tomorrows when given the opportunity to cheat life out of another day. They haven't learned a missed opportunity might just be a blessing. It's not old age that is their enemy but growing old. As for the puppies, they will lick and love us long after the cows come home."

In their silence, Eldra reflects on her own marriage. At age fourteen, she was a child bride. Times were different back then. College was not any more in her future than the ninth grade. Early on in her marriage, she understood her job was to keep house, cook a hot meal, and iron clothes fresh off the line. It was never in her cards to host five-course dinner parties for her husband's business associates, plan summer vacations in Europe with their children, or dress in the latest fashions she admired in storefront windows and magazine covers.

Six years her senior, Buster Medera had shown promise. Every Sunday after church, he arrived at her parents' house on South Washington Street. Shielding his eyes from the morning sun, he asked her mother about her day while offering to weed her garden and trim the trees in the same breath. In the next breath, he asked how many folks she expected for supper. Her answer was always the same: *Seven, just like last Sunday. Eight, if you promise to join us.*

Wearing a wide smile and an old straw hat, Buster set out to fish the neighboring waters. Later in the afternoon, long after the crows returned to their branches high in the river birch trees, he arrived in her mother's kitchen with a proud grin and enough black drum, collard greens, and vine-ripened melon to feed the neighborhood.

Days into their marriage, Eldra accepted that this would not be a union in which they enjoyed fireworks in the bedroom. Although he lacked imagination under the sheets, he proved to be a good provider,

and like her, a faithful reader of the Bible, allowing her to overlook
his shortcomings in the early evening hours when their bedding was
pulled back and the lights turned out.

"My marriage was never a Cinderella story," she tells Peggy, "but
I believed it was rock-solid. That is, until Peaches Swindell came to
live with her aunt, a jezebel who smoked unfiltered cigarettes with
the men and drank Old Man Parsky's moonshine when her arthritis
flared up, something she swore happened the second she opened her
eyes in the morning until she passed out on the couch soon after the
cocktail hour.

"Before Peaches brought her bad ways to town, Buster and I spent
our Sundays cracking pecans we gathered from a neighbor's yard,
a generous stretch of land deep in the Delta's floodplain. I may be
mistaken, but the dark corner in my history leads me to believe her
name was Mrs. Glur," she says, reliving the memory. "We used the
broken bits for sweet pralines and pecan pies we shared at the church's
weekly social. We sold the whole pieces, the pretty ones that looked
like angel wings carried on a cloud, to local restaurants and sundries
at two cents a pound.

"A young girl with a woman's figure, Peaches caught the eye of
every single man and the roving eyes of married ones, including my
Buster. Like our pralines, I could see she was sweet on him from the
get-go. When the day was warm and a light breeze moved through
the trees, she pranced by our house barefoot and in a dress made of
cotton. Sometimes she would sing songs—nothing like the hymns we
sing in church every Sunday along with Reverend Abramson's choir,
but those I worried were written by the devil himself.

"On a day much like today, I stopped by Mr. Dedy's Sundry
hoping the price of eggs was fair and his homegrown tomatoes were
affordable. Instead, I found my husband sampling Peaches' painted
lips in the dry goods section. A woman of faith, I kept my feet planted.
Those who bothered to look found the Holy Bible peeking out from
under my arm. Buster's sorry eyes and pitiful self followed me all
the way home. While the setting sun brought light to our kitchen, we

shared fried chicken and sugar snap peas. Later, when curtains were pulled and doors were locked, we shared only silence. Days later, I heard through the church's grapevine that Peaches had hitched a ride to New Orleans."

Growing silent, she allows the painful memories to fade. When she turns to Peggy, she is met with wet eyes. "It's not for you to save a broken person, but to save yourself," Eldra says. "Take as much time as you need. I'll sit here with you. This old floor can just wait. We both know it isn't going anywhere."

Seated next to a stranger who is reaching out in kindness, Peggy continues to question Preston's actions. She wonders if they were meant to send an uncaring message to her heart. The what-ifs continue until her racing heart threatens instant death. A flashback has her laughing at a televangelist who, decades earlier, asked his faithful viewers to place their hands on the television set while guiding them through prayer. Her grandmother, a woman of strong faith with a liking for gin, raced open-handed to the old black-and-white before falling to her knees. Forced to look at her own future, something tells her she just might embrace the television when she returns home.

"I once knew a man who shaved his chest when his hair started to gray. He went on a crazy diet. Poor soul, his breath smelled like that toilet," Eldra says, pointing to an open stall a few feet away. "Not good, I tell you. Not good. Turns out he was trying to erase the years his aging body could no longer hide."

"My husband isn't old."

"In the eyes of a young child, everyone over twelve is prehistoric. Age places us at different stages in our lives, and our hearts know only to beat. For some men, having a young woman on their arm validates them—if only for a moment or until she grows tired of early-bird specials, midday naps, and, if he has them, grandkids. Don't even get me started with the changes in the bedroom." Again, she takes Peggy's hand. "Fools are what they are."

"I feel like I'm on the verge of a nervous breakdown. When I look to my future, I'm afraid I'll see only my shadow." Although her heart is breaking and shows little promise of becoming whole again, Peggy forces a smile. "What am I going to do? I feel like I've been shot out of a cannon only to be thrown into a lion's den. He doesn't care how much or how deep this pain he put on me hurts. It seems all I do is wallow in self-pity."

"Relax your shoulders, unclench your jaw, and remember to breathe," Eldra advises. "When you feel planted, do what it is you must do to make yourself happy. It's not for you to carry the shame. My grandmother, a wise woman with a lifetime of learning, used to say how we embrace today determines who we become tomorrow. You can choose to wail in misery or make each day memorable.

"The way I see it, you have three choices: You can go after what is yours and not waste your time wallowing or licking open wounds: we know nothing good comes from that. You can fight like the dickens for him and your marriage. Or you can accept what you can't change. My advice is to let the sweet essence of time play it out. Whatever path you choose, always wear the face you want others to see."

Giving a stretch, she shoves the sheets with the rubber soles of her shoes. "That woman wants what you have. She's never happy for long. She's eaten up with jealousy and envy. As for your husband, only you know if he's worth the emotional distress, pain, and anguish. I believe your heart will know when it's time to hold your feet to the fire. I'm not suggesting you come in swinging. When the time is ripe, throw out simple words he will understand. Tell me, though—what kind of prize causes such pain to the woman whose hand he asked for in marriage?"

Foregoing an answer, she taps Peggy's wedding ring with a weathered finger. "As his wife, you hold all the cards. Royal flush, I believe they call it. Give that some thought for a minute," she says, looking back to the open stall. "Now, let's wash your face and fix your makeup. Forgive me if I dust you off a bit. When you walk out of here, you will wear the face of a strong woman—one with morals and values. Now let's get up from this nasty floor. We both have our work cut out for us."

"Thank you for your kindness and your wisdom. I'm sorry, but I didn't catch your name."

"Eldra. Eldra Medera. Never forget—time is an asset. And one last thing: if you ever come across a woman named Peaches Swindell, please give her a swift kick in the ass for me."

CHAPTER 30

Although Preston's schedule requires him to be at the office, he returns to the boat. A greasy smile crosses his face when he finds the tray has been picked up. Inside, he catches a hint of perfume. Although he enjoys the fragrance, caution suggests he give the room a spritz.

An uneasy feeling washes over him when he searches the slim cabinet under the sink. The glance warns something is not right. He takes inventory—reading labels, securing caps—until he realizes a can of spray paint he keeps on board for quick touch-ups is missing. While his heart races, he runs through the salon to the aft cabin. Finding the bed stripped, he checks the laundry basket where the cleaning service is instructed to leave the dirty laundry. Except for the hand towel he used earlier in the day, the basket is empty.

Panic travels his veins until he remembers Peggy's luncheon. A glance at his watch tells him she would not have had time to swing by the marina. It only made sense that the cleaning service took the bedding and forgot to remake the bed. Taking fresh sheets from the drawer, he does their work for them. While tucking corners, a warning in his head cautions it is only a matter of time before he will learn all is not what it appears in his little world.

CHAPTER 31

"Molly has lost all interest in me," Clay blurts out. "I've racked my brain trying to recall what I could have said or done, but nothing jumps out at me. Maybe that's the problem. Doesn't matter what I say or do, she's tired of me. She doesn't care about anything but herself. Given our history, I can't say I'm surprised."

"I'm sure you're seeing something that's not there," Preston reassures. "Is she nagging?"

"Sometimes I find myself believing she's a first-grade teacher—giving me directions and shouting out orders. Other times, she is downright mean. I'd call her a bully, but I'm afraid she'll put me in the corner. She's keeping me in line with what I like to call *constructive criticism.*"

"That's borderline nagging."

"I suppose. She complains that extreme headaches continue to haunt her. She's not alone. Look at me. I'm finding the grief I suffer every day threatens a stroke. I have dark circles under my eyes, and the few times I'm given a reason to laugh, I suffer a threatening pinch in my chest. There was a time in our marriage when we discussed parting ways. My lawyer suggested we attend a couple's retreat. It was some sort of healing therapy meant to guide us back to the happy place where we once saw the best in each other. Her lawyer was on board, but hours before our plane was to depart, he had a change of heart. I had the feeling he was she-banging her on the side. That SOB continued to charge her by the hour. I'm still pissed I ended up paying for a bang I didn't get to buck. Turns out, she fed me false promises, hoping to convince me she would change her ways. I'm guessing her lawyer knew she followed her morning coffee with a little pink pill."

"Birth control?"

"Of course. Truth is, once she pops the pill, she puts on a different mask."

"Do you know this to be a fact? The lawyer, I mean."

"His father-in-law was the firm's managing partner. Leaving his wife for Molly would have put a blemish on his dossier. At this point, what I know and don't know no longer matters."

Earlier, when Clay asked if he had a minute to talk, Preston believed they would be discussing payroll. Recent increases to their employees' salaries has put a pinch in the firm's slush fund, and although their partnership in the practice has spilled over to a friendship, he does not want to be Clay's Dutch uncle—giving advice and getting caught up in his drama with Molly.

"I've nicknamed her Trouble," Clays says, throwing him the side-eye.

"I'm guessing there is a story behind this."

"She's always in it. Just yesterday, I suggested we meet friends for dinner. I threw out their résumés hoping she would find them interesting. After hours of hemming and hawing, she told me to go alone. I continued to beg until she said she wanted to stay home with the dog."

"As good a reason as any."

"We don't have a dog. She has a drawer of lacy getups she wears when she wants playtime. Call me blind, but I haven't seen a stitch of these pieces in a month of Sundays. Weeks back, she told me she was going to visit her sister in Arkansas. Two days into the trip, Celeste, that's her sister, called the house. There was something in her voice that had my radar up. I told her I thought Molly was with her. There was this awkward silence and then she came up with some crazy, lame-ass story. A round of questions followed. In the next breath, she came at me on all fours."

"I think you mean on all twos."

"If you heard her words and felt the tone in her voice, I believe you would agree she went animal on me. I pictured her in a military helmet, camouflage clothing, and desert combat boots."

"On all four feet?"

"I'd bet my last dollar. It ended with her telling me she meant to call someone else, but somewhere in the misdial ended up with me. We shared a laugh until I asked to speak to Molly. Caught in a trap, she made up a cockamamie story too ridiculous to believe."

"Have you considered hiring a private eye?"

"It's crossed my mind a time or two, but I'm trying to remain hopeful our pieces will fall back together. Another divorce would ruin me, and not just financially. There was a time when I was able to read her like an open book, but now I'm thinking she is skipping over our life chapters and writing her own love story. I'm worried the last page will close with a doozy I never saw coming."

"It's possible she suffers with what I like to call *seasonal disorder*."

"I'm not familiar with this."

"Spending too much time recalling happier moments. Perhaps she is a dreamer."

"The dreamer in her is becoming a nightmare in our marriage, and now I'm left questioning why she goes to great lengths to hide the truth. Sometimes I'm left believing she has underlying anger issues. Some days, I feel like I'm living with an ankle-biting adolescent. Other days, I'm struggling to manage a teenager. I often find myself wondering if she's a terrorist."

"Knowing Molly, that's quite a stretch, but you might be on to something. Do the country a favor and notify the authorities—CIA, FBI, and Homeland Security. If time allows, you might study the want ads. The fine print often hints at the truth. If you have access to them, study her passport and travel visas. I might also suggest you search any boxes she might be hiding under the bed or deep in her closet.

When you're through there, get a court order to search safe deposit boxes and offshore accounts. Prepare your heart for any surprises. I've never experienced divorce," Preston shares, "but I've witnessed outcomes where only the attorneys come out as winners. If you're concerned about matters of the heart, talk with her. You might be surprised to learn that's what she is wanting. I'm not suggesting you charge in like Rambo, but go at her with a gentle approach."

"Yeah, maybe," Clay replies. "I don't know. I fear she is eager to put a syringe in my arm. Our history has me worried she will find a way to turn this around and point the finger at me. If she sticks with her usual plan of attack, she will twist my words in such a way, I'll be left feeling guilty for bringing it up. Making matters worse," he admits, "our schedules are crazy, upside down, and backward. She stays up watching late-night television, and I'm dead asleep before the nightly news. The hours in between leave me planning my own hoopla and homecomings. It doesn't help that she's had a headache since Christmas. It appears everyday is National Period Day—a clear message our bed is for sleeping only. That said, she can be a pill at times. I'm a doctor, for crying out loud. I know something is not right."

Frustrated and embarrassed, Clay turns away. Left floating on the silence, his thoughts turn to the day he threatened Richard outside his home. What a day that was. His promises to Tank, leading up to and including the moment, were misleading. One false move, and he would have opened fire.

"Again, my advice is open dialogue. It can't hurt," Preston says, interrupting Clay's thoughts.

"It's too late. Who am I kidding? Molly's not pulling away. She's already gone. I think she is suffering buyer's remorse. Every time I call the house, I'm sent to voicemail." Chewing at his lip, he hopes his words will go unquestioned. "There was this guy Richard. He was all over her. I caught them naked and in the moment. I was ready to shoot him dead."

"And Molly?"

"She was next in line. She tends to go away when things don't go her way. The affair is why we moved here. I thought we needed a fresh start if we wanted to save our marriage."

"I recall hearing she grew up in Sugar Ditch Alley," Preston says, donating information.

"Not that I'm aware, but I wouldn't be surprised. While she never plays hard to get, I understand she bounced around in her forming years."

"What happened to Richard?"

"He fled the house believing I set him up for a crime he didn't commit. He went straight to the police station in soiled slacks and carrying what he believed was stolen jewelry and a hot gun. He told the lieutenant he was framed. Officer calls me. I tell him about catching Richard with my wife and that the jewelry was costume and the gun was scrap. We enjoyed a few laughs before he let Richard walk. After meeting up for a few brewskies, the officer agreed to chalk it off as a case of mistaken identity. As for Richard, I never saw him again, but I've smelled his presence a few times. I'm not proud of my actions," Clay reflects, "but at the time, it seemed like a good idea. When his wife got wind of the affair, she didn't waste any time filing for divorce. Not to be outdone, Richard tampered with her computer, moved money into a friend's bank account, and when the house went on the market, he hurried to cut the electricity. I heard the judge was not very happy with him. As for me and my actions, I'm guessing planting churches isn't in my future."

Although Preston nods in understanding, he questions whether they are discussing the same Molly. He has never known her to run from anything. History shows she digs in her heels until she believes she has won the war. Forcing those thoughts aside, he leans in, giving his best shot at brotherly advice.

"I knew this doctor in Atlanta," he tells Clay. "Handsome guy with reddish-brown hair and blue eyes. Picture a young Paul Newman, if you will. He had the body of a trained athlete. He was not only successful in his career but also an avid tennis player, marathon runner, and triathlete. Young chicks chased after him, and old age couldn't catch him. Older women tried to buy him. Married women hinted at unhappy marriages. On the flip side of the coin, some might argue that educated women ran from him and lesser women couldn't resist him. His girlfriend was a cute young thing with breast implants, collagen lips, and from what I understand, a healthy appetite for sex. The girlfriend crawled into a hot tub in the lady's locker room at the country club with his wife and her double's partner. By that, I mean tennis." Recalling the story as he heard it, Preston lets go a grin. "Doctor's wife commented on the girlfriend's necklace. The story goes it was a seven-carat diamond on a gold chain. Dingbat girlfriend proudly shared to all who moved close that her boyfriend, a member of the club, gave it to her days earlier, along with a membership to the club, when he swept her away to Santa Barbara for a long weekend. Small talk, or what I like to call the interrogation, continued until the wife's tennis partner asked about the boyfriend. Beans were spilled, his name escaped full lips, and a catfight ensued. Call it what you will, but all hell broke loose. Water splashed everywhere. Names were called, and words were exchanged. The girlfriend was held under water, splashing about like salmon swimming upstream, until a bite to the wife's thigh shot her to the surface where slaps were traded, claws worked double-time, and threats turned nuclear and life-threatening. By this time, a circle of women had gathered to cheer on the wild brawl. When the hot tub's rising water threatened a flood, security was called. After biting the wife's hand, the girlfriend ended up with the necklace in her clenched fist. Wife goes home, packs her bags, and when she backs out of the garage, a miscalculation nearly rips the driver's door off a brand spanking new Jaguar. Damn door hung on by a hinge all the way to her lawyer's office. I was told the car's side mirror didn't fare much better."

"That's it? That's the end of the story?"

"Yep."

"Was the wife tested for rabies?"

"I can't answer that," Preston admits, "but charges were dropped. The daily rag had fun calling it an ugly seduction. Those in the know knew better. Like most affairs, this one had more than two sides—he said, she said, mistress implied. In the following days, it took on more weight as the rumors picked up speed. Maybe Molly thinks you have some bimbo on the side."

"That's ridiculous. I don't have time to please one woman, let alone two. That said, what happened to the doctor's girlfriend?"

"She stayed in it for the long haul. Months later, when wounds healed and the doctor and his wife reached a record settlement, he and the girlfriend married on a secluded beach in Cabo and honeymooned on the Sea of Cortez."

"That might just be the worst story I've ever heard."

"Listen, buddy, what I'm trying to say is, Casino Beach is a small pocket. If Molly were unhappy, you would hear about it. Take it from me: the gossip train travels faster than a speeding bullet along the Low Mile."

CHAPTER 32

The bridge's slow-moving traffic gives Molly time to mull over her plan and rehearse her scheme. As always, she has a few tricks up her sleeve, and the time to use them is fast approaching. It was a stroke of luck when Preston was called into the emergency room. She struggles to understand why he would assume she would stay on the boat until his return. "Oh, Preston, you should know by now I have better ways to spend my time," she says aloud.

More than once, and longer than she could stand, he went on and on like a broken record about Peggy's visit to her alma mater. As his words play over and over in her head, the threat of projectile vomiting has her worrying she will have to pull over to the bridge's narrow shoulder.

Searching the area for familiar landmarks that will guide her to Preston's home, she cuts three lanes of traffic before taking the exit ramp to Banyon Hills. Slowing her speed, she throws a steady finger to the turn signal. Cruising through the intersection, she makes an easy turn onto Starlight Cove, a cul-de-sac leading to the Faynes' home. As she nears the house, the sweet fragrance of pearly white gardenias welcomes her once again to the rich side of town.

Coasting at a speed the car's speedometer fails to register, she taps at the brakes and pulls up to the sidewalk's low edge. Through fresh eyes, she surveys the street and its neighboring houses. Except for a graying Labrador lifting a hind leg to a hydrant on his afternoon walk, the winding road is quiet. Moving at a snail's pace, the Lab sniffs a soiled phone directory parked at the curb before fertilizing a young magnolia.

The window shades on the house to the north are closed, and a pile of newspapers collects runoff water from the home's automatic sprinklers. A 1965 Buick Riviera with concealed headlamps is parked across the street. A Dodge Viper GTS, rumored to have once been an Indy pace car, gathers a fresh layer of dust under the English Tudor's carport. A weathered tennis ball rests against the car's rear tire. Letting her thoughts drift, she wonders if it belongs to the Lab.

Careful not to draw attention, she inhales the gardenias' aroma. Finding the coast clear, she shops the Faynes' mailbox. She has read enough mysteries to know it is best to convince nosy neighbors she belongs here. Making her way to the home's front door, she skips over a monthly rag, but pauses when a delivery package on the porch's welcome mat piques her interest.

"Well, well, well. Peggy Fayne has a gift from Willa's Lighting," she says, removing dark sunglasses. The label's fine print tells her Peggy has been shopping online again. Tucking the small box under her arm, she hopes she will remember to grab it on the way out.

Thinking about Preston and his habit of returning to poor choices, this is another one of those times she is grateful for his trust. Now is not the time for him to learn she does not deserve it. Although it is to her advantage, he was foolish to explain to the housekeeper, who interrupted their alone time, that the home's spare key was tucked up the downspout at the right of the front door. She was all ears when he shared that the home's alarm system is never activated.

Worried Peggy may have changed her plans at the last minute, she gives the doorbell a press. If needed, *I was in the neighborhood* will be her excuse for standing at the door. Venturing over the porch to the downspout, she swipes the key from safekeeping. Returning to the door, she gives the bell another press before turning the lock.

A smile travels over her face when the front door opens without so much as a squeak. Her heart is racing, but not fast enough to send her running back to the car. When images of Clay's surprise attack when he caught her playing house with Richard rush at her, she turns the lock. She cannot risk another snafu, especially one involving the Governor, Clay's favorite handgun.

Barely breathing, she absorbs the room's art, scents, and framed photographs. Pierre Deux wallpaper appears out of place in the stucco house. "Who are you trying to impress?" she questions aloud. Except for a model sailboat perched high on a shelf in the entry hall, she notices for the first time that the house is without any coastal decor. She expects to find one of those whimsical lighthouses offered to tourists vacationing at the beach during high season or an antique helm. After all, they live in Casino Beach, not the White House.

A wicked smile crosses her face when her eyes fall on the sheepskin rug. Recalling the spill she so beautifully orchestrated, she marches over the floor like a trained soldier. Stomping spiked heels into the hardwood, she thrusts a trio of bracelets up her arm. With a sweep of her hand, she flips over a corner of the rug. Anger builds when she finds there is not the slightest hint of the red wine that once bloodied the rug. With no thanks given to Dana, club soda was a great suggestion but not a fix. Falling to her knees, she rakes the rug with angry fingers. Preston's failure to mention he replaced the rug has forced her to come up with another way to skin the cat, Jupiter included.

Standing tall, she slips out of her shoes, unbuckles her belt, and while screaming inside, pushes denim jeans down to her ankles. The voice of reason shouting in her ear does not keep her from falling into a necessary squat. Moments later, when her bladder is empty, she pulls her jeans up to her hips, buckles her belt, and steps from the soiled rug into waiting shoes.

Although she's drawn to a porcelain rabbit and a gold basket filled with colorful crystals, Peggy's prized aquarium is her next target. Tapping at the glass, she pulls the slim cord from the electrical outlet. Her thoughts return to an afternoon, decades earlier, when her school's librarian, a short, plump woman who smelled like mothballs, warned of the dangers the fish in the science lab might suffer. The memory now blurred, she recalls learning the harm in overfeeding. Letting go the memory, she brushes her hand through the water.

When the fish rush the glass, she is ready with a mesh spoon. One by one, she scoops them from the water. Careful to not cause injury, she places them on the tank's flat edge. Captivated by their desperate search for air and water, she sits in wait. A science experiment in Mr. B's third-grade class reminds it is only a matter of time before they give up the good fight.

The Oscar-winning performance is interrupted when she hears the roar of an engine. Stepping up to the window, she pulls the rich drape aside. A quick look up and down the street lets her know the coast is clear. A second glance confirms there is not a soul in sight. When she turns back, Jupiter rushes at her feet. Recalling their last encounter, she gives a cold stare and bares her teeth.

"You better watch your back." Just as she turns to walk away, she eyes the lifeless fish parked in its mouth. For a brief moment, she considers a rescue attempt, but recalling the seahorses are Peggy's favorite, she slides over the hardwood.

"*Bon appetit,*" she says, waving the miniature pony in the cat's round face. She finds it apropos that the other seahorses are the last to surrender. Once they take their last breath, she tosses them behind the tank. Bidding them adieu, she wipes her hands of their untimely demise.

"Nice house you have here," she says, treating the visit like a realtor's open house. Traveling the hall's generous space, she explores rooms never included in Peggy's tours.

The guest bedroom's walls are papered with a small floral pattern she believes is meant to match the bedspread's large print. A mirrored vanity displays a collection of porcelain flowers she finds ugly and worthless. "Who smells fake flowers?" she questions in a low voice.

Down the hall, in an area unfamiliar to her, is a paneled study with a stone fireplace and leather recliners the color of sweet, creamy butter. The hearth holds a cardboard tube of matchsticks, several logs, and a stack of magazines. Flipping through the pages of the monthlies, she believes the sailing journals belong to Preston while the design catalogs are meant to hold Peggy's interest.

A carved door she believes once welcomed guests inside a castle somewhere in the South of France allows passage into the spacious bedroom. Except for four walls and a floor beneath her feet, the room bears no resemblance to her bedroom in the rental. There is not a single fiber of seafoam green carpeting or a display of urine stains on cheap curtains she was told the previous tenant's cat was determined to leave behind.

The sitting room leading to Peggy's bathroom displays a gold ornate mirror worthy of a grand museum. In a flash, Molly's thoughts turn to her own bathroom and the dime-store mirror that slaps the door at every closing.

Folded towels anchor a window seat, and in the room's far corner, Preston's shirts fall over the back of a tufted chair. A rainbow of reading glasses circles a floor lamp's small shade. She recognizes a tortoise frame she once saw on the boat. Promising to return to the generous space, she makes her way into the bathroom.

Beneath a chandelier draped with jewels is a pedestal table. A sleek toilet claims a small closet. Limestone vanities hug curved walls and candles of every shape and fragrance invite her to soak in the jetted tub. She pulls at the faucet's handle, feels the water's temperature, and when the water reaches the tub's lower jets, strips down to her birthday suit. Although tempted to light a candle, she shops a row of bath beads. Vanilla Bean is the first to catch her eye, but taking a whiff, she scoops up light purple beads and holds them under her nose. The familiar scent of sweet lavender puts a smile on her face and Vanilla Bean to shame.

Reclined against the tub's contoured pillow, she wraps a gathering of wispy stray hair behind her ear. Giving a dramatic sigh, she hopes the warm water will relieve the tension in her neck that Peggy's absence has brought on. Unfamiliar with the tub's many gizmos and gadgets, she grows frustrated when a button she expects will move pulsating water against her aching back responds with a nasty cough. Sliding deeper into the tub, she invites the water to massage her tired shoulders.

"I could get used to this. The life of luxury suits me. One day soon, all of this will be mine—except for that tacky curtain. I've seen better at garage sales. And the door pulls are boring. Once the ring is on my finger and Fayne follows my name, I'll replace them with colorful knobs like those in the house Clay shared with his stupid ex-wife. It's no wonder Preston chases after me. I have good taste." Wrapped up in the life she is meant to live, she pulls the cell phone from her purse and presses Preston's number.

"Hey, baby. How much longer are you going to be? I'm so lonesome here all by myself."

"Give me thirty to forty minutes to wrap up here and another twenty to run by my house."

Losing traction against the tub's slippery bottom, she sinks low into the water. "Can't that wait? This is our time now. Peggy is out of town, and I planned an evening I know you'll enjoy." It will be the death of her if he finds a single drop of water in the tub or gets a whiff of the scent the bath beads will likely leave behind.

"You're right. Give me an hour. Order dinner from the hotel. Oysters for me and a Caesar salad—no anchovies."

"Of course," she says, planting her feet, one foot over the other, on the tub's satin faucet. "Consider it done."

She is reaching for the tub's release when she looks up to find her painted nails and crossed-over feet worthy of a magazine centerfold. Phone in hand, she snaps a picture—one certain to include the bath's marble tile and the room's green and pink wallpaper. "Just in case a little blackmail is needed," she says, thinking about the possibilities.

Across the room, a monogrammed towel hangs from a gilded bar. She struggles to ignore a folded hand towel near the basin. Believing it is giving her the evil eye, she looks away. Escaping the tub, she shoves the hand towel into her purse. "Surely Peggy will not miss one little towel."

Wrapped in a bath towel she rips from the window seat, she explores perfumes displayed on the dressing table. She gives each a healthy spritz before returning the bottles to the mirrored tray. When her eyes fall on a bottle she recalls having seen in her teen years, she lets go a laugh. *One would think she shares the bathroom with her grandmother.*

A quick glance in the walk-in closet has her questioning the rack of clothes she recognizes as belonging to Preston. In a snap, her mood changes. He swore, at her insistence, that he is sleeping in the guest room. A rise in her temperature warns there will be hell to pay if he is lying.

With fast steps, she races down the hall to the room she skipped over earlier, at the beginning of the tour. Determined to know the truth, she pulls back the bed's pink-on-pink chenille spread. The pounding of her heart drowns out her screams when she finds the mattress bare. A quick glance in the closet reveals extra blankets, bed pillows, and empty hangers. Spewing expletives, she circles back to Peggy's closet.

Perfume samples likely torn from magazines anchor a shelf of folded sweaters. Inches from Peggy's clothes, Molly brushes the wardrobe with her hand. The closet soon fills with the scents the clothes hold close. She rakes through the hangers like she is shopping the sale rack at Bloomingdale's until a designer dress catches her eye. A hard push at the padded hangers leaves the dress in its wake. Ripping the dress from its hanger, she holds it against her slim frame. A glance in the mirror shows a heartless smile threatening to expose her thoughts.

Returning to the perfumes, she snatches up the blue-ribbon bottle. Racing back to the closet, she aims the bottle at the sad-looking dress. Holding the bottle at arm's length, she sprays until it coughs up and spits out its last drop. Placing a hand over her nose, she returns the saturated garment to its rightful place, pulls the clothes east until the hangers are inches apart, and returns the empty bottle to the dressing table.

She is turning to escape when her eyes fall on Preston's bathrobe. It is identical to the thick terry cloth robe he keeps on the boat. The familiar scent of his favorite cologne—a woodsy scent she pretends drives her wild—envelops her senses.

Determined to destroy his marriage, she returns to Peggy's closet. She strums through a collection of beaded necklaces hanging from a rack near the closet's door but moves on when they fail to hold her interest. She pushes along the clothes until she comes upon Peggy's bathrobe. Just the sight of it nearly kills her. If she were decades older, death either by stroke or an untimely heart attack would be imminent.

White with red stitching, the robe is identical to Preston's. Pulling the cotton wrap from the hanger, she slips thin arms into its generous sleeves. A gift tag attached to the cuff has her questioning why it has not been worn. When she notices the simple monogram, she knows it is meant for her, and she must have it. She is caught by surprise when her thoughts turn to a time not so long ago when she briefly borrowed Sally Hanson's nail polish, Frutti Patootie, from a discount store she frequents when money is tight. Polish in hand, she raced into a changing room where she enjoyed a manicure on the house before returning the bottle to a shelf on aisle six.

A further search uncovers leather-bound yearbooks, moth-eaten sweaters, and carnival trinkets she supposes were won while shooting metal ducks with long-handled rifles jerry-rigged by a posse of underpaid carneys—something similar to a scene she once watched on *The Andy Griffith Show*.

Returning to the bathroom, she sidles up to the dressing table, where she falls into the vanity's low-back chair. Curious what the table holds, she rifles the shallow drawer. Giddy like a schoolgirl at cheerleading tryouts, she squeals when she comes upon Peggy's jewelry. She slides an art deco ring onto her finger and holds a gold stone to her neck. The chunky pendant feels heavy against her skin. A herringbone necklace protected in a satin pouch is more to her liking. Later, she will think of a way to thank Preston for the bauble.

Ruby earrings soon replace the silver hoops she has had for so long, she can no longer recall how she came to own them. As if sitting for a photo shoot, she poses in front of the mirror. Throwing a hand to her neck, she models a Tahitian pearl ring until a fire of diamonds catches her eye. She recalls admiring the ring some time ago, when she first met Peggy on the boat. Just as she did then, she laughs. *Harry Winston, she called it.* Unable to take her eyes off it, she slides the diamond cluster onto her finger. She waves it about until a glance at her own simple ring reminds her that not only does the ring belong to Peggy, so does Preston. If she has her way, she will stake a claim to both before Peggy knows what hit her.

The dressing table's middle drawer holds the usual suspects—cotton swabs, tweezers, hand lotion, and dental floss. It is in the bottom drawer that she strikes gold.

A fat folder holds the typical honeymoon memorabilia. A cork from a champagne bottle is the first to draw her in. *Veuve Clicquot,* she reads in her head. Someone had taken the time to pen their wedding date and the moment of their toast—right down to the second. Their wedding announcement is tucked inside a recycled envelope that also holds a recipe for grilled chicken, chickpeas, and twice-salted avocado. A penciled list tells of the pots and pans, sets of china, and picture frames they received from friends and family so close, only first names are provided. A three-paragraph note from Babs, a woman signing off as Peggy's cousin, begs forgiveness that a family reunion on her husband's side prevents their attendance.

It is the wheel of birth control pills in the drawer's dark corner that sparks her rage. Preston swore he is jumping through hoops dodging Peggy's advances. She sweeps up the plastic compact and, one by one, flushes the yellow pills down the toilet. It is only after the last pill circles out of sight that she regrets her actions. If Preston and Peggy are sharing a bed, the last thing she wants is for Peggy to get knocked up.

A reflection in the mirror stokes an already hot fire. There it is—the marital bed, all four corners and the playing field. She throws aside happenings under the boudoir's duvet while growing curious about the oil painting above it.

Loosely wrapped in what appears to be imported bedding and wearing a smile and a diamond-studded choker, Peggy resembles Angie Dickenson's iconic magazine cover. Although Angie wore a baby-blue sweater and white pumps, the message is the same: sultry and seductive.

Through unblinking eyes, Molly reads the sentiment above the artist's signature: *To My Veiled Lady, Love always and forever, Preston.* A burning rage races through her, and foam fills her mouth. Preston never mentioned his innocent little Peggy posed so scantily for him nor his talent with a paintbrush. Pushing aside poor judgment and the possibility of prison time, she jumps onto the bed, grabs the frame with both hands, and with the strength of a superhero, tears it from the wall.

"I'm going to rip your face out of our lives," she screams at the canvas. Greedy hands leave her staring at a moment Preston never thought of sharing. She hates that he captured every detail, right down to the sparkle in Peggy's eyes. Once he belongs to her, she will demand he paint her portrait. If she has her way, it will be much larger and displayed in a room for their guests to admire. As for Peggy's portrait, she will later tear it to shreds and throw a match to it.

Drawn to the bed's coverlet, she brushes a hand over the toile pattern. Sliding her hands over the silk fabric and believing it is expensive, she tosses the robe aside. In a flash, her thoughts turn to her own bed where she sleeps under a simple flame-stitch bedspread she has had since high school. Sweeping up the large decorative bed pillows, she curses each one when it meets the floor with a thud. Catching her reflection in the mirror, she scoops up her bra—a plunging piece she usually wears after dark and not for long—and tucks it under the silky pillow Peggy rests on each night.

"Good luck explaining this, Preston Fayne, artist extraordinaire," she shouts in a voice only a dog will hear.

Crouched on a bended knee, she reaches into her purse, rummaging its contents until she feels the lipstick's familiar tube. Pursing her lips, she applies a thin layer of Tempest, a fiery-red color she knows Preston will recognize from the many getups she wears to hide her true identity. As she lifts the bed skirt, a devilish grin claims her face. Before regret can dissuade her, she tosses the lipstick under the bed. She cannot be certain when Peggy will find it, only that she will—and when she does, Preston will be caught in a trap. She wants to feel sorry for him for the pain he will surely suffer, but sympathy is not in the cards. *Oh, Preston, you are old enough to know there is no trophy for acting stupid.*

In her rush to the front door, she nearly blows a gasket when Jupiter cuts her off at the pass. While the fur ball watches her every move, she retrieves the fish from behind the tank. Pulling back a corner of the sheepskin rug, she tosses the lifeless creatures to the floor.

A sweep of the room has her drawn to a small cassette on the wet bar's marble counter. A narrow strip on the tape's slim side knows only to taunt her. *Margaret and Preston Fayne.* Their wedding date is written in ink below their names. Allowing curiosity to get the best of her, she tosses the cassette into her purse. She will watch it the next time Clay is called away to deliver another crying-ass baby.

Set to exit the house, she studies the room with inquisitive eyes until honing in on the home's thermostat. A smirk comes over her as she presses the keypad to ninety degrees—its hottest setting.

In her hurry to escape, she sweeps up Peggy's portrait, the robe, and the package from Willa's. Once she is on the flip side of the door, she gives the key a hard shove up the downspout.

CHAPTER 33

A sour stench and a cloud of thick, hot air greets Peggy at her home's side door. Steps behind, Preston panics when he, too, comes face-to-face with the vile odor emanating from the house.

"It's a sauna in here," he says, waving a hand at the air in front of him. "What is that smell?"

"It might be Jupiter. Here kitty, kitty, kitty." When Jupiter does not run to greet Peggy, worry wastes no time rushing at her. "Where can she be? I hope she didn't get into something." With a hand over her nose, she races from room to room—opening closed doors and looking beyond open ones. Frantic, she peeks around corners and under furniture, all the while calling for Jupiter to come out of hiding.

Preston travels the house, checking doors and windows. Finding them intact and locked, he steps out to the porch. A search of the downspout confirms the spare key is in its rightful place. Returning indoors, he trips over Jupiter, who, wide-eyed, scrambles over the floor into Peggy's outstretched arms.

"My poor baby." Holding the cat close, she brushes a loving hand along its side. "I wish you could tell me what happened here."

In a flash, Jupiter jumps from her embrace and races across the living room where she paws at the floor. Recognizing the orange and black tailfin caught in Jupiter's clenched jaw, Peggy lets go a scream.

Searching the tank, she prays her beloved fish have taken refuge in the castle or among the living reef's many nooks and crannies. Surprised to find the mesh scoop on the tank's rim, she sweeps it through the water—a tactic that usually attracts Elli, a Blue Ribbon eel.

"My fish! They're gone!"

Left asking questions, Preston takes the scoop from her trembling hand. Brushing through the water, he hopes to lure the fish with the same tactics she used. Unlike Peggy, he rolls back his sleeve and shoves an arm into the tank. "The water is warm—too warm for the fish."

"Preston, there aren't any fish." She points to the small, colorful tailfin Jupiter continues to slap about. Heartbroken, she makes the long walk through the house, wondering with each step what took place in her absence. She is waving away a veil of fumes when her eyes fall on the empty space above their bed. "Preston, where is my portrait?"

"Maybe it fell behind the bed," he says, coming up behind her.

"That's impossible. There's not enough space between the wall and the bed."

"It couldn't just disappear into thin air."

"Well, it appears a brush of magic swept it off into the next universe. Next, you're going to tell me David Copperfield paid a visit." Left rolling her eyes, she enters the bathroom—a place, until now, she called her sanctuary. A quick sweep of the room sends a shiver down her spine.

A towel gifted to her when she and Preston exchanged vows is missing, and a collection of perfumes she displays on an antique silver tray she inherited when her grandmother passed are rearranged. Eyeing the empty bottle, she feels certain it holds a secret begging to be told. The odor escaping the closet has her fearing it will be shared behind the double doors.

"Preston, I need you in here," she says, stepping into the closet.

"What in the hell happened?"

"Who would do such a thing? Saturate a dress to the point where it's ruined?"

"I can't imagine." Fidgeting about, he knows the time to turn serious has arrived. "We'll get to the bottom of this."

"Did you have friends over?" Believing there is every indication someone has been in their home, she forges on. "Anyone stop by? Any deliveries?"

"No. And no one was here. I slept …" He catches himself before the slip-up. "I wanted to sleep late, so I canceled the housekeeper when I returned from the airport. Now I wish I hadn't."

Looking away, Peggy eyes the table's open drawer. "Someone has been in this house. Argue if you must, but my jewelry drawer has been explored and shopped. This home invasion was personal. We were targeted."

Trying to hide his confusion, he peruses the space. "Are you thinking we've been robbed?"

"Ransacked. Someone rifled through my things."

"Likely young hoodlums or a gang of punk street rats."

"Punk street rats? We don't have street rats here. This is an upscale neighborhood." She wants to remind him of the silhouette outside the window days earlier, but watching him grow silent and withdrawing to a place she will never be invited to visit, she decides to do the same. Another scenario, one with evil calculations and the work of the devil, grabs her, but she quickly brushes it off. Surely he would not bring his mistress into their home.

"We might not have been robbed, but I think we will agree our home was vandalized," she says. Growing quiet, she wonders if now is the time to come forward with the gossip she is hearing. A sweep of the room convinces her there will never come a better time to learn the truth. "I'm hearing things."

"Voices? Footsteps?"

"Rumors, gossip, mostly spoken in whispered voices."

"Are you saying you overheard someone planning this?"

"Rumors of an affair. Word on the street is you're seeing someone."

"Do us both a favor and skip over the street and the nonsense that comes with it. Whatever rumors you're hearing, you must believe they're not true. Let them flounder. Humans get off creating drama, tension, and when necessary, unnecessary chaos. Decades of documented research show the seedy cell of jealousy and envy seep deep within the spinal cord. I've been told it sprouts from the third vertebrae. My training doesn't allow me to elaborate. Do us both a favor and ignore the busybodies. They are just trying to stir up trouble."

"I'm telling you what I'm hearing."

"Ignore it, and it will go away."

"People are naming names."

"Oh, so more than one. What names would that be?"

"I'm not naming names, but that doesn't keep me from listening."

"Enough with the palaver. I'm calling the police. Go next door and wait for me there."

"What about the other women? I deserve to know the truth. You should know better than to lie to me."

"I've given you the truth, and I'm done talking about it. Now, please go next door and wait there until the police arrive."

"You've given me what you believe I need to hear."

"You're talking nonsense."

"I beg to differ."

"Differ all you want, but please let it go, Peggy. I believe you'll agree we have more pressing matters."

"I've checked the house. It doesn't appear anything else is missing. The petty cash I hide in my shoes is still there, and the spare key to the house is on the hook. I'm telling you, my gut instinct tells me this is personal." Biting back tears, she holds him with her eyes. "Do you think our lives are in danger?"

"Perhaps. Better to be safe than sorry." Lifting the phone to his ear, he places a call to the sheriff's office.

While he gives their address, Peggy eyes the house for clues. Looking back at him, she finds worry in his eyes.

"The police are on the way," he says, ending the call. His thoughts are all over the map, taking him places he is ashamed to visit, especially in her presence. "We will let them take it from here." Growing frustrated, he runs a hand through his hair. "Please, go next door until the police get here."

"Not until you tell me you and your cheating ways have not put our lives in danger."

"If you want to call my long hours at the office and late nights at the hospital a threat to our marriage, then go ahead. I've been faithful to our marriage since the day I placed that ring on your finger."

"One can only hope."

"Surely you don't believe I'm cheating on you."

"Is that a statement or a question?"

"I'm not sure what you are hinting, but I believe you will agree I don't deserve the finger you're pointing."

"Forgive me for my stupidity. We all know this is the finger you deserve," she says, offering the middle-finger salute.

"If you shoot me the finger one more time, I'm going to tell you where to shove it."

"Good luck with that."

He is turning to walk away when a trio of squad cars pulls up to the curb. Leaving Peggy behind, Preston makes his way out to the street.

"Thanks for getting here so quickly. I'm giving fair warning, the place is a wreck."

"I'm Officer Whelan, and this is Officer Vance," a big man with a straight face offers. "We have officers canvassing the neighborhood, going door-to-door asking if anyone saw anything unusual or suspicious. On the drive in, we noticed several of your neighbors have security cameras. I just heard from one of our officers that one of your neighbors saw an older model car parked on the street near your driveway. She couldn't make out the plate, but when she put on her glasses, she was able to see a doll-like figure on the dashboard. It's not much to go on, but maybe we'll catch a break."

Preston's stomach rumbles its concern. If there are leads to catch and breaks to be had, and they point to Molly, he, too, will have some explaining to do. "We appreciate it. If you're ready, let's go inside."

"The house reeks of perfume," Peggy warns. "They killed my fish, my portrait is missing from above our bed, and it smells like urine in here."

"Looks like Jupiter's been here," Preston says, pointing to a stain on the rug.

"She's never done this before. How do you explain the aquarium? Whoever broke in is sending a message."

"Do you have any reason to believe this isn't a random burglary but an intentional act?" Whelan asks.

"Nothing concrete, just a gut feeling. It's rumored that a mafia group recently rented a house in the neighborhood, a Colonial with a privacy wall and gated driveway," Peggy offers.

"I suggest you hold your horses. Let's not get too far ahead of ourselves. For your own safety, and for those you love and hold dear, I think it is best you put any rumors to rest. We're not seeing a growing number of hits in your zip code involving multiple vehicles, rapid gunfire, and skid marks. I would be quick to bury any rumors involving street gangs and organized crime. When it comes to these people, it's best to turn a blind eye. They are not looking to steal microwave ovens, laptops, washers and dryers, or any other household goods, portraits included. There is little money in pawning those items. When the Mafia feels they have been crossed, they seek revenge. When initial threats and tactics fail, they turn to sadistic torture and intricate carvings. Unless you're dealing in money-laundering or stolen goods, I suggest you refrain from pointing fingers. Given the facts, it appears what happened here in your home is the work of a femme fatale."

"I don't understand or speak your language. You're going to have to break it down for me," Peggy says, rolling her hands.

"Green-eyed monster also known as jealousy. This looks, and smells, like the work of a jilted lover marking her territory."

"My husband is a doctor," she says, giving Preston the once-over. "Believe it or not, women are always coming on to him."

"That's not true," he argues. There is no denying he is hit on and flirted with, but his suitors usually move on—except Molly, who appears to enjoy the challenge.

"I wasn't talking to you."

"Peggy, show them into the bedroom," he says, pulling up a corner of the rug. A whiff of something akin to cheap beer and canned sardines has him holding back vomit. When Peggy's precious fish give him the cold eye, he hurries into the bathroom to give them a proper burial.

Down the hall, in the bathroom they share, Peggy points to an open drawer. "I haven't touched anything." Searching the drawer for the pieces she values, she sighs in relief when she eyes the ring and pearl necklace Preston gifted her the previous summer when they celebrated their anniversary on Maui.

"Everything appears to be accounted for," Preston says, sneaking a peek over her shoulder.

"So far." Another search has her gasping for air. "My mother's diamond ring is missing."

"Don't touch anything. We'll need to fingerprint the drawer and the vanity," Whelan reminds.

"I'm sorry, Peggy. I'm finding all this hard to believe. It's just that we have several pieces of art far more valuable than your jewelry." Preston glances at the walls, intentionally skipping over the empty space that previously showcased her portrait. "The art is still here."

"Let's take a look in your jewelry drawer."

A quick search of a slim, velvet-lined drawer reveals diamond cuff links, priceless timepieces, and a collection of insignia rings have gone unnoticed.

"Whoever broke in wanted my jewelry. It's easier to sell than a Picasso," she says, expecting a rebuttal. "I have photos of all my pieces. Our insurance agent wanted pictures and appraisals when he drew up the rider," she tells Whelan.

Preston's uneasy expression gives her cause for concern. She will ask him about it later, when the officers leave.

When Whelan moves to examine the drawer's contents, she closes in over his shoulder.

"Those earrings," she says, pointing to large silver hoops, "are not mine."

"Are you suggesting someone came here to rob you, and while doing so, left these earrings behind?"

"I'm not suggesting anything. It's the truth." Pausing, she crosses her arms over her chest. "I don't wear hoop earrings."

"Why is that?"

Raising her hand, she points to a small flaw on her earlobe. "Scar tissue."

"All kinds of crazies out there. Never know what they're thinking or going to do next. You might want to visit the local pawn shops," he says, sneaking a peek at her ear.

Standing in the shadows, Preston's stomach does a flip. Molly almost always wears hoops, and thinking about it now, he cannot recall a time she wore anything else. Still, he is not convinced she would stoop to this level. Besides, they were together all weekend.

While Peggy shows the officers the soiled dress, he revisits the last seventy-two hours, right down to the minute. He is preparing to remove all doubt regarding his lover when he recalls the hours he was called away to the ER.

CHAPTER 34

"I got here as fast as I could. Traffic on the boulevard is bumper-to-bumper," Molly explains.

Believing Preston is about to propose marriage, her heart races. A glance at her nails reminds her that last week's manicure is suffering some wear and tear, but until her next appointment, these broken and chipped nails will have to suffice. As for the ring he will soon place on her finger, she will need to find a clever way to hide it from Clay. There is always the space in the basement. If that doesn't work, she will tuck it away in the luggage she keeps in the rental's crawl space. Should the ring display a generous diamond anchored with large stones, she will keep it nearby, perhaps in a drawer in the bedside table, allowing her to admire it in the hours Clay is called away.

"Have a seat next to me," Preston says, patting the bed.

"What's going on? You sounded desperate on the phone, and now, you look so tense. Are you working too many hours at the office?"

"Everything is fine at the office."

"I'm sure I can convince Clay to put in more hours."

"Forget the office. It's moments like this when I find myself wishing I could be like Trehan," he mumbles under his breath.

"I'm sorry, I don't understand."

"I said, I should be like my friend, Trehan."

"I don't know who that is."

"He's a guy I once knew. He's a staple at a restaurant in New Orleans. About midweek, he takes his business and slim wallet to Darrel's, a pick-up joint. It wasn't long before he became known as the ass man. You don't need to know why. Please understand, I don't mean for this to sound like a smear campaign. Trehan is a good guy who just happens to be at the wrong place at the right time. All I know is he sticks with a routine that always works in his favor. He's a happy-go-lucky single man who, when it comes to women, lives by three rules: no rent, no ring, no ride. For what it's worth, that man is onto something. I can only imagine how my life would have turned out if I had learned his secret to making mushroom soup."

"You're losing me here. For what it's worth, I hate mushroom soup."

"It's not about the soup. He's convinced chicks are waiting in line for a home-cooked meal."

"I don't see how his stupid rules have anything to do with me. Is he why you called me here? If he's saying stuff about me, he has me confused with someone else. I swear I don't know the guy. That's the truth, or it damn sure ought to be."

"No, of course not. This has nothing to do with him. Please forgive me, but you need to understand this is serious." Pausing, he takes a deep breath. "Molly, I need to ask if you were in my home in recent days."

"I'm not admitting or denying anything. You know the truth. You know where I was all weekend. If I'm on trial here, I'd like to retain counsel."

"Someone was in my home. Damage was done and jewelry was stolen. Police dusted interior surfaces, confiscated perfume bottles, and the front door and its bell were fingerprinted. They have a team going door-to-door asking my neighbors if they saw any suspicious activity. I've been made aware many of these homes have security cameras. I wouldn't want to learn you were involved."

"What's wrong with you? You need a chill pill. Take a Valium or something. I've been in your home many times—as an invited guest, I might add. I'm no expert, but I'm guessing my prints are all over the place. You should know I resent the accusation."

"I'm not accusing. I'm asking. It appears my wife was targeted." A scowl weighing on his face does not prevent the words from rolling off his tongue. "You should know hoop earrings were left behind."

"You know I don't have a key to your house."

"I'm not suggesting you do."

"Are you suggesting I slipped in through the keyhole?" Biting at her lip, she wants to kick herself for being so careless. She has watched enough crime shows to know prints can be lifted from silver. "Are you so naïve as to believe I'm the only woman who wears hoop earrings? Why would I want to damage your home? We both know I want to live there with you. Am I a suspect?"

"No one is at this point. I just felt I had to ask. I've heard it said it's best to know the law before breaking it."

"If the interrogation is over, I'd like to leave."

She is steps from the door when she circles back around. Words do not come, but the way she holds her ground leaves him wondering about their future. He is walking a fine line, one that does not promise an outcome he can live with. He loves his wife, but a struggle deep inside reminds he wants Molly on the side. Forcing a choice will do nothing but weaken his heart. He is a man in love with both his wife and this woman he often finds unlovable.

"I'm sorry, Molly."

"You know what hurts most, Preston? You felt you had to ask. Have you so little faith in me that it's impossible for you to believe in me?"

Foregoing an answer, she races from the boat, all the while damning Peggy for reasons she does not have or understand. If the police come knocking, they will find a new twist in their investigation. She will lead them to believe Peggy stole the hoop earrings and is making false statements. Picturing Peggy in prison garb and forced to join a gang returns a smile to her face.

CHAPTER 35

Red-knuckled and fighting the onset of hunger, Peggy grips the car's steering wheel with such force she fears she will break it in two. Up ahead, a homeless man pushes a shopping cart into traffic, forcing her to slam on the brakes. Lifting a gloved hand to the air and pointing his finger, he pretends to take aim. Worried for her safety, she presses the door locks and activates the car's emergency flashers.

Near the corner of Hanley Road and Bienville Boulevard, a sheltered bus stop marked with graffiti and cryptic gang symbols offers little shade to a young mother with a lively toddler at her side and a swaddled newborn at her breast. Standing at attention, a spirited pit bull defends his family. Unable to quiet the newborn, the mother shifts about. When Peggy steps on the gas, the dog falls into a butt roll and performs a half-nelson before taking refuge under the bench.

Passing by a cigar shop that until recently was a yoga studio, Peggy crosses over to the far right lane. She studies the storefronts until her target is in sight. A-Z Pawn is located on an isolated road veering east of South Main, a crossing familiar only because local crime reports continue to warn of carjackings, drug dealing, and aggressive panhandling.

Up ahead, industrial steel gates part just wide enough to allow her to pass. Used syringes and crushed soda cans peppering the lot's busted concrete send a chill through her. The stench of feces drifts on a northerly breeze. Believing it is a campsite for the homeless, she scans the area. A building permit posted near the curb announces the adjoining property will soon be home to a massage parlor, a glass and mirror shop, and a fast-food joint—places she doubts she will ever visit. She considers placing a call to A-Z Pawn asking if anyone has dropped off jewelry in recent days, but a shadow passing by the shop's barred windows lets her know her presence has been detected.

Inside a cramped space no larger than a two-bay garage, parked between a welding shop and a used parts store, a surly man no bigger than an elf waits behind the counter. Cauliflower ears own his face, and a varsity sweater struggles to cover his thick arms. If it were not for the flesh-colored patch over his eye, he would be the spitting image of Tiny Tim, the novelty singer famous in the sixties. All he needs to complete the ensemble is a long-stemmed tulip.

"Close the door. You're letting out the cold air," Elf says, tossing back a ponytail he has likely been growing since birth.

"I'm sorry. I thought it closed behind me." She looks about the space until eyeing the height strips next to the door's frame. "Are you robbed often?"

"Daily," he says, taking a long drag off a short cigarette. Through a plume of gray smoke, he flicks a thimble of ashes to the concrete floor. His wide smile displays a chipped tooth.

"At gunpoint?"

"Annoying customers."

"I thought height charts were meant to discourage theft."

Again, he gives her the once-over. "I'm guessing you're about five three. If pressed to give your weight, I'd round you at about one fifteen."

"Regarding your poor guesses, I'm guessing I need to move along."

Peggy's exit is interrupted when the door swings open and three young men with Ping golf clubs nearly run her over. Curious if they are here to pawn stolen goods, she fakes interest in a fur vest she fears is home to body lice and field mice.

"Hey, guys. What are you selling?" Elf asks, pulling the patch from his face. Blinking eyes fall on club-issued shirts he recognizes from a course known for its rolling hills.

"New clubs still wrapped in plastic," the dark-haired guy says with a grin. "Distributor shipped the wrong clubs. Boss says we'd save money selling them here."

"Is that so? You should know the morning paper reported those clubs stolen from a pro shop in Ocean Springs. I suggest you either return them or take your business elsewhere."

Worried a shooting might occur, Peggy hurries to make her exit.

Quick Pawn, a business operating out of a shady trailer on a dead-end street, is Peggy's next stop. A big man with a pencil neck and tight-fitting jeans stands guard at the door. A toothpick rests between thin lips holding up a handlebar mustache.

"Howdy," he greets with a Texas accent. "How can I help you?"

"Do you carry women's jewelry?"

"Watches and rings. What are you looking for?"

"It belonged to my mother," she says, handing over the folded paper she pulls from her purse.

"Nice ring. Are you looking to sell it?"

"It was stolen in a home invasion. The officers who took the report suggested I look into area pawn shops."

"I have some smaller pieces, but nothing like this. Have you been to Dirty Larry's?"

"It's next on my list."

"That's your best bet. He gets a lot of gamblers. When they're down on their luck, they hurry to pawn jewelry, guns, and televisions to pay their bookies. On the flip side, winners rush to spend their dollars on Rolex watches, and, if they have a special someone, a diamond ring for their lady. Just be careful. Sometimes the table winners are followed and robbed."

"I'll be sure to remember that. By the way, is there a story to go with Dirty Larry's name?"

"He used to manage a landscape company until he threw out his back hauling river rocks and flagstone."

"In more ways than one, I'm sorry to hear this. Once I heard his name, I imagined a better story—one involving a criminal's life," she says, making her way to the door.

Dirty Larry markets his goods in a small shed a block south of Roger Street at an intersection where rugged asphalt meets loose gravel. A flashing light near the door warns that surveillance cameras are activated and recording.

A step over the shed's threshold reminds Peggy of a visit to a high-end jewelry store on New York's Fifth Avenue. Crystal chandeliers light up the small space and rich, oriental rugs protect hardwood floors. When a church bell chimes her arrival, she feels she might just be stepping through heaven's gates.

Dirty Larry's collared shirt is as crisp as a new dollar bill, and his full-quill ostrich boots appear to have enjoyed a shine. A quick glance at his hands suggests he recently had a manicure.

"Welcome. I'm Larry. Are you looking for anything special?"

"I'm just here to see what you have. You know, something my friends often call window-shopping."

"If something catches your eye, let me know."

Shopping a jewelry case, she studies a necklace similar to one Preston gave her. "I'd like to see this piece," she says, pointing to the glass drawer. "Can you tell me who brought it in?"

"Not without a warrant."

"I don't have a warrant. I just want to see if the necklace is mine."

"Listen, lady. I don't want any trouble," he says, reaching for a button on the underside of the counter. "I don't deal in stolen goods. Amateur gamblers, experienced pickpockets, and unwed mothers hock things all the time. Just last week, a young mother pulled her crying toddler out of the stroller she came rolling in. That baby screamed all the way out the door. Again, people pawn things all the time. I'm not in the business of asking why. Every item that comes in here is photographed, and the seller is fingerprinted. I also ask for ID, usually a driver's license, if they have one. Are you aware loose stones, diamonds included, have identifying stamps? It's called a Maker's Mark. Helps identify stolen goods."

"I understand," Peggy says, "and I don't mean to accuse you. I'm aware of identification marks. I've been told the same applies to breast implants. It often helps identify the dead. Regarding the necklace, I once had one identical to this."

"See that fancy expresso machine over there? It came out of a restaurant. A lot of people have that same model. In this case, my client needed to sell it. Again, I'm not in the business of asking why. That guitar there," he points to the far wall, "is a 1931 Martin worth about nine grand, even more to a collector. Owner has an autographed picture of Elvis strumming it inside Sun Studio in Memphis. If the name isn't familiar to you, it's a recording studio. The man hated to part with it, but he's fallen on hard times. That Rolex," he says, throwing a finger to the counter, "arrived here after the owner lost an eye when a baseball bat met his face in a dark alley behind a steak house in Oxford. Robber got away with one just like it, and now the old guy is afraid to wear this one out in public. Every item that arrives here comes with a story and proper identification."

Although nodding, she continues to plead with her eyes. "Can you at least tell me what the person who brought in the necklace looked like? Male, female, the color of their hair? Speaking of Elvis, you might consider getting your hands on the ambulance that transported him to the hospital. I understand it is parked in a backyard in Memphis. It might be worth something to a collector."

"Look, I'm giving you until the count of five to walk out that door and out of my life. To be clear, I'm not interested in an ambulance."

"Please, I just need some answers."

"Have it your way." He whips out his cell phone and taps at the screen. "This is Dirty Larry. I need the police to remove a belligerent customer."

"All right, already. I'm going. You can be sure of one thing—I'll never step foot in here again."

"Once again, I'm reminded to be thankful for small blessings."

CHAPTER 36

"Good morning, Mrs. Fayne. My name is Carole, and I'm with the *Sun Herald*. How are you today?"

"I'm fine. May I ask the purpose of your call?"

"My call has two purposes, actually. I'm hoping your service resumed this morning."

Caught unknowing, Peggy finds the question puzzling. Since the day she and Preston married, he has started each morning with a cup of coffee and huevos rancheros topped with a heavy pour of his favorite hot sauce. The sports section, the comics, and the daily crossword hold his attention until his presence is required at his office or the hospital. A glance at the kitchen table confirms he studied the paper's cover.

"Delivery as usual," she says.

"Would you like delivery of the papers you missed?"

"There must be a mistake. We didn't stop delivery."

"Let me take a look-see here."

Pressing her ear to the phone, Peggy listens to the familiar sound of fingers tapping a keyboard.

"Mrs. Fayne, I'm showing a recent stop in service."

"What days would that include?"

"Tuesday through Sunday."

Taking a place at the table, she falls into the chair Preston sat in earlier before rushing off to work. Holding the phone close, she listens to the caller read off the dates. Learning they match the days she was away, her heart falls to her stomach.

"I appreciate the call, but I won't be needing those papers. Believe me when I say I've had about all the news I can handle."

A glance beyond the table into an open closet has her eyeing the boat lamp she purchased in recent weeks. Curious if the order she placed with Willa's, a lighting store in Memphis, has arrived, she makes her way to the study where deliveries are usually placed. A clean desk confirms the sailboat finial is still out for delivery. Lifting the phone's receiver, she taps at the numbers.

"Willa's," a woman answers in a singsong voice.

"This is Peggy Fayne. I'm calling to check the status of a finial I ordered weeks ago."

While on hold, she worries the package may have been taken during their home invasion, but a clear mind reminds this makes little sense. Burglars do not usually take decorative lampshade toppers. Her thoughts are interrupted when she hears what sounds like a phone traveling over a counter.

"Mrs. Fayne, we have confirmation the package was delivered last Friday."

"Did someone sign for it?"

"I don't see where a signature is required. It appears it was left at the door."

CHAPTER 37

"I read this quote today by William Hutchison Murray, although some argue it was written by Johann Wolfgang von Goethe." Consumed with guilt, Preston wrestles with the article he tore from the morning's paper. "No matter the author, I think it captures my situation: 'Until one is committed, there is hesitancy, the chance to draw back, always ineffectiveness. Concerning all acts of initiative (and creation), there is one elementary truth, the ignorance of which kills countless ideas and splendid plans: that the moment one definitely commits oneself, then Providence moves too.'"

"Preston, where are you going with this nonsense? I didn't come here for a poetry reading," Molly interrupts. "Did I mention I shaved my legs?"

"Please quit interrupting and let me finish." Pausing, he runs his eyes over her legs. "And it's not poetry. It's meant to be mind-thinking."

"Cut to the chase. We have better ways to share the afternoon. I'm talking mind-blowing."

As his thoughts drift to their last rendezvous, one thing becomes certain: she always delivers. Clearing his throat, he continues with the quote: "'All sorts of things occur to help one that would never otherwise have occurred. A whole stream of events issues from the decision, raising in one's favor all manner of unforeseen incidents and meetings and material assistance, which no man could have dreamt would have come his way. Whatever you can do, or dream you can, begin it. Boldness has genius, power, and magic in it. Begin it now.'"

"If you were an artist," she says, giving him the once-over, "I'd ask what picture you're painting. I'm sure you'll agree we make the magic happen all the time."

"It's never easy to say good-bye, but we have arrived at a place that is no longer healthy." He folds the paper and returns it to his pocket. "I'm sorry, Molly, but I think it's best we go our separate ways."

"How dare you? Do you know how much time I've invested in you?"

"What does that mean?"

"You know darn well what it means." She wants to come at him with angry words, but knowing to tread carefully, she holds back. "Don't start this unless you mean it."

"Molly, we are over. I hope we can part ways without spewing ugly words we may later regret. I'm not asking for a formal good-bye, but one where we agree our time together has expired."

"Why now, Preston?"

"This is where the rubber meets the road. I've heard it said it's hard to please one woman. Believe me when I say jockeying two is insanity."

"Are you serious? I'm leaving all that I know and have to be with you."

"What is it you are leaving?" he asks.

"Please don't pick at words. You must understand I'm walking away from everything to be with you."

"I never asked you to."

"I see it otherwise," she replies. "I thought we wanted to be together."

"I can't give you what I don't have."

"Cliché much?"

"Listen, Molly, I'm not free to be with you. I have obligations."

"Ever hear of divorce?" she snaps back.

"Heard of it? Yes. Want it? No. It is what it is. I don't want any drama or a scene I might have to explain. Let's agree to shrug it off, part ways, and move on."

"I've loved you through three seasons now. Four, if we let our hearts skip over the years we can't discuss. Given you talk all the time and get off on hearing your voice, I find it interesting, if not sad, that you choose a poem—excuse me, a mind-thinking whatever—to end our relationship. Not that it matters to you, but thinking for myself is kind of my thing." Moving toward him, she narrows the space between them. "Why, Preston? For entertainment purposes, I'd like an answer."

"What am I supposed to say?"

"Let's start with the truth. Just so you know, I'll be understanding, but I won't be foolish. Let me remind you, words have consequences."

"Guilt is not something I let alter my behavior, but I can no longer ignore its warnings." Fighting the pinch in his chest, he understands she is right. No matter how painful, she deserves to hear the truth. "A sixth sense has me fearing that one day I'll be forced to answer for my sins. I love my wife. If I'm going to save my marriage, I have to hit the reset button. That includes saying good-bye to you."

"Well, now I know it's not the roll in the hay that excites you." Knowing his precious Peggy would never act out in anger, she lets her words take aim. "I think you'll agree you're hitting below the belt. You're not being fair, and that silver spoon you were born with hasn't served you well."

"Have I mentioned it was covered with diamonds?"

"Once or twice, when you believe it works to your advantage."

"Think what you will, but I'm wheels up and out of here. Just to be clear, I want to go home with all my limbs."

"You're a spineless coward, Preston Fayne."

"While that may be true, I'm also a married one." Pausing, he lets a sneer cross over his smug face. "Tell me, what does that make you?"

An open hand to his face returns the sting.

CHAPTER 38

"You're looking kinda lonely, girl. Would you like someone new to talk to?" a man at the bar asks while tweaking his ear with a hand kissed by the sun.

Taking a healthy sip of her cocktail, Molly turns away. Given her spat with Preston, she wants only to be left alone. "Who do you think you are? Dr. Hook? Go back to the seventies," she screams in a deafening voice.

The bartender shuffles by but, recalling the many times he has been the victim of Molly's unleashed tongue and childish tantrums, quickly retreats to a dark corner.

"You're a weak specimen of a man," she mutters at his backside.

"Hey, we're sitting here in the corner of a bar. When I'm not looking at you, I'm watching the clock. It doesn't appear someone is coming to meet you. I'm here because I'm lonely. Given the late hour and the fact that you're nursing straight-up bourbon, I'm guessing you're lonely, too. I'm …"

"Get lost. What I drink and when I drink it is none of your business."

"That's uncalled for, don't you think? Allow me a proper introduction. I'm Joran Lindquest. I just moved here from Paris. A recruiting coach saw promise in me when my own tennis coach didn't."

"Does it look like I care?"

"You're still here."

"If you don't mind, I'd like to enjoy my drink."

"Of course. You drink, I'll talk."

"Have at it."

"Do you come here often?"

"If I answer, I'll be talking. Not that it's any of your business, but I prefer the Sand Bar. I'm going there when I leave here."

"I was there last night. My scotch and soda was a little weak, but the service was above par. Have I mentioned my tennis career is taking off?"

"Twice now. I found you a bore both times."

"I've been told a time or two that it helps that I'm ambidextrous."

"A useless skill only a guy would brag about."

"Think what you will, but the next time I play Wimbledon, the grass courts will work in my favor."

In the blink of an eye, the thought of scoring with a worldly tennis player appeals to her long-term goals. "I met Andre Agassi and Patrick McEnroe, big John's baby brother, at a tournament in Memphis. If memory serves, I believe it was at the Racquet Club. That young man scores in the looks department."

"The same can be said of you. Let me buy you a drink."

She is ready to give up the bark and go for the bite when she turns to him. Giving him the once-over, she is surprised to find he, too, is easy on the eyes. "I guess I don't see any harm in it."

"I gave my name, but didn't get yours. I've heard it said a guy has gotta know a girl's name before he kisses her."

"Molly. Don't even think about going in for a kiss." She finds his innocence refreshing. Because he is new in town, she wants to make a good impression. There will come a time, perhaps within the hour, when she is sure to damage his heart and destroy his faith in women. In the interim, she will play him for the fool he is.

"That's it? No last name? If you're worried I'll bite, I won't. At least not without your permission." Wearing a grand-slam grin, he moves in close. "I'm sure you've heard this before, but you are drop-dead gorgeous."

"Don't try to get cute with me," she says, giving up the stink-eye. Although she appreciates his humor and playfulness, she worries Preston and Clay might get wind of this encounter. Drunk from the bourbon, she still looks to her future.

"I suggest we finish our drinks."

"What's the hurry?"

"I know a quiet little speakeasy where we can better get to know each other."

Throwing back her drink, she follows him out of the bar into a waiting elevator. "Just so you know, I'm not going to bed with you, and I'm not into any kinky shit. No exploring anal cavities—yours or mine. Stay out of my private parts. No tools, no toys, no pets. You're no Harry Reems, and I'm no Linda Lovelace. Forget a third party. I'm sure you know what they say about three's a crowd."

"I understand."

"I would hope so. Rules are rules."

Joran's third-floor room at the Palms offers a glimpse of the gulf and a bird's-eye view of Beach Boulevard. A thin drape blocks out the hotel's air-conditioning platform and a stepladder. A weathered sticker from a wholesale warehouse grips the ladder's bottom rung.

Molly moves about the room like she is the only bug not invited to the Lady Bug Ball. Flapping her arms about, she stays near the slim window and a stack of tennis rackets. Eyeing the network of strings, she sits armed and ready to defend herself. When Joran secures the door's chain lock, she maps out an escape route.

"Don't be nervous. I'm a tennis player, not Ted Bundy."

"Who is Ted Bundy?"

"A good-looking serial killer who fancied college girls."

"Never heard of him."

"Count your blessings. He drove a Volkswagen Beetle outfitted with reclining seats and steel handcuffs."

"This history lesson is irrelevant and immaterial. I thought we were going to a quiet little place for a drink."

"I believe you'll agree it's quiet here."

"Maybe."

"We have a fully-stocked bar. I'm having bourbon on the rocks. What may I pour you? Wine, perhaps?"

"Rum and Coke, easy on the rum. I have to drive home."

"Where is home?" he asks, searching the minibar.

"Not far. Less than a mile." She wants to kick herself for sharing even a hint of her personal life with him, a stranger she met in a bar, but she is both lonely and angry. "And for you?"

"I'm fixing up a house off Irish Hill on a narrow street near Guice Place. Contractor tells me it'll be finished by the end of the month. We both know it'll be another forty-five to sixty days," he says, looking back over his shoulder.

Minutes later, they are tossing the sheets about and making their own racket. As the moon rises over Casino Beach, he becomes the man of the hour, while Clay and Preston become a distant memory.

CHAPTER 39

The sensual voice of Diana Krall greets Preston on the flip side of the Sand Bar's brass door. A lone stool sits unclaimed at the horseshoe bar. Shuffling over the floor, he hurries to take it.

The five-star bar serves its drinks with thick cloth napkins and a generous sampling from its signature charcuterie board. When dinner is served, the staff whips out playful placemats designed by a young woman who often makes known she attended art school in Atlanta.

Later, when the happy hour crowd begins to thin and single patrons couple, Strode Broussard, a concert pianist who returned to his roots after eight years of East Coast living, plays smooth jazz on a black-lacquered Steinway in a mirrored corner of the room.

"Hey, Preston, what are you drinking tonight?" Trude asks.

Though their fling ended with Trude calling him weak and desperate, they later found a way to enjoy an honorable friendship.

"I'll start with water."

"Sparkling or Mississippi's finest?"

"Tap, and I don't want any fruit in it."

"How about a Franc?"

"I've never had a good Franc."

"There is a joke in there somewhere, but I'll let it slide."

Eyeing the bar's patrons, Preston throws back salted peanuts the bar serves free of charge, and with a quick swipe, brushes the salt from his hands. "I need something to help me forget. You know what, I'll have a gin and tonic. Add a twist and a splash of testosterone."

"Gin and tonic will do that for you. Are you on call tonight?"

"Nope. Not to worry. I'm not putting anxious mothers on edge or tiny newborns at risk."

"Good to know."

"How's business?"

"We have a full house even on nights not named Wednesday."

"Is that live music night?"

"Better than that. Complimentary appetizers and half-price bar drinks."

"Good to know some things never change. I'm going to need a thin-crust pepperoni pizza to go. Hold off on the gin and tonic. I'm going to live a little," he says, matching her smile with one of his own. "Make it a dirty martini—Ketel One, two olives, and a twist, and another bowl of nuts when you have a minute. By the way, how's your father?"

"He's declining," she shares. "It wasn't that long ago he was a rollin' stone. His wild spirit and rambling ways made him bigger than life, but when his memory started to fade and we became strangers to him, we knew we had to bring him home. During my last visit to the nursing home, his clothes were soiled. When I asked his caregiver to change him, she found fungus growing on his genitalia and infections on his hips and tailbone likely brought on by neglected bedsores. His chart indicated he had not been bathed in months. That same day, he rolled out of bed to the floor. He turned his ankle and broke his nose in the fall. Although his memory is fading, the poor man understands he is living on borrowed time. He doesn't have his teeth, and he can't hear worth a darn, but he's managing. We're all managing. Elliot is sitting with him tonight. I think you'll recall he is one of the misfits my mother inherited with her second marriage. After failing Georgia Tech's first semester's required courses, he realized his future was better served making cocktails and lending the occasional bartender's ear. Soon after returning to Casino Beach, he opened this bistro and added me to the payroll. When word of his success made the front page of the newspaper, marriage soon followed."

"I'm not surprised," Preston notes. "Good men are hard to come by."

"His wife is a good person. Raised in the school of hard knocks, she's always willing to help. When my dad is not struggling with fatigue, mood swings, and chronic idiopathic urticaria, he is in a state of confusion and restlessness, especially at night. One of the nurses called it Sundowner's Syndrome. It has something to do with fading light. It's another reason for the doctors to overmedicate him. There is nothing behind his eyes, and right before mine, they are slowly turning him into a vegetable. There was a time he flirted with the nurses—playfully, of course—but now, he's just downright ornery. He yells, kicks, and when dinner doesn't suit his fancy, he throws the tray across the room. Before he dies, these doctors and their test trials will kill his mind and steal his soul. Don't get me started about the morphine. I would move him in with me, but I don't think I can properly care for him."

"I'm not suggesting you take your father home," Preston says, "but I know remaining at home gives my father a longer life, even when he pretends he doesn't want it."

"My dad says nursing homes are for old people."

"At least he still has his sense of humor."

"Your father is a good man," Trude says. "My father will turn eighty-two on his next birthday. Until his stroke, he was set in his ways. Now he's drooling and decaying right in front of us. He's always cold and hungry. The older he grows, the more I'm afraid poor circulation will become the least of his problems. We're moving him into hospice care at the end of the month."

"I have to hand it to you," Preston replies. "I'm sure it wasn't easy when your father skipped town, leaving your mother to remarry to help make ends meet." It was rumored through the grapevine that doors were slammed, curfews went ignored, and when her mother thought necessary, a venomous temper jumped off leash. When Elliot outgrew his brother and his hellion ways, he helped Trude get back on track.

"Your old friend, the she-devil, was in again last night."

"Molly?"

"The one and only. She bellied up to the bar, and when opportunity knocked, jumped at the chance to play pool with the regulars. She was wasted when she got here. Man, what a mess. I bet she dropped the F-bomb a dozen times. She was wearing these thick bangs, you know, the kind aging women turn to when trying to hide age spots and a roadmap of deep wrinkles. Now that I think about it, it may have been a wig. I couldn't tell. Either way, she looked desperate. I can't put my finger on it, but something about her leaves a bad taste in my mouth."

"Are you sure it was last night?"

"I was on the clock."

"That's odd. I overheard Clay say she made plans for the evening."

"She had plans all right. She was making the moves on Virgil over there." She points to the busboy, who, hearing his name, gives a sheepish grin. "The band was taking a break when she grabbed the microphone and called Virgil to join her."

Pausing, she recalls the fear in Virgil's eyes and the lively crowd cheering him on. "By this time, she had the attention of everyone in the bar. The kitchen crew came out to see what all the fuss was. She took Virgil's hand and looked into his eyes. When she belted out that she once dated a man named Virgil Caine, the crowd roared. She went on to tease him, but when his face turned red, she apologized, telling him *The Night They Drove Old Dixie Down* is her 'favortist song.' Her words, not mine. I was laughing so hard, I nearly peed my pants. She's a train wreck waiting to happen. When she said something about the weather growing nippy, I tried to rein her in. I'll give her this: she has an appetite for adventure. A few drinks always loosen her tongue. When I called out her name, she thumbed her nose at me. I won't go into details, but you should have heard her mouth when we sent her home in a cab. That girl swears like a drunken sailor."

"I gather she's a handful." Familiar with Molly and her antics, he is not surprised to hear she lost control of her tongue. The fact that she spent the evening entertaining the bar's patrons causes him concern.

"Believe me when I say we've had enough of her entertainment."

"About last night ... was she alone?"

"Best I can tell. I thought maybe she was waiting for someone, but no one showed. She closed down the bar at last call. Her car is still out back."

"What was she drinking?"

"Whiskey. She threw me a curve ball when she ordered a glass of wine. I suggested she try the Water Witch, a blend from Washington State, but she ordered a glass of Crazy Mary, a red wine from Columbia Valley—both fitting, in my opinion."

Caught off guard and deep in thought, Preston is startled when a thirsty patron races through a slim crowd to claim the stool next to him. He tries to look away but is drawn to the young man's tremors. His hands and arms shake uncontrollably. He is about to offer his jacket when the man's bloodshot eyes meet his. He watches as the man's pupils grow smaller than the head of a pin. Caught staring, he turns away. Hearing a low growl, he takes his drink and scoots down the bar where a trio of overhead lanterns shed little light on those patrons wishing to go unnoticed.

"Trude, go ahead and take care of him. When you have time, I'll have another drink, and water with ice. Lots of ice."

In the passing minutes, a leggy blonde takes a seat at the bar. Preston gives her the once-over and his winning smile. "May I buy you a drink?"

"Piss off," she says, storming off. The words she mutters under her breath are unclear, but the finger she throws over her shoulder is loud and clear.

Wearing a look of surprise on his face, he turns to the beefy guy at the end of the bar who, minutes earlier, was chatting up an empty stool. "Did I insult her?"

"Her husband called."

"I hate when that happens." In the following minutes, his thoughts turn to Molly. The breakup has played in his head so many times he is growing a headache. The imprint of her hand still owns his cheek. He was lucky Peggy bought his story about getting in the way of the boat's boom. Unable to get Molly out of his head, he reaches for his cell phone, but returns to the television's small screen and the hand-rubbed oak bar when Trude moves his way. When she moves down the bar, he hurries to make his call.

"Wrong number," Molly snaps in a voice sounding like Faye Dunaway's character in the film *Mommie Dearest.*

"Please, don't hang up."

"Why are you calling?"

"I want to apologize." Careful not to speak her name aloud, he keeps his voice low and the phone close to his chin. "I didn't mean to hurt you."

"Hurt me? You call what you've done to my life hurting me? You make me laugh. It's not hurt I'm feeling, Preston. I'm boiling. Do you know what follows that? Getting over you. That should put a smile on your face. After all, that's what you asked for."

"I don't want you to get over me," he says, dropping his voice. "I want you under me, on top of me, beside me, always with me."

"Are you leaving her? I believe you would agree I've given you plenty of time to think this through and get your affairs in order. No pun intended. I doubt that you care, but I'm one breath away from calling cat-rope."

Resigned, he rubs tired eyes. In recent weeks, there has been a shift in their relationship. While she presses for more, he remains content with the secret passion they share. Each time she demands more of him, he wants only more of the same. Some might give in to her pressure, but he knows the boundaries. Still, he understands that if he wants to see her again, he needs to placate her growing outbursts.

"It's been said a closed mouth doesn't get fed, Preston. Give it to me straight. Are you going to leave her?"

"I'll tell her after the regatta. You have my word."

"You're lazy when it comes to us. It's time to put up or shut up."

"Cut me some slack. I have a lot at stake."

"Excuses are for the weak, and you should know by now it's not your word I want but you. If we're getting back together, we should have our own song."

"Am I hearing you right? Did you say 'our own song'?"

"Like goldies from the oldies we hear at cowboy bars."

"Have you ever been to one?"

"One what?"

"A cowboy bar."

"Enough with the games. How do you feel about '*I Got You Babe*' by Sonny and Cher?"

"How can that be our song when I can't recall hearing it with you? What do you think about '*The Bitch is Back*'?"

"That's not funny."

"I don't mean for it to be. How about '*Devil Woman*' or '*Witchy Woman*'?"

"Can you be serious for one minute?"

"How about that song about Virgil Caine? Oh, what is it? It was written by Robbie Robertson."

"No idea," she says, wondering if he got wind of her night out. "Never mind. I'll give it some thought and get back to you."

"You know I'm crazy about you." Fidgeting about, he wishes he had time to meet up with her on the boat.

"Well, you got the crazy part right."

"So I'm a little crazy, but that includes being wildly in love with you."

"Do you mean it? I don't want to be misled."

"Of course I do."

"Say it in a full sentence. Be sure to include my name."

"I can't right now. I'm at the Sand Bar."

"Worried T-Rude will hear you?"

"Listen, I'm down on my knees here."

"Are you offering a ring?"

"You know I'm not in a position to propose marriage, so why ask? Just know I love you."

Seated with his back to the door, he does not see Bunni Varozza, but she spotted him the second she entered the bistro. She also heard his words. Not finding Peggy, she decides to pull a playful prank on her best friend. Tapping Preston's shoulder, she snatches the phone from his hand.

Caught off guard, he pushes away from the bar and rushes to his feet. "What's going on here?"

Giving a wink, Bunni stops him with an open hand and, offering a knowing grin, holds the phone to her face. "Who is whispering sweet nothings into my husband's ear?"

"Who in the hell is this?" Molly screams.

Bunni recognizes the voice, its tone, and foul language. Foregoing a response, she slams the phone to the bar. "Your girlfriend talks like a trucker," she says, turning away. "When you see your wife, tell her I'm here for her when she's ready to talk." In the blink of an eye, she slows her exit, and catching him by surprise, throws an open hand to his face. "You know she will. Want to talk, I mean. As for you and Molly Lambert, yours is a match made in hell."

"Do you want to talk about what just happened?" Trude asks, catching Bunni's scowl as she marches off.

"Not during this lifetime," he says, throwing down a stack of cash and sweeping up the pizza.

Across town in a house she hates, Molly paces the floor. In her rage, she throws pillows against the wall and slams chairs against the floor—and those that dare to survive are flipped over. An overturned table sends a lamp crashing to the floor. A glass figurine takes a bounce on the hardwood before shattering into pieces. She continues to call Preston's cell phone, growing angrier each time the call goes to voicemail. As for the damage, she will now have to come up with an excuse Clay will believe.

CHAPTER 40

Clay is nursing a beer and mingling with neighbors and friends when a clip of the Mardi Gras parade travels over the room's flat-screen television.

Trapped in the kitchen with women who prefer to engage in idle chitchat rather than talk of the games leading up to basketball's March Madness, Molly is slicing and dicing limes, onions, tomatoes, and avocados—the makings for guacamole—when she hears the television's climbing volume.

"Molly, come look. Preston and Peggy are on television!" Clay shouts over his shoulder.

Like Moses parting the Red Sea, the women huddled around her move aside, giving their hostess a view of the screen. Along with her friends, who are nothing more than acquaintances, Molly watches Preston slide his arm around Peggy before lifting her face to his. When they exchange matching smiles, her guests swoon in envy while she is left tightening her grip on the butcher knife. Although the reporter is not on camera, he is heard congratulating the Faynes. The ticker tape at the bottom of the screen continues to introduce them as King and Queen of the Mardi Gras Regatta.

Finding it odd that neither Peggy nor Preston mentioned they were in the running for the regatta's prestigious title, she wonders why she was not invited to share in their celebration. A sweep of the room reminds that anything would be more exciting than listening to these Betty Crockers exchange recipes and discuss diaper brands. Just as she turns back toward the television, she catches Preston leaning in to place a kiss on Peggy's cheek. Her temperature rising, she returns to the kitchen, where she stabs an avocado with such force, the knife's blade pierces the seed. Feeling a presence, she looks up to find curious and inquiring eyes.

"Are you OK?" Clay asks, rushing to her side.

"I forgot to buy limes," she mutters under her breath.

"They're right here, next to the sink. You've already sliced them. What happened here?" he asks, pointing to the knife stuck in the seed like a sword in a stone.

"Blame it on the tequila."

She waits for Clay to return to their guests before sneaking off to their bedroom. Tucked behind the door, she grabs the remote and flips on the television.

"There you are, Peggy and Preston, all dolled up in velvety fur capes. You're royal, all right—a royal pain in the ass." She wants to call Peggy to let her know purple is not a color she should wear in public, but time does not allow. Preston's ear-to-ear smile adds to her growing anger.

Crouched low in the closet's far corner, she grabs the phone Preston demands she use when calling him. She laughs when the reporter's microphone picks up the ringing of his phone. When her call goes to voicemail, she is ready to pounce.

"Preston Fayne, go to hell and shove that aluminum scepter up your kazootie."

Minutes pass before she feels the phone's vibration. She hesitates to answer, but because she has a lecture he needs to hear, she takes the call.

"What now?"

"I'm sorry, Molly. I wasn't in a position to discuss the celebration with you. Hell, I didn't know until last week that I was going to be crowned. Surely, you will agree I couldn't take your call."

"How do you feel about making it up to me?"

"Name it," he says, expecting her to ask for his hand in marriage, "unless you're asking me to sign a letter of intent."

"Don't be silly. Meet me on the boat tomorrow. We'll take it from there."

CHAPTER 41

"Preston, let's look for a place to call our own," Molly says, pressing the newspaper against her chest. "I'm thinking we should get a boat."

"I've said it before, and I'll say it again: we must keep our relationship on the down-low."

"Is this a good time to remind you that you promised to leave Peggy after the regatta?"

"I'm working on it. These things take time. That said, I'm not in a position to purchase another boat. I understand why it's easy for you to forget you're tied to Clay, but how is it you keep forgetting I'm married? If I buy a boat, word will spread like wildfire. Peggy will hear of it, and I can't afford the consequences."

"I'm tired of hiding behind closed doors and jumping through hoops. Besides, Peggy is onto us, and this boat is the first place she'll come looking." Knowing it will drive him wild, she runs a hand along the small of his back. "You wouldn't want her to catch us in the act, would you?"

"You're talking nonsense. Remind me why you're reading the paper when we should be having fun? As for Peggy, trust me when I say I would know if she suspected anything."

"Oh, really? I'm hearing otherwise."

"What are you talking about?"

"She's afraid I'll get pregnant or give you something you might accidentally share with her, like herpes. I don't understand how that can happen now that you're sleeping in the guest room."

A spray of warm spit escapes his lips. He regrets telling her that made-up story during one of their spats just to get her off his back. He learned early on in their affair that she has the memory of an elephant and, at times like this, is not afraid to prove it.

"What is it you want now?"

"I found a boat. An Albin. It's docked at Point Cadet. It's perfect for us. It's away from the harbor, tucked between ocean-going vessels and mom-and-pop fishing boats. If she bothers to come looking, she'll never find us."

"I don't want another boat."

"Please don't take that tone with me. If I didn't love you, I wouldn't be asking."

"Is it possible for you to love me a little less? And please quit hounding me."

"I don't *hound*, Preston. If you want me, you'll want this boat. I've arranged for us to see it. The agent, I forget her name ..." Pausing, she searches her purse for the note she scribbled earlier. "Wanda Raye Harvey is meeting us in twenty minutes."

"Twenty minutes? I can't stay out all day. I'm supposed to bring home dinner."

"Well then, we best get dressed."

"Cut to the chase. What else do you want from me? Today, tomorrow, down the road, and every idle moment in between? Give me the whole ball of wax. Keep in mind I don't have much to give. If you're thinking about asking for a Land Cruiser with a custom gun safe, forget it. The last thing I want is being forced to hide under the bed while you come at me loaded up and pointing a weapon."

"This boat. Nothing more," she promises. "Except marriage, but we can talk about that later."

"Sometimes your mood is like a circus wheel."

Planting one foot and leaning on the other, she stops dead in her tracks. "Who do you think you are? Fleetwood Mac?"

"My circus, my wheel," he says, giving her the once-over. "Sometimes I'm convinced you suffer with atelophobia."

"Cut the crap. Speak to me in English."

"The fear of never being good enough."

"You can toss that diagnosis to the curb. I'm good. I'm really good. Isn't that why you're here?"

"Touché."

"Whatever."

"I suggest we take two cars. We can't risk being seen together."

"I'll ride gangster-style."

"In the trunk? Could be a bumpy ride."

"In the passenger seat."

"I'm kind of digging the trunk. I could use some peace and quiet."

"You can be so funny at times."

When they arrive at Point Cadet, the agent is waiting for them on the pier. "I'm Wanda Raye Harvey."

"I'm Dr. Fayne, and this is my wife," he says, skipping over first names that could later come back to haunt him.

"You are going to love the Albin." Monster arms invite Preston and Molly to have a look inside the boat's cabin.

"She has shoulders better suited on a wide receiver and looks like she'd enjoy an evening of polka with Big Joe," Molly whispers.

"Who is Big Joe?" Preston whispers in return.

"He had a polka show called *Happy Music, Happy People*. Tell her we want a swim platform."

Falling back, he puts space between them. In the blink of an eye, his thoughts shift to Peggy. She never asks for more than he can deliver. Thinking about her now, he understands that she asks for very little, especially big-ticket items. The few times she made a suggestion, it was easy to see her heart was in the right place. Heart palpitations have him worrying he cannot take much more of Molly's constant demands. A poke to his rib reminds a response is waiting.

"We'd like a swim platform," Molly says, ignoring Preston's eye roll.

"And transom storage," Preston throws out.

"Please tell me your name again, young lady. It seems to have escaped me," Wanda Raye says.

When Molly pauses to offer her hand, Preston fills his cheeks with air. A knot in his throat has him fearing she will blurt out her real name. He shoots a look she understands to mean she is to get her act together. Still, the uneasy feeling haunts him. The look in her eyes and the way she moves about leaves him worrying what will escape the wheels spinning in her head.

"I'm Peggy Fayne."

Aghast, he nearly chokes on his tongue. If it were not for Wanda Raye watching the minutes unfold, he would kick the snot out of her. When the agent steps onto the boat's deck, he pulls at Molly's sleeve. "Dial it down a bit."

"You didn't expect me to give her my real name, did you?"

"I was hoping you would make up one."

"Well, Peggy, this is your lucky day." An aging woman with an unblinking eye and a frightening look of surprise on her face, Wanda Raye claps her hands in delight. "It just so happens this beauty has both."

An uneasy feeling returns to Preston's stomach. The agent's piercing shrill adds to his discomfort. "Molly, if Peggy gets wind of this, she will kick me to the curb," he whispers.

"Won't happen, unless you talk in your sleep."

Unaware she has lost their attention, Wanda Raye continues. "This boat is designed to provide all the comforts and needs for a weekend escape. The owner recently installed a Bose sound system and a Garmin GMR Fanton 54. I know firsthand this beauty has been professionally maintained."

"I agree it's a great boat, and I appreciate the two heads and double cabins, but my wife and I would like to think it over."

"Darling, there isn't anything to think over. I love this boat. It has everything we've been looking for," Molly says, resisting the urge to stomp her feet. "Do me a favor and paint on a happy face," she adds in a low voice.

"Sweetheart, this is the first boat we've visited."

"Oh, but Preston, I can just picture a sheepskin throw on the bed."

"A lightweight fleece would be more fitting," he says, knowing she is fully aware he has already shelled out big bucks for a sheepskin rug.

"How about a compromise? I prefer sheepskin, but this is something we can discuss later." Refusing to make eye contact, she looks south toward the water. "We can motor out to Anchor Island. With the time we'd save, we can picnic on the beach and swim in the lagoons."

"I hear there are alligators in those lagoons."

"Are you worried they'll spy on us?"

"I'm afraid they'll eat us."

"Well, we can spend our free time searching for arrowheads on Osprey Island. I don't think they will eat us."

"I think we should talk this over. My dear darling, perhaps we should visit the other boats on our wish list." Exhausted, he wants only to end the conversation. "Thank you for your time, Wanda Raye. We'll get back to you when we reach a decision," he says, pushing Molly toward the car.

"Preston, I want this boat."

"You have the patience of a branch-hanging squirrel."

"Waiting is not something I do well. I live in the here and now."

"You should learn to enjoy the moment."

"What makes you think you can tell me no?"

"Don't take your anger out on me. It's my marriage speaking."

"Forgive me if I fail to share in your humor. I'm so embarrassed, Preston, and I don't really care for your tone. I didn't tell Wanda Raye we are shopping for a boat. I told her we wanted this one."

Startled by her tone, he expects she will try to win him over in the bedroom, but she will not succeed. The stakes are too high. "Why would you tell her that without having seen it?"

"We deserve our own place, and this boat is perfect in every way. We can motor out, and when we want, drop anchor for the night. Best of all, we won't have to be on the lookout for self-invited guests."

"Listen, Molly, a boat is not in our future. Not today, not tomorrow, not next week or next year."

"We will just have to do something about that."

A cramp in his stomach warns now is a good time to drop the subject.

CHAPTER 42

"Peggy, I've been wanting to talk with you about something," Molly says. "It's personal."

"Of course. What's up?"

"I hate to be a busybody. We know nothing good comes from meddling into someone else's business." A juggled stammer carries her pause. "I ran into Preston a few days ago at the Sand Bar. Well, he didn't see me, I don't think, anyway."

"He was picking up pizza. We agreed a quiet dinner at home was just what the doctor and his wife ordered." Although she has said this a hundred times, it still makes her laugh. "I just hope all is quiet this evening at the hospital."

"Again, I want you to understand I debated talking about this, and I'm not intending to pry or be nosy, but from one woman to another, especially doctors' wives, I believe you would want to know this. I hope you understand I'm only looking out for you."

"Go on."

"I saw Preston with a young woman. If pressed, I would guess her to be in her late teens. He kissed her in a way I found disrespectful. Something didn't ring right. The kiss wasn't a simple peck on the cheek, you know, the kind you give a good friend when reuniting or parting. Theirs lingered. When the lip-lock was over, he continued to hold her in his arms. Again, I don't believe he saw me. If he had, I think he would want to explain his actions."

Although struggling to take Molly at her word, Peggy remains silent. Their marriage has suffered some bumps and bruises, but Preston's attention toward her in recent weeks tells her it is on the mend. Broken pieces stay broken, but they are learning from their rough times and working to make better ones. At the end of each day, when she rests her head against her pillow, she wants to believe he is faithful to her and their holy union.

Molly's reference to doctors' wives is meant to cloud her vision. She has heard countless times that young women turn to nursing in the hope of catching the eye and attention of a young or seasoned, single or married, physician. She knows it is all hogwash.

"I'm certain you are mistaken. Looks can be deceiving," she says, hoping her message is understood. "Please don't give it another thought."

"Of course. Please, then, I hope you won't mention this to Preston. I don't want to ruffle any feathers or stir up trouble. Hey, let's step into Valeggia and Whiting. They are having their annual sale today. If you have time, we can do lunch after."

Peggy and Molly are shopping the store's racks when Molly's phone rings. Recognizing Preston's number, she lets the call go to voicemail.

"I'm heading to the changing room," Peggy announces.

"I'm ready, too," Molly says, snagging a sheer nighty off a well-put-together mannequin. She is posing in front of the changing room's mirror when her phone rings.

"Hey, gorgeous. What are you doing?" Preston asks. "I left a message on your phone."

"You've caught me in the changing room."

"What are you wearing?"

"Lace thong and matching bra." Given he prefers her naked and on her back, something tells her he does not want to hear about a velveteen caftan she intends to lounge in on a lazy Sunday morning.

"What color?"

"Black, but I'm thinking I'll get it in chocolate brown, too. Your thoughts?"

"Grab both and meet me on the boat."

"Oh, I wish I could. I'm with Peggy, and we're heading to lunch when we leave here. I'm sure she wouldn't mind if you join us."

"How can I possibly join you? I don't want lunch. I want to rip that lacy getup off you."

"Can it wait until later?"

"I guess it'll have to. For the love of God, please do not tell Peggy I said hello."

She sweeps up the pieces and steps from the changing room to find Peggy waiting for her.

"I didn't mean to eavesdrop, but I couldn't help but hear your conversation with Clay. If you need to rush home, we can do lunch tomorrow."

"No, no, no. He's a grown man. He can wait."

"In that case, show me where you found the lace thong. Something tells me it will put a smile on Preston's face."

"Oh, I'm sure it will," she says with a knowing grin.

CHAPTER 43

Horned up and ready for action, Joran pulls Molly behind the hotel room's door. Taking her by the hips, he places her on the small kitchen island. Leaving her spread-eagled, he sweeps a basket of strawberries from the minibar's refrigerator. In the coming minutes, he traces her body with the cold juice the berries leave behind. When she begs for more, he lifts her from the cool granite and carries her off to the bedroom.

"I'm glad you dropped by."

"I thought you'd enjoy my new purchase," she says, tossing her bra across the room.

CHAPTER 44

"What's up?" Preston asks, pressing the phone to his ear. "Do you think you'll be home by five? I've invited friends to the house to celebrate your win," Peggy says.

"Not a problem. Five it is. Do I need to pick up anything?"

"I've taken care of everything."

"Perfect. I'll be home in time to grab a shower."

Turning to Molly, he fears the coming minutes will turn the boat into a war zone. Shots will be fired, words exchanged, and a chain of endless threats will soon follow. After many misdials, he learned early on in their relationship that breaking bad news to her is never easy and often painful.

"I have to turn back. Peggy is planning a celebratory dinner," he says, tossing his phone to the table.

"What's the occasion this time? Jupiter's birthday?"

"That's next week. We're celebrating the regatta."

"Why?"

"It's a big deal, and she's proud of me."

Tired of feeling second in his life, she comes at him with fire in her eyes and fisted hands, and jumps about with catlike reflexes. Quick on his feet, he dodges the first punch but not the blow to his chest.

"I have to be there. I'm the guest of honor, for crying out loud."

"I don't care if you are celebrating your best-in-show win at the Westminster Dog Show."

"You've lost me. What do you mean by that?"

"Everyone knows you are her bitch. Next thing you know, she'll throw a spiked collar around your neck and plug your bottom with a rubber tail. In the blink of an eye, she will come at you with greased up hands begging to rub your tummy."

"Only on those nights when the moon is full."

"It appears you agree. When you come looking, I'll be waiting in the shadows for you to tell me she put the screw to you."

"History tells me I'd be foolish to attempt such humor."

"Acting foolish is something you do well."

"Molly, give it a rest already. I understand you are upset, but you must understand I have obligations."

"With or without your heart? Do me a favor and don't bother with an answer. This is supposed to be our time together. We made plans, and now, in the final hour, you're bailing on me." In her attempt to close the space between them, she loses her balance and falls against the wall. When he turns his back on her, she rips his cell from the table.

Inside the cabin, Rick and Valerie are engaged in a game of cards with Poppy and Shay when they hear loud voices and a wild commotion one might expect on a Saturday afternoon at a small-town rodeo.

"Here we go again," Shay whispers in Poppy's ear. "I told you this was a bad idea."

"As long as we have ownership in the boat, we are forced to deal with Preston and Molly."

"If we end up sharing a room again, I call dibs on Preston. If I'm going to be up all night, I might as well be having fun. Rick, it's time for you to break up the brawl before things escalate."

"I'd rather we roll the dice. That woman is a handful."

"We'll be cheering for you. Now, go," Valerie says, pointing toward the door.

Rick's presence goes unnoticed until Preston and Molly's wild behavior forces him to move between them. "Hey, you two lovebirds. What's the problem?"

"Preston started it. He promised this was my weekend with him." Lunging forward, Molly presses an angry finger at Preston's chest. "Tell her about us or I will."

"Quit horsing around. Rick, would you ask her to give me my phone? Be careful. She might be tiny, but she's strong."

Holding Preston at arm's length, Rick points a fat finger at the phone pressed against Molly's chest. "Is that his?"

"Maybe." Wearing a challenge on her face, she dangles the phone over the water. "Does it matter? He's cheating on me."

"Give me the phone," Preston demands, knocking her to the floor.

"Get off me. You're hurting me!"

"Preston, take a corner, buddy," Rick throws out like a referee in a heated boxing match. Offering a hand, he helps Molly to her feet.

"She's acting like a feral dog backed into a corner. If you get too close, you may need to be quarantined. I'm sorry, Molly. Please, just give me my phone."

"Not until you promise to tell her about us." Quick on her feet, she pulls the ring of keys from the boat's ignition. Taking flight, she races over the deck. Aware Preston is hot on her tail, she swirls around and plants her feet. "We are over."

"What a shocker. Every time you don't get your way, we are over. You're acting crazy, and your temper tantrums are growing old. Now, give me the keys. Need I remind you we are not the only people on this boat?"

"At this point, do you really think I care? I'm sick of the disguises, sneaking around, and sleeping in separate beds. I'm beginning to think you're still in love with your wife."

"You know I love you. For everyone's sake, can we please talk about this back at the marina?"

"When it comes to us, everything is always later."

CHAPTER 45

"Are you free?" Molly asks when Joran answers his phone.

"Give me a second." Placing a hand over the phone, he turns to the young woman he has been entertaining for most of the afternoon. "This is my boss. Would you be a love and step into the bathroom?" When she passes by, he gives her tush a gentle tap. "Your hot body is a distraction that could get me fired, and given your young age, five-to-ten in the slammer." He listens for the door's familiar squeak before returning to the call. "Sorry about that. I'm going over a video with one of my students. What's up?"

"I'd like to see you. That is, if you have time to squeeze me in."

"I always have time for you, and I'll squeeze whatever pleases you. Do you want to meet someplace, or would you prefer some downtime in my room? If you like, I'll order champagne."

"I'm thirty minutes away. Get my side of the bed warm and call room service. I'm craving strawberries."

Darting through traffic, she arrives at the hotel in under twenty minutes. Expecting to find the elevator empty, she inches toward the brass doors when they begin to part. Stepping forward, she is nearly run over by a young girl rushing through the doors. In her hurry to jump aside, she eyes the girl's wet hair and the tennis bag falling over her shoulder. When she brushes by, Molly gets a whiff of the sweet scent of jasmine.

Several floors later, Joran greets her at the door with a lingering kiss. When they part, he gives a low whistle. "How's my gorgeous Molly today? My, you're looking saucy."

She is about to tell him her day just got better when her eyes fall on the bottle of perfume on the bedside table. Marching over the carpeted floor, she rips the top off the bottle and gives the room a quick spritz.

"Did you sleep with her?"

"Who?"

"I saw her stepping out of the elevator. She darn near knocked me over, and she smelled like this perfume. I don't have to tell you she had a tennis bag over her shoulder."

"Please tell me you are joking. Tess is a teenager. Sixteen, I believe. I'm coaching her."

"Define *coaching*."

"We were breaking down the video from her practice session today."

"Where's the camera?"

"I let her take it home. When you called, I hurried her out of here."

"I bet you did."

"Why would I sleep with her when I have you?"

"Having seen her, I was wondering the same thing." Years of sneaking off to hotels have her eyeing the bedding. The sheet is not tucked at the corners, and the pillows are inches off center. Flipping back a corner of the bed's duvet, she lets go a laugh. "Well, what do we have here?" she asks, waving a blonde hair in his face. "You lying sack of …"

"Hold it right there, crazy woman. I never agreed to be exclusive."

"You are an ass."

"For what it's worth, I've heard it said every toilet needs one. And don't go throwing a nickname at me I don't deserve."

"She probably earns more than you."

"Those are mighty big words coming from a woman who saves pennies."

"How dare you," she says, coming at him with an open hand.

Ducking the swing, he catches her wrist. "I'm not just another pretty face you can easily manipulate. You would be foolish to think I haven't done my homework."

"Like I care."

"Oh, but you will. I know you're married to an obstetrician who is up to his ears in debt, and when time allows, you entertain a lover on his boat. *Open Wide*, is it? Not to worry. Your secret is safe with me—that is, as long as we continue our little liaison. I believe you'll agree it's a win-win for both of us."

"Are you threatening me with blackmail?"

"Where I come from, we call it insurance. I'm sure you can come up with the money. I'm hoping the good doctor you're bedding on the side will make a sizable contribution to a bank account I keep just for this purpose."

Stomping over the floor, she swings open the door. "Good luck with that. If I have my way, he will see to it you never swing another racket. As for me, I've been dirt poor since the day my mother's doctor slapped my ass."

CHAPTER 46

The restaurant's patio is buzzing with activity, and valet parking is at a premium. Guests mill about, often pausing to admire the breaking waves and its oceangoing vessels.

Seated at a table reserved for the restaurant's most gracious guests, Preston signals for the waitress. "Tiffany," he says, reading the name tag resting against her perky breast. "That's a lovely name." Giving her the once-over, he offers his signature smile. "Any specials today?"

The waitress, barely into her twenties, flips through a pad the size of a cell phone. "Shrimp and grits and the shrimp po'boy."

"What do you recommend?"

Flirting with her eyes, she lets go a young girl's giggle that always guarantees a generous tip. "The po'boy is my favorite."

"Well then, the shrimp po'boy has my name written all over it."

"So will a gravestone, if you keep flirting in my presence," Peggy whispers. "And put her clothes back on her."

"I'm sorry. I didn't hear you."

"You were undressing her with your eyes." Staring him down, she hopes he understands the look of disappointment on her face.

"Anything calling out to you, Clay?" Preston asks, changing the subject.

"The shrimp platter sounds good. What do you think, Molly? Want to share?"

Before she can brush him off, a woman interrupts with a hand to Preston's shoulder.

"Hello, Dr. Fayne. I'm Wanda Raye Harvey."

He looks up from the table to find his reflection in large sunglasses popular in the sixties. The round face behind the frame is familiar, but he struggles to place her.

"I'm not sure if you remember me. I showed you and your lovely wife an Albin over in Point Cadet. I'm in the boat business," she says, offering her hand to Peggy.

Seated across the table, Molly digs into the bowl of salted chips. Hoping to ignore the confusion growing around her, she hides behind the restaurant's menu.

"I'm Peggy Fayne. I'm Preston's wife." Peggy folds the napkin and returns it to the table. "You'll have to forgive me, but I don't believe we've met."

The agent eyes the table, sweeping over Clay before resting on Molly. She finds her familiar, but a little birdie suggests she save recognition for another time. She meets dozens of people every day, and before long, every face becomes familiar. "We met at Point Cadet. I believe you wanted a boat with a swim platform," Wanda Raye says, turning her focus on Preston.

Peggy looks to Preston for an explanation, but he offers a look she is to interpret to mean the woman is either crazy or mistaken, possibly both. Still, a knot forms in her stomach. It pains her to learn he is parading his muse out in public, and given Molly and Clay are now holding hands, she believes it is best to play along. "Oh, yes. That's right. I do recall the Albin, however, the asking price escapes me."

The agent taps at a notebook she pulls from her pocket. "One hundred thousand US dollars. By the way, the rolls here are my favorite. I've been told they have more fewer calories than the breadsticks."

Preston withholds a laugh. Hoping he does not appear nervous, he reclines into the chair and crosses his arms over his chest. He is not surprised Peggy chooses to take the high road. It is like her to avoid conflict, especially in public or among friends.

"That's a good chunk of change. Is it still for sale?" Peggy asks, faking interest.

"We have a pending contract, but should it fall through, I'll give you a call." Retrieving a card from her purse, Wanda Raye places it on the table in front of Clay. "If you find yourselves looking for a boat, please give me a call."

Peggy sits through lunch planning her interrogation. She wishes she could slam Preston with a wall of questions, but with Molly and Clay rushing lunch, she knows the time to attack is not in the present but on the horizon. "I'm sorry we have to cut lunch short, but we are expected at home."

"What are you talking about? This is our day of leisure," Preston reminds.

"I'm sure I told you the repairman is coming by."

"What man, and what is he repairing?"

"I guess I didn't mention the leak under the kitchen sink. Clay and Molly, I'm so glad we were able to catch up, but I hope you'll forgive us for running out. You know how these repairmen can be. If we aren't there to answer the door, they race off to the next job."

"No problem. Go take care of that leak," Molly says with a smile.

Peggy pushes back her chair and, leaving Preston in her wake, marches through the restaurant's patio out to the parking lot.

"Slow down there. Are you training for a marathon?" Preston asks, catching his breath.

"How could you humiliate me like that? In front of our friends, no less."

Preston slides into the driver's seat and, pressing the accelerator to the floorboard, grabs at his chest. "I'm telling you, that woman is mistaken."

"I didn't see you jumping to set things straight."

"What was I supposed to say?"

"That she is mistaken are the first words that come to mind. Who is she?"

"Wanda Raye Harvey."

"Not her, you fool. The woman who was with you."

"Peggy, please believe me. She has me confused with someone else."

"She's not the only one. By the way, were you flirting with the waitress? Don't bother with an answer. I was waiting for you to reach out and grope her. Your lies are growing by leaps and bounds, and your eyes know only to roam. I've noticed your head is always in a swivel."

"What do you mean by that?"

"You know exactly what I mean."

"Enlighten me."

"I know about the other woman," she says, focusing on the windshield. "You've been crying out in your sleep."

"The boat is wearing on me."

"You shouldn't sleep with her."

"I'm talking about the boat. I'm telling you, that broker is mistaken. I've never seen her before in my life. You heard her say the rolls have more fewer calories. I've never heard such nonsense. The lady's a fruitcake."

"She called you by name." She pauses until hurt feelings give her the nudge she needs to continue. "I also know about the woman you met up with at Trude's bistro."

"It's not Trude's bistro and I didn't meet up with anyone. You're talking crazy. You'll recall I was picking up dinner. For us, I might add."

"Molly saw you kissing a young woman. There, I said it. The hole is in the bucket. As for Molly, she is nothing more than a rented friend."

Learning Molly has thrown him under the bus has his heart skipping a beat. "You're making this up for reasons I don't understand."

"What I'm doing is growing tired of this love dance. With you, there's always another partner waiting under the sheets."

"That's not true, and you know it."

"Don't try to minimize the damage."

"What damage? The crazy lady's made-up story? You know me well enough to know if I want a boat, I'll damn sure buy it."

"That said, I'm guessing you didn't care for the Albin."

"I'm telling you, I didn't look at a boat at Point Cadet."

"You used to be so attentive. Now, nothing with you is what it used to be."

"You don't mean that."

"I know about Trude."

"Are you crazy? She was long before I met you."

"That's what you want me to believe, but it's not true."

"She's a friend, nothing more."

"You have her address in your car's navigation."

"You searched my car?"

"You gave me the key."

"Not for you to spy on me."

"Spy on you? You're my husband."

"Didn't stop you from searching my car."

"Is that guilt I'm hearing in your voice? By the way, where's your wedding ring?"

"I forgot it on the boat."

"I'm not surprised. It has come to my attention that you forget a lot of things when you're on the boat."

"That's not true."

"Has Trude been on the boat?"

"I don't know where you're coming from or what finger you are pointing, but Trude DelCamp is a friend. Nothing more."

"We'll just have to wait and see about that."

"I'm guessing this is not the time to bring up that I'm taking the boat out tomorrow."

"Stay out as long as you like."

"Remind me later to thank you for the permission slip."

CHAPTER 47

The agent at Easy Rental does not intend to be nosy, but he grows worried when Peggy's unsteady hand accepts the rental agreement. He is on high alert when she drops the pen and, once she has it in a firm grip, scribbles her signature on the date line.

"Are you OK?" he asks. "You seem a little rattled."

He is spot-on, but Peggy is not about to share her plans for the day. Instead, she leans in and, with a slight tremble, invites him to do the same.

"I'm being followed," she tells him. She keeps her voice low while canvassing the space around them. "Stalked, maybe. Not this very minute, but in recent days. Every time I'm in line at the grocery store, complete strangers offer a smile. Just yesterday, when I was at lunch, a man pointed in my direction. Gloria Woodland, my friend since high school—well, she's married now and has a different last name—anyway, she met me for lunch. You would like her: everyone does. She has an easy way about her and always makes a stranger feel like a long-lost friend, and although she never lets alcohol touch her lips, she's always up for dessert. She tried convincing me the man at the counter, the one who took our order, was pointing to the chalkboard behind us—you know, the one with a short list of dishes meant to draw in diners—but I'm certain he was tailing me. Not once did he take his eyes off me. Just this morning, a car drove by my house. By the way, I like your sleeveless sweater."

"It's a vest."

"So it is."

Amused, the young man leans in with great interest. "I take it you live in the middle of nowhere."

"Well, no. My neighbors live next door. Every morning since the day they moved in, we've exchanged a wave from the kitchen window, but you know what they say: better to be safe than sorry." She had not intended to tell such a tale, but her actions on this night are not his concern. "I'm convinced my husband is swinging with one of our neighbors," she throws out like she is dealing from a gambling boot. "I saw them with my own eyes."

"For real? Swinging?"

"I've seen them at the park. Next thing you know, they'll be coming down the slide and building castles in the sandbox."

"I'm an anti-stalker myself. I study the patterns of people I want to avoid."

"I'm no expert, but isn't that stalking?"

"I guess it could be. All depends how you look at it." Returning to his computer, the agent, a clean-shaven man with genuine eyes, chalks her up as another crazy. People like her are not unusual in his line of work. Still, he cannot wait to share this encounter in the employee break room when his coworkers run out of similar stories and cold pizza. "I'll need a copy of your driver's license and proof of insurance."

"Of course—unless it's for anti-stalking purposes."

"You got me there," he says with an easy smile. "Here is your contract, and if you will sign at the bottom, I'll have you on your way in no time. Your car is around back." He points a long, thin finger due east. "Go out those doors and take a left. There will be an agent there to assist you."

"By the way, I'll be leaving my car here."

"No problem."

Minutes later, she scoots over the seat and settles behind the rental's steering wheel. Tossing her tote bag to the passenger seat, she grips the steering wheel at its ten and two o'clock positions. Memories of the summer she attended driving school with her best girlfriends try to weave into her thoughts, but her racing heart will not allow it. Snippets of Mr. Ruthee and the orange and white traffic cones she navigated in reverse on a dare are best forgotten.

Falling against the headrest, she invites a deep breath to fill her lungs. The coming hours will change not only her future but also the one she'd hoped to share with Preston.

"I don't know who you are, but you better be ready. It will be a cold day in hell before I let you break me. I'm stronger and wiser. I'm coming, and I'll be fighting like the dickens to save my marriage." In a voice meant to be heard around the world, she again cries out, "If you don't believe me, stick around." After a violent lunge, the dark two-door hugs the road with all four tires.

The marina's fueling station is battened down for the night, and the night guard's absence allows her presence to go unnoticed. Large lanterns offer just enough light to alert passing boats of the fueling station's lengthy structure and its floating dock. She catches a break when she rounds the harbormaster's house, a place she once visited when Preston needed fishing tackle and batteries. A quick glance confirms the lights are out and the parking area is empty.

Dimming the car's headlights, she inches along toward the far end of the station. It takes only a breath for the smell of diesel fuel to fill her lungs. A glance at the rearview mirror confirms she has not been followed. This is a huge relief, as she has no words to explain the rental car, her need to stay low, and the open bottle of vino she brought along for the ride.

As she idles along, the alarm on her wristwatch breaks the eerie silence. Ten fifty-five—five minutes shy of her usual bedtime. It is late, but she is not going anywhere, especially to bed. Perched against the headrest, she kicks off kitten heels and rummages in the tote bag until she finds the deck shoes she almost forgot to pack. She is pulling the cork from the wine's bottle when she realizes she has forgotten to bring a glass. Biting at her lip, she pins the blame on Preston. One thing is certain: anything that goes wrong tonight will be his fault.

Lifting the bottle to her lips, she observes the covered slips through fresh eyes. A seasoned sailor, she notices that the marina's barrel ceiling shelters the boats not only from pouring rain and blistering heat but also the faint sliver of light tonight's low moon offers.

She is not surprised when Dana enters her thoughts. In a well-put-together package, she is all Preston admires and craves—young, naïve, and lying in wait for the next best experience of her life. Until recently, before moving to Casino Beach, access to six television channels after the late-night news fulfilled her greatest wishes. A lover, especially one with a title before his name, would surely be the sprinkles on her cupcake.

Thinking about it now, she understands Dana is only one of the many young women who catch Preston's roaming eyes. There is the neighbor's daughter, too. A handful for her parents, she left them no choice but to send her off to boarding school after she disappeared for five weeks to travel the Gulf Coast with her boyfriend, a street thug released from juvenile detention with only the clothes on his back and a dream in his heart.

And then there is Brandie. There will never come a time she will talk about the advances the young woman made after too many cocktails were served at the club's holiday party. It took three visits to the dry cleaner's to get her scent out of Preston's jacket and months to erase the memory.

When a flickering light on the *Wet Hen* catches her eye, she returns the cork to the bottle. Although it was some time ago, she recalls hearing that its owner moved onboard the thirty-foot Catalina the same day a smug processor served him with divorce papers.

A search of the marina has her studying *About Face*, a luxury yacht in from Miami. It is rumored the sixty-foot Fly belongs to a cosmetic company's recently retired CEO. A sweep of the remaining slips tells her only one is vacant—28W. Out of the corner of her eye, she follows a narrow beam of light coming over the water. When the vessel nears the channel, her palms grow sweaty. Like the incoming boat, the time to act is fast approaching. Although tempted to chug the last of the wine, she keeps her eyes on the water.

As the trawler makes its approach into slip 28W, Peggy prepares her heart to meet the enemy. Expecting a battle, she rolls her fists and cracks her knuckles. When her conversation with the old woman in the marina's bathroom enters her thoughts, she pushes fear and uncertainty aside. There was great wisdom in the woman's words, and if she learned anything in their brief time together, it was to watch and listen even when bad news comes first.

Rick and a woman unknown to her are the first to exit the boat. Their heads bowed and faces covered, they walk in silence to the *SlipNFall*. It was a stroke of luck when she learned at the trawler's christening that the Sundancer belongs to Rick Finley, one of Preston's partners in *Open Wide*.

Oh, how she hates the name. She turns red in the cheeks each time she is pressed to say it. The afternoon when Preston came home with personalized all-weather gear, sun visors, and pullover T-shirts, she put her foot down, refusing to partake in his excitement while threatening to stay on terra firma. This was probably his plan, and in hindsight, another one of the many mistakes she adds to finger-pointing and her growing list of blames.

The couple following behind Rick is not familiar to her. The man, who stands inches shorter than the woman at his side, keeps his nose to the ground. The woman is struggling with a large suitcase whose rear tire appears to have suffered a blowout. Although her voice is loud, her words are unclear.

Peggy watches in anticipation, expecting them to join Rick on his boat. Instead, they rush to a car parked near the marina's roundabout. Minutes later, when the car passes under the light, she gets a glimpse of the tag attached to its rear bumper. The *N2TEETH* vanity plate tells her the car belongs to Poppy.

When minutes pass without any movement onboard *Open Wide*,

doubt begins to enter her thoughts. Perhaps she is mistaken, and Preston is not on the boat. Worried something may have happened to him, and growing concerned for his safety, she tosses the bottle into the backseat. She is placing her hand on the key when a beam of light from the boat's aft cabin brightens the night.

CHAPTER 48

"Well, well, well. Not only does the cauldron boil over, but the plot also thickens. I never guessed you, a person of so little means, to be the other woman," Peggy says, throwing open the cabin's door. "My husband and Little Miss Goody Two-Shoes. Two little lice-infected lovebirds. I suggest you set your aim on the tree's lower branches, something closer to home. I must say, this is sobering."

"How would you know?" Molly asks, shooting sarcasm off her tongue. "You're a boozer. I've never seen you without a drink in your hand. Do you ever think to eat before you drink?"

"Molly, don't go there," Preston warns.

"I don't know whether to laugh or cry," Peggy continues. "One would think you would know to stay on your side of the tracks. I can choose to cuss like a dollar hooker—much like you, Molly—or I can be an example. Only a worthless person would do what you've done."

"Think what you will, but dismissing me is a mistake," Molly fires back. "You come off like June Cleaver with the perfect house and a strand of pearls around your neck, but the real you is boring. If you don't believe me, ask Preston. He tells me the only time you can accept the truth is when you're drunk."

"Peggy, that is not true," Preston says, stepping between them. "Molly, please stop."

"It appears you know only arm-twisting tactics. Truth or myth, you stole my marriage," Peggy shouts with hate in her eyes.

"Preston comes to me willingly."

"You two are mirror images of a double-edged sword." Turning away, Peggy shoots a look at Preston. "It appears you've lost your faculties and the ability to think. I believe you know the old saying: *If they'll do it with you, they'll do it to you.*"

"Peggy, please let me explain. If you will just hear me out, I'm sure you will understand."

"Are you asking to share something with me? Don't try to obfuscate the truth. You know, Preston, you always speak in a tone that suggests you are giving a gift. As for understanding, it's not happening in this lifetime."

"I'm prepared to tell the truth," he insists.

"With another lie? You have an opinion about everything and everyone, and you make sure those around you know it. Something tells me you should have been a lawyer. I'll say this: I hope there will never be another love like ours. I wouldn't wish this pain on anyone."

She fights the urge to throw a bitch-slap across the room, hoping to take both Preston and Molly down with a single strike—but holding her head high, she keeps her hands at her sides. Each swallow feels like shards of glass are traveling through to her heart. Standing before her is a woman she invited into her home and into their lives. She wants to ask how long they have been sleeping together, but learning the truth will do nothing but cause more pain. The stab to her heart tells her their history no longer matters.

As reality sets in, surprise begins to fade. The moments she witnessed, the exchanges they shared in her presence when they thought she was not watching, and the gossip she heard inside the club's old walls come rushing to the surface. It pains her knowing they played her for the fool she is.

"Let's get you home. We can talk there," Preston says, moving toward her.

"Not happening. Preston, I believe you know what they say: *You can lead a whore to culture, but you can't make her think.*"

"Who's saying that?" Molly asks, locking eyes with Preston. "Who is calling me names?"

"It's an expression." Preston freezes, not wanting to believe he is seeing Molly for the person she is while understanding he failed to see Peggy in the light she deserves. Although he turns away, he cannot escape Molly's cold smile.

"In this case, it fits." Peggy points a firm and steady finger to the open door. "Molly, it's time for you to leave. I can't put into words the damage you've caused."

"No one asked you to. Tell her, Preston. Tell her it's over. Tell her we were lovers long before she came along. We are like Romeo and Juliet—in love till death and forever after."

"Molly, let me handle this. Go home."

"Remember that finger I broke?"

"The one you slammed in the car door?"

"The one and only. Now that it's on the mend, I can't decide who to give it to."

"I'd laugh, but I've forgotten how. You clowns belong together like Bonnie and Clyde," Peggy says, enjoying their squabble.

"Whatever," Molly says, lifting her voice. "As always, you've had too much giggle juice. Will you call me later? When it's over?" she asks, cutting her eyes to Preston.

"Go home, Molly."

This scenario had never played out in his head or in his heart. In his next breath, his body language changes from the cocky confidence he has carried his entire life to something small and insignificant.

"Cat got your tongue all of a sudden?" Molly snaps. "I'm tired of being used. Every time you have your way with me, you tell me I matter. It's only when you are under Peggy's fat thumb that I'm left believing otherwise. I'm not leaving until you promise you'll call when it's over."

"I don't want to say something you might regret hearing. I'm staying here. Peggy shouldn't be alone tonight." Reaching for answers, he searches for words to reassure Peggy. Knowing anything he says is sure to spark a fire in Molly, he treads carefully. "Molly, go home. We'll talk tomorrow."

"With you, every day is tomorrow. I'm beginning to think you enjoy sitting on your hands. If I'm sorry for anything, it's that I didn't have time to delete the nude photos we've been exchanging," she says, throwing her phone to the table. "As for you, Peggy, you're all washed up." Giving the door a hard push, she slams it behind her.

"Preston, you and your actions leave me feeling empty, alone, and without purpose. What little remains of our marriage is ashes. My heart is hanging on by a thread. Just tell me it's over between you and Molly in real words I'll believe."

"I wish I could, but I'm stuck in a place I fear I can't escape."

"When did you decide to give up on me? Was it something I said? The words I used to say it? Do I move about in a manner that says I'm not good enough? Why did you stop being an honest person?"

"I messed up, Peggy, and I'm sorry. I've been an ass."

"Well, what do you know? We finally agree on something. We've done the denying, fighting, and screaming only to be left with a basket of empty promises. Your mistress talks a tough game, but when she's backed into a corner and forced to shed her skin, you'll see nothing but broken pieces. Earlier this evening, I watched a plane fly overhead. I don't know where it was going, but I wanted to be on it."

"I was hoping you would never find out," Preston replies. "Believe me when I say she means nothing to me." He waits for her to correct him, but when the moment passes without questions and explanations involving the *why* and *how could you* drama, he is forced to do some self-searching. He will never let slip that Molly makes him feel young again. It is only now he understands that Peggy is always without a list of demands. She cheers his successes and comforts him when his efforts fail. As for Molly, she knows only to put the heat on him.

"My dear Preston, having experienced you, your charades, and your constant shenanigans, I believe I'll be better off without you. I've learned from you and that hooligan of yours that no vow is sacred. You walk through life without a care in the world. Looking back on our marriage, I wish I had learned to be more like you." The drop in her voice warns he should listen and pay attention. "I will no longer live and fall imprisoned to you. Our marriage is no longer a game of rock, paper, scissors. You can wave your hand about, but mine is out of the game. She can have you. I take some satisfaction knowing you will do to her what you've done to me. I'm convinced you can't help yourself."

"I know it's not for me to ask, but I hope you will find it in your heart to forgive me. I'm begging you will not let this night end our marriage."

"This night? Have you forgotten about all those nights before this one? Preston, you're an attractive man, but beyond that you offer very little. You're old enough to know begging is unattractive. You embarrassed me this evening in so many ways and on so many levels." She wants to ask if he is sleeping with any of the women who gather to celebrate his achievements, but something tells her those women, her true friends, would not have him.

"I'm begging you to give our marriage another chance. I'll go to counseling. We can go together. Whatever it takes. I'm in it for the long haul."

"People like you and your mistress tend to ask for second chances when they've already been given a baker's dozen. I've given you far more chances than your cheating ways deserve. Do us both a favor and put a cork in it. Need I remind you that it has been said trust is like uncorked Bordeaux? Once you put the screw to it, it's never the same." The humor's truth pulls at her heart. "You want to know how I sum up our marriage? I stay up every night hoping it will keep another tomorrow from coming."

He moves to take a seat beside her, but she is quick on her feet.

"Step back, mister," she warns, tucking her knees at her side, leaving little space for him. "I remember the day you brought me here to see this boat. I listened as you described the ins and outs, the teak, the draw, even when you busted out with a name so ridiculous to call your sea mistress, I thought you'd lost your mind. When your excitement grew, I encouraged mine to follow. It was because I loved you that I was on cloud nine. That was until I realized you never said *us*, *ours*, or *we*. It was always about *you*. I knew then our life was turning about. Through your eyes, you wanted me to see the adventures you would embark upon. You were so wrapped up in your life that you failed to see a growing distance in ours. There has never been an adventure in my eyes that you were not part of. The blurred line in our vows where we agreed to forsake all others sailed not only by you but also *with* you. I met a woman recently," she says, pausing. "Funny, isn't it? Those are words I've come to expect from you."

"That's not fair."

"Don't talk to me about fair. This woman offered comfort in my darkest hour. In our short time together, I was in awe of her great wisdom. At her suggestion, I let the cards play out while watching you shuffle and break the deck." Lifting her chin, she looks him square in the eyes. "I feel like Alexander the Great—left with nothing more to conquer. My dear Preston, I'm not here to engage in marital warfare. That said, I'm through fighting for our marriage, and I'm tired of being alone in it. Make no mistake, I don't wish for you and Molly Lambert the best, but I do pray you survive."

"I would give anything to right the many wrongs I have come to regret," Preston pleads. Looking away, he studies the floor beneath him. "I swear I can feel my heart breaking. All the good in me is because of you. I know you don't believe me, given the way I've treated you and our marriage, but I love you, Peggy, with every ounce of my soul. I love loving you."

"Loving me? Don't go there. Those nights you went missing, failing to answer your phone, ignoring your pager, leaving me to imagine you with two-bit hookers in push-up bras and hot pants, I was ashamed to know I had failed you. After years of sleepless nights and gut-wrenching pain, I've come to understand that it isn't those things I failed to give you that sent you away, but all those meaningless moments you need to up your ego that ultimately killed our marriage."

"I'm begging you'll give me another chance."

"I was not in love with you, Preston, but loved you, even in those times when you didn't deserve it. I vowed to love you for a lifetime, longer if God and time allowed." Broken, she lays her pain on the table. "Do you think I've forgotten the many times I asked if you love me?"

When the memories come rushing, his face turns serious. It was not that long ago she insisted they visit a marriage counselor. They rode in silence until the elevator reached the third floor of the old Hammond Mercer building. The fifty minutes they shared inviting a stranger into the dark side of their marriage did not go well. Even then, he would not share his true feelings. Now, he wishes he could go back to each of those times and shout for the entire world to hear, and to whisper into her heart, his love for her. Ashamed of his actions, he remains silent.

"The three words I needed to hear from you never slipped through your lips. I gave you my whole heart when we started this journey. I wanted the same from you. Tonight's events tell me your affair is still fluid. I believe you'll agree your mistress is hanging in the background pulling strings."

"I'm sorry." Closing his eyes, he rubs at his chin. It is only now he understands her pain and is taking responsibility for it.

"You know, I bet your whore is watching us now."

"Why would she?"

"She's been watching us since the day you invited her into our lives. For the love of God, Preston, do you not understand the mess you created and the gravity of your actions?"

"Peggy, I swear I will work to make all of our tomorrows better— days we will look forward to for the rest of our lives."

"Oh, Preston, save it for someone who cares. Rough patches are bumps in the road most couples experience at some point in their marriage. Our patch is different. We can't slap a Band-Aid on this open wound and expect it to heal. This is our last dance. Your baggage tells a story I no longer care to hear. Surely you realize Molly's been rented many times before you, perhaps while she's been entertaining you. She is like a feral cat—always on the prowl." The look she gives is not of pity but disappointment. "What a fool you've been. Do you realize you have given up all of this?" she sweeps her eyes over the boat's cabin, "along with our home, your practice, the respect of our community, only to be stuck in a withering lease with used merchandise most men would turn away? Some would call her a floozy. Others, words far worse." She sits in wait, watching the wheels in his head take a knowing spin. "I hear more in your silence than I've heard from you in our entire marriage. What I hear the loudest are the words you're too weak to say."

"I'm sorry, Peggy. I swear it was never about hurting you."

"Still, this is what you've done. This is why you no longer matter. You have a way of spinning the truth to suit your fancy."

"Surely you don't mean that."

"Oh, but I do, and if you keep talking like this, with scripted words and false promises," she grabs a wine glass from the bar and holds it in the air, "I'm going to need more wine." Fighting tears, she lets a laugh escape. "The picture you're trying to paint isn't the real truth, but one you hope I'll believe." Offering a look of disappointment, she scoots over the bench, grabs the bottle, and tops off her glass. "I can't change you, but I can fix me." Pausing, she swirls the wine like a sophisticated sommelier. "Ours is a marriage crippled by broken promises. I loved you until you gave me reason not to. In the moment when you were no longer lovable, I found a way to believe in you. But now, my heart is cold. You no longer have a place here. Again, you've done nothing but damage my soul. You are an idiot, and you should know it has been said every village has one."

"Peggy …"

"Don't *Peggy* me. As for Molly Lambert, that tramp will lead you into rough water. You must realize that high forehead of hers doesn't live up to the promise of great intelligence." Steeling her spine, she points a finger at the only man she has ever loved. "You want my advice? Strap on a life jacket, jump overboard, and swim like hell. That woman will drown you faster than this bottle drowns my sorrows. Please go. Just get out and leave me alone. Your actions tell me this shouldn't be too difficult for you."

He wants to take her in his arms and brush away the pain, but the angst she wears warns he should remain planted. "What are you going to do?"

"What I should have done a long time ago. I'm going to chart my own course. I'm moving on. Should the opportunity present itself, I might consider trading up."

His belief in his self-worth tells him another man will never take his place. His only concern is that a hero will not only steal her heart but also comfort it.

"Please go, and take that phone with you," she says, throwing her eyes to the table.

"Come home with me. I promise I'll change."

"Promise all you want, but we both know you'll never change. Given your actions, my heart tells me I can't do forever with you."

Every moment when her heart fell deeper in love with him races through her mind—the cotton candy they shared at the county fair when they threw out names for the prized pigs, comforting words he offered when their plane nearly missed the runway at Reagan National, and the time he reassured her a missed turn off the highway was an opportunity to explore a new adventure—and pulls at her heart.

"I think I'll stick around for a while. I assume our tax returns are in order." A glance at his hand has her wondering why he is not wearing his wedding ring. The image of the circular band has her envisioning a rope around his neck. In the blink of an eye, she worries about the future of their shared bank accounts and those he has likely gone to great lengths to hide. "Given that our marriage has come down to dollars and cents, you might consider calling Bad Bob."

"The insurance guy?"

"The lawyer."

"You can't be serious," he says, understanding the consequences of such a call. Bad Bob jokes about financial obligations one might have to a first, second, or third wife. In an earlier time, when their marriage was on solid ground, they laughed along with the commercial during late-night television. A quick glance at her face tells him she is not laughing now. "You're talking nonsense. Gather your things and let's go home."

She wants to believe he is speaking the truth, but Molly's presence here tonight tells a different story. The thought of foregoing the damage and surrendering into his arms has her heart racing, but knowing he has taken refuge in the arms of another, she keeps on point. "Hold your horses, two-timer. I'm staying put."

"It's late, and I believe you will agree you've had enough to drink."

"I'm not drunk, but we can agree I am drinking."

"I'll drive us home. We can get your car in the morning. That said, I don't believe you should be taking the wheel tonight."

"Preston, I vowed to love you till death us do part." Although her eyes soften, she does not ignore the pinch in her heart. "I waited my whole life to love you. We've been through the good, the great, and now this—the truly ugly. I've wasted so many hours agonizing through monumental events hoping you would see me and perhaps fall in love with me all over again, only to be stuck here."

"Peggy, I think we've said enough for tonight."

"I'm just getting started."

"Fine. I'm listening."

"It wasn't long after we married that I heard whispers that your father wanted you to marry Kaye Sherman. Preston, I didn't want to believe you settled with me."

Reflecting on recent events, she circles the rim of her glass with an unsteady finger. "You do know Kaye attends most of the charitable events at the club. She rarely volunteers, but she's the first to bring out the checkbook. At first, I felt guilty, but now I think her attendance and contributions are her way of thanking me for sparing her the pain she knew you would one day cause."

Guilty of loving him, she holds him with her eyes. "I'm sure you're aware her husband is always one rank ahead of you. You failed to hide your disappointment last year when he was chosen Mississippi's Sailor of the Year. Are you aware he tripled in one phone call the money you raised in one year, not only for the club, but also in every fundraiser he feels passionate about? Something tells me Kaye must be thanking her lucky stars."

"Peggy, you're not being fair. And I didn't, as you so eloquently put it, settle with you. I love you."

"Fair? You're not worth the game. Oh, Preston, all this time I thought you were just selfish. Now I understand you are foolish, too. What I find interesting, especially for a man who has so much more to offer, is that it appears you believe your greatest asset is tucked behind your zipper—that is, when it's not out roaming the streets. As for loving me, perhaps you should reflect on the evening's events." Tired of the banter, she turns away, holding tight the words that ready themselves on the tip of her tongue. "Once you lose respect and the light burns out, the gig is over."

Left with nothing but memories of poor choices, Preston fumbles with the pockets of his jeans.

"As a young girl, I looked to my parents' marriage to determine what I wanted in mine. You know what I learned? You don't measure up to my dreams and expectations."

"Peggy, I apologized for my indiscretions. I wish you would find it in your heart to forgive me."

"Indiscretions? Not happening. When I learned of your cheating ways, I set aside my dreams of having children. I was so worried you would leave me, I knew I couldn't put children through such pain. To think all along it was Molly who cast her spell on you."

"I'm sorry, Peggy. Thinking about it now, it's more like she put the squeeze on me."

"Seriously? What is she? A boa constrictor? I'm guessing that makes you her titmouse."

"A titmouse is a bird."

"Next, you will swear she had you by the short hairs."

"If that's what it will take for you to forgive me."

"Don't count on it. You're the one who foolishly exposed them. Your excuses tend to go sideways. As a result, we've landed in a foreign place where you are no longer my hero. Where you once made me feel safe, I now worry what lies ahead. It's easy to see our roles have changed. From this day forward, I am my own navigator. As for your future, you can give Molly all you have, but she will never be anything but empty."

"We can start over. Have a baby or two. I'll do whatever it takes for you to stay with me."

"You invited this hell into our marriage. Do not ask me to turn a blind eye to your cheating ways. You left me living in the here and now. I'm no longer accepting false promises or elementary pledges that you will do better. I miscarried last year, days before the Chapman Regatta," she whispers into her glass. Months of pain and anguish allow her to forgive the lie. "A baby wouldn't make you mine. Just to be clear, I know what I lived. You, however, can't hide behind your sins and shame."

Caught unknowing, he searches for words, but when they fail to come, he hopes his silence will be mistaken for words too painful to speak. The Chapman Regatta is the oldest and most prestigious interclub race in the United States, but the look on her face suggests now is not the time to remind she had insisted he go. "Why didn't you tell me about the miscarriage?"

"Given the state of our marriage, I doubted we would weather the parenting stage." The look she gives validates her actions. "I washed my hands of you when I learned you were playing house with another. You were supposed to be my protector, and here you were throwing me in harm's way. Time with you has a habit of beating the dreams out of me. All you talk about is taking last year's title away from Shep Bingham and his crew. For what it's worth, he's a better captain."

"That's low, Peggy."

"Trust me when I say I know the truth hurts. All those nights I was left alone—including the night you left our bed and walked out of our home having me believe you were called to the hospital—prepared me for this day. I kept waiting, counting empty minutes for you to come home to me. I watched the clock tick away the seconds, accepting that I no longer mattered. In the dark moments, when the minutes turned to hours, doubt entered my thoughts. Can you blame me? Imagining you in the arms of another, whispering words I longed to hear? In those moments when suspicion entered my thoughts, I resisted the urge to fight for what I believed was rightfully mine. Now, in the final hour, my heart warns me to beware. Pacing the floor with scenarios of you and your lover playing out in my head didn't bring answers but insanity. Believe me, I've found a way to believe my miscarriage was a blessing."

"You must believe I'm sorry."

"Do not make me a pawn in your board game."

"This isn't a game."

"Great. Because I'm not playing."

"I would have stayed with you," he offers with little commitment.

"Oh, Preston, you rip off so many lies I'm beginning to think you believe them. I don't want guilt, yours or mine, to play a hand in our future. You've always been worthless, but in recent months, you've become a liability. You know, it's interesting how we adapt to disappointment." Once again, a deep sadness blankets her face. "What pains me most is knowing you were faced with a moment when having an affair with her meant more than honoring me. Your twisted behavior boggles my mind. Apparently, you've never been told that when in doubt, don't. Did you ever worry about getting her pregnant? Don't bother with an answer. I'm guessing her eggs are either cracked or rotten."

"I'm sorry."

"You chose this for us."

"Peggy, you must believe I never intended this pain."

"What about Clay? I'm sure he will lose respect for the trash he married, and I'm guessing once he learns you were part of the affair, he'll feel the same about you."

"As for getting pregnant, Clay told me she was on birth control."

"Are you having me believe he discussed this with you?"

"He offered the information."

"Knowing you are sleeping with his wife?"

"He needed an ear and brotherly advice."

"I'm guessing you're the Cain to his Abel. Don't bother responding. You're pathetic."

"Please, don't say that."

"You clowns deserve each other. I hope you will agree she's not the motherly type. We've said enough," she says, slurring her words. "Surely you know me, the woman you placed a ring on, well enough to know it's not in my nature to be offensive. This tiff between us calls for my defensive team to enter the field."

For the first time in months, a sense of relief sweeps over her. "When we married, I didn't believe in divorce. However, my dear Preston, you deserve a pat on the back. I'd do it for you, but I don't trust my own strength. You've changed my mind, but you can't change history. I'm prepared to accept this is my last day with you."

Resigned, he crouches low and rests his tired body against the wall. "Let's call it a day. I'm exhausted. You must be, too. We can talk about this tomorrow."

"You can go. I'm staying. I'll spend the rest of the night reliving every time you damaged my soul. I believe you will agree those moments far outweigh the ones when you left me feeling disappointed."

"That makes no sense."

"Perhaps not to you, but for me, they opened my eyes to the man you will never become."

"What will it take for you to forgive me?"

"If I were to forgive you, we'd end up arguing about what's for dinner and who left the lights on. Each time your phone rings, I'd ask who's calling. We'd end the day with you arguing my accusation that you're lying."

Reclined in the salon's banquette, she looks at him through fresh eyes. Once a man she loved and adored, he now appears small and desperate. She wants to believe he worries about being alone, but that would be giving him credit he does not deserve. If he does not intend for Molly to be in his future, a new candidate will make her presence known once word is out he is a free man.

"I've always given you the benefit of the doubt. Your mistake was accepting what you didn't deserve. I believe you know the phrase 'separate ways.' Mine is the road to recovery. Yours is the road you and your cheating ways pave." She reaches for her drink, but wanting a clear mind, pulls back her hand. "Although each day with you is an adventure, my heart tells me I won't grieve our ending marriage. I'll be over you before the sun rises. I shudder to think what will become of you should you continue down this forbidden road. I pray you will make time to heed your personal well-being. This game of life we play far outweighs happenings in the bedroom. As for me, I believe the next chapter in my life will be the best one ever."

In the passing moments, a starboard light catches her eye. Believing her future is out there somewhere, she manages a smile.

"Please give me a chance," he again begs.

"You have blown all your chances. What a fool I've been. Your place at the mirror will remind you've been a bigger one. I find it sad that I'll never see you again, at least in the way I once believed in you."

"Let's agree that tonight's events are water under the bridge. Let's get you home. Again, I'm concerned you've had too much to drink."

"For what it's worth, I may be drunk, but you are worthless. I won't be drunk tomorrow, but you'll still be worthless. Besides, you know I drink only when I'm celebrating, or perhaps I drink not to forget, but to accept. The reasons go way back, longer than should be allowed."

"What is it you're celebrating and accepting?"

"All of my tomorrows." Growing a smile, she waves a finger in his face. "Without you, I am onward through the fog."

"Are you quoting the head shop owner in Austin, Texas?"

"If you say so. As for the old Colt," she throws a nod to the gun cabinet near the door, "it's loaded and so am I. Mark my words, I'll use it if I have to."

"Are you threatening me?"

"Promising. You asked for this shit-show the day you stepped outside our marriage."

"If we come at this together, we can fix it. I don't want this snafu to change anything between us."

"Snafu? What are you? A third-grader? My dear Preston, if I stay with you, our future promises nothing but trouble." She brushes him away with the wave of her hand. "I'm done chasing a cold heart that belongs to Molly Lambert, and I'm through playing *I love you* and *I love you not*. Every night, I evaluate how my day delivers. I'm not talking about the hours I spend volunteering at the club or the recipes I prepare hoping to make the picture pages of the annual cookbook, but matters of the heart. I realize this must be a blow to your ego, but I'm finding you don't have a place in my tomorrows. While we're at it, I'm finding people look so different when you no longer care about them."

"I'll make it up to you. All this heartache, this pain we are feeling, I'll make it right. You have my word. Believe me when I say I'm drowning here."

"Slap on a life vest. You're old enough to know it takes two to tango and three to *huachinango*."

"That makes no sense. What does red snapper have to do with us?"

"Not a damn thing. I just like saying it."

"You've lost me."

"I'm not surprised. Years of loving you had me believing in you. There was a time I believed with you at my side, I could walk on water. Now you've left me drowning. In your absence, especially in the late-night hours when you tell me you are needed at the hospital, I often find myself looking about our home and wondering if it's our bed you'll come home to or if your lover has you making a stop along the way. Those hours are a struggle. When the questions come rushing, I'm left wondering if I matter. In those moments, it takes only the blink of an eye for you to become a stranger to me. You know what I just realized? The more I drink, the more stupid you sound. I'm no longer arguing with you. I feel certain that once word of our separation is made public, a parade of ambulance-chasers will darken our doorstep. In their excitement to climb the industry's food chain, they will come at us with bumper stickers, signature coffee mugs, dollar-store key chains, and refrigerator magnets. Next thing you know, ads will be placed in Sunday's paper encouraging seasoned lawyers to skip over the racing ambulance and chase our case. I wouldn't be surprised if we end up presenting our case to Judge Judy."

"There are worse places."

"I'm not so sure."

"Ever hear of soap operas?"

"My begging words and your false promises will never return you to the man I once believed would make all my dreams come true. Before we point fingers and assign blame, you should know I'm neither upset nor angry, but I am through competing for your love and attention. If our brief marriage holds any merit, let it be that we will find a way to agree this is our crash-landing. It's not the ideal place, but my heart assures me we will find a way to survive."

He reaches for her, but knowing he cannot change her heart and his cheating ways, pulls back his hand.

"That said, you will go your way, and I'll go mine," she tells him. "Should we speak again, it will be through my lawyer. The way I see it, I need only two things—fresh air and Perry Mason."

"Raymond Burr's been dead for years. And he only played a lawyer."

"Well then, I'll call John Grisham."

"The author? Whatever for? Have you forgotten the typo you found on the pages of *Ford County*? Allow me to remind you he opened dialogue with a closed quote. I might suggest you study the chapter where Freda was fired."

"Forget Freda. She is no longer on my radar. Even in my most drunken state, I'm convinced he could turn this into a best-seller. If he's not interested, I'll call that Memphis lawyer. Oh, what is his name?"

"I'm begging you won't go making this into a novel or a life sentence."

Ignoring the warning, she searches the ceiling until the man's youthful face comes to her. "He helped that preacher's wife. In repeated interviews, the newspaper called him the best criminal lawyer this side of the Mississippi."

"If memory serves, his client shot her husband in the back with a twelve-gauge."

"What is better than a great memory?"

"Aim, I suppose."

"I'm guessing his back was her target. Although her actions are not those I would hurry to take, I give the woman credit for her steady hand. I would have shot him between the eyes and asked questions later when his pulse laid out the truth." Using the back of her hand, she wipes at a wayward tear. "I'd find a way to forgive you if you had only flirted with your eyes." Her abbreviated pause comes back with a punch. "There's an old Southern saying: *Just because you eat your soup louder doesn't mean it's better.* You have your whole life to regret your actions. That said, I wish you many birthdays."

Leaning forward and resting on her elbows, she allows a scowl to anchor her face. "I'm sure my attorney will want to speak with the usual suspects—Rick and that dentist friend of his. Let's not forget mudhen Molly. I'd love to be a fly on the wall. Oh, but I will: after all, there will be depositions. Forgive me, Preston, but I'm actually looking forward to great lawyering."

"It sounds like you're holding court here."

"Don't be silly. I'm saving that for the judge. You asked for this. Every time you turned your back on our marriage, you invited trouble. I understand her crush on you, but one should never go after another bitch's bone. Your Molly gets off manufacturing chaos. Common sense tells me you two birds of a feather deserve each other. If I ask one last thing, please let it be that you go away and leave me alone."

"Can you stay sober long enough to accept my apology?"

"I wouldn't want to."

"Are you going to be OK?"

"I got this. In recent months, in those lonely moments when you left me believing I no longer matter, I worked on my life. In the takeaway, when the silver-lining moment replaced disappointment with strength, I learned to navigate the ups and downs at a pace I'm comfortable with. My beating heart tells me I'll always land on my feet. Early on, in my learning years, when I observed happy marriages and witnessed the pain of failing ones, I knew I wanted something better than a two-star review. You should know that living with you hasn't been easy."

"Again, you're not being fair."

"Our marriage is dead in the water."

"I need to know you'll be OK."

"I'm still going to breathe and eat, and if life treats me right, I might travel the coast and play some golf."

"You don't golf."

"You haven't met the new me."

"I'd like to."

"Forget it. That ship has sailed. I may just make the Florida Keys my new home. After a morning of diving, I'll rest on a warm sandy beach, looking out over crystal clear water with a cold tropical drink in one hand and a roll of cash in the other. I think you'll agree I'll be having the last laugh."

"Peggy, please be serious."

"I'm serious as a heart attack. If I'm kicking on this side of the dirt, I'll be fine. Please go, and take that filth with you," she says, throwing her eyes to the phone Molly left behind. "One last thing: you might want to give your street-type girlfriend a Group B strep test. In the end, when you get the results, I'm betting you'll be glad you did."

CHAPTER 49

Tucked in the shadows, Molly keeps her eyes focused on the trawler. Flicking a lighter she lifted at a gas station, she takes a long drag off a cigarette. Raising her face into the night, she blows a gray plume through thin nostrils. A trio of smoke rings soon follows. The ringing of her watch's alarm has her tossing the butt to the ground.

She is set to light another cigarette when she sees Preston pacing the boat's cabin. Twice, he steps toward the door. Both times, he turns back. Minutes later, when he steps out to the dock, she paints on a winning smile. Still, an uneasy feeling warns she may have won the fight, but the battle to win Preston is far from over.

Once his Jeep clears the rolling gates and his taillights fade out of sight, she crawls out of hiding and falls into a runner's sprint. Dodging wet sand, she stomps over the golden stems Peggy admires. Thunderous skies and pulsating waves drown out her labored breathing. Going unnoticed, she makes her way to the boat.

"Who's there? Preston, is that you?" Peggy asks, looking to the door, wondering if perhaps he has realized in their final hour the pain he has caused her. Forgiveness is not in the cards, but she will hear him out. She almost feels sorry for him. He is stuck between a rock and Molly.

Earlier, when he cowered with his tail between his legs, she hoped he would tell her that Molly is nothing more than a midlife crisis. Believing he has come back to beg like the dog he is, she is surprised when the door swings open and Molly steps through it.

"Not you again," she snaps. "Your mother should have named you Boomerang."

"It appears you are drunk once again," Molly vollies back. "When it comes to you and your next pour, I'm always left waiting to see which way the wind blows. You should consider working on a cruise ship. I understand the crew pays a dollar for a cocktail. I'm guessing the bucks you take in will have you dancing on the tables."

"It has come to my attention that you're a frequent visitor to this boat. Have you nowhere to go? No place to belong? Allow me to answer for you: your actions have me believing you should be put down like a rabid dog."

"We need to talk. Woman to woman."

"Where is she?" asks Peggy.

"Who?"

"The other woman."

"What woman?"

"To talk like one requires being one."

"Peggy, knock it off. You have to know Preston belongs to me."

"You have some nerve coming here. It appears your dreams are not easily met, and your goals, however simple, are impossible to reach." Her anger growing, she worries that in the coming minutes, she might go postal. "Should you stand strong in your game to take hold of my husband, I pray the ground below you will open and suck you back into hell. As for my poor, misguided Preston, I hope he will turn his life around. If you came here looking for him, I have four words for you: better luck next time. He is probably at home washing his hands of you. Given the pain and suffering I was forced to endure today, it's only now I regret not going with him."

"I came here to talk to you."

"*To* or *with*? Surely you know the difference. I've had enough of your Tom and Jerry routine. If revenge is what you are seeking, you're in over your head."

"I'm no cat, and you're no mouse."

"I think we will agree you are something far worse."

"Take a look around. You will find I arrived here armed and dangerous. That said, I need a drink."

Peggy is quick to notice that Molly moves about the cabin with ease and familiarity. Closing in on cabinets near the sink, she opens a door knowing it is the salon's wet bar. "Might I suggest a Molly-tov cocktail? I'm sure we have plenty of fuel on board."

"To think you used to be the perfect hostess," Molly says, pouring from the bottle she enjoyed earlier in the day with Preston and his friends. "Care for a pour?"

Surprised by the gesture, Peggy turns away. "I wanted to believe we were friends."

"That was the plan."

"We welcomed you into our home."

"That was your mistake, not mine. I accepted the invitation knowing I'd end up there."

"As my husband's mistress or his secondhand mattress? I can't speak aloud what I wish for you."

Sitting tall, Molly steadies her posture. "My aim is bigger than your pea-brain can imagine on its best day. In the coming days, when Preston adjusts the scales of justice, you will be forgotten."

"Let's agree to disagree. What about Clay?"

"Don't lose sleep over him. He will be a free man. No longer a concern of mine. He's buried in debt up to his eyeballs. When he learns our marriage is over, he will rush to bid me adieu."

"And Whitt?"

"I don't give a rat's ass about Whitt. He's Clay's problem. I'm not here to kiss and make up and slap a Band-Aid on our friendship, and I sure as hell am not here to discuss them. I'm here for one reason, and one reason only. I want to know what it will take for you to let Preston go."

"To think you believe this is your place. How dare you come here placing fault on the people you pretend to love. Listen up, you trifling imbecile. From sunrise to sunset, from dawn to dusk, you and your untamed tongue have nothing to gain when you attack me. It's best you pick a lesser war—one to match your intelligence. When daylight comes and your senses are heightened, throw open your eyes. You'll find I'm still here."

"You should know this game you insist on playing, I'm playing, too. I'll win, and I'm playing for keeps. Think what you will, but you need to accept that I'm moving in."

"I'm not surprised to learn that you've failed to do your home-work." Turning away, Peggy sweeps her eyes over the salon and its black-and-white photos taken in happier times. "This is my family." Looking about the cabin, her eyebrows rise, and a challenging sneer moves over her face. "If you came here thinking you can take me on, have at it. I've never been more ready."

"He doesn't love you. He quit loving you a long time ago. It's time for you to accept that he loves me."

"Something tells me Dr. Phil would agree you're out of touch with reality. He might take the roundabout, throwing out medical jargon and referring to case studies he was once part of, but I'm pretty sure he'd arrive at the same assessment." Pausing, she allows a knowing smirk to cross her face. "Your ill-bred self is coming out in full color."

"Preston wants me."

"You are both naïve and stupid. Everything Preston says, does, and shares with you, he has said, done, and shared with me." Tired of the wine, she slides over the banquette's leather bench and makes her way to the cabin's minibar. A quick search has her mixing a gin and tonic. Adding a twist of lime, she gives the glass a gentle shake. "Here's to Preston. He introduced me to this drink on the night of our first anniversary."

Hearing these words, Molly cringes. He had done the same with her. It was not an anniversary they celebrated, but an afternoon they shared in the waters off Osprey Island.

Enjoying a lengthy sip, Peggy throws her head back, allowing the gin's slow burn to travel her throat. Feeling Molly's eyes on her, she admires the ten-carat diamond perched on her finger. "I'm guessing you didn't know that throughout our marriage, including tonight, Preston tells me my face is the one he wants to see at the end of each and every day. You tell me, does that sound like undying love?"

"Do me a favor and cut the bedtime story. He's mine." Growing quiet, Molly struggles to hide her anger. Her temperature soars as she imagines the intimacy she is denied. She would give anything to hear Preston say those words to her. If she were honest with herself, she would ask the same of Clay. There was a time he was all she wanted. Soon after they met, he wined and dined her, hoping to win her heart. When she learned he was married, she stepped up her game, demanding more from him, knowing he could only offer less. Listening to Peggy's words has her worried fire might shoot from her fingertips.

"Surely you understand anything you've experienced with Preston, he experienced first with me."

"He has done things with me he has never done with you," Molly counters.

"Oh, what a fun game. Promise you will let me play," she says with an easy laugh. "Recite the alphabet? Paint by numbers? Reading picture books? Perhaps, teaching you how to tie your shoes?"

"It's easy to see you're toying with me. Preston swore you are no longer intimate, and regarding things you've shared, you're only saying these words to get a reaction."

"Tell me, is it difficult living with a small mind?"

"I excite him," Molly snaps back. "Isn't that why we're here?"

Peggy feels the sting but will never give Molly the satisfaction of knowing how deep it hurts. She wants to shout that Preston entertains her because she is easy, cheap, and always available at his beck and call. Holding her head high, she remains on point. "After we make love, he steps from our bed, drops to his knees, and thanks the Lord for placing me in his life. I can't recall a single time he hasn't given thanks. It's interesting that in recent days he has added to his prayer.

What is it? Oh, yes. Something about our marriage is an everlasting one. Speaking of bedtime, shouldn't you be returning to your coffin in a dark dungeon somewhere?"

"Unlike you, I know and encourage his sexual fetishes and fantasies. I believe we agree I deliver on both. While he was down on his knees, did he find my lipstick under your bed? What about the bra I left under your pillow? If you're not wearing it, I'd like to have it back."

The knife to Peggy's heart takes a hard and deep turn. She found the lipstick and the bra, but when asked, Preston half-heartedly intimated the cat had something to do with it. While she did not buy his story, she hoped he would turn his life around. "Tell me, Molly, is it me you're trying to convince, or is panic seeping under your decaying carcass? Perhaps, it's the face looking back at you each time you darken a mirror that gives you cause for concern."

Searching for words and waving her hand about, Molly attempts to respond.

Throwing out her hand, Peggy cuts her off. "I think you need to leave. You are a horrible breed of evil. Your actions here tonight, and all those leading up to this night, will no doubt lead to your downfall."

"Preston despises you. You don't stand a chance. He wishes you were …"

"Dead?" she interrupts. "Quite the contrary. He needs me."

"You're mistaken. I'm what Preston needs to further his career."

"Further his career? Forget the future. One might say it appears you're living in the past. Trust me when I say your ticket to the future expired when our dear Preston returned to me. The community will shun him if he leaves me for the likes of you. My words aren't meant to belittle you. You do that in your own actions. You came here tonight, your reasons unknown to me, but should push come to shove, I'm willing to bet a trifecta ticket you will fail to win, place, or show. I'm not begging for you to leave my husband alone, but simply talking woman to woman, much like the time you shared with me that you caught Preston kissing another woman." Along with a smirk, she gives a knowing laugh. "In spite of his faults, and there are many, he's a man to be respected. If he were to leave me for you, a ruthless commoner, his reputation will be forever tarnished. Tell me, is this what you want for him?"

"As for his reputation, he will rise above this. He tells me your marriage is over and without passion."

"My dear, ignorant Molly, I'll give you this. It appears you take destroying another's marriage to a whole new level. If you are anything, it's a dreg of society—nothing but dead weight. If these words are foreign to you, I'll break it down. You are a failure on many levels. When it comes to our nation's population, you are the most undesirable. I'm sure Preston has told you many things, simple words he knows you need to hear. I would be willing to bet he had to explain these words to you as if you are still learning the alphabet. With you, he pretends to be a badass. I, however, know him as the ass he is."

"You're wrong. You know nothing about him. You talk a big game, but all he wants is to live on the boat and venture out to sea. He loves me. We are soul mates and best friends. I swear he said these words to me. Why can't you accept that you are no longer important to him?"

"This coming from a backwoods mistress defending her sea captain," she says with a laugh. The blow hurts, but she will cut off her arm before she will let it show. "Such poetic words for a home-wrecker. Sounds a bit cliché, would you agree? Why did you come here? A lover's spat, perhaps? Or is it ignorance and insanity that guide you?"

The fight with Preston was far more than a spat. She had no way of knowing she would end up here having this conversation with Peggy. "I've already told you. I came here to tell you your marriage is over."

"To think you believe this is your duty amazes me. I would think you would be hounding Preston to leave me. Despite your assessment, Preston and I have survived some tough times. I must assume because you're sleeping with my husband, your marriage has as well. In my marriage, however, as love would have it, Preston and I have grown closer through all of them. We will survive this … oh, what should I call it?" she says, snapping slender fingers, "this *nonsense* with you. Seriously, I don't understand what he sees in you."

"His future. I know everything about him and what makes him happy—things you no longer do for him."

"Given your presence here tonight, and all those when your actions were meant to destroy my marriage, I'm left believing you are fully aware Preston is not a grower, but a show-er. When asked about his low-hanging fruit, he tends to give a grin before looking away. Accepting little rises after the midnight hour, he hopes his words to you are his ego speaking. You're obviously not bright enough to notice, but he takes satisfaction in watching your insecurity fester. Are you aware he leaves the night-light on in the bathroom? Poor Preston. His bladder is the size of a peanut. Perhaps you're referring to the foot massage his tired feet require after a long day at the hospital. I'm certain you've learned he likes to have his bottom rubbed in a circular motion, much like a windmill, until your hands tire. Speaking of hands, did he share with you that he falls asleep holding mine?"

Rolling her eyes, Molly sits ready to come unglued. Preston has never once reached for her hand or asked for a massage. "Cut the crap. We're not writing a romance novel here. You can't fool me with your nonsense. We both know Preston is not a hand-holder."

"It amuses me that you think eye-rolling bothers me. You can't fool me. You've been watching us. You were outside our window, looking in at a life you want." Images of Preston alone with Molly race through her head. A lonely tear threatens to escape, but she will not allow it. "Surely you've noticed the baby in him still needs to be burped. Perhaps you are unaware I still flavor his scrambled eggs and grits with a dash of hot sauce. Should you need to hear more, he over-salts his food, yawns loudly while stretching his back, and although I argue the echo, whistles tunes in the shower I've never heard before."

Growing silent, she wants only to put an end to this game of Ping-Pong Preston. "That afternoon when I first met you, we were on the boat. Clay whispered that you were from a town of not many. You laughed along, but the look on your face was one of shame. I find it interesting your husband intentionally embarrassed you."

There is no denying Peggy's words strike a nerve, but Molly is not here to talk about herself or her marriage, only to destroy one. "Preston needs me. I give him what you don't. I'm not here to debate who owns the stake but to claim it."

"That's it? Your best argument wrapped up in three simple sentences?"

"I'm speaking the truth. If I'm not in Preston's future, he will soon be with someone else. You don't do it for him. I know it must be a hard pill to swallow, but it is what it is."

"I have to say, if I'm grateful for anything, it's knowing we were not cut from the same cloth. It's becoming clear to me that you've been engineering this since the day Clay joined Preston's practice."

An evil grin creeps over Molly's face. "You opened the door, and I'm stepping through it. I'm ready to come clean, even if it means tangling with hell and its consequences." With bated breath, she slams an open hand on the table. "I've been orchestrating this since the day I first laid eyes on him. The beauty of it is, you both played right into it. I was eighteen at the time."

"So, even then, your faculties were in question."

"It's the fire in me."

"I believe you mean the bitch in you."

"That too, but you must admit I'm an expert. The Expert Mistress. Perhaps, I should write a how-to book."

"What are you going to call it? *The Home-Wrecker*? *My Cheating Ways*? *Messed-Up Molly*? Any words you put in print will never be fine qualities any man would admire. Preston can be so foolish at times. I find it sad he prefers circus to class. Given my upbringing and the life I've lived, I believe a woman like you would know her place. One would think Preston would grow tired of your games and getups."

"I own the game, and I make the rules," Molly retorts. "Not that it's any of your business, but my getups have him leaving your bed and jumping into mine. These are my tools for a solid future. In case you haven't noticed, I'm good at taking what doesn't belong to me. Remember that white rug? Planned the spill. Your fish tank?" she says, clawing the air. "Blame it on Jupiter. I wish you could have seen her pawing away at your precious seahorses. I had to look away. It was more than I could stomach. Thanks to your kitty cat, I now look at sushi through different eyes. Tell me, have you been missing your robe?" Wrapping her arms around her shoulders, she purrs like a feral cat. "Fits like a glove."

"On top of all your other faults, which are many and continue to multiply, it appears you are a killer and a thief. When the time comes, and it will, you will be judged not only by your peers but also your victims. Look around and listen closely. I'll be front row and center. Mark my words, my voice will be the loudest. You should know, I'll be holding the gavel and the first to cry out for a public hanging," she says, resisting the urge to throw her hands around Molly's neck. "Go home, Molly. There isn't anything here for you."

"I disagree. Ready or not, here I come, and I'm coming for Preston. Your marriage is over. He tells me, quite often I might add, that you are jealous of me."

"I'm neither jealous of you nor wish to be you. Once again, that's Preston's ego speaking and your insecurity showing. It appears you're so desperate for a man, you'll settle for a married one who cheats on his wife. I once found you amusing and, often, entertaining. Now I find you psychotic. I see in you a woman filled with evil, doubt, and fear." Holding her breath, she pauses to watch the stab go deep into Molly's thick skin. "You're living up to your reputation."

"While that may be true, there is no stopping this freight train."

"I've heard enough. I've already forgotten you and the pain you've thrown at me. Please go and take your mean spirit with you. If you can't find the door, I'll map it out for you."

"You should know I'm moving into your marriage one visit at a time. I'm not going anywhere. You can count on it. One more thing. You know those famous Peggy-ritas you brag about? Well, they're not so famous. They taste like suntan lotion."

Peggy brushes a stray hair from her forehead and tucks it behind her ear. Sitting tall, she allows her posture to speak of unyielding confidence and growing strength. "It will be over my dead body that he will go to you."

"Don't think for one second that hasn't crossed my mind. Just so you know, he's worth killing for," she says, making her way to the door.

"This is not your marriage to step into," Peggy shouts at her back.

"Oh, but it is," Molly says, slamming the door behind her.

A glance at her watch tells Peggy it is long after midnight. Her speech is slurred, and in her attempt to walk the floor, she sways from side to side. An untimely trip over a chair leg sends her sailing through the cabin. A crash-landing against the wall and a bleeding elbow convinces her driving home is no longer an option.

Alone on the boat and forced to revisit the evening's events, she wonders how long sanity can carry her. There will be no therapy, marriage counseling, or holding hands in prayer. She and Preston will never again share a bed, home, or marriage. Holidays will be lonely, and her role at the yacht club will slowly come to an end. Should the board beg her to stay, she will explain that she will not risk running into Preston, especially if Molly has him on a short leash.

An annoying growl from her stomach reminds her she needs to eat. A glance in the boat's mini-fridge offers little. Except for a trace of mold the housekeeper continues to overlook at each cleaning, the top shelf is empty. A block of smoked Gouda, thinly sliced Prosciutto, and a sleeve of saltines rest on the middle shelf. A peek inside silver foil she tosses to the galley's counter reveals a sliver of dark chocolate. When a handful of limes roll about in the pullout drawer, she entertains the idea of making a margarita, but a brewing headache suggests now is not the time to mix wine and gin with tequila. Another cry from her stomach has her calling dibs on the chocolate and saltines.

Hearing only her breathing, she questions why the last night of her marriage should end this way. Better memories come at her—returning her to the best of times she now wants to go after with a chainsaw.

Forced to leave Preston, she curses into her heart that she will never forgive him. In a passing moment she will never forget, she eyes the glass and lipstick Molly's lying mouth left behind. Rushing out to the poop deck, she hurls the glass and her love for Preston into the water.

"Good riddance. As for you, Poseidon and Neptune, this boat has been cursed from the beginning. Legend tells me a renaming ceremony removes its curses, but I've experienced only pain. Unless weaker gods guide you, the blessings bestowed on this vessel are empty and worthless. My husband is a cheat, and his mistress is a bottom-dweller. I want all the world to know she can have his sorry ass."

Too tired to think and with her vision blurred by the alcohol, she wishes to numb not only the pull in her heart, but the pain she has been suffering for so long, she cannot pinpoint its onset. Returning inside, she makes her way to the aft cabin—the scene of Preston's broken promises and countless sins.

Outside the open window, a raging wind moves in from the south. Growing quiet, she listens as it circles the deck like a drunken sailor. Deprived of adrenaline and fresh air, she moves to the window, where she invites the salty air and the light of the moon to embrace her. Earlier in the evening, when the sun floated on the water, she admired a gentle wave as it moved over the marina like silken velvet. Given the evening's events, she wishes she had jumped on it or held Molly under it.

Observing the cabin through hungry eyes, an uneasy feeling has her believing the old teak walls beg to whisper secrets she is not ready to hear. Kicking off her shoes and crawling over the blanket, she rests against the bed's pillows. The last time she slept on the boat, Preston's cries pulled her from sleep. Pacing the floor and sweating at the brow, he swore a sea monster tangled up in sea grapes and wild brown algae was calling out to him. Now, she blames his twisted affair for the nightmare.

As the evening's events play over in her head, one thing becomes certain: she needs a lawyer. Accepting that her breath smells like a fraternity house during rush week, she understands the time has come to call Neyland, the attorney she and Preston turn to when matters require legal advice.

In the string of misdials, she apologizes to a woman who shares she is about to snake her way up the dance pole, a mother with a crying baby, and a man who begs to meet up for a nightcap. It is after the next call goes to an answering machine she realizes her mistake. Searching the phone's directory, she places a call to Neyland's office, where a recording promises he will return her call.

"Neyland, this is Peggy Fayne. I need you to handle my divorce. I might suggest you read up on that Mississippi case—the one where the jilted spouse of the cheating wife sued her lover on the grounds of alienation of affection. I believe it is referred to as the heartbalm tort." Although exhausted, she provides her cell phone number before ending the call.

Moving about like a drunken slug, she slips out of her clothes and into the cabin's slim shower. It takes the blink of an eye to regret a glance in the vanity's slim mirror. Unlike Preston, the mirror never lies. Ashen circles under her eyes remind she has not slept in days. While a stream of warm water travels over her tired body, she blames the thirteen pounds she has lost in recent weeks on stress and deceit. Although the chill she felt earlier has passed, a shiver runs through her. An uneasy feeling warns that her struggles are just beginning.

Returning to the unmade bed, she holds the blue and white pillow against her chest. Memories of the afternoon she found the pillow in a small boutique at Hilton Head's famed Harbour Town pull at her heart. Preston had gone sailing with seasoned sailors he'd met that morning at breakfast. She was invited to join them, but instead chose to explore the island's local shops and boutiques. She was over the top when she presented the nautical pillow to him on his birthday. It is only now she questions his forced interest.

Pressed against the bed's headboard, she reaches for a bed pillow. A hint of Taboo, Molly's signature perfume, comes flying at her, nearly sending her over the edge. Positioned like a punter at a championship game, she kicks the pillow across the cabin. Squeezing her eyes closed, she imagines their conversations. She would not be surprised to learn they shared a laugh or two at her expense. Envisioning their lovemaking sucks the air from her lungs. Forced to face the truth, one question continues to play over and over in her head: *How could he do this to me?*

CHAPTER 50

M olly steps over the small gate onto the deck. Finding the cabin's door unlocked, she creeps inside and turns the lock.

A low light over the sink guides her through the salon to the aft cabin, where she expects to find Peggy sprawled out on the bed. Low snores floating on the air let her know the lush is sleeping soundly.

"If these walls could talk, you would never rest your head on those pillows," she whispers. "Look at you, Peggy Fayne, all used up and nowhere to go. Looks like you don't have a wooden leg after all." Lifting Peggy's arm into the air and releasing it from her grip, she watches it take a hard landing on the bed. "You should stick with those Peggy-ritas you're so fond of."

Inches from her lover's wife, she is surprised when her thoughts turn to her childhood, her parents' screaming matches, and the punches they threw soon after beer cans hit the dinner table. Rumors and whispered voices told her she was conceived out of wedlock in a room without love. Looking back at her life, she understands she has come a long way since the cold-water flat her parents rented in a rooming house without air-conditioning or a fresh coat of paint.

At a young age, she embraced the aquamarine two-door fridge her mother rescued from the curb in the early morning hours before the garbage truck traveled the narrow street. Shoved deep into a dark corner inches away from a four-burner cooktop held hostage by the once-popular cane-printed wallpaper, it held the barest of essentials. On a good day, when her stepfather scored a paycheck, a crusty ketchup bottle shared a shelf with a six-pack, a staple on their dinner table. When money was tight, a cracked drawer was home to table scraps and a slim package of bologna her mother would later fry in a cast-iron skillet with garlic and onions.

A rotary phone mounted on unpainted plywood inside the home's small vestibule was shared with three households and answered by Myra Elfring, the county's party-line operator. Sundays were spent crawling over old logs and bouncing on discarded tractor tires her stepfather swiped from the city dump. When their neighbors were away, she picked apricots from a row of trees planted decades earlier to divide the properties.

Asbestos threatened the clapboard house, and their apartment had electricity only when her deadbeat stepfather remembered to pay the bill. After months of nonpayment, the utility company was forced to install a coin-operated meter. "No quarter, no lights," the old man reminded each time he came to collect the coins.

In his spare time, her stepfather salvaged used car parts. Although he never made a sale, he roamed the neighboring counties like a worldly collector. It was not long before bruised fenders and blown tires lined their gravel driveway. When her stepfather had gas money, he drove an older-model Starcraft van. Vinyl seats held dirt, nail clippings—some painted, others torn from the bed—and food crumbs. Knotted fur circled the steering wheel. One night, in the late evening hours, a smiley-face sticker was slapped onto the mangled bumper. Unlike the neighbor's van, the Starcraft's foldout sleeper never saw any action.

A beer-drinking fool, her stepfather threw back the lager like tomorrow was not on the horizon. When dinner hit the table, he slopped his food like a fat pig in a sty. Decades of smoking unfiltered cigarettes left him diagnosed with nose cancer. His diagnosis came from a hospital in Jackson, but given the distance, he sought treatment at

Mercy General. He was celebrating the all-clear when his body was found afloat in brackish water. Although his family argued he died from natural causes, a death certificate confirmed he choked to death on a chicken wing. As a young child in a small town, she grew tired of the jokes intimating her stepfather chickened out.

Weeks before his passing, her stepfather, whose tired name was no longer remembered by the locals who often drank beer with him, cleared pastures and moved dirt for a local landscape company owned by two brothers and a young woman built like Brigitte Bardot who was rumored to be the owner's mistress. He did not know a hill of beans about Mississippi's soil, but when cornered, he promised a fruitful garden to the farmers who shucked out big bucks for his dedication and hard labor.

Six months after his untimely death, her mother married a balding man she met at a horse auction. He owned a modest cabin on a lake several miles from the town's main road. It was not long before the man—who she was initially unsure about, but eager to call Dad—sexually abused her. In the early evening, while her mother threw together a simple dinner, she was encouraged to sit on her stepfather's lap. Believing his actions would go unnoticed, he caressed her bottom and fondled her budding breasts.

Her mother observed these violations on several occasions, but afraid to rock the boat, she turned a blind eye. Few tears were shed when he lost his life in a car accident the following summer. Soon after his passing, Molly's mother skipped town in the dead of night.

Left without parents, she was ordered by a county judge to live with relatives she had never met. She packed up and shipped out to a rent-controlled unit where she slept pressed against a wall in a small bed she shared with her grandmother, a bitter woman who shuffled about in a plaid duster from sunup to sundown and all the hours in between. Each night before turning out the room's floor lamp, she closed the room's accordion door. A pee-pot propped against the paper-thin door kept it closed until morning.

The elderly woman drank like a fish and smelled like low tide.

Each time she wet the bed, which was almost nightly, Molly backed up against the wall and locked bent knees into her grandmother's back. She moved to the sofa when her grandmother's trickle changed direction. Instead of keeping with the southern flow, it streamed due west. The sofa did not smell much better, but it was dry.

Penniless and dirt poor, she tossed aside sidewalk chalk and stuffed toys. In the rare moments when she was encouraged to speak of her future, she spoke of living among the wealthy in a life free to order a second round of drinks without counting on fingers a tip to the check. She scribbled in a nickel diary her wish to travel the world. First on her list was California's rocky coastline and its treacherous Big Sur. If time allowed, she wanted to take a swing on Pebble Beach's seventh hole overlooking the Pacific Ocean, and later, order a cocktail with one of those fancy umbrellas. Dinner would begin with an onion loaf and end with two scoops of butter pecan, her favorite ice cream.

In recent years, she has come to understand that she is like her mother: lost and lonely, and often confusing quiet moments with a sense of loss. It is only now she realizes it is not Preston she wants. He is a necessary temptation, and she wishes only to be appreciated in the many ways he adores Peggy. She knows all too well he has a difficult time remaining faithful to those he pretends to love: after all, he had done the same to her years earlier. She had not meant for their affair to turn out like this—a game she must win. The cards just fell that way.

Still, she has fought too hard and too long to throw in her hand, and giving up now will not solve her problems but add to them. No man will ever match the fire she and Preston enjoy. If she ends their affair, she can never return to his office. Idle gossip among the staff would drive her crazy, and if Clay got wind of it, he would kick her and her cheating ways to the curb. A myriad of questions rush at her, but one is the loudest: *Why must I always be the victim of another's poor choice?*

She pulls a cigarette from the soft pack and lights it with a butane lighter she retrieves from the bedside table. She is enjoying the burn when a smile crosses over her face. Tonight's performance was nothing short of stellar. Preston is all hers, and that is better than any Hollywood trophy. When a yawn escapes, she glances at her watch. The late hour tells her it is time to go. Preston is surely waiting for her. She is preparing to adios Peggy when her eyes fall on her purse.

She pokes Peggy's leg, and for good measure, pokes it again. "Peggy Fayne, I do believe you are three sheets to the wind. Two, if you were on a sailboat."

Quicker than a common purse-snatcher, she grabs the bag. "Well, well, Peggy's got a brand-new bag." The smooth leather feels like warm butter, and its rich, gold chain smells of money. She considers taking it with her but quickly realizes she has bigger fish to fry. A quick search with sticky fingers has her thirty dollars richer and the proud owner of designer sunglasses.

Taking a long drag off the cigarette, she casts the burning butt toward the open window. When the cigarette misses the window, she watches in horror as it meets the wall and ricochets to the blanket. Pressing her hands together, she wonders what to do until a rich, earthy scent floats on the air. She considers dousing the bed with water, but if this is a false alarm, she will be forced to deal with a drunken Peggy and, possibly, an angry Preston. On the other hand, Peggy might roll over and put out any fires that might be growing.

Panic sets in when a slim tower of gray smoke catches her eye. As if on cue, smoke fills the cabin, and with each hot ember, the fire grows. When a hungry flame travels over the crumpled bedding, she jumps aside, taking the cash and sunglasses with her. Worry comes flying at her when she understands that her actions, whatever they might be, will forever alter the future—not only hers, but also Preston's. Just when she decides she cannot risk crawling over Peggy, a spark ignites her hair. Fearing for her own, Molly tosses long tresses over her shoulder.

Rubbing her hands together, she worries she will never find the words to explain her presence here tonight, especially to Preston. While her heart threatens to implode, the voice of reason arrives and hurries its way to her head. There is no way she can do time in prison.

She learned early on in her childhood that orange is not a color she should wear. If convicted, she will promise to turn over a new leaf while demanding a black jumpsuit: one with a gold zipper down the back and a matching belt.

The thought of being the bitch to a Cajun named Yolanda who takes liberties with an iron towel hook stolen from the community shower sends a chill up her spine. Should solitary confinement be in her future, the sound of a prison door slamming behind her sends a shiver through her. A sensitive stomach warns blanched prison food and twice-cooked beans will throw a cramp into her digestive system. If sentenced, she will likely miss a warm breeze at her face, sunbathing on the beach, and late-night television.

"There is no way I can do time in the slammer. I have weekly manicures scheduled with that crazy lady every Friday," she says, hoping her whispered words will not wake the dead. Hearing only the beating of her heart, she decides to push aside any guilt and move on. After all, it is only a cigarette. If she is going to survive, now is the time to run. Grabbing the cash, sunglasses, and the leather purse, she makes a beeline for the door where she washes her hands of the pickle Peggy Fayne got herself into.

In her rush to escape, she does not notice when the purse slips from her hand.

CHAPTER 51

It is long after midnight, and Casino Beach looks like a scene out of a Tom Clancy novel. Helicopters circle overhead, sirens blare, and reporters sit ready to share breaking news. Blue and white lights flash in rhythm while approaching officers outfitted in Kevlar vests with ballistic plates, military-grade combat helmets, and gun-mounted weapon lights race to the slip.

A symphony of sirens drowns out the roaring crowd, and police whistles go ignored. SureFires, Nitecores, and smoke bombs light up the sky, while search dogs trained to sniff out arson and contraband are taken off-leash. Those in the know understand that answers will come long after the questions.

Captains aboard neighboring boats alert the harbormaster, police, and fire department of soaring flames and the ashy scent of burning wood. Worried for their own crafts, they cut rope and pull anchor.

Slips away, in a space east of the lighthouse, the captain of a sixty-eight-foot red-hulled Azimut places an emergency call to the marina's security guard.

"A spark is threatening my craft," he says. Should he step out to the yacht's generous deck, it is likely he will jump ship, as thick, gray clouds warn a fire is underway and possibly heading his direction.

Fearing the growing fire will jump onto their boats, owners of large crafts motor out of the marina and into the channel.

Engines from nearby fire departments arrive on the scene equipped with heat-resistant TAC lights, battle-vision glasses, and night-vision goggles. Ready to enforce state and federal laws regarding boat and water safety, a team from the Department of Marine Resources Dispatch and Emergency is close behind.

While many questions drift over the water, "Is anyone on the boat?" is the loudest.

CHAPTER 52

"Dr. Fayne? This is Kenny from the harbormaster's house. You need to get down here. Your boat is on fire."

Preston struggles to match a face with the name. Shaking the cobwebs from his head, he quickly recalls the pimply-faced boy who almost always wears a look of surprise. "I'm sorry, Kenny, what are you saying?"

"Your boat is on fire. There are huge flames coming from the aft cabin. I was told to call you. I'm not really sure what's happening, but there's a filming crew near your slip."

"Filming crew?"

"There's a guy with a camera and a lady in a dress. I think she's a reporter with one of the local stations."

Sleepy-eyed, Preston sweeps a searching hand over the bed. Forgetting the events that took place earlier in the evening, he is surprised to find Peggy's side of the bed untouched. "I'm confused. I have two boats at the marina. A sailboat and a trawler."

"The trawler, sir."

"I'm on my way."

Tossing the bedding aside and flipping on lights, he calls out Peggy's name. Running through the house, he steps into each room along the way. Finding the rooms untouched, panic grows, and breathing becomes a struggle. He does not need a doctor to know his pulse is racing faster than his legs. Struggling to recall bits and pieces of the evening's broken conversations and left fearing the worst, he grabs the phone.

"Kenny, this is Dr. Fayne. It's possible my wife is on the boat. Please have someone search it. The spare key to the cabin is in a copper box just left of the bell."

Knowing seconds matter, he throws on the scrubs he stepped out of before this nightmare began. Grabbing a ring of keys, he races from the house.

Ignoring posted speed limits, he blows through red lights, stop signs, and, in posted areas, failing to yield, all the while praying there has been a mistake. Fueled by fear and uncertainty, he slaps the steering wheel. Through an abbreviated breath, he realizes Peggy is the only woman he has ever loved. Ignoring the state's cell phone laws, he calls her phone. When the call goes to voicemail, a sixth sense warns she is in trouble.

A roadblock flooded with rubberneck traffic, likely composed of curious onlookers who sit ready to snap photos they will later share on social media, has him inching along in traffic. When an opening allows, he pulls over to the road's slim shoulder. Stepping from the car, he watches an ambulance, its lights flashing and sirens blaring, fly by him. A contingent of police cars follows close behind.

On his approach to the marina, a dank, heavy odor rushes at him. In the coming minutes, thick smog rushes his lungs. He prays the stench is a camper's fire and not burning flesh. In a flash, the pungent smell of diesel fuel and burning wood makes its way over the marina while searchlights falling from a chopper likely stationed at Keesler Air Force Base expose the growing crowd traveling the Low Mile. Shielding his face, he eyes dark, growing clouds. Looking out over the water, he watches the *Wet Hen* making her way out of the channel.

Kicking up sand, he navigates slow-moving cars exiting the marina until a uniformed officer cuts him off.

"I'm sorry, sir. No one is allowed beyond this point," the officer says, throwing out a hand.

"You have to let me through."

The officer, a rookie with dark hair and ruddy cheeks, does not budge. His face is serious, and his hand sits ready on his holster.

"That's my boat," Preston shouts over sirens and moving traffic.

"I'm just following orders."

"You're not listening. That boat on fire is mine."

Overhead, a helicopter travels the Low Mile. Coming in from the east, a fast-moving Mooney Ovation 2 DX travels over the coast. Turning south, it trails behind a drone circling the marina. After a third go-round, the chopper flies due east of the marina while the Mooney heads south. In the blink of an amateur's eye, the drone circumnavigates the coast before returning to the sand.

Out of the corner of his eye, Preston watches a police car, its lights flashing, escort a tow truck with a small car strapped to its flatbed trailer. It is not an unusual sight in general, but rare at the marina. Believing its driver parked the car in a restricted area, he brushes off any thoughts of foul play.

"What is your name, sir?" asks the officer.

"Preston Fayne."

"I need you to stay right here," the officer says, displaying a no-nonsense face.

Standing under the lights the search planes offer, Preston watches the officer talk in a whisper to someone on the radio. Although only minutes have passed, it feels like hours when the officer finally returns.

"Someone is coming for you," he says.

"You don't understand. It's possible my wife is on the boat."

Left standing on the sidelines, Preston watches rescue units and fire engines surround the marina. Within seconds of parking their tires and cutting their engines, they watch as angry flames engulf the boat. An explosion at the fueling station throws a threat toward the marina's west side, coming within inches of moored boats and anchored vessels. Thick smoke rises from the rubble, and growing flames hurry to light up the sky.

Breaking through the crowd, Preston pushes onlookers aside and elbows those who refuse to budge. He dodges officers in uniform and serpentines through the parade of cars parked along the beach. In his race to the boat, he loses his breath and a leather loafer. Stumbling to the ground, he kicks wet sand into the faces of curious onlookers who deny safe passing.

"Watch where you're going," a voice shouts.

Foregoing apologies, he hurries along the marina's west side. Up ahead, a woman holds a cell phone to the sky. When she turns to share a laugh with the crowd growing around her, he stops dead in his tracks.

"Dana," he yells over the commotion.

"Hey, Dr. Fayne. What are you doing here?" Lurking in the dark, she tears away from the crowd.

"I was about to ask you the same question."

"I was driving by the marina when I saw smoke."

"Have you seen Peggy?"

"No. I've only been here a few minutes."

Sirens and flashing lights up ahead force him into the shadows. "Come with me."

Uniformed officers stepping out of black-and-whites are next to arrive on the scene. A large man whose jacket identifies him as the fire marshal greets them. The respect shown him reveals he is a seasoned officer.

A tall man in a lightweight jacket throws a beam of light over the marina, forcing Preston to take cover behind a slide-out fifth-wheel camper.

"What are you hiding from?" Dana asks, lowering her voice.

"I'm not hiding. I'm trying to get to my burning boat. I have reason to believe Peggy might be in danger," he says, peeking around the camper's spare tire. "She was on the boat when I went home."

"Stay with me. I'll be your alibi."

"I don't need an alibi."

"You might if your wife is on your burning boat."

"Stop right there, Dr. Fayne," a voice booms. "I'm Detective Ray Robak."

"Stay here, Dana," Preston orders. "No need for you to get involved."

"But I'm worried for you."

"Go, Dana. There is no reason for you to be dragged into this."

"I want to help you."

"Dr. Fayne, please step into the light," Robak throws out.

"Run, Dana—run like the wind and don't look back. I'll explain later."

"Dr. Fayne," Robak says, putting the spotlight on Preston. "I'm hoping you can shed some light on what took place here tonight. Step out here where I can see you, and bring your friend with you."

"Return to the crowd," Preston whispers to Dana. Wide-eyed and wearing a look of fear on his face, he staggers over the sand.

"Go after the girl," Robak orders an officer standing nearby. "Are you Preston Fayne?" he asks, throwing the light on Preston's face.

"I am."

"Are you carrying any weapons?"

"No."

"How about a cell phone?"

"Since when is a cell phone considered a weapon?"

"I repeat, are you carrying a cell phone?"

"I use it to stay in contact with my office."

"I'm going to need it. You might be surprised to learn there wasn't a call for help."

"You are not getting my phone without a warrant."

"It's coming."

"I've done nothing wrong."

"I can't agree or disagree. I repeat, I'm requesting your phone."

"Why?"

"It's what we do in these circumstances."

"What are you talking about?"

"Foul play. Possibly murder."

"How can you accuse me when we don't have answers?"

"I'm not accusing."

"I don't understand."

"Reasonable cause and circumstantial evidence."

"Am I to believe that while I'm concerned for my wife's safety, you're worried about my phone?" A glance at the detective's large, rough hands hints he has done construction work, or perhaps toiled with an engine. Scuffed leather loafers show signs of wear and tear while fraying laces slowly lose their stronghold. "I don't know what happened here tonight. I've been home for hours."

"The harbormaster confirmed you were here tonight. We also have witnesses who claim to have heard loud voices coming from your boat."

"Peggy, my wife, and I argued. It was nothing, really. She said something about staying on the boat. I went home. Is she OK? Where is my wife? If she's still on the boat, she is in grave danger."

"Dr. Fayne, if you will, please come with me."

"Not without my lawyer."

"That can be arranged."

Hearing an explosion, Preston turns to find a growing tower of red-hot flames. A cloud of black smoke fills the air. Throwing his hands over his ears, he tries to tune out the high shrills and gut-wrenching screams from those who have gathered to watch, including Dana, who, giving a wink, hurries to position her phone's camera.

CHAPTER 53

"It's too soon to tell, but it appears the fire originated from a burning cigarette," the fire marshal shares with a straight face.

"How can you be sure?" a voice cries out.

"I applaud the work of first responders and law enforcement. The area is still active," the marshal shares. "We are not taking questions at this time, so I'm asking that unless you are a member of law enforcement or the immediate family, please withhold all questions and comments."

Before proceeding, he gives a heads-up to Detective Robak, who, walking at a Southern pace, joins him at his side.

"The mattress was ignited. A partially burned body was found in the aft cabin." The marshal, a big man with reddish skin and a raised scar from his elbow to his thumb, widens his stance. "The aft cabin was a death trap."

"What are you saying?" a woman asks.

"Are you with law enforcement?"

"No, sir."

"I'll let it slide this time. Again, I'm asking that questions be kept to a minimum. The engine room is beneath the salon. When a match is thrown to it, hundreds of gallons of fuel can cause a great deal of damage."

"I've never seen Peggy light anything more than a candle," Preston lets go.

"Burning candles are responsible for over 18,000 fires annually," the fire marshal reminds.

Searching the crowd, Robak calls a stone-faced man to his side. Lowering his voice, he whispers words meant to instill fear. When the man returns to his place in the crowd, Robak puts his eyes on Preston. "It appears we have a Jane Doe on our hands." Expecting Preston to collapse, he is caught by surprise when he witnesses a look of relief.

"It's not Peggy. It's someone else."

An officer carrying a clear plastic bag comes forward from the crowd. Instructed by her supervisor, she hands it over to Robak.

"We believe this purse belonged to the victim," he shares, holding the bag close to his chest.

Preston recognizes the purse. If memory serves, he gave it to Peggy last year in the days leading up to Christmas. He reaches for the purse, but pulls back his hand when the detective's face gives warning.

"As long as we have a Jane Doe on our hands, this purse is evidence."

"Where is she? Where is Peggy?"

"Have you filed a missing person's report? Anyone know where she might be?"

"If you are trying to pin any foul play on me, you are wasting precious time. She was alive and well when we parted."

"What's your definition of *well*?"

"The events of the evening weren't perfect, but I left the boat believing we would work out our problems. She just needed time."

Robak throws on forensic gloves he accepts from an officer standing at his side. Wanting to share the truth's evidence, he questions the driver's license recovered from the purse.

"Do you mind telling me your wife's legal name?"

"Margaret Fayne."

"She have a birthmark, scars, or any imperfections or identifying marks?"

Fearing any words he says will come back to haunt him, he answers with only three: "Peggy is perfect."

"The body will be transported to the state crime lab in Pearl, where pathology reports will take place. I can't say when, but you'll be notified for identification."

Dead-eyed and shaken, Preston staggers over the sand. Inching along, he refuses to accept Peggy has become known as *the body*. "Her car isn't here," he says. Waving a hand, he invites the detective to see for himself. "You have to believe me. There's been a mistake. I know how it must look, but I'm telling you, you are wrong."

"It is not my place to hold court on the sand. Experience and convictions always tell a different story. The facts tell that a woman suffered and died from smoke inhalation on your boat. We've been given reason to believe your wife rented a car this afternoon." Hoping to gain useful information, he does not disclose that charred remains of the rental agreement were rescued in the search.

Revisiting the evening's events, Preston's thoughts turn to the tow truck and the car it carried on its flatbed trailer. Hanging his head, he struggles to wrap his head around the night's unfolding. It is not like Peggy to go great lengths to corner him. He confessed to the affair and, in the same breath, begged forgiveness. Surely when cooler heads prevail, she will find it in her heart to forgive him and return home.

"I'd like to go aboard," he says.

Once again, the fire marshal positions his large frame like a wide-end receiver. "That's not going to happen. The FBI, the Department of Marine Resources, and the Mississippi Fire Investigators need to do their jobs. They don't need anyone, especially you, underfoot."

"I just need to show that you are mistaken."

"Water hoses have caused a great deal of damage to the boat, and we're still extinguishing hot spots in the aft cabin and engine room. No civilians, you included, are allowed on board." Puffing his chest, he stands ready to act should Preston attempt to bolt by him. "I'm sorry, Dr. Fayne. As of now, the boat and the surrounding area is a crime scene. You should know there will be an inquest."

"A judicial inquiry? My wife isn't dead."

"I can't comment at this time," he says, displaying an easy nod meant to convey understanding.

"I understand you own the boat with two partners," Robak interrupts.

"If you are wanting an answer, then yes."

"My job comes with paperwork and government forms," he says, displaying a look of shame. "Another example of our hard-earned tax dollars at work. Listen, if I'm going to keep my job—and I need it with five kids and a wife who doesn't understand credit card charges have to be paid at month's end—I'm going to need their names."

"Surely you're not thinking they are in any way involved in this."

Raising a hand, Robak points to his badge. "Just so we're clear, and as I said earlier, I'm not a judge. I've seen a lot and lived on the edge when it was against my better judgment. When I was a young man, in the days leading up to the week I was expected at the police academy, I spent my entire life's savings exploring the great state of Mississippi. Three days into my trip, I was slammed with a speeding ticket on an exit ramp near Cleveland. The officer was a big beefy guy with a personality to match. He was the second toughest cop I've ever seen. The toughest was sidled between a grove of mature trees leading curious tourists into Hattiesburg. That bad-boy cop was from Chihuahua. A chain tattoo circled his neck. If I were a betting man, I'd guess those links continued down his legs all the way to the soles of his feet. There was a large cross under his left eye and a smaller cross owned the tip of his nose. You know, the bulbous part," he says, throwing a finger to the center of his face.

"You tell me who does that," he continues. "Can you imagine what that cross will look like down the road? It's going to stretch across his face and flap about like a dime-store umbrella. How is he gonna justify that when old age has him wearing a baby's bib around his neck, slurping pureed pumpkin out of a can, and letting go a burp while filling adult diapers?" Pausing, he allows Preston to paint a visual. "Listen, I'm just doing my job like that cop. Dotting the i's and crossing the t's."

"Rick Finley is very single. He is like that little blue pill: fast-acting." Robak's expression has Preston regretting his choice of words. "What I mean is, he's like Baskin-Robbins. Every time I see him, he introduces a new flavor." Again, Robak's curious look leaves him struggling to find the right words. "What I'm trying to say is, he avoids commitment at all costs."

"Would one of those costs include murder?"

"Oh, no. That's not at all what I mean."

"What about the other guy?"

"Poppy?"

"You tell me."

"He's married."

"What's his last name?"

"Epstein. He still chases skirt, but I'm not saying he catches it. Think what you will, but given his age, I have to give him credit. Rejection doesn't stop him from trying."

"Poppy? Is that his real name?"

"I believe it's Barry. I heard his wife call him by that name one time on the boat. I don't want to cause either of them any trouble. They're good guys."

"Forgive me, doctor, but this looks, and smells, like murder. Pure and simple."

The wheels in Preston's head begin to spin. A gut feeling has him worrying that any minute Navy SEALs equipped with combat boots, dual-sided earphones, and combat earplugs will escape breaking waves, throw aside buoyancy compensators, and tear away scuba tanks and night-hero binoculars before coming ashore. Throwing their muscles about, they will bust through the crowd and, while he ponders where he went wrong, tackle him to the ground. "Are you suggesting I'm a suspect?"

"Not suggesting anything—at least not at this time."

"Unlike you, I know the truth. Peggy is alive."

"You must understand that in our eyes, you're all rowing the same boat." Widening his stance, Robak flips the pages of a thick notepad. "Now, I'm gonna need phone numbers to go with those names. Let's start with Finley."

On the far side of the marina, Molly lets her eyes pass over the fire ladders, smoldering flames, and lingering explosions that rock moored boats and create thrashing waves throughout the marina.

Walking along the sand like a seasoned tourist, she hopes to blend in with the growing crowd standing ready with cell phones and pricey full-frame cameras perched on compact action tripods. Wallet in hand, she is ready should vendors offer freshly popped corn and ice-cold beer.

An approaching van has her heart racing. She does not need a lawyer to know her smile is illegal in most counties and neighboring states. When the van nears the marina, she recognizes the bold print on the driver's door from a clip she saw on the news in recent weeks.

"Harrison County Coroner," she whispers when it passes by. "Checkmate, my friend. When it comes to love and war, casualties are expected. No proof—no pudding. I'm guessing this is what amateurs call a game-changer."

CHAPTER 54

A lone in the house, and hearing only the steady ticking of the clock, Preston stares out the open window. Darkness circles around him, and questions come shooting at him like rapid gunfire. He has been home for only a short while and has already checked the clock a dozen times. The minutes tick away, but the worry in his heart makes their passing feel like days.

The events of the evening play out in his head like recurring nightmares. The night is filled with conflict, and while he finds comfort nestled beneath the sheets in his own bed, he cannot ignore that the late-night hours have turned deadly. He refuses to accept that Peggy has fallen in harm's way—or that, while hoping to escape her pain, she succumbed to suicide. His actions and lies may have left her feeling rejected and humiliated, but surely she is not powerless.

The words she spoke have him believing she did not mean them. She fired back at him out of hurt and disappointment. The hate in her eyes left him resenting Molly and her actions. It was not her place to throw their affair in Peggy's face and muddy his marriage.

If harm has come to Peggy, his cheating ways will forever haunt him. It is only now, in this eerie silence, that he understands the years of deceit and dishonesty are coming at him with a price he never expected to pay. The way she looked into his eyes told him he deserved a lecture and a hard-and-fast kick to the curb—perhaps to the groin as well.

It was foolish to make a so-so promise to Molly that he would call when the events of the evening had found closure. Lowering his head, he prays she will not show her ass by coming to the house. The thought of her face at his door throws a cramp in his stomach.

Perhaps it would be a small blessing if it is her body they found on the boat, he thinks, allowing a slim smile to cross his face.

CHAPTER 55

"What can you tell me about the women who visited Dr. Fayne's boat?" Robak asks, running a hand through his hair.

He has spoken with Kenny for only a handful of minutes and is already questioning the young man's competence. More than once, he wonders how anyone could have given Kenny the responsibility for guarding the marina. He is certain his eight-year-old granddaughter is better qualified.

"Are you looking for a person of interest? In case you're wondering how I know to ask this, I watch a lot of detective movies," Kenny assures him.

Robak wants to reach over the table and, with short, stubby fingers, poke out the young man's eyes. He stops short when a pinch in his back pocket reminds he needs this job if he wants to make ends meet. "I'm sure you do. Tell me, Kenny, what is it you do when you're not guarding the marina or watching movies?"

"When the weather heats up, I practice fire-spinning, but most of the time, I shoot a longbow at medieval festivals. I'm sort of a warrior. Maybe you've heard of me."

"Can't say I have." A devout fan of superhero Clark Kent, Robak has seen his fair share of *Superman* episodes and is familiar with the comic's super friends. "Are you something akin to the Green Arrow?"

"Exactly," Kenny says, hinging his arm and pretending to pull back a bow. "Is there a reward for information?"

"That remains to be seen. Have you ever had a girlfriend?"

"I had a crush on a girl named Pamela. I met her in Sioux City, Iowa."

"Recently?"

"The summer after seventh grade. We had a song."

"What song would that be?"

"Can't remember. I gave her a promise ring."

"What might that be?"

"A worthless ring with an empty promise of marrying her someday."

"Have you ever sought or been in counseling?"

"Nope. Never. I'm on an even keel."

"Tell me, what did you do before you started your job at the marina?"

"You don't want to know."

"Legal?"

"In some parts of the world."

"Underground?"

"Only when needed."

"Did you receive a 1040?"

"The aerosol lubricant?"

"That's WD-40. A 1040 is an income tax form. You file it with the IRS. It determines what you owe the government or the refund you can expect."

"Maybe. I don't know. If it looks like junk mail, I toss it in the trash."

Robak ponders his actions for a moment. There is little doubt a psychiatrist would have a field day with this guy. "How do you feel about cops and robbers?"

"If forced to choose, I want to be the robber," Kenny exclaims.

"And miss the opportunity to slap cuffs on the bad guy?"

"Don't judge. It's your scenario."

"How did you get this job?"

"My second cousin knew somebody who knew somebody. I think the somebody he knew owed Darren, my second cousin, a favor."

"Did you finish high school?"

"Heck yes. Right after my sophomore year."

"Why the early checkout?"

"Algebra."

"And Pamela?"

"She dropped out the following year."

"Why is that?"

"Geometry."

"Any reason you didn't go back?"

"Calculus. If my dreams allow, I want espionage duties. If that doesn't work out, I'd like to be a drone operator." Born the middle child in a family of seven, Kenny is rarely given attention on the home front. Being seated across from a big-shot detective has him basking in the limelight and believing a career change is in his future. Kicking aside his dream of working in martial arts, he hopes to land a job in law enforcement. Given his memory and attention to detail, he believes the FBI and CIA are better suited to his intelligence. "I'd be happy as a television chef. Hey, can I have some water?"

Robak reaches for the plastic pitcher and, giving a necessary stretch, fills two paper cups. "Now, let's get back to these women," he says, pushing a cup across the table.

"They are always dolled up, you know, lots of makeup. Sometimes they smell like the perfume counter at Target on Saturday. They strut their stuff like they belong on television."

"How many women are we talking about?" Years on the force assure him Kenny is about to surprise him with a wealth of information.

"Six, maybe seven."

"Did you talk with any of them?"

Kenny searches the ceiling for several seconds before answering. "Only the blonde and the white-haired lady. You might have heard I'm known as the Casanova of the marina. Sometimes I think it's a curse.

I've never flirted with any of the women who pass through my gate, but just between us, I kind of had a thing for the blonde. We flirted back and forth—until she lit a cigarette."

"Do you happen to recall the brand?" he asks, skipping over Kenny's wet dreams.

"No, can't say I do. I didn't have a beef with smoking, until my mother died."

"Lung cancer?"

"Cancer didn't take her, but the driver of the other car did. He swerved into her lane when he tried to reach for a cigarette that slipped from his fingers and jumped to the floorboard."

"Sorry to hear that. No disrespect to your mother, but I'd like to get back to the blonde for a moment. Did she give a name?"

"My memory is a little fuzzy," he says, exercising his fingers with a game of *Here is the church, here is the steeple.*

Robak pulls a fiver from his wallet and slides it over the table. "Perhaps this will help jog your memory."

Reaching over the table, Kenny sweeps up the bill faster than an industrial vacuum. "It's helping."

"Does the name Dana mean anything to you?"

"Doesn't ring a bell."

"You sure about that?"

"Sure as rain at a picnic." He places the empty cup smack-dab in front of him, and with the flick of a finger, sends it flying. When it misses the wastebasket, he lets go a laugh. "I'm guessing shooting hoops isn't in my future."

"Neither is counterintelligence," Robak mutters under his breath. "If you don't mind my asking, how old are you?"

"Twenty-four."

"I would have guessed younger. Only because of your skin."

"Good genes, I guess."

In the following minutes, questions bounce off Kenny until Robak narrows in on the cars. "Do you recall what they drove?"

"You know, it's kind of weird. It didn't occur to me until now that they all drive that car with the Olympic rings. You know, the swooshy-swooshy circles." Leaning back in his chair, he draws rings in the air with a pointed finger.

"An Audi? You sure about that?"

"At first I thought they were part of our Olympic team. You know, Dara Torres, Katie Ledecky, and Lindsey Vonn."

"Two of those women are swimmers and the other is a skier, but if I search deep enough, I can see your point. What about the color?"

"Come to think of it, they all drive black cars. For an old man, Dr. Fayne must be quite the Romeo."

"That old man is in his forties."

"Go figure."

"Are you aware Dr. Fayne owns the boat with two partners? It's possible these women were invited on board by those men."

"I know those other guys, and they don't spend much time on the trawler. The big guy keeps another boat in a slip on the far side of the marina."

"And the other guy?"

"He's always with his wife."

"What can you tell me about the white-haired lady?"

"She told me she was having lunch with the Wessons. They have an eighty-foot yacht. I threw out my hand to give her a high-five, but she sped off. That's when I noticed her car tag was about to fall off. I was going to chase after her, but I'd get into deep trouble if I left my post."

"Do you recall anything specific about the car's tag?"

"It was a regular old plate, so-big-by-so-big," he says, holding his hands inches apart. "There is one more thing. There was a crazy hula dancer on the dashboard and a Razorback sticker on the bumper. By the way, the harbormaster has footage of cars coming and going."

"Surveillance cameras?"

"All over the marina."

"Paying members aware of this?"

"Why are you asking me? I'm new to the rules."

CHAPTER 56

A large iron clock is striking straight-up ten o'clock when Robak passes through Easy Rental's automatic doors. Coffee in hand, he waits in line until a portly fellow with a receding hairline waves him up to the counter.

"Donnie, I'd like to speak with your manager," Robak says, eyeing the young man's magnetic name tag.

A puzzling look comes over the man's round face. "My manager? Do you mean Mr. Pue?"

"I do—if, in fact, Mr. Pue is your manager."

The young man bobs his head, adjusts large-frame glasses, and, with a fat finger, searches a menu of telephone numbers before settling on four digits near the bottom of the page. While he struggles with the call, Robak observes the small roped-off reception area and its waiting customers.

A young mother with a toddler is at wits' end with his antics. When the young boy crawls behind the room's drinking fountain, his actions appear to wear on her last nerve. In the corner of the room, against an unpainted wall, an elderly couple is disagreeing about where lunch will be shared. Raised voices let those seated nearby know she has a hankering for fried chicken while her husband is craving grilled catfish. A second look around the room tells him a smile is nowhere to be found.

After a few minutes, a middle-aged man pushes through the swinging door. Crossing over the worn carpet, he moves over the floor like he is tap-dancing. He walks along the counter, shoving reading glasses up and over the bridge of his nose. Along the way, he pauses to read the name tags of employees he knows only as shifters—a small crop of kids whose job is to complete applications and leave him alone so he can tend to more important matters, like reading the paper, conquering the daily word-search puzzle, and debating if dinner will be Salisbury steak topped with mushroom gravy or meat loaf with mashed potatoes and green beans. He almost always chooses meat loaf, but only if the frozen dinner's aluminum tray includes a brownie.

"I'm Pue. How can I help you?"

Although a joke waits on his tongue, Robak bites at his lip. Now is not the time to share it: after all, he needs Pue's help. "I'd like to speak with the agent who signed off on this rental agreement."

Wetting his thumb with the tip of his tongue, Pue studies the contract for several minutes. "The agent's personal code number isn't familiar to me. I have eight employees working under me. Given my many responsibilities, I find it impossible, and sometimes tiring, to keep up with two four-man shifts. I'll need to check the date to learn who was working that shift." Needing the computer, he elbows Donnie off the stool. "What's your password?" he asks.

"*Stud Muffin* with a dollar sign," Donnie says, turning red in the face.

"Following muffin?"

"In place of the *S* in *Stud.*"

Pue looks away from the screen and into Donnie's dead eyes. "We will talk about this later." Studying the screen, he looks up at Robak. "That would be Chad. It just so happens he's here today." Lifting the desk phone, he presses the three digits connecting him to the employee lunchroom. Minutes later, a young man arrives without a smile.

"What's up, Pue? I'm on my break," Chad squawks. "I just ordered beef tacos. Microwave is out in the lunchroom again, so make it snappy."

"You rented a car to Margaret Fayne. This man here ..." Pue points a bent finger at Robak. "What's your name again?"

"Robak. Detective Robak."

"He has some questions for you. Do I need to stay, or can I go back to my office?" he asks, turning back to Chad.

"So you can watch your game shows? Like you're ever going to win a trip to Vegas."

"Somebody has to win. Might as well be me."

"Keep dreaming, my man." Waving away his boss with a sneer and an eye roll, Chad directs his attention to Robak. "How may I help you?"

"Do you recall anything about the afternoon Margaret Fayne rented a car from you? Rather, Easy Rental?"

"I'm sorry, it's Robak, right?"

"Correct."

"Other than putting up with Pue, this is a decent job. Hours are good, pay is fair, and the rental discount comes in handy when I can afford to travel. Last week, when the calendar in the lunchroom announced my birthday, my shift surprised me with balloons and cupcakes. On the downside, no one ever hints at meeting up for happy hour."

"How long have you worked here?"

"It'll be two years next month. I'm working this job to cover my living expenses until I start my job at Oak Ridge, a laboratory in Tennessee." He pauses to scan the contract. "I remember this lady. She was a wreck. She was all over the map. She dropped the pen and messed up the contract. I had to walk her through it twice. What I found interesting was she thought she was being stalked. When I asked her about it, she made up some lame story, but I knew she was trying to hide something. She was either running from something or searching for answers. My gut feeling was neither would arrive with a positive outcome."

"Do you recall if she was with someone?"

"She didn't appear to be."

"She make any phone calls?"

"I don't recall seeing a cell phone, and I'm positive she didn't use the house phone."

"How can you be sure?"

"You wouldn't use it once you saw the scum and mold. Don't get me started with the fingerprints. That's why I keep my cell phone close by."

"Thanks for your time. You've been very helpful. Congratulations on Oak Ridge."

Robak's next stop has him driving north to Southaven, a sleepy one-horse town a handful of miles shy of Tennessee's state line where the Epsteins live in a newly planted community of single-story brick homes dipped in white paint. Although he called ahead, Shay Epstein appears surprised to see him.

"You've wasted your time coming here. I really don't believe I'll be of any help to you. Aside from the marina and the outer islands, I'm not familiar with Casino Beach or the people who live there."

"Not a waste of time at all. I enjoyed the drive. I've never been in these parts of Mississippi. If time allows, I might just skip over into Memphis for some barbeque."

"Well, that will certainly make it worth the drive."

"I understand you were on the boat the night of the fire. Do you have any thoughts as to what might have happened?"

"Once we docked, Poppy and I headed home. That's all I can tell you."

"I'm sure you understand there is a marked difference between *can* and *will*." He pauses, allowing his words to sink in. "If you know anything more, I'd like to hear it."

"Molly was always dressed in a different getup and angry for reasons I wasn't privy to," she says, squealing like a pig.

"What do you mean?" Curious to learn what she is about to share, he puts down his pen and closes the pages of his notepad. A senior on the job, he trusts his memory to capture the coming words.

"The first time I met Molly, she was in a neck brace and a maternity dress, or that's what it looked like. It was a swing dress, you know, cut short and full at the bottom. I thought she was pregnant until she whipped a pillow out from under it. She mentioned something about an audition. It took only a few visits for me to notice that each time I met up with her on the boat, her hair was different. One day, she arrived with a mess of curls. The next time, she had a bob. Other times, she had big hair. Another time, she arrived in a striped poncho and vinyl go-go boots. The last time I saw her, she had fiery red hair and a tattoo. Once we were out of the channel, she ripped away the masquerade—except for the purple contact lenses, which were almost always hidden behind dark sunglasses."

"Are you certain she introduced herself as *Molly*?"

"That was the only name I knew to call her. I'm not sure I should be telling you this. Poppy will be all up in arms. He would prefer I keep my eyes on my own plate." Feeling anxious, she rubs nervously at her knuckles. "We once shared a hotel room with them, Preston and Molly. The minute we arrived back at the marina, Preston was dodging someone named Peggy."

"Am I to believe you don't know Peggy Fayne?" he asks, wondering if she is drinking Kenny's Kool-Aid. "Didn't Dr. Fayne ever speak of her?"

"I only know Molly. She is always with Preston. Where he goes, she goes. Until that night at the hotel, Poppy and I believed she was his wife." Feeling the heat, she throws her hands to her face. "They argued in whispered voices, but within minutes, voices were raised when she talked about her sister, Cecilia. No, that's not right. *Celeste.* Her name is Celeste. Molly was supposed to be with her in Arkansas."

"That night in the hotel room, did she remove her lenses?"

"Come to think of it, she did. She was wearing glasses when she came out of the bathroom."

"Did you happen to notice the color of her eyes?"

"Did I mention she was naked?"

"Not until now. Well, thank you for your time. If you think of anything else, please give me a call."

The twenty-minute drive to Poppy's office gives him time to place a call to Rick Finley. Searching his notepad, he slides a fat finger under Finley's telephone number.

"Mr. Finley's office," a voice answers.

"This is Detective Robak. If he's available, I'd like to have a few minutes of his time."

"Will he know what this is regarding?"

"So I've been told."

Waiting on hold, Robak watches the minutes tick away. Instinct tells him Finley will not be available for quite some time. Just when he considers a redial, the receptionist comes back on the line.

"One moment while I transfer your call."

"What can you tell me about Molly?" he asks when Finley gets on the line.

"What Molly might you be referring to?"

"I understand you shared some time with her on the boat you own with Dr. Fayne."

"The only Molly I know is married to Preston's business partner. If memory serves, she was there for the boat's christening. If it helps to put an end to your line of questioning, Peggy and Molly are good friends."

"Are you saying Peggy Fayne knows Molly?"

Believing he does not have a role in the play, and knowing he has nothing to lose, Finley lets a smirk own his face. "Peggy and Molly are good friends. I've witnessed nothing less. Should you continue this ridiculous investigation, I suggest you take your line of questioning elsewhere." Expecting a rebuttal, he ends the call.

Poppy is a nervous wreck when Robak arrives at his office. His bowels give a threatening rumble one would liken to booming thunder. He cannot sit without shaking, and a glance in the mirror confirms his face is the color of young strawberries. A cramp in his stomach has him worrying the detective has already spoken with Shay.

"If you'll excuse me for a moment, I need to use the men's room." Placing open hands on his desk, he stands ready to make a quick and timely exit.

"This will take only a minute," Robak promises, blocking the door with his large frame.

Wiping at the beads of sweat forming above his lip, Poppy has little doubt Shay told of the night they shared a hotel room with a woman they believed, until that night, was Preston's wife. "I really need to use the bathroom."

Robak lowers his chin and gives it a slow side-to-side. "It might calm your nerves knowing I've already spoken with your wife."

"Oy vey," Poppy mumbles, falling into his chair. "I'm guessing she mentioned our sleepover. It wasn't our idea. We were just along for the ride."

"The ride?"

"We were out on the water when the situation turned threatening."

"The situation?"

"I don't want to get involved. If someone had lost a tooth, I'd be the first to lend a hand. Well, not a hand, but dental forceps."

CHAPTER 57

Tucked behind a sheer drape, Clay watches local media vans rush the driveway leading to his rental. When a camera crew sets up sound systems and positions a camera facing the house, he knows the time has come to take action.

"How can I help you?" he asks, stepping out to the porch.

In their eagerness to nab a juicy headline, the crew has turned a blind eye to the posted warning giving notice that beyond the marker, they are guilty of trespassing. The blank and bewildered expressions facing him show they are fully aware of the laws they briefly debated and ultimately ignored. A desperate and hungry gang of three—a long-haired kid from the *Sun Times*, a thin-faced biker representing a weekly rag, and the Einstein of the group, a scholar from a junior college who has taken a foothold on the steps leading up to the door—demand answers.

"You're on my property," Clay says, waving a cell phone in the air. "I've called my attorney and the police. According to my best estimate, you have about two minutes to get off my property." A double-action revolver pressed against his hip backs up his words.

"We want to know about the redhead and blonde seen coming and going from the marina, specifically, Slip 28 West," Einstein says, throwing out a microphone.

Before Clay can respond, all eyes turn to watch a four-door sedan roll up to the curb.

"What's going on here?" Robak asks, making his way up the driveway.

Believing he is best in show, Einstein offers his hand. "Just trying to eke out a living."

"Eke somewhere else," Robak says, foregoing the handshake.

"We're just doing our job," the reporter from the rag sasses. "We want details."

"We are not prepared to share details."

"Surely you are aware details were leaked about an hour ago."

"Stop right there, young man. That's a false statement, and you know it. What is it they call it these days? Ah, yes, *fake news*. This is still an open investigation. Now, if you boys will run along, I'll see to it you're the first to get the scoop. Capiche?"

"We want a story."

"Not happening, at least not today."

"Then when?"

"Later."

He waits for the reporters to scatter before offering a hand to Clay. "I'm Detective Robak."

"I was expecting a patrol car."

"I'm investigating the death on Dr. Fayne's boat, and because you work with him, I took the call. What can you tell me about Peggy Fayne?"

"She's bright, well-traveled, and the perfect hostess. She is always kind and generous, not only with her money, but also with her time."

"How would you describe their marriage?"

"I don't have a bird's-eye view, so to speak, but in the times we've shared together, it appears they're happy."

"Any reason to suspect Dr. Fayne is having an affair?"

"Only if you consider his love of the water a threat to their marriage. He's a stand-up guy. Sometimes he flirts in her presence, but not in a threatening way."

"What do you mean when you say he flirts in her presence?"

"If you've seen him, you know Preston is a handsome guy. Women flirt, he flirts back."

"Are you saying Mrs. Fayne is comfortable with his flirting ways?"

"I can't swear to it that she's comfortable, but I get the feeling she's used to it."

"Twenty years of marriage to the missus has me finding it hard to believe this is something a wife gets used to."

Clay's thoughts turn to Molly and her devious ways. When his first wife learned of her, there was hell to pay. "I've learned every marriage develops its own set of rules."

"Maybe, but I have to believe it's not only difficult but painful watching your husband's cheating ways."

"I haven't witnessed anything more. Again, I get the feeling Peggy is used to it."

"I appreciate your time. If you think of anything, give me a call," Robak says, offering his card. "If those bozos darken your door again, don't hesitate to call me."

CHAPTER 58

The three-hour drive along US-49 allows Preston to prepare his heart for the worst moment of his life. With each passing mile, he continues to hope a mistake has been made. Knowing Peggy's strengths, he continues to believe she found a way to escape the boat's fire.

Tossing what-ifs about, he forces his heart to believe she is still angry with him. He is willing to accept open wounds exist, and if she needs time to clear her head and mend her broken heart, he is on board. With a little bit of sweet talk on his part, and perhaps a bauble or two, he is convinced she will forgive his shortcomings and return home and to their marriage. When the building on Allen Stuart Drive comes into view, a lump in his throat threatens to take his life.

Seated at the wheel, Rick navigates the parking lot. He wonders if he, too, is stalling. It is only now he questions his place in such a private moment.

"How are you holding up?" he asks.

"I need forty winks," Preston mumbles.

"Rest when you can."

"I've been reading the Bible."

"Have you found forgiveness and resolution?"

"Nope. Only words, places, and names I can't pronounce or find on any travel map. I got so frustrated, I closed the book and threw it across the room. Later, when I reached the Acts of the Apostles, I begged for a translator."

"There is always the Lord's Prayer."

"I'm no longer certain I'm worthy of forgiveness."

"Do it for Peggy."

"Let's see what today brings. When I took the call from that detective, I was expecting to hear good news. I wasn't prepared to learn my presence is needed here today."

"I've never been in your shoes. My only advice is to hang in there, buddy."

"I guess I should be grateful our presence isn't expected in Greene County. I've been told the dead bodies they take in are zippered up and laid out on a table in a room without air-conditioning."

"I think the holding pattern applies to inmates who pass after midnight," Rick shares. Rounding a corner, he takes a narrow spot in the parking lot. A glance out the window has him staring at the brown four-door parked next to him. "Don't look now, but that detective friend of yours is sitting shotgun in the car next to me. A uniformed officer is behind the wheel. You're not going to like hearing this, but the detective is wearing a serious face. His sidekick is wearing the same mask."

"For real? Do they have nothing better to do than shadow me?"

"At this point, all we can do is play by the rules and hope for a miracle."

"I didn't kill my wife. I hurt her in ways she didn't deserve, but I'm not a killer," he says, stepping from the car.

"Good morning, Dr. Fayne. How are you doing?" Robak asks, throwing open the sedan's passenger door.

"Managing. I'm living minute by minute."

"I thought you would want to know we've ruled out suicide. Before I forget, here is your phone. You will need to sign for it," he says, offering a form.

"Thank you. I didn't know suicide was on the table."

"Everything is on the table and under investigation when a life is taken."

"Forgive me if I can't find a reason to celebrate your news."

"I understand," Robak nods. "I thought you might want to know your wife made a call to Neyland Waters. Do you know him?"

"He's our lawyer. When did she call him?"

"The night of the fire. She wanted a divorce." Always on duty, a recorder in his pocket captures the conversation. "We have a witness who is ready to testify."

"Testify to what?"

"That your wife was aware of your affair and wanted out of the marriage. Have you given any thought to lawyering up?"

"If you'll excuse me, I'm needed inside."

"No problem. We're heading that way ourselves."

"Regarding my wife?"

"To learn what a dead body has to share."

CHAPTER 59

The coroner's office and the state's crime lab occupy several floors of the State Medical Examiners Building, a glass-and-concrete structure built in recent years. Tall pines and mature magnolias frame the center's large automatic doors, and cream-colored plumes of pampas grass and Lady Banks' roses shoot up from lilyturf grass. Large stone-cast lattice planters display hearty hibiscus and hydrangeas whose colors match the midmorning sky.

"I get the feeling the gardener is a plant addict," Rick chimes. "One thing you never want to watch is someone fighting addiction."

"Battling a beast is painful for all who live and witness the pain," Preston says in a low voice.

Two badges in leather jackets rush to meet Preston in the building's atrium. The taller badge wears a preacher's comb-over and tired shoes. Blinking nervously, his sidekick saunters along flat-footed with his hands on his hips.

Upon their approach to a bank of elevators, Preston stops to admire a charcoal piece set against the room's white wall. The artist is unknown to him, but he will study the man's work when time allows. He is slowing his step to take in a sailboat done in pastels when he notices the officers' bulky hips. Common sense suggests they are carrying more than a few extra pounds.

When the elevator's steel doors part, an antiseptic odor rushes at him. Memories of the hours he spent studying and exploring cadavers rush his memory. Believing he might vomit, he doubles over. Although he appreciates the effort, Rick's hand to his back offers little comfort.

Stepping from the elevator, his eyes drift over the sterile environment. Lost in thought, he finds the walls white as rice and the floor pristine and unsoiled. Other than the beating in his chest and the squeak his shoes offer with each step, he hears only the low hum escaping the building's backup generator.

Moving forward, he sets his focus on a covered gurney parked near a large window. Easing up, he steps aside to allow preacher cop to step around him. When preacher cop moves on, he hurries to follow.

The room across the hall brings back memories of the science labs he practically lived in during medical school. Test tubes and microscopes line the wide stainless steel table, and a flexible life-size anatomy skeleton waits in the corner for a chance at the next dance. Human road maps and drawings of medical instruments paper the walls. A caged metal clock ticks away the time—not that it matters to the dead, who no longer rush off to work, shuffle to carpool, or race to board the ever-elusive on-time flight. X-rays on a wall-mounted light box reveal a skull fracture in the victim's cranium, a dislocated nose, and a fractured rib. Turning away, Preston prays the image is not of Peggy.

"Hello, Dr. Fayne. I'm Dr. Henry. Miles Henry. Given our careers and our medical history, I'm sorry we're meeting under these circumstances." Walking with a noticeable limp, the coroner opens a slim file and flips through the pages. "A rape kit ruled out sexual assault, and nail clippings indicate a struggle had not ensued. Findings after the first set of photographs indicate there are no bruises, bites, scrapes, or defense wounds, other than a small wound on the victim's elbow. A body rinse and second set of photos confirm the initial findings. Toxicology reports were studied and histology slides are concluded. Smoke inhalation was determined to be the cause of death. There were burns to the face, nose, and mouth. I see here a box indicating singed head and nostril hairs. Blood alcohol concentration was 0.33, making alcohol a contributing factor." Returning the folder to his side, he invites Preston to follow him to the holding area.

Fighting the knots in his stomach, Preston wants only to change the past and return to a time when he and Peggy laughed at the simplest of things and spoke of far-off dreams they wished for their future. The pain in his gut reminds that his careless actions forced their future and, ultimately, determined this outcome. Dragging his feet and giving a deep sigh, he enters the room. Pushing aside his fears, he is drawn to a cardboard tag hanging from Peggy's big toe. He does not have to look to know a case number typed in large, bold print on the tag's flip side identifies her name, hair, and eye color.

Placing his hand on hers, he finds her body cool to the touch. It takes only a moment for him to recall that the human body is preserved in a chamber kept at fourteen degrees Fahrenheit to reduce decomposition. When he leans in to place a kiss on her forehead, he is surprised to find her hair damp.

"Give it to me straight, Doc. Did she suffer?"

"Given her BAC, the blood alcohol concentration I mentioned, I would say she suffered long before the fire broke out."

"I don't understand."

"It is likely she experienced tremors and memory loss. Body weight is also a factor. At 51.36 kilograms, her low weight didn't help. The autopsy revealed there was little food in the stomach. I'm sure you're aware females tend to keep more alcohol in their blood than males. That said, it will take weeks for officials to give a full report. Are you aware your wife was pregnant?"

"I didn't know," he says, turning quiet. It is difficult to hear Peggy described in medical jargon, and learning she was carrying his child sucks the air from his lungs. "How far along?"

"Between ten and eleven weeks. Elbows and knees could bend and genitals were developing."

Growing silent, he rubs at his face. "I'd like to be alone with her."

"Of course. Take as much time as you need. As a doctor, I'm sure you'll agree healing comes after grieving. In all my years, I've come to learn grieving comes at us in different directions. If I may do so, I suggest you listen to your heart. I'll be right outside if you need me."

"Thank you."

"Again, take all the time you need."

"I'm struggling to find the words," Preston says, falling into a chair next to the gurney. Surprised by his tears, he lets them flow. "Today has me believing I lost you yesterday. As crazy as it sounds, yesterday had me struggling to accept the passing of time. I woke up at the crack of dawn with a pain in my chest. I'm beginning to believe it's a reminder that my heart is no longer whole. I don't want to grow old without you.

"Just this morning, I thought I heard you cry out for me. I raced through the house calling out your name. Last night, I drove along the beach just to feel a little closer to you. I must tell you, the waves seemed rougher and the sky seasons darker.

"In everything I do, I am aware of your absence. No matter the hours I sleep, I'm exhausted. My body is screaming out for you. Be it good or bad, the first smile we shared remains etched on my heart.

"I fear that in the coming days, I'll ask my heart to erase our last minutes together—a time I should have made more loving. I've spent hours staring at the phone waiting for you to call. When those hours grew tiresome, I walked in circles wondering where you were.

"Until yesterday, I woke up each morning expecting to find you at my side. At the end of the day, it takes all I have to return home knowing you won't be there to greet me with a loving hug and a hot dinner, and to tell me about your day after asking about mine. In our greatest moments, you made me feel alive.

"As I neared this building today, I felt complete destruction. My world is in utter chaos. The pinch in my heart tells me nothing will ever be the same. Left struggling in the here and now, I'm finding my world is dark without you. I've been told this feeling of loss will pass with the sweet essence of time, but I'm beginning to have my doubts. I'm left believing I'll never love again—not in a way like ours.

"Every minute of every day, I'm missing you. When I walk by your dressing table, I'm reminded of our Saturday night dates. This morning, while I was preparing for this moment, I grew so frustrated, I swept up your perfumes, tray and all, and threw them into the trash. When sunrise threatens her arrival, I find myself dreaming inside a broken heart only to wake up disbelieving. I struggle getting out of bed, knowing this pain and emptiness will not go away.

"There was so much more we were supposed to do together. Nothing feels right. I'm growing to hate this life I'm forced to live without you, but I must accept this is the cross I have to bear. The doctor in me reminds I can't continue to live this way, carrying this haunting emptiness that does nothing more than eat away at my core.

"Much like you in your final hours, I'm left feeling I deserve better. While my heart encourages me to surrender to the pain I'm suffering, I realize it is best to accept my loss and move forward. To do this, I must be strong. It's time to get my mind and body healthy. That said, I'm hoping time heals my wounds.

"I will leave here believing you were an angel on this earth. You were the best gift I've been given and my greatest adventure. It was easy to see you weren't like the other women who hurried to latch on to me, hoping to become my wife." He reaches for her, but pulls away when the burns to her face become too much for him.

"There was something about your smile and the ease in which you reached out and touched others, especially strangers—the valet guy at the club who always compliments the photographs you exchange, the homeless man on the corner who asked only for a handout so he could feed his family, and the old lady, the one who walked with a stick, who bummed the parking lot trading hard candy she likely lifted from the laundromat down the street for bones to feed a stray dog she could not shake. You gave them hope and made them smile, if only for a short time.

"I've always admired your strong character and sincerity. It kills knowing I let you down. So today, in this sterile room, I'm taking a deep breath and moving on. I'm hoping you will agree it's time to rebuild the walls in my head and outline my future. Just so you know, I'll remember you today, and if my memory allows, in all of my tomorrows."

Moving close, he brushes a hand along her chin, and with a finger to her lips, kisses the air. Gathering his thoughts, he hurries from the room.

"Excuse me, Dr. Henry," he shouts down the hall. "I believe my wife's body arrived with jewelry. I'd like to take it with me."

CHAPTER 60

"We didn't get the morning paper," Clay says, looking out the kitchen window to the street.

"I canceled it," Molly says, looking away.

"Why?"

"In case you haven't noticed, the *Sun Times* continues to run old pictures of Peggy at charity events, photos of her hammering away at construction sites, and several days ago, they published a three-page spread of black-and-white photos taken on her wedding day."

"Forgive me if I don't see the problem."

"Of course you don't. Other than your divorce, you haven't lost anyone. This is different. I'm grieving the loss of a good friend. You know how close we were—closer than sisters. Celebrating her life is premature. We should be nurturing those dandelions she treasured, making a donation to the gallery where she studied, and if money allows, adopting a stray cat from the animal shelter."

"While I agree with you, I'm allergic to cats. As for celebrating Peggy's life, I'm on the same page as the newspaper."

"Of course you are."

"I'm hearing there is a litany of suspects. Officials have hinted a vagrant is responsible for the fire. I don't want to bring it up with Preston, so I was hoping to read up on it today."

"Every day there is something about her accomplishments and the many ways she will be missed in the community."

"That's to be expected. She was a staple in Casino Beach."

"If you must know, and it pains me to share it with you, I canceled the paper for personal reasons. It's just too painful to be reminded of her death."

CHAPTER 61

"Peggy died on the boat," Preston shares with his father.

Remaining silent, Duncan shifts his wheelchair into drive. With both hands on the gears, he travels over the floor to the window. "I've been sitting on my blistered ass in this cold chair waiting for you to find the guts to tell me about the fire."

"I didn't know you knew."

"It's foolish of you to think I don't read the paper or watch the news."

"There was a possibility it wasn't Peggy's body. I didn't want to tell you until I was certain."

"Paper said Peggy was alone. Why was that? She catch you with your mistress?"

"She learned of her."

"Way to go, slick. I believe you'll agree that's equally as painful."

"I suppose."

"What kind of response it that? What happened to you, Preston? You used to be a proud man who stayed on the right track. This woman comes along, and in the blink of an eye, you become a stranger to all who believed in you."

"I never intended to leave Peggy."

"I beg to differ. You left her when you stepped outside your marriage."

Searching for answers, Preston shares the first to come to mind. "I didn't think it would come to this."

"Still, it has. Are you still involved with this woman?"

"No."

"Is this the truth I'm hearing, or another one of your lies you have no problem telling?"

"There was a moment I wished she was the one who suffered in the fire."

"If that's the truth, I'm sorry I asked."

"Will you come to the funeral?"

"You should know better than to ask."

"I don't understand."

"Will your mistress be there?"

"She's married to my partner. I have to assume they will attend."

"I can only imagine what your mother would say. She was always so proud of you."

"And you?"

"Not any longer."

"I'm sorry to hear this. I hope you'll have a change of heart and attend the funeral."

"You're speaking words you should have lived by."

"Give me some space. In the same breath, I'm left losing my wife and my lover."

"If you had changed your heart, your wife would still be alive. As for your lover, you deserve the consequences."

"I want you to attend the funeral. If not for me, do it for Peggy."

"I suggest you record it. Perhaps someday, when your head is on straight, we can watch it together. I've changed my Last Will and Testament. My assets will be divided between Veta and Sergio. It's not your place to ask why."

"At least you got her name right."

CHAPTER 62

Rick arrives at the Rest in Peace Funeral Home with a bombshell at his side. Taking the young woman by the elbow, he works his way through the crowd. When an opening allows, he pushes aside lesser beings, allowing him to rub shoulders with Preston.

"Although I wish we were somewhere else and under different circumstances, I'd like for you to meet Brittani." Stepping aside, he pushes young Brittani into the spotlight.

Regaining her foothold, Brittani steadies her posture. A wide smile displays a chunky metal track running along her upper teeth. "I'm sorry about your wife. Ricky told me she was a nice person." Surveying the room with lollipop eyes, she rubs her hands along her arms. "This place gives me the creeps. I don't know if Ricky told you, but this is my first funeral. I've never seen a real-life dead person before."

"Brittani, dear, one should never refer to the body of a dead person in such a manner," Rick says, growing red in the face.

"Not to worry," says Preston. "After all, this is her first funeral. We're all entitled to such a mistake. Brittani, allow me to assure you a funeral is for grieving the loss of a loved one, something I'm sure, given your young age, you've not had to experience."

"I lost a cat once. She didn't die, but she ran away during prom weekend. Did your school have prom?"

"Best I recall, but time has a way of fading memories."

"I was so busy with hair appointments, dress fittings, and manis and pedis, I forgot all about her. Now that I think about it, I can't even remember her name."

"That happens," he says, giving her hand a gentle squeeze. "It is not for you to carry the guilt."

Across the room, Molly watches Preston massage the young girl's hand. She also notices the way his hungry eyes move over her five-foot frame before taking a crash-landing on her cleavage. "Scoundrel," she mumbles under her breath.

"I'm sorry. I didn't understand you," Clay says, leaning in.

"I said, this is such a shame." Pushing him in Preston's direction, she picks up her pace when she notices an elderly couple's hurried attempt to reach Preston.

"I'm Eldra Medera," the old woman says to Preston. "My face and name are unknown to you, but when I read of your wife's passing, I knew I had to come here—not only for her, but for all the women who suffer knowing their husband's bad behavior and poor choices. This is Buster, my husband," she offers, placing a hand on Buster's shoulder.

"Thank you for joining us here today. I'm sure your presence puts a smile on Peggy's face," Preston says, faking one of his own.

"I didn't know your wife, but believe me when I say I've heard an earful from Eldra." Backing away, Buster prepares for a poke to his ribs.

"I understand your wife had a liking for Pronto Pups," Eldra throws out.

"I didn't know this," Preston responds in a weak voice.

"Oh, Preston. I am so sorry. Peggy was like family to us," Molly interrupts. "She was a force of nature and a pillar of strength. She had a bigger-than-life personality. I think it is fair to say we are all going through the grieving process. Just last night, I wanted to run away from all the madness. Our hearts are hurting for you. How are you managing?"

"I'm breathing. When that becomes a challenge, I place one foot in front of the other and force my heart to come along."

"I'm sorry," Clay offers. "I can't say I know what you're going through. I've never suffered such a tragic loss. My father, a known thief when it comes to adages, tends to borrow a saying and often takes credit for it: *There will always be an absence of presence and the presence of absence.* Peggy will always be with us. I'm hoping you'll find comfort in the memories."

"My heart breaks for those who never had the chance to meet her, and for those who loved and lost her. She was always one to strike up a conversation, and she had a large network of genuine friends," Preston says, pausing. "Your presence says all I need to hear. The love shown here today is a great testament to what a special person she was to all those blessed to know her. My Peggy was the salt of the earth."

"Of course she was. Those who were blessed to know her are fully aware she was heavy-handed when it came to the salted rims on her signature margaritas," Molly says with an easy laugh.

"I'm sure you mean that in the nicest way," Clay throws out.

"I believe Preston knows exactly how I mean it," she says, placing her hand on Preston's.

Dumbfounded, Preston scans the room. A camera near the dais meant to record the funeral, a last minute request from his father, is parked in neutral. Right from the get-go, he did not want any part of it, especially if Molly brushes by the lens, but because his father asked, he pretends the small camera is capturing the evening's events. Should the time come to explain the blank video, he will gently remind his father of his growing forgetfulness.

While Molly yammers on, he watches Poppy work the crowd. A quick sweep of the room confirms he arrived solo. Given their last outing and the night they were forced to share a room at the hotel, he is relieved to find Poppy left his wife at home.

Out of the corner of his eye, he finds Trude and Bunni watching from the shadows. He attempts to look away, but their whispers have him curious. The grimace on Trude's face confirms his fear. Always the rat, he is convinced Bunni told her about the phone call she intercepted at the Sand Bar.

When Bunni gives him the evil eye from across the room, he turns back to the pink pearl casket. His disappointment grows when Molly does not do the same. The last thing he wants at Peggy's funeral is a fracas.

"Again, we are so sorry for your loss," Clay offers, unaware he has lost Preston's attention.

"I appreciate your being here and thank you for your continued friendship and support. I have gained a new respect for life's happiness and the value of true friendships. As I look around this room, I come to understand how lucky I was to be a part of Peggy's life. Friends she held close knew she was loyal to the people she loved. She saw the best in people, even when they failed to show it. While I search for words, I can't begin to describe the magnitude she had in my life. I couldn't have made it through these last days without the love and support of everyone in this room. Lost and alone in the mayhem, I expect I'll find a new breed of emptiness. I hope we can move on from our sadness and grief. Peggy should be remembered for the good moments she brought to our lives."

"Look at it this way: You'll always have the memories. Clay, be a dear and get Preston a glass of water," Molly says, giving him a gentle shove.

Once she's alone with Preston, Molly's voice softens, and her demeanor becomes familiar. "Peggy gave us this gift. Imagine our life together." A slow, sexy smile softens the lines in her face. "Preston, do you see what I see?" Waving her hands about, she cuts him off. "Don't bother with an answer. In my eyes, and surely in yours, we're free. No more sneaking around, always on guard, looking around every corner. We can now play house on our schedule. Preston, this is all behind us now," she says, throwing a hand on the casket and giving it a gentle tap. "Peggy wants this for us. By the way, nice casket. Please tell me it didn't cost a fortune. If you act quickly, I bet you can still plant her in a pine box, and should you need to ease your guilt, slap a bow on it. Unless it's a treasure chest laden with jewels, cold hard cash, and pirate's booty, anything buried six feet under isn't worth the money. Have you considered having her buried in Dead Man's Park? Think of the money you will save."

Worried their conversation might be recorded and their alone time documented and photographed, Preston tilts his head in understanding. Fearing what those around him might think, he moves to brush her hand off the casket.

"I want to spend the rest of my life with you, starting today, especially now that her life is over." Leaning in, Molly slides her hand into his. "The moment you first entered my life, and again, when you brought Clay into your practice, my heart told me we were meant to be together."

Somewhere in the near distance, a church bell rings out. "Do you hear that?" Molly asks. "Even heaven agrees. It's been said death can't be trusted if it brings us together only to keep us apart. I want to explore the outer islands with you, sail virgin regattas in the Caribbean, and with the sun shining down on us, prepare meals the envy of every gourmet chef. I want to sail uncharted territory, dance in your arms under a blue sky, and when day turns to night, share a bed we can crawl into without guilt."

Pulling him close, she gives his hand a lover's squeeze. "Let's make our own memories. We're off the hook, and you are finally free of the albatross around your neck," she adds, tossing a jovial nod toward the casket.

CHAPTER 63

"Would you mind repeating the payout?" Robak asks, sliding his large frame into an infant's chair.

"I can't quote the final payout, but the contract hints at two million dollars. That's a two with six zeroes," Dewey shares.

"Seems odd, don't you think?"

"How so?"

"That's a lot of money."

"Dr. Fayne lives big, and he's tired of the late-night hours. He's going to take some time off to teach me how to swim."

"Swim? As in laps?"

"We're going to work on our breaststroke. Months back, he invited me to go out on his boat, but I'm not comfortable doing that until I learn to swim."

"Back in the day, we started with the crawl."

"Dr. Fayne says it's all about the breaststroke."

"Imagine that. I'm guessing he'll find peace and tranquility on the water."

Robak's next stop is the eighteenth floor of the State Bank building, home to Waters and Briddle, a law firm specializing in admiralty law and offshore drilling.

A young woman struggling to stay upright on three-inch heels several sizes larger than her elflike feet escorts him through the office. With each step, he gets a peek at the discount sticker slapped on the heel of her left shoe.

Traveling the generous corridors, he looks into the rooms along the way. A corner office, overlooking Main Street, is decorated with a large painting he believes was created by Monet himself. A walnut armoire owns a wall opposite a carved writing table. Holding up the center of the room is a pedestal table with a marble top resting on a hand-knotted rug appearing centuries old.

An interior office, one sans a window, is home to a modest desk and matching chairs. A filing cabinet hugs the room's far corner, but it is the old fireplace mantel that catches Robak's eye. A step into Neyland Waters' office has him eyeing antique beams.

"Nice office. Must be rich in history."

"You'll find most of the buildings in the Historic District have stories to share. If we can, please get to the point of your visit. I'm a busy man, one without time for small talk. Such talk shrinks the take-home pay."

"Of course. The rug doesn't look like anything I'll ever be able to afford," he says, falling into a leather chair the color of cognac. "Me and the wife bought our rugs at a closeout sale."

"This is centuries-old. Keep in mind, it's been said practicing law is the only career where you can be employed and unemployed on the same day."

"I'll be sure to remember that. I work out of a makeshift cubicle with broken tiles and worn carpet. Before I was added to the payroll, it was a coat closet. The first month, I would come in every morning, grab a cup of warm coffee, and shuffle off to my desk only to find a pile of coats in my chair. When it wasn't coats, wet umbrellas and tote bags greeted me at the door. Either way, it was always something. It was years before my request to have the door removed was granted. It's not much, but I'm proud of it. I have a picture of my wife on the wall. She's not on the wall—the picture is. For what it's worth, that little closet stays warm." Settling into the chair, he admires the room's generous windows. "I don't have a window, but the copy machine is right outside my door. Well, if I had a door, it would be right outside it. I'll say it again, and you can take it to the bank: I love that little space."

"Why?"

Parking envy at the curb, Robak throws his eyes about the room, observing family photos and framed awards. "It's mine."

"Perhaps you would be better served going out on your own."

"Maybe someday." Leaning forward, he places an elbow on the rich mahogany desk. "Listen, I'm hoping you can tell me about Preston and Peggy Fayne. There has been mention of an affair."

A seasoned lawyer who demands a five-figure retainer, Neyland knows to remain tight-lipped. Prior to Peggy's death, he represented the Faynes as a family. He found Peggy's phone call disturbing. If time had allowed, he was prepared to suggest she seek counsel elsewhere. It was not a conflict of interest that concerned him, but Preston's friendship.

"Ours is much more than a professional relationship," he says. "We are friends. My actions may challenge the courts and its settlements, but I make it a rule to live on the right side of the law."

Accepting the answer, Robak gives a simple nod. "How did you come to represent them?"

"That's confidential."

"I suppose. Tell me, do you practice family law, too?"

"Only when asked."

Again, Robak responds with a nod. "Anyone ever tell you that you look like Hannibal Lecter?"

"Twice. Both ended in divorce."

"For real?"

"It wasn't so much that they said it. It was the fear on their faces when they made the comparison," he says, tapping the edge of the desk like a concert pianist. "They mentioned something about a movie role I could have played. Now, if they had said I looked like Tom Selleck, I'd still be married." Laughing, he sneaks a peek at his watch. "I have a client due any moment. Is there anything else?"

"One last question, and I'll be on my way. Are you in possession of Mrs. Fayne's phone message from the night of her death?"

"A copy was turned over to the proper authorities this morning."

"As evidence?"

A slim grin crawls over Neyland's face. "As ordered."

"In that case, I shall find a copy waiting for me when I return to my closet."

The medical center where Preston has his practice is Robak's next stop. His stakeout near the building's revolving door is cut short when Dana steps off the elevator. Calling out her name, he rushes to catch up with her.

"I'm Detective Robak. I'd like to ask a few questions about Dr. Fayne," he says, catching his breath. "Do you mind if we slow down a bit?"

"I tend to walk fast when I'm in a hurry."

"Don't we all."

"This isn't a good time. I'm already running late. Perhaps another time."

"Are you walking to your destination?"

"I believe that is what they call this, and I don't see where my destination is any of your business."

"I'll walk with you. I can use the exercise," he says, throwing a hand to his stomach. "I understand you are Dr. Fayne's personal assistant. I must tell you, all this jargon is new to me. Back in my day, my doctor had a nurse—plain and simple. Forgive me for asking, but what are your responsibilities?"

"I shadow him."

"What does that mean, exactly?"

"He is required to have someone with him when he's with a patient. I'm that someone."

"Do you take phone calls for him when he's not available?"

"Surely you don't think I had anything to do with Mrs. Fayne's death?" she asks, stopping dead in her tracks.

"Oh, no. That thought never entered my mind. You see, my job is to gather information. In this case, I channel the victim and shadow persons of interest."

"Am I a person of interest?"

"I'm talking with the people who have the most to gain. Forgive me, but you look familiar. Did I see you with Dr. Fayne on the night of the fire?"

"I was at the marina. I was on my way home from a mixer when I bumped into him."

"Excuse me, miss, but you're giving me another foreign word."

"I was at a party. I bumped into Dr. Fayne on the way to my car."

"That's right. You were the young woman I saw taking pictures on your phone."

"Is that a crime?"

"You might want to read up on the Anthony Weiner scandal."

"Is he that creepy hot dog vendor on Quince?"

"I'm not familiar with the vendor, but Weiner's best known for his photography. Do you know if Dr. Fayne was at this mixer?"

"I don't recall seeing him there."

"Do you know if he was involved with another woman?"

"He would never cheat on his wife." Clenching her jaw, she recalls the many times she stood at his side, wishing he would find her interesting. When her crush turned into an obsession, guilt had her avoiding his wife. Now that he is alone, she hopes he will reward her loyalty, but this is not information she cares to share.

"Word on the street hints otherwise."

"I'm telling you, Dr. Fayne was faithful to his marriage."

"How can you be so certain?"

"If you must know, I threw myself at him many times, and not once did he give me the time of day."

CHAPTER 64

Rounding the corner, Robak is surprised to find a sold sign in the Faynes' front yard and a moving truck in the driveway. His eyes fall on the van from a women's shelter idling at the curb. Wearing a forced grin, he makes his way to the porch. Finding the front door ajar, he steps inside. "Dr. Fayne?"

"I'm in the kitchen," Preston shouts.

Robak weaves his way around the movers and stacks of boxes, nearly turning an ankle when he trips over a wild mess of bubble wrap.

Lifting her hand, an elderly woman points toward the back of the house.

Aware eyes are on him, Preston looks up to find Robak propped against the refrigerator.

"Sorry for the interruption. I was in the neighborhood, so I thought I'd stop by. Lots of activity going on here."

"I hadn't planned on having everyone here at once. It just ended up that way."

"I noticed the sign out front. This going to your new place or the shelter?" Robak asks, shopping a box on the table.

"What's in it?"

"Tupperware."

"The women's shelter. Listen, I appreciate your stopping by, but as you can see, it's a zoo around here."

"Yeah, I understand. I moved last year. Wife insisted on doing the packing herself. The money we saved was spent on curtains and area rugs. Either way, my wallet took a beating." Moving over the floor, he searches a small box filled with spices. "I love the smell of ground cloves. Takes me back to being a young boy in my mother's kitchen."

"You can have it. Where I'm going, I won't be doing much baking."

"Where would that be?"

Preston fills his cheeks with air and draws a deep sigh. "Not sure. I just can't stay here. Peggy wouldn't want me to. Listen, let me walk out with you."

Traveling the lawn, Robak watches as shelter volunteers haul armloads of clothes and boxes of shoes and handbags out of the house. A middle-aged woman built like a fireplug carries a large portrait out to the van.

"Hey, do you mean for your wedding picture to go to the shelter?"

"They can sell the frame. They might get only pennies on the dollar, but every little bit helps."

"Are you holding on to anything?" Robak asks, rolling the spice jar in the palm of his hand.

"Not even the memories."

CHAPTER 65

It was not by happenstance or coincidence that Bunni was drawn to Molly and Preston during Peggy's funeral. When asked, Trude agreed they looked a little too cozy, especially when Molly took his hand in hers. She does not want to point fingers, but things are starting to add up. It would not be the first time a jilted lover or disgruntled and desperate mistress murdered her lover's spouse. It is her love for Peggy that forces her to make the call.

"Robak here," the detective answers.

"My name is Bunni Varozza. I understand you're investigating the death of Peggy Fayne."

"That's correct," he says, pressing the phone's record button.

"Peggy was a good friend. The sister I never had. You should know Preston is having an affair. If you have time, I'll fill you in with what I know."

CHAPTER 66

Sunset is making its approach over Casino Beach when Robak arrives at the Lamberts' rental. The detective in him observes their house and its neighboring properties. When time allows, he will canvass the area, seeking information and looking for answers.

Navigating deep cracks in the concrete, he makes his way to the home's front porch. Peeking through a window, he raps at the door.

When Molly inches open the door, he flashes his badge. "Mrs. Lambert, I'm Detective Robak. I hope you'll give me a few minutes of your time. I have some questions I'm hoping you might be able to answer."

"What is this regarding?"

"I'm investigating the death of Peggy Fayne. I understand you two were close."

Although her heart withholds a beat, her smile turns upside down. "Thick as thieves. I miss her more than you can imagine."

"I understand. Good friends are hard to come by and harder to lose. Hey, would you mind if we step out to the carport? I'd like to take a look at the blue two-door."

"It's a 1973 Plymouth Duster. It belongs to our landlord. For what it's worth, he didn't cut the rent when he demanded it remained parked in the rental's garage. I don't have the key, but I don't see any harm in looking if you don't get too close or leave a scratch. It's not a car I'd want, but I've been told it's worth a great deal of money."

"It's the dream of every collector." Changing direction, he skips over the concrete to a dark four-door. "I noticed the Lexus when I was walking up to your house. My wife's been asking for one." Circling the car, he gives a low whistle. "I've seen them on the street, but I haven't seen inside," he says, placing a hand on the door handle. "May I?"

"Help yourself."

"She's a beauty. My wife drives a Slug Bug. Darn thing is held together by mud and rust. Just last week, she dang near rolled it when she missed a curve in the road."

"The Slug Bug is a classic." Finding his admiration of the car awkward, she wishes he would go away. "We bought it used."

"Same with the Bug. It came with one of those crazy hula dancers on the dash. I wanted to toss it to the curb, but my wife likes it. She even gave it a name. What am I gonna do?"

"You know what they say: *Happy wife, happy life.*"

"You don't have to remind me. I learned early on in our marriage, it's best to keep the missus happy. So, about Peggy Fayne. I take it you've been in her home."

"If that's a question, then yes. Many times. She is, I'm sorry, she *was*, my best friend. It still seems unreal that she's no longer here."

"Given your close relationship, have you been on the Fayne's boat? Forgive me while I search for the right words. Did you sail together?"

"The trawler moves under engine. My husband is Preston's business partner. We've been their guests a dozen or so times."

"Have you ever been given reason to believe the Faynes' marriage was in trouble?"

"Not once. If you're suggesting Preston would cause her harm, you are mistaken. He adored her. His love for her was the envy of every woman."

"I'm hearing this from many of her friends. I have found in my career that envy oftentimes leads to murder. When was the last time you saw Mrs. Fayne?"

"At her funeral."

"Allow me to rephrase my question. When was the last time you saw her alive?"

"I don't recall the exact date, but it was several days before the fire."

"Do you recall under what circumstances?"

"I wanted my earrings."

"Earrings?" he repeats, throwing a hand to his earlobe.

"She borrowed silver hoops, and I wanted to wear them."

"Did you get them?"

"She couldn't find them."

CHAPTER 67

"I received my check from Maritime," Poppy says. Too restless to take a seat, he paces the floor. "I'm sorry Peggy lost her life in the fire, but I have to be honest with you: I'm relieved to be out from under the debt. Maybe this will put an end to Shay's constant demands for a far-off vacation and an upgrade on her diamond."

"I'm still waiting on my check," Rick shares, shrugging beefy shoulders. A creature of poor habits, he cracks his jaw and fingers his ear.

Turning to his friend, Poppy catches him picking at his teeth. "I have floss for that," he says, tossing a wheel across the room. "Where's the boat now?"

"Hasn't been released yet, but I understand Maritime sold it to Coastal Avenue Salvage Harbor, a boat yard in Pensacola known as CASH."

"What are we going to do?" Poppy asks.

"Should we sue him?"

"Why are you asking me? You're the lawyer. You should know you can sue anyone for any reason, but it won't guarantee the outcome you want. What are our damages? Insurance paid out."

"I say we chalk this up under the law of unintended consequences and move on," Rick says, offering a high five.

CHAPTER 68

"I'm sorry about Mrs. Fayne," Dewey says, offering a hand and a sympathetic smile.

Searching for words, Preston offers a nod and a simple handshake. "Her passing was unfortunate."

Crossing the floor, Preston settles into the chair opposite Dewey's desk. Feeling eyes on him, he hurries to place a leather bag in the chair next to him. Recalling the fishy odor he suffered on a previous visit, he searches the calendar on the wall behind the desk. A red circle reminds Vinnie's Bait and Tackle is two days out from their fresh bait delivery.

Sitting low in the high-back chair, Dewey pretends to admire a coffee cup he found in a stall in the building's restroom. "Your wife was a wonderful lady. I know I only met her once, but in the few minutes we shared discussing high-end jewelry and the growing cost of living, she seemed genuine. I've been reading about her in the newspaper. Something tells me the community will mourn her passing for a good long time."

Biting at his tongue, Preston refuses to believe Big Roy Ridolphi, his underwriter, shares the same sentiment. Several conference calls tell him Big Roy is not thrilled about shelling out big bucks on the insurance policy, and as the underwriter for Maritime, his pocket took a beating with the trawler.

Throwing his chair in reverse, Dewey rolls over the tiled floor to a metal file cabinet. When a pull at the slim handle fails to free the drawer, he gives the tin box a necessary kick.

"Try putting a quarter in it," Preston says, tossing a silver coin into the air.

Catching the coin, Dewey gives the cabinet a winning kick. Gliding over the floor, he returns to his desk, where he shuffles through a stack of papers. Letting loose a finger, he travels along the fine print while his lips move silently about. "I'm going to need a copy of the death certificate and your driver's license."

"I have both. Here is the death certificate. I have another original, if you need it." Leaning forward, he reaches into his back pocket, opens his wallet, and with a knowing grin, throws down a plastic card. "My license."

"Let's talk about the payout. There are several options available. You can take a lump-sum payment or take interest-only with the body of the benefit remaining intact."

Reclined in the chair, Preston relaxes his shoulders and rests his elbows on the chair's slim arm pads. "Finding myself with unanswered questions, I consulted with my tax attorney. At his advice, we decided to take a single payout."

Hearing these words, and understanding their consequences, the short hairs on Dewey's knuckles rise to the occasion. Although Preston is sporting a hint of gray at his temples and behind his ears, he is still a young man with a successful medical practice. Turning away, Dewey hopes the look on his face does not reveal his concern.

"Big Roy, I mean the underwriters, advised me it would be several months before the funds are released," he tells Preston. "I assured them you're not living paycheck-to-paycheck." A crooked smile follows an untimely laugh. "Do you have any plans laid out for your future? Many of our clients take some time off. First on their list is a trip to rest the soul."

"As for my soul, it will have to wait. After I tie up loose ends, I'll slow down and enjoy a relaxing lifestyle."

"Are you thinking of retiring?" Dewey asks, nearly choking on his tongue. "You're still a young man."

"Age has nothing to do with it, my friend. I'll find a nice boat and either sail away or motor out. I don't mean any disrespect for my wife—rather, my late wife—but in many ways, I feel liberated."

"What about those swim lessons? Are you ready to work on your breaststroke?"

"What are you talking about?"

"We were going to take swimming lessons, you know, so I could go out on your boat. Look at me," Dewey says, pounding his chest like one of Jane Goodall's chimpanzees. "I'm a Sam. We were meant to be partners. Don't you remember? McNickle and Fayne?"

"Who in God's name is Sam? I'm here to settle my insurance claim. My precious Peggy lost her life in a fire."

Sad and sheepish, Dewey tries to hide his disappointment. Hoping to mask the pull in his cheek, he throws a hand to his face. "I've been told the open sea is a nice place to reset your future."

"Speaking of the future, let me hear from you if you know anyone who wants a cat."

CHAPTER 69

Slowing his speed, Preston shifts the lava orange Porsche into first gear. Coming to a stop, he watches the 911's iconic flyline, a contoured fiber carbon roof, fall out of sight. Brushing a hand through his hair, he dons the automaker's signature sunglasses—a gift from the dealership. They pushed coffee mugs and hats at him, but he prefers coffee at home. After a brief rebuttal, he accepted the hat while making it perfectly clear he wants the wind in his hair.

When he paid the six-figure drive-out total with a personal check, the sales team treated him as though he was the only customer at the dealership. The pricey figure put a dent in his savings account, but once the insurance money comes in, he will return to his place high on the hog.

The owner of the dealership, a frail man who carries a walking stick and moves about flat-footed, never complained or let on it was a bother arranging a trade for the car with a dealership in Tallahassee. After all, at the end of the day, the trade put money in his pocket, too.

In addition to the sporty frames and hat, a windbreaker and leather driving gloves were handed to him when he was given custody of the key. When the car's speedometer climbs to eighty, freedom moves through his hair.

CHAPTER 70

A mechanic covered in engine oil and specks of paint greets Preston with a genuine smile and a greasy handshake.

"I understand my trawler is begging to get back in the water. I can hardly wait to see her," Preston says.

"She looks better than brand new," the mechanic adds. "Hey, Randy, someone's here to see you."

They turn to watch a big guy travel the yard, navigating potholes and rows of worn boat seats and fuel tanks.

"It's a pleasure to meet you, Dr. Fayne. I'm Randy Keller. It's always nice to match a face with a voice," he says, offering his hand. "I took over the salvage yard about ten years ago when my father passed, and I have to tell you, I've never had more interest in a boat. We've had calls from all along the gulf coast, California's Catalina Island, and a guy from St. Croix—each offering to buy it sight unseen."

"My wife and I built a scrapbook of memories on that boat. Something tells me she would want this old trawler to stay in the family."

"She's in dry dock," Randy says, shooting his eyes across the marina to a roofed structure. "I think you'll agree she's a beauty."

Crossing over the lot, they pass by a big guy in bib overalls and a young kid holding an engine tester. Although Preston is familiar with the tool, he has never needed it. Feeling their lingering stares at his back, he keeps with his stride. There is little doubt they are aware of Peggy's accident. Exchanging words spoken in low voices, they share a laugh. Steeling his spine, Preston walks with renewed confidence. After all, he is now a man of great wealth and renewed freedom.

"Watch your step," Randy says, pointing to a wide crack in the lot's concrete. "We've had a few mishaps here—most of which took money out of my pocket and put it into the hands of bloodsucking lawyers."

"I understand. They're like the plague—best to avoid at all costs." Approaching the trawler, Preston slows his step. His thoughts return to the day in Stuart when he made the purchase. Looking at her now, he finds her more beautiful than the day he knew he could not live without her. "You and your team have done a fine job. You'd never know what a mess she was when the fire department was through with her."

Preston's words send a quake up Randy's spine. He expects to see grief, but seeing the glisten in Preston's eyes, he wonders if, perhaps, he is misinformed.

"Forgive me, but I understand you lost your wife on the boat."

Throwing a hand to the air, Preston waves him away like an annoying fly. "She'd want me to move on with my life. I've always loved the water. Something tells me she's smiling down on me."

Although hesitant, Randy pushes open the small gate. "Let's go aboard. By the way, we found this photo in the wreckage," he says, holding a slim frame. "I thought your wife might be the beauty in the bikini."

He recognizes the photo, and although it had caused quite the stir with Trude, he wants only to let a sleeping dog lie. "I don't know these women. I'm guessing the previous owner or one of my old partners left it behind. Feel free to toss it into the trash. Regarding the boat, were you able to get rid of the odor? I've been told the smell of lingering smoke is often worse than the fire."

"One would never know she suffered a fire."

The familiar scent of fresh paint and teak oil greets them at the door. Preston is quick to notice the banquette's old cushions have been replaced with the blue and white fabric he approved weeks earlier. Although the window shades suffered only water damage, he had them replaced with a pattern to complement the seat cushions.

"When you're ready, of course," Randy says, moving toward the aft cabin.

It is only now Preston worries about this moment. Slowing his pace, he allows baby steps to carry him to the door. "Good job, my man. I love what you've done with the place."

CHAPTER 71

"I'm retiring at the end of the month," Preston says, folding his hands behind his head. "I'm hoping you're interested in buying the practice."

Caught by surprise, Clay taps a pencil against his desk. "Are you sure you want to do this? Retire, I mean? I believe the day-to-day grind will keep your mind busy. I just think you should give it some thought. I've heard it suggested one should wait a year before making any major decisions."

"I've given it plenty of thought, and I keep arriving at the same conclusion. It's time to move on." Scanning the room, his eyes fall on the framed degrees and diplomas holding up the wall. "I sold the house lock, stock, and barrel in twenty-four hours. Neighbor knew somebody who knew somebody. Regarding the practice, I just need to know where we stand."

"Of course I'm interested. I've made Casino Beach my home. In all fairness, though, I'll need to run it by Molly."

"That's fine. I don't anticipate a problem. My accountant promises a figure by the end of the week."

"If you don't mind my asking, what are you going to do with your free time?"

"What I've always wanted to do: live on the water," he says, flashing a rich man's smile.

CHAPTER 72

As if posing for a magazine cover, Molly falls into a role she perfected earlier in the day when Clay was away at the office. Open hands are perfectly placed on her hips, and an orphan's frown owns her face. A quick glance in the mirror has her grateful for the forced tear's cooperation—the first she has shed all day.

"I have arrived at a point where I need to decide if moving forward with you is worth the effort. That said, I'm finding I want out of our marriage. I want a fresh start—one that takes me out of the shadows and puts me in the spotlight. I can't live in a neighborhood where we touch walls with people who make art out of toothpicks, chart bowel movements of the neighbor's dog, and pour drinks and pop corks until after the midnight hour. Call it a sixth sense, but I'm guessing the neighbors who moved in last year are either drug dealers or gunrunners. If you haven't noticed, they keep their garage door closed, the blinds pulled, and when night falls, cars come and go."

"It's possible they work the graveyard shift."

"Think what you will, but I'm tired of sleeping in a bedroom lined with gym lockers. The room stinks of sweat and running shoes."

"I bought them at an auction."

"The shoes or the lockers?"

"If memory serves, it was buy one, get one free."

"Have you ever considered an armoire?"

"Not until now."

"I want a divorce."

"You must be joking. We're newlyweds," Clay reminds. "Our marriage is still young."

"Our marriage might be young, but it's no longer healthy. I need to unplug for a while. If we want a life together, we need to move far away. Given your financial obligations, you're not in a position to do this. I've made poor choices I'm ashamed to revisit, but marrying you tops the list. Although the here and now might work for you, it's not home for me. When I dream about my future, I don't see you in it. If I stay with you, I'm afraid I'll lose all of my dreams."

"I don't understand where you're coming from. We have big dreams for our future. If you've been drinking, I'd like to believe it's the bourbon talking."

"No, Clay. This isn't about a power struggle, and I haven't been drinking. While I'll agree our romance was once golden, I'm finding I don't want to be the booby caught in your trap. I'm tired of riding a dead horse. Each day with you adds a wrinkle to my face. The door to our future is closing. Stand where you want, but I don't want to be stuck on the wrong side. This ho-hum marriage might be working for you, but it's not working for me. Half the time, I'm left feeling like my neck is in a noose. I worry, if I stay, I'll be shaved and shackled and left for dead in a prison camp. I may not be holding scissors, but I'm ready to cut rope. I'd rather get out now while I'm still young. Perhaps I'll meet the man I'm meant to be with. To do that, I need to divorce you. Life is short, and there is no better time than right now to carve out the life I was born to live."

"While you're carving, do you mind keeping a safe distance? I don't trust you with a knife. I worry you'll try to neuter me."

"Don't think I haven't thought about it."

"I'm finding your cold and empty heart keeps me on my toes. Is this a good time for me to hide behind a bulletproof vest?"

"Can you be serious for one minute? I'm tired of living like a nomad. I'm ready to put down roots, and that can't happen in this rental."

"Why now? What are you thinking, Molly?" Searching her face for compassion, Clay is left astounded when it does not show. "Your poor timing leaves me to worry about so many things."

"Death and disparity?"

"Worse."

"What could possibly be worse?"

"Diarrhea and Peyronie's disease."

"Enough with the medical jargon. Give me the short version."

"Not always short, but painful. Scar tissue develops in the penis."

"So?"

"Leaves the big guy looking like a diseased cucumber."

"Please be serious. With you, I'm forced to accept that little should be enough. I'm tired of begging for a kitchen with open shelving, a dining room table with custom chairs, and a set of matching lamps only to be told I should be thankful for plastic deck chairs, a roof over my head, and a ping-pong table with a net in the middle doing double duty as a dining table. In case you haven't noticed, I never fall back in the recliner with the cup holder. I've grown tired of cleaning, scrubbing, and rushing to the dry cleaner. Can't you wear the same lab coat more than once? Do us both a favor and forego an answer. I've come to understand this is your way of making me feel necessary. There are days I can't afford a pack of gum. Don't get me started about filling my car's gas tank. I have to top it off when it nears the cash in my pocket. Let's talk about the toilet. After each flush, it whistles like a soaring skyrocket on Independence Day. I'm worried it will lift off the floor and shoot through the roof. I've named her Lady Liberty. Have I mentioned I'd like a drawer for our good silver?"

"We don't have silver. We eat off stainless steel. Not that it matters, but I'm promised a hurricane lamp and a wicker rocker when my uncle Seymour dies."

"Never met the guy, but I'm sure he would agree we get only one life to live, and I'm ready to live mine to the fullest. Unfortunately, I don't see you at my side."

"Given these are economic facts of life, it's never wise to cut off the hand that feeds you. Given our means, I worry you will leave me living on a shoestring."

"There are worse things," she says, taking a cross-court swing over the table with a hard paddle. "You listen to gospel while I prefer rock and roll. I don't see us meeting in the middle. I'm tired of riding a wave of emotions."

"Maybe you should get out of your own way. If memory serves, I believe we would agree you've lived in squalor—a condition far worse than the living conditions I provide."

"Way to insult the person you pretend to love. Not that it's any of your business, I am more than I ever dreamed possible."

"Because you're potty-trained and walk upright? Sometimes, you're like living with a toddler. Every time I turn my back, I fear you will come at me with war paint."

"How many fingers am I holding up?" she asks, throwing a hand into the empty space between them.

"Four. One is a thumb."

"Pick the one that's speaking my mind."

"Trust me, I don't need to choose a finger. I hear you loud and clear."

"You should know by now I don't start fights I can't finish."

"Believe me, I know. I'm always left guessing the next time your plans don't go your way, you'll stick your tongue out at me."

"Every Sunday, when you are off making rounds, I search the paper's real estate section hoping to find a house within our budget, and then I'm reminded we don't have a budget because the home of our own is on the bumpy road known as alimony and child support. I worry our next home will be a pup tent."

"It's always comforting to be reminded what you don't do for your spouse or in your marriage."

"Tell me about it. I've been rooked. I'm sure you've been told life with you is no picnic. Living with you is like touring the safari. I never know what's hiding in the grasses."

"I'm guessing once the ants move on and the rain moves out, you will accuse me of spousal abuse."

"Well, it's true."

"Only in your mind."

"My mind is the only one that matters."

"This is poor timing," Clay points out. "Not that there is ever a good time to have this conversation. You are aware I'm buried in debt. You know I agreed to purchase Preston's interest in the practice. I told you he's retiring. That said, I still have ten years of alimony and child support."

"That's what happens when you cheat on your wife."

"Well, this is golden. You seem to have forgotten I cheated with you."

"Your problem, not mine."

"May I ask a question?"

"If you're asking to ask, I suggest you should be prepared to accept the answer."

"Do you love me?" he asks.

"Not like I should."

"Not the answer I was hoping for or expecting, but I guess I deserve to hear the truth."

"Every time you leave the house, I'm left feeling like I'm on lockdown."

"You're free to do what you want."

"Can't afford to. I'm tired of counting pennies."

"Divorce won't change your means."

"No, but it betters my odds."

"Perhaps you should consider a part-time job."

"I'm considering a lot of things," she retorts.

His thoughts shift to the distance growing between them in recent months. "I'm finding that you're becoming too much for me. Is there someone else?" Turning silent, he revisits their marriage counseling and her endless promises to be true to their vows. "Is Richard back in the picture?"

"I can't believe you would stoop so low as to ask. I would be willing to bet he's still battling post-traumatic stress syndrome. You should know couples divorce for a myriad of reasons. My reason? Look at this place. I'm not happy."

"If you are worried I can't provide for us, I promise we'll be fine. It may take a year, perhaps two, but we'll be on our feet in no time." He steps toward her, but sidestepping him, she dodges the hug he needs. "Where will you go?" he asks. "Have you forgotten I walked away from my marriage and a life with my son for a life with you?" When she does not respond, he continues to beg for answers. "Will you stay in Casino Beach?"

She knows the look on his face all too well. It was not that long ago she coached him into saying similar words to the wife he left behind to be with her. Still, she pretends to ponder the question. "I'm hoping to house-sit or rent a live-aboard at one of the marinas. I'll work it out so I won't have to pay living expenses beyond my means."

"You have no means. You haven't worked a day in your life."

"That's simply not true," she replies. "You seem to have forgotten how we met."

"You asked for a ride."

"That's not working? I passed up several offers before I accepted yours."

"Sweetheart, please believe I'm doing my best to provide for us."

"If I stay much longer, I'll turn into one of those carpool moms with plastic hair clippies, yoga pants, and when school lets out, making eyes at Whitt's soccer coach."

"Miss Morris?"

"Maybe."

"Is that such a bad thing? Not Miss Morris, but becoming a carpool mom?"

"Only if it involves volunteering at bake sales in the school's gymnasium or organizing the parent-teacher association's annual potluck.

Do me a favor and take a quick trip down memory lane. I think you'll find how we arrived here."

"If memory serves, you put the squeeze on me."

"You enjoyed it. I wanted us to be different. We've had years to build a solid relationship, but in the last inning, you've thrown me a curveball."

"What are you talking about?"

Frustrated, she pushes away from the table. "Your obligations to your first family are always a priority."

"We discussed this when we first met. Hell, I'm lucky my ex allows my son to visit, given you had a hand in breaking up the marriage."

"Unlike you, I hadn't sworn to forsake all others. I'm leaving you, and I won't come back. Nothing good comes from returning to a place where I was never wanted."

"That's a new one. History shows you self-invite into places where your presence isn't welcome. It pains me to ask what evil scheme you might be planning. Given our marital challenges, I can only pray I'm not high up on your list of victims. I hope I haven't failed to mention great heights and deep ravines send a chill up my spine. Should I tumble to my death, what will you do about money?"

"In case you haven't noticed, I've lost three pounds this week—two last week. Stress is eating me alive. Regarding money, I've been saving pennies, enough to get me through."

"Well, what do you know? There is a silver lining. A court of law might agree those pennies are marital property."

"Where are you going with this?"

"It might just be I own half the pie. I think you'll agree we've reached a place where another glass of wine replaces a tumble under single-thread sheets."

"Are you really going to deny me the chance at a fresh start? Is it too much to ask for my own parking space and a house key on a knitted ring? If you want to talk about changes in the bedroom, I'll pull up a chair."

"Only if your rebirthing involves Richard, the dick, and my hard-earned money. As for the bedroom, you should see a doctor about your growing headaches."

"Let's not go there, Clay. You seem to have forgotten I was a witness, too. Regarding my headaches, I'm convinced you bring them on."

"It appears to have slipped your memory that I have Tank and Denise in my corner. A sitting judge in a court of law will hear my testimony, view the winning photo, and rule in my favor."

"In that case, I want spousal support. I've earned it."

"Stop with the malingering."

"Listen up, Noah Webster. I don't need a dictionary lesson. I don't know what you're talking about. I never linger, and you know that."

"Enough with the nonsense. You can make up stuff for attention and financial gain, but your words are nothing more than flat-out lies."

"Say what you will, but I want out of our marriage, and there is nothing you can say or do to change my mind. I'm ready to take life by the reins and ride that puppy like there is no tomorrow. I'm reaching for the mother lode."

"Are you prepared to take such a risk?"

"It's been said you can't put a price on freedom."

"What will your freedom bring to the table?"

"Everything I've been denied. After years of heartbreak and loss of sleep, I'm willing to roll the dice."

"What is it you've been denied?"

"A happy ending."

"You might be biting off more than you can chew. You know I can't support two households."

"I always land on my feet, and I'm sure I'll be awarded alimony."

"Have it your way. Getting over you will be painful. I have the feeling that speaking your name will leave blisters on my tongue. You have my word, one sealed in blood, that I'll see to it you receive everything you deserve."

"Would you like to take a stab at the words I'm holding back?"

"I fear I'll be asked to wash my mouth with a bar of soap."

"The tone in your voice has me worrying about my future."

"Something tells me you will always be known as the Bitch from Sugar Ditch."

Stopping dead in her tracks, Molly shoots cold eyes at him. "What are you talking about?"

"Let's just say a little birdie whispered in my ear the pieces of your history you're hoping to skip over."

"Would that little birdie be Celeste? She knows only to cheat death."

"Are you thinking your sister would sell you out?"

"She'd sell her soul to the devil. She always wants the lion's share when she gives only grief. She's a bit snarky—always throwing out words believing she is one up on me."

"In doing so, breaking your sisterly bond?"

"She's done far worse."

CHAPTER 73

Under an indigo sky, the trawler drifts along Antigua's serene waters. To the south, the island's signature regatta is underway. Observing the race through binoculars, Preston is quick to recognize *Karma*, a sailing vessel he once captained. Although he knows its call letters and frequency, he resists the urge to radio his old friend. Something tells him his call might not be welcome. Bridges were burned when he sold out and escaped Casino Beach, taking his partner's wife with him.

Standing at the helm, he throws a hand to his chin. A rub over the short hairs tells him the week's stubble will be gone before sunset. Glancing about, he thanks his good fortune and lucky stars. He never imagined in his wildest dreams he would be here, admiring St. John's rocky shore, while captaining the boat he is certain will take him into adventures he has only dreamed about.

Passing like a ship in the night, a similar trawler sounds its horn, announcing safe passage. Letting go a hand from the helm, Preston returns a wave. As he slows his approach into Jolly Harbor, a popular tourist destination on the island's western coast, the Caribbean's smooth water beckons him to shore.

"This is *Hot-Ta-Molly*. We are requesting permission to come ashore," he says, holding the radio near his face. "You might want to change out of that bikini. Best not excite the locals," he says, blowing a kiss Molly's direction. "Grab our papers from the safe."

Following the sun's ray as it casts a beam on Molly's hand, his eyes fall on the diamond cluster ring. He does not have to search his memory to know it is the ring Peggy inherited from her mother and later reported stolen when their home was violated. Overhead, an ominous cloud throws shade over the boat. For a passing moment, he fears it is an omen—or worse, a warning from Peggy's recently decorated grave.

Arching her back, Molly invites the returning rays to warm her face. Knowing he is watching, she throws on sunglasses. "I work hard to keep this body, but if it pleases you, I'll throw on a cover-up."

Watching her perform for him, he is caught by surprise when again his heart skips a necessary beat. It takes only a memory to know he has seen those sunglasses before.

Holding him with her eyes, she blows a kiss off her hand while holding a slim cigarette in the other.

"What are you doing, Molls? I thought I made it clear I won't tolerate smoking, especially on the boat."

"Oops," she says, tossing the burning cigarette overboard. "I keep forgetting I no longer need a disguise. Once again, I'm handed another example reminding that old habits are hard to break."

CHAPTER 74

Saturday morning finds Clay rummaging the crawl space under the rental's side porch, a two-by-six area he was unaware existed until now. He sweeps away the remains of curious creatures that have fallen victim to growing cobwebs and layers of dirt the wind blew in. Taking a seat on a wooden crate, he sifts through college papers and a doctoral dissertation he once believed important to keep. Old letters and holiday cards from friends he has not heard from in years are tossed into the trash. Too tired to carry a box of pictures belonging to Molly to the curb, he kicks it out to the street.

Returning to the crawl space, he hauls an unmarked box shoved deep into a far corner into the light. Resting on yellowed papers and black-and-white photos of people unknown to him is an envelope from Seth's Storage. An address in the top left corner provides a Casino Beach address. He finds it odd that it is addressed to Celeste, Molly's sister.

Although curious, he knows a phone call to Molly is out of the question for two reasons—he never again wants to hear her voice, and when she fled their marriage, she did not provide a forwarding address or telephone number. It appears they are on the same page when it comes to severing ties.

He entertains the idea of calling his sister-in-law but doubts she will be of help. Every living soul knows blood is thicker than water. He stares at the sealed envelope until curiosity gets the best of him.

"Hey, Celeste. This is Clay."

"I knew this day would come," she says with indifference. "What's up?"

"Please tell me what I don't know about Molly."

"I don't want to get involved in her drama."

"This isn't drama. It's real life."

"Is she going to come charging in here?"

"I don't know. She's become a stranger to me."

"I don't have much to tell you other than she pays my rent and promises I will get the car and everything in the storage unit," she says, believing the call is the beginning of Molly's downfall.

"The Lexus?"

"From what she's told me, it's an Audi. I gather I'll probably have to put more money into it than it's worth."

"I'm not aware of any Audi. Molly drives a Lexus. I get that you're her sister and if you needed it, she would want to help. That said, there is money owed on the Lexus. As I mentioned, I'm also calling about the storage unit. I'm guessing it's the same one you just mentioned."

"I don't want to stir up any trouble. I haven't done anything illegal."

"I'm not accusing you of any wrongdoing. I'm just trying to put the puzzle pieces together and connect the dots. It's not my intent to stir up any conflict or cause drama between you and Molly."

"Are you two on the outs?"

"Divorcing. She has flown the coop."

"She might come back. She's a little weird when it comes to keeping in touch. There are times when we talk for days, and before I know it, she goes ghost on me. Don't blame yourself. That girl is out of touch with reality. She's always ready for a cage fight she's determined to win."

"While that may be true, she's leaving a mess behind."

"I can't say I'm surprised. She's always reaching for the stars and stretching the truth to fit her needs. Instead of making an impact, she tends to always be on a mission to destroy everything around her. I learned early on that every word she spits is self-serving, and that's not her name," she shares, realizing she is up against a struggle to win a car she is no longer sure she wants. Looking to her future, something tells her next month's rent and the stuff in the storage unit are not looking promising either. "You're going to learn sooner or later we're not sisters. If I ask anything, I beg you will not shoot the messenger."

Clay's mind races with questions and his head threatens to explode. "I don't understand. You were a witness at our wedding."

"Your Molly is a one-trick pony. You should know by now her gene pool is a recipe for disaster. Aside from that fancy watch she wears, she doesn't know shit from Shinola. As for your wedding, she paid me fifty bucks. Don't judge. She drove a hard bargain, and I needed the money."

"I'll take a bite at your bait. If that's not her name, what is?"

"Cindi. Cindi Presley. No kin to Elvis."

Picturing the King of Rock and Roll, Clay withholds a chuckle. "Do I dare ask your name?"

"Celeste Ortega. We shared a night in a holding cell. She was arrested for breaking and entering—home burglary, maybe. No reason for you to know my story, but it involved a propane tank, a bag of ReddyIce, and a fast-food drive-thru. I was arrested on a bench warrant. Before that, my only run-in with the law involved double-parking. No need for you to know more." Growing silent, she laughs at the memory and the mistakes she made. "By the way, that lawyer friend of hers posted bail."

"What lawyer friend?"

"I don't remember his name, but I believe he lives in Casino Beach. One more thing: you should know she's not welcome back in Sugar Ditch Alley."

"Why is that?"

"She left town in a stolen car."

"With or without a partner in crime?"

"An older man she called Mac. If memory serves, he was in law school. She was later found guilty of giving false testimony."

Forgoing small talk, he ends the call and hurries to dial up the telephone number listed on the statement.

"Seth's," a voice answers.

"Good morning. My name is Clay Lambert. I've lost my key to our unit. Any chance you have a spare?"

"We sure do."

"Perfect. I'm on my way."

A quick dash into the house has him grabbing his wedding ring and a photo he is saving for reasons he does not understand.

CHAPTER 75

The storage facility is held hostage by a scrap metal graveyard near the airport. Acres of damaged cars and heaps of used parts awaiting trial surround a two-story Class C building. A rotund man with a graying beard shuffles through a wall of cardboard boxes until he finds the contract.

"Your next payment is due at the first of the month. You wanna pay it now?" he asks, sliding a key over the counter.

"Remind me again how long we've had this unit?" Clay's words hang in the air, and questions come to him so fast, he cannot dodge them.

New to the game, the man licks the ball of his thumb before using the wet stub to search the file. "Twelve months. You were given a free month when you paid in advance."

He wants to wish the old man good luck in collecting a copper penny from Molly, but worries his words might raise eyebrows. Instead, he fills his lungs with secondhand air. Truth is, he does not give a shit. For all he cares, her items can be sold at auction to the highest bidder.

"Give me a day or two to think it over."

"I'll need to see your driver's license."

"Of course." Throwing open his wallet, he hopes the gold band on his finger and the picture taken on their wedding day will convince the manager that he and Molly are happily married. After studying the compound's map, he hurries out the door.

The unit's metal door rattles along the track before crashing into a plastic box near the far wall. Desperate to uncover the secrets the ten-by-thirty unit holds, Clay follows the midmorning sun into the generous space. At first glance, it appears the Audi has done nothing but gather dust. Circling the car, he finds it familiar, but for the life of him, he cannot recall when or where they crossed paths. Placing an open hand on the trunk, he rubs a hand along the car's rear bumper. Eyeing the car's tag, he hopes the questions forming in his head will soon be answered.

Popping the trunk, he takes a step back. Cases of cigarettes, an assortment of matchbooks advertising local restaurants, and piles of clothes and running shoes he does not recognize stare back at him. Deep in the trunk's far corner are several cans of Fix-A-Flat. He questions whether Molly is smart enough to attach the quick fix to a low tire. Shopping the clothes, he holds a floral blouse to his face. The lingering fragrance brings back memories of a better time. Tossing the blouse to the floor, he makes his way to the driver's door.

A pirate's smile owns his face when he finds the key in the ignition. Their history reminds it is like Molly to leave the car unlocked and loaded. A glance at the hula dancer has him recalling the many times she hinted at visiting Hawaii.

A search of the car's glove box and the papers it holds is quick to put a knife through his heart. Learning Preston is paying for the insurance has his head spinning. It takes only a moment to believe his old partner likely paid for the car, the storage unit, and private moments with his wife. Throwing a fist to the windshield, he escapes the car.

His eyes race over the long table hugging the unit's far wall. Stepping up to its flat surface, he studies the generous display of necklaces and rings—each piece offering large cuts of Indian turquoise and Wall Street diamonds. Painted faces display wigs of all cuts and colors. It is the platinum wig that begs him to come close. Dolled up and ready to hit the scene, the foam face appears melancholy. He cannot help but believe her dark eyes and painted lips cry out for a quiet evening at home. As he runs his fingers through the tresses, it takes only a moment to imagine the evil part the hairpiece may have played in Peggy's death and the downfall of his marriage. Offering his condolences, he walks along the table, pausing to read hand-written notes Molly left behind reminding of the role each wig played in her devious scheme.

Although Molly's actions tend to surprise him and often prove him wrong, he does not expect she will show her face again in these parts—that is, until these items land in a court of law. Whipping out his cell phone, he snaps pictures of each corner of the unit and the generous space in between.

A basket of sunglasses in all shapes, sizes, and colors, brings a chuckle. He is not surprised to learn she turned to an aging pop singer to keep on top of the latest fashion trends.

Embroidered letters on a monogrammed towel convince him it once belonged to Peggy. The name and address on a small box from a store in Memphis begs to tell a story he does not want to hear. A chill runs through him when his eyes fall on the painted canvas shoved in the corner. Moving closer, he wonders how Molly came into possession of Peggy's portrait. Recalling the affair they once shared and Celeste's words, he guesses she has returned to her old ways—this time with honed skills and another willing victim. When mental images of Molly and Preston's affair rush at him, he struggles to accept that his old partner would step outside his own marriage and into his. Reliving the morning he sat ready with a loaded handgun to take the life of her lover, he wonders now if, perhaps, his aim was on the wrong target.

Recalling a cigarette is to blame for the fire and ultimately Peggy's death, a sick feeling rushes through him. He does not want to believe Molly is responsible, but the time has come to learn the truth. Escaping the storage unit and the lies it holds, he pulls a slim card from his wallet. When his call goes to Robak's voicemail, he sits ready to pounce.

"This is Dr. Lambert. Clay Lambert. Do us both a favor and check your email. I think you'll enjoy the photos I just sent. Regarding the death of Peggy Fayne, I believe I know who you're looking for. I suggest you start with Cindi Presley. For what it's worth, I've been told she's not related to Elvis. Don't expect an apology. She doesn't know how to give one. I believe you will find she tends to fall short when it comes to separating *never* and *always*.

"One more thing: don't believe everything she tells you. The lies she tells are whoppers. Skate around it, but don't ask for the truth. She tends to shade it. Believe me when I say she's a pathological liar. When you draw up the growing list of charges, you might add breaking and entering. If I may be granted one last request, let it be that you speak with Preston Fayne. He's the man sleeping with my wife."

CHAPTER 76

S crolling through names and pages of legal records, Robak continues to tap away at the computer's keyboard. Believing he's hit
the mother lode, he throws on reading glasses and leans forward in
his chair.

The State of Mississippi issued Cindi Jean Presley a learner's
permit, and later, soon after her sixteenth birthday, a driver's license.
Other than a thinner face and several visits to the orthodontist, Molly
Lambert remains the spitting image of the young girl in the black and
white photo.

Young Presley received a speeding ticket on the outskirts of Sugar
Ditch Alley the day following her birthday. Radar clocked her doing
sixty-two in a thirty. Three weeks later, she was ticketed for failing to
yield, leaving the scene of an accident, failing to furnish information,
driving without valid registration, and the unlawful taking of a vehicle
parked in front of an electric company.

It is further down the list of charges that his eyes light up. One
month shy of her seventeenth birthday, she became a resident of a
youth detention center where she served time for the ever-popular
breaking and entering, threatening a witness, and vandalism when the
owner of an old cotton gin insisted on pressing charges.

In the next screen, a simple paragraph draws him in. A seated judge, an old coot who refused to retire after a series of strokes left him dependent on blood-thinners, granted Presley a name change. Nothing unusual, except for the fact she was a minor at the time.

Staring at the screen, Robak grows curious about Cindi Jean and her criminal background. Cindi Jean Presley, known later as Molly Green, and now, Molly Lambert, is running from something. His gut instinct suggests a life of crime. Perhaps she wants to skip over the cracks in her history. In his line of work, cracks matter. His job is to learn who, what, and why. If he had the money to gamble, he would bet the fiver in his pocket she is running from herself—something she just might believe is far worse than any criminal charges.

CHAPTER 77

A violent gust of wind sweeps over the trawler's deck. Paper maps, takeout menus, and plastic cups float about before taking a hard landing on the sea. Making way for the rising sun, a wave of billowing clouds drifts through the lavender sky. In the coming minutes, Preston checks the weather radar. Knowing the time to worry is fast approaching, he rubs a hand along his chin. "Molls, a storm is coming in from the east and it's building," he cries out over the wind.

Wrapped in the robe she lifted from Peggy's closet, Molly shuffles over the deck. "Are you thinking a hurricane?" Caught up in Preston's weather forecast, she does not see the helicopter or hear its whirling flutter.

"Temperature is dropping, and the air is damp."

"*Red sky in the morning, sailor take warning,*" she says, pointing to the darkening sky. "Preston, is that a boat on our starboard? It looks like the Coast Guard," she says, eyeing the boat's wide girth.

"I can't imagine why they would be approaching us."

In the coming minutes, a loud siren and deep horn interrupts their conversation. Before they take their next breath, the helicopter circles overhead.

"*Hot-Ta-Molly,* this is the United States Coast Guard. We are requesting permission to come aboard," a voice commands over the water.

"What could they want?" Molly asks, throwing on the sunglasses she swiped from Peggy's purse.

"I don't know, but I suspect we're about to find out." Taking the Coast Guard's order to heart, he slows the engine to a crawl. "You might want to put on some clothes."

"That's not something I hear every day."

"Grab the Colt. Make sure the clip is in."

"Are we in danger?"

"Never know. Better to be prepared. Slip the gun into your waistband."

"Tell me you are not expecting me to shoot at the Coast Guard."

"Only if our lives depend on it."

"I have faith in the Coast Guard."

"You might have to rethink your loyalty."

In the coming minutes, a cutter races over the water. Breaking through dark, rolling waves, it sidles up to the trawler's swim platform.

Uniformed guards and a sheriff's deputy accompany Detective Robak, who, standing tall, is ready for battle. Binoculars fall from his neck and a smile is nowhere to be found.

"Preston Fayne, we have reason to believe Molly Lambert is on board."

"She's Molly Fayne now. She was granted a divorce in Santo Domingo and we married in San Juan." Searching for answers, Preston turns his eyes to the armed guards and their aimed weapons. "What's this about?"

"Is Molly Lambert, now Molly Fayne, on board?" Robak asks, brushing aside Preston's question.

Hearing her name, Molly steps from the shadows. With each step, her heart races. The look on the faces staring her down hint this moment is the precursor to judgment day. Something in the detective's eyes tells he learned of the storage unit and the life she hoped to leave behind.

"These men weren't sent here to learn of our marriage. They are here to discredit me and separate us," she says, hoping Preston hears her whispered words. Knowing their history, she believes Clay had a hand in Robak's discovery. In an eerie silence, she moves to Preston's side.

"I'm Molly Fayne," she says, reaching for a hand Preston does not give. "I'm guessing these men are here to knock me down a peg," she whispers in a voice for only Preston to hear. Turning back, her eyes travel the boat before falling on Robak's hips. A standard service pistol, likely a Smith and Wesson, sits ready for action. Metal handcuffs fall from a clip on his belt. Holding her breath, she again reaches for Preston's hand. This time, she catches it. "How did you find us?"

"You used your passports."

"I'm sorry, Preston. This isn't what I wanted for us."

"Molly Lambert, you are wanted for questioning in the death of Margaret Fayne," the deputy sheriff advises.

Hearing the charge, the blood drains from Preston's face and an upturned lip shows doubt. "Molly would never cause Peggy any harm. Tell them, Molly. Tell them they are mistaken."

"Preston, this is all a big misunderstanding."

While questions come at him, and answers and logic jump overboard, he tries to stand strong. He looks toward the team of rough-looking men who stand ready with sniper rifles. A machine gun and grenade launcher mounted on the vessel have him feeling like a hunted criminal. "Is this legal? The use of the Coast Guard?"

Robak gives an approving nod to the Coast Guard's captain, and with the sweep of his hand, invites him to his side. "We have evidence for probable cause. Judge Randall Vanhese issued a warrant for her arrest this morning," he says, nodding to a rugged man who stands prepared with a hand on his pistol.

"The Coast Guard has several duties, including the right to act as transportation police for law enforcement. Please cut your engine and raise your hands above your head," a uniformed officer demands.

Leaving the cutter, Robak shifts his weight over the boat's slim ladder. Placing one tired foot over the other, he climbs aboard the trawler. While the Coast Guard prepares for conflict, he moves to Molly, who waits with wet hair and little makeup.

"Molly Lambert Fayne, we are transferring you without delay to state officials. If my gut instinct is spot-on, I believe we might just end up in a court of law."

"You're making a mistake," Preston cries out. "My wife hasn't killed anyone."

Breaking from the group, Robak moves toward him. "It appears you couldn't choose between your wife and your lover. In the end, she chose for you."

"What have you done?" Preston asks, turning to his bride.

"She has what I call the O'Brien Effect. She suffers from self-inflicted wounds. It's not documented anywhere, but the end result is always the same," Robak offers.

"I'm far from suffering. My actions, however misinterpreted, were meant to be aboveboard. A fair and just court will find me innocent when the jury hears murder was never my intent. Preston, all I ask is that you find it in your heart to believe me," Molly says, pulling the gun from her shorts.

Surprised by her action, a team of officers rushes over the deck and tackles her to the floor.

Lifting her head, she throws cold eyes to Preston. "I believed with you at my side, I'd be happy. Turns out, it isn't you who makes the magic happen. My dear Preston, you were foolish to step outside your marriage and into mine. For what it's worth, I'm not blaming you."

"I can accept the blame, but the pain I'm feeling comes with a long list of questions I would like answered."

"Your actions put your wife in harm's way."

"Molly Lambert, now Molly Fayne, you are wanted for questioning in the deaths of Margaret Fayne and her unborn child," the deputy interrupts.

"Unborn child?" Throwing her head into a wild spin, she looks to Preston with fire in her eyes. "You son of a bitch. You lied to me."

"Careful there. You don't want to add an assault charge to the list," the deputy advises, placing her in handcuffs.

CHAPTER 78

Months before Russell Berhost walked across the stage at the University of Mississippi School of Law, he accepted an associate's position at the law firm of Goodwyn, Maxwell, and Lacey. Three years later, when he made partner, he was rewarded with a corner office on the twelfth floor of the First Mississippi Bank Building. His success as a criminal defense lawyer earned him the Readers' Choice Award, and later, he was named one of the "Top 50 Leading Attorneys" in the *Mississippi Business Journal*. Weeks later, he was selected as one of "America's Top Criminal Defense Attorneys." Although his wife was dead set against it, he recently accepted an adjunct position at Ole Miss, where he will teach criminal law.

An older man long in the tooth, he would seldom be described as *handsome*—but the same was true in his youth. Acne left his wide face patchy and pocked with scars when puberty moved on. Although he dodges beach vacations and waterskiing, humid weather and spicy foods continue to trigger outbreaks.

A glance at his watch reminds that he is due at the Downtown Grill, a popular pub located on Courthouse Square near Jackson Avenue. Carla, the pub's manager, never asks if he wants the daily special with sweet tea or catfish served with black-eyed peas and peach cobbler. She knows her regulars and their lunch orders. She is often heard whispering that her best customers are bankers and lawyers. "They never linger behind a menu and always end the lunch hour with a generous tip."

"Excuse me, Mr. Berhost. There is a woman here to see you," his secretary says, entering his office.

"Does she have an appointment?"

"No, but she claims it's urgent."

"Is she a client of the firm?"

"No sir, but something tells me she's aiming to be."

"Tell her I'm on a conference call."

"I tried that. She said she would wait all day if need be."

"I'll see her," he says, sighing heavily. "Please call Carla. Ask her to deliver my lunch."

"Same as yesterday?"

"And the days before. Gently remind her I want extra mushrooms and skip the bread. By the way, what's this woman's name?"

"Molly Fayne."

CHAPTER 79

"Fingers are pointing," Molly says, holding back tears.

"Have you been served?" Russell asks, handing over a tissue.

"Yesterday."

"The charge?"

"Wrongful death. I need you to represent me."

"We'll get to that in a minute. I'm surprised you've been released. That said, you must understand I have partners, associates, and a mean-spirited secretary I have to answer to. I'm also forced to appease my wife when my wallet takes a beating. To pacify their concerns, I'm often reminded I can't rush into anything until I know all the facts. For my own sanity, let's start at the beginning. Who is Preston Fayne?" he asks, flipping through the papers Molly pushed over his desk. "His wife is the deceased?"

"Late wife. I'm his wife. I've been made aware he's annulling our marriage. He requested an aerial survey, a copy of the autopsy report, cell phone records, and crime-scene photos."

"Are you telling me he believes you're responsible for his wife's death?"

"He's been told I left her for dead. Rumor has it he's building a list of witnesses, including fact witnesses and expert witnesses."

"Sounds like he's putting the screws to you."

"It wouldn't be the first time he screwed me. Mr. Berhost, I didn't murder his wife."

"Graham Waterman is a seasoned lawyer," he says, reading the papers she gave him. "He trained in trial science. He studies eye movements, hand activity, and breathing patterns of plaintiffs, defendants, and members of the jury. I understand nothing gets by him. It has been said he can spot a fake tear before it is shed. Dan Meyer, his partner, is a recipient of the Frank Carrington Champion of Civil Justice Award. He is also listed in past and current editions of *Best Lawyers in America*. I'm guessing he will do all the preliminary work. He will spend hours mulling over and chewing on evidence and witness statements. I don't know Mac McKenzie. You can be sure they will come prepared. That said, do you know the legal definition of wrongful death?"

"Is it anything like OJ Simpson's trial?"

"Death caused by the wrongful act of another," he says, skipping over her question. "If you are found innocent, is forgiveness in the cards?"

"Preston doesn't forgive or forget."

"Should he forgive, forget, and regret, will you find yourself in love with him?"

"I'm not sure I ever truly loved him. I needed passion." Knowing Russell is hanging on her every word, she goes in for the kill. "I want a man to love me with his heart. I want to be one with my lover." Reaching over the desk, she takes his hand in hers. "I couldn't so much as hurt a fly. You must believe me." Faking tears, she forces his hand to her chest. "I need you to believe me."

Taken by her beauty and rising to the occasion, Russell moves to her side. Holding her with his eyes, he pulls her into his arms. "Whatever the outcome, I'm all yours," he says, pressing his body against hers.

From that moment on, he is putty in her hands.

CHAPTER 80

Pressing his aging frame into his chair, Judge Lavaca shuffles about until his back is comfortable. Sipping a bottle of water, he rubs at the fine lines on his forehead. Placing a finger above his lip and his thumb under his chin, he runs curious eyes over the row of witnesses who hurry to put a knife in the defendant's back. A stirring in his slacks tells him if he were married to the blonde beauty at the defendant's table, he would find a way to forgive her sins and shortcomings.

Observing the courtroom and its attendees, he finds Clay Lambert a handsome guy. In a different setting, one outside a courtroom, he believes the good doctor is likely a stand-up guy with a good heart. Returning his eyes to the defendant's table, it takes only a breath for his aging eyes to envision the defendant stark naked and raring to go.

Mac McKenzie's professional career is nothing short of stellar. A young man in his forties, he has prosecuted over four hundred cases. Although it has been decades, the two cases he lost continue to haunt him. When he is not in the courtroom, he takes to the open road. Tall, lean, and clean-shaven, he has medaled in dozens of marathons. It is rumored the long runs often bring peace to his troubled soul. It takes only a memory to place the defendant in his history. Catching Molly's eye, he runs his tongue over his upper lip.

Seated in the witness booth, Clay has quite the stories to share, right down to his own troubles with Molly and the evidence she left behind when she fled Casino Beach.

"I learned of the storage unit soon after that wife of mine asked for a divorce. I found an envelope from Seth's Storage in the crawl space under our porch and the papers for the car in the storage unit." Pausing, he gives Molly the evil eye. "She's a two-timing little devil."

When called to testify, Celeste Ortega hurries to put into record she was paid to keep secrets. "Cindi pays my rent."

"By Cindi, are you referring to the defendant?"

"Yes," she says, looking straight ahead.

"Are you related to Molly Fayne?"

"Not by blood. There was a time when we shared a holding cell. I didn't know her as Molly Fayne."

"By what name did you know to call her?"

"Cindi Presley, and later, Molly Lambert."

"Are you telling the court you spent time with the defendant behind bars?"

"Just one night. The next morning, she went her way and I went mine."

"Do you know why the defendant was arrested?" Russell interrupts.

"That night or now?"

"Let's begin with that night."

"I can't swear to it, but she implied she was falsely accused of extortion."

"Still, you stayed in touch with her."

"I did, but I didn't do anything illegal. I stayed with her for the money."

"What do you mean by that?"

"Cindi paid me to pose as her sister when she married Dr. Lambert. After weeks of tossing terms about, we finally agreed she would pay my rent and give me her car and everything in the storage unit."

"Why do you think the defendant is here today?" Russell continues.

"She barks at her own shadow and bites at her victims. Forgive my French, but that bitch is messed up."

After swearing to tell the truth, the whole truth, and nothing but the truth, Preston falls into the witness stand. "I never suspected Molly of any wrongdoing. She and Peggy, my late wife, were close. When my wife passed, I gave her several pieces of my wife's jewelry. I believe this is what Peggy would have wanted."

"How do you explain your wife's portrait in the storage unit?" McKenzie asks with little interest. If he is going to rendezvous with Molly, he understands he cannot make her mad.

"I can't, but if Peggy were here, I'm sure she'd have a logical explanation."

"A police report shows your wife was convinced your home was targeted and that particular painting was taken."

"If you must know, my wife had a drinking problem."

"Would you say she was an alcoholic?"

"Functioning. The pages of her desk calendar will confirm every hour of her day was a happy one. Although her actions were sometimes nebulous, I came to understand she often made up stories to fit her mood."

When Rick Finley is called to testify, he shuffles over the floor like he is wearing spurs. When he passes by Molly, he shrugs his shoulders as if to apologize.

"Mr. Finley, if you will, please tell the court your relationship with the defendant."

"We've boated together. Nothing more."

"Do you have any knowledge of the alleged affair between Molly Lambert and Preston Fayne?"

"I've never witnessed anything more than mutual respect," Rick says, remaining tight-lipped. "If pressed, I would say Dr. Fayne had his hands full with his personal assistant."

"Could you be more specific?"

"I know her as Dana."

"Have you been given reason to believe Dr. Fayne was in an intimate relationship with his personal assistant?"

"Nothing concrete, but I caught her making eyes at him."

"How would you describe Dana's relationship with Mrs. Fayne?"

"Pure envy. Actually, seething might be a better word."

"I would like to call Shay Epstein to the stand," the prosecutor says, shuffling through a stack of papers.

Licking dry lips, Shay skates over the floor. Placing her purse at her feet, she runs a hand through her hair. Feeling eyes on her, she cracks a smile.

"Would you please state your name?"

"Shay Epstein."

"I'm sure you heard Mr. Finley's testimony. I'll ask you the same question. Do you have any knowledge of the alleged affair between the defendant and Preston Fayne?"

"Yes, I do. That woman, right there, is just awful," she says, pointing a firm finger at Molly. "I don't understand what Preston sees in her. As for Finley, he should be disbarred. Judge Judy might reprimand me for speaking another's mind, but Rick is fully aware of Preston's affair. The night we were forced to share a hotel room, he offered to hide Molly's car. That woman is no Girl Scout."

Hearing Shay's words and witnessing her expression, the courtroom fills with laughter.

"Order in the court," Lavaca demands, slamming his gavel to the bench. "This frivolous lawsuit is filled with nothing but potholes, hearsay, and scandals."

"Mrs. Epstein, if you will, please stick to the facts," McKenzie reminds.

"Preston and Molly were having an affair."

"How can you be sure?"

"As I said, Poppy and I were forced to share a hotel room with them. I want to make it perfectly clear that I was against it from the start."

Again, laughter fills the room.

"Let me remind you that you're not on trial. Please accept understanding does not make a moment truthful," the judge reminds.

"Until that night at the hotel, I believed she was his wife," Shay continues.

"Is there an event that had you believing differently?" McKenzie asks.

"When we docked, Rick told Preston that someone named Peggy was looking for him. In the coming minutes, we put two and two together and the next thing I know, Poppy and I are hiding under the covers. With all the commotion in the other bed, we didn't get a wink of sleep."

"To be clear, are you telling the court you shared a room with another couple?"

"Yes, indeedy."

"Will you tell the court who shared the other bed?"

"Preston Fayne and Molly."

Seated up front and center, the court reporter, a young woman with a million-dollar smile, follows Lavaca's eyes as they pass over the floor to Molly's shapely legs. She entertains the idea of typing the judge's interest into the transcript, but worrying such actions may place her job in jeopardy, she instead gives him the evil eye.

Ignoring the court reporter's eye roll, Lavaca puts his focus on Molly. Admiring her beauty, he finds her poised, alert, and stunningly gorgeous. Undressing her with his eyes, he is grateful his robe hides his growing interest. Positioned to decide her future, he lets his mind wander to far-off places where island music, captivating sunsets, and intimate moments allow them to enjoy one another without lawyers preparing their closing arguments. Giving her the once-over, he questions how much time he should let pass before reaching out to her.

CHAPTER 81

"My handsome Russell, I have no doubt you will be victorious. The jury has heard the truth and will return a verdict in your client's favor," Molly says, placing a kiss on Russell's forehead. Memories of the brief trial that set her free sweeps over her. "Look what you did for me—for us. I was thrilled to death when the judge called it a frivolous lawsuit. I will be forever grateful that you took the attention off me and threw the dirt on Dana." Throwing an arm around his neck, she pulls him close. "I was misguided and blind. It took loving you to realize I'd been played."

"I meant it when I said I was all yours. From the moment I first laid eyes on you, I felt like I won the lottery."

"I felt the same way. When you took me in your arms, I threw caution to the wind. Never before have I believed in love at first sight."

"Baby, we've hit a home run. My divorce will be final by the end of the month." Ring in hand, he struggles to get down on one knee. "Molly, will you marry me?"

"I want nothing more than to be your wife, but I'm not certain Preston was granted an annulment. My only concern is I don't have any assets to bring to the table. I worry that if you leave me, I'll be as poor as a church mouse."

"Regarding your annulment, I'll call Preston's lawyer. I will never leave you, and you will never have to worry about money ever again." Fumbling about, he pulls a note from his shirt pocket. "As a token of my undying love, I opened an account in the Cayman Islands in your name. This is the account information. I transferred funds this morning, but just say you'll marry me."

"Yes, yes, yes! I love you, Russell, with all my heart. I'm only sorry your wife put up such a struggle. I know, in time, she will come to accept your marriage was over long before I entered your life."

"The passion faded years ago. As for us, we're fortunate the Great State of Mississippi dismissed all the charges. We caught a break when the videos from the marina's surveillance cameras went missing. I admit, they had me worried when the wrongful death charge didn't stick, they would try to pin the home invasion, vandalism, and theft on you. It served in our favor when Dr. Fayne admitted inviting you into his home and giving you several pieces of his late wife's jewelry. I'm still surprised his lawyers didn't advise him he was coming into court with dirty hands. The old stick and rudder routine almost always fails."

"I'm not sure what you mean."

"He acted in bad faith and engaged in wrongdoing, while pointing fingers and pinning the blame on you. Some may say he was guilty of witness tampering."

"He certainly was. I can't believe Peggy lied to the police about the theft. It was by happenstance Preston found the missing pieces when I went by his house to offer my condolences. If I had known accepting them from him would cause such a stir, I would never have agreed to keep them."

"All that is behind us now. You are the best thing that has ever happened to me," he says, cupping her chin. "I'm due in court, but I'll be home in time for dinner. A celebration, perhaps."

"Every day with you is a celebration. I'll prepare duck à l'orange. When dinner is over, we'll move to the bedroom, where I'll satiate you with dessert."

"Maybe I can stay a minute longer," he says, placing a hand on his zipper.

"You know I want more than a minute with you," she says, recalling the little blue pill's lengthy response time. If forced to wait that long the next time, she will dash out for a manicure and a car wash. "If you hurry anyone, let it be the jury. I'll be waiting to celebrate. Now, off you go." Placing a kiss on the tip of his nose, she brushes his face with an open hand.

"If it's all right with you, we can skip the duck."

"Whatever you desire," she says, moving him toward the door.

Tucked behind the curtain, she watches from the window until his car is out of sight. Admiring the diamond he placed on her finger, she moves it to her right hand.

Keys in hand and with a smile on her face, Molly slides behind the Jaguar's leather steering wheel. Five months old, and the new-car smell continues to linger. In the following minutes, her thoughts turn to the old Audi. There was never a day it did not reek of cigarette smoke, sweat, and her profound cries for a better future. She would have given anything to see Clay's face when he toured the storage unit. Knowing his heart, she would bet her life he struggled to understand the secrets it held.

It was easy to avoid eye contact during the trial, but she could not dodge his mean-spirited words: *Conniving, heartless, evil bitch* he had called her, but Russell did not bat an eyelash. She had him under her spell since their first visit. It was an Oscar-winning performance when she fell into his arms, faking tears while pressing her hungry body against his. She has since learned it takes some time to sculpt the putty, but the bank receipt he forced into her hand will keep her motivated.

Easing up on the car's accelerator, she makes a left turn into the marina. The drive brings back a million memories—the good, the bad, and the horribly ugly, but none involving Peggy. Lifting her foot off the pedal, she cruises into a parking space and cuts the engine. A quick glance in the mirror puts a smile on her face. The days of wearing disguises are over. Stepping into the sun, she inhales the salty scent of the gulf. With a skip in her step, she makes her way to the *Hot-Ta-Molly* and into Preston's outstretched arms.

"I've missed you," he whispers, moving in for a kiss.

"Hold on, Preston. You know I love you and want to be with you, but you burned me."

"You started the fire."

"In the eyes of the court, I was found innocent. I need proof that you intend to be with me."

"Are you proposing?"

"I believe we are still married." Pulling away, she looks at him with sad eyes. "I need for you to be serious."

"What is it you want?"

"I would like for us to renew our vows. After that, I want fifty-thousand dollars in my bank account. I also want health insurance, a new car, and an engagement ring from Tiffany's. Don't choke on the size. I want at least eight carats."

"While I agree with you regarding our vows, how do you feel about wearing Peggy's ring?"

"Just between us, I can't believe she wore that pitiful thing out in public. Do us both a favor and trade it for a larger diamond."

"Are you serious? That 'pitiful' ring is worth a good chunk of change."

"We both know you have plenty of money. Your insurance policy came with a sizable payout. Some believe I helped put that cash in your wallet. I think you owe it to me, given what you've put me through."

"Regarding the fifty thousand, will you accept a check?"

"You should know better than to ask."

"How do you feel about gold?"

"If you're talking jewelry, I prefer platinum."

"Bars. I'm talking bars."

"Tell me how often you exchange gold bars in lieu of money."

"This will be a first."

"Cash, Preston. Make it a wire transfer."

"Can it wait until tomorrow?"

"Not if you want me today."

"By the way, what's up with you and your lawyer?"

"I'm staying in the guesthouse."

"Is his wife OK with this?"

"She hasn't said anything to me. I don't know if I should be sharing this with you, but she's not well. I'm taking care of her to pay my legal fees."

"How much do you owe?"

"Seventy grand."

"I'll give you the money. Pay him today and move to the boat. It doesn't look good for you to be seen coming and going from his house. On that note, I would like for you to meet my father. It's important to me."

"I have an aunt who raised me, along with three of her own, when my mom skipped town. We're not close."

"Do you know where your mom is?"

"In the rare times I am forced to say her name, I call her Rose. She wasn't much of a mother. When she walked out, I let her go."

Recalling the conversation he had with his father when Molly first arrived on the scene, the wheels in Preston's head take a hard and fast turn. "Where does your aunt live?"

"Outside Lula, near Clarksdale."

"Near Moon Lake?"

"You've heard of it?"

"Years back, I attended the Annual Juke Joint Festival. When my father was a young man in his early years, he spent some time in that part of the state. He had a relationship with a woman named Rose." Looking at her through different eyes, he gives her the once-over.

"Although I'm enjoying your walk down memory lane, I suggest we visit the bank."

"It'll have to be quick. I have a meeting with my insurance guy."

"Be sure to mention my name."

Chapter 82

"Thank you for seeing me," Molly says, taking a seat.

Rolling over the floor, Duncan studies the curl in her hair, the fire in her eyes, and the way she shifts about before settling into the chair. When she tosses her hair back and crosses her legs at the knee, he sees a bit of his mother in her. "Why are you here?"

"I thought it was time for us to meet."

"I know who you are and what you've become."

"Is that any way to talk to your daughter-in-law?" Looking across the room, she sets her focus on the picture above the fireplace. "Who is the bearded guy?"

"That bearded man is my great-grandfather."

"Kudos to family pics. I think I see a bit of myself in him—mostly in the eyebrows and our heart-shaped lips. I always say, every family should have a photographer."

"Enough with the Kodak moment. Let's get back to your future."

"Preston suggested we renew our vows," she says, waving the diamond ring she accepted from Russell. "He thought we should meet. I didn't have the heart to tell him I've known you my whole life."

"He can be so foolish at times."

"While that may be true, the same has been said of you. You left my mother to raise me. Your actions and negligence forced her to rely on public assistance."

"I provided for you. Every month, a check was sent to your mother. When your health was threatened, I paid the doctors. We never came to terms regarding your education, but your mother assured me she had it covered. As for supporting her, it wasn't my job. She was the state's responsibility. I had a wife and son to provide for."

"You should have thought about *them* before bedding my mother. It appears the men in your family have no problem planting seeds."

"What do you mean by that?"

"I'm expecting. Unlike my mother, I'll have it taken care of before the week is out."

"Does Preston know?"

"No."

"Best news I've heard all day."

"Tell me, do you honestly believe a check in the mail every month provided for me?"

"That ship has sailed. Tell me, what brings you here?"

"I told you. Preston wanted me to meet you."

"Why didn't he come with you?"

"I arrived here on my own for reasons he wouldn't understand."

"What do you want from me?"

"The list is long, but I'll start with cash."

"Lost moments can't be replaced with extortion."

"I'm making new memories. Preston tells me you've told him to stay away from me. Given his love for me, I think you will agree your fatherly advice isn't working."

"Given the pain and suffering you put Peggy through, I'm surprised he feels anything for you. Tell me, do you love him?"

"Much like you, I don't believe in love. I'm just moving through life. When the moment serves me, I dance to the music. Your generous deposit into my account will have me walking away and never looking back. I believe you'll agree your son isn't much of a catch.

He mirrors every man I've avoided. I believe these fools are meant to be briefly borrowed."

"When it comes to matters of the heart, my son travels his own road. I'm not giving in to blackmail."

"Forget blackmail. That's a piss in the bucket. I'll tell him about you and my mother. Knowing Preston, I'm not sure which will hurt him the most— understanding he's madly in love with his half-sister or learning you knew the truth all along. We have genetic sexual attraction. If this is foreign to you, it's an intense attraction between biological family members. It could be said you had a hand in this. Well, perhaps not your hand so much."

"He'll be over you before the next sunrise."

"Have it your way. In the coming minutes, Preston and I are heading to the courthouse. Would you care to join us?"

"You are something else."

"I am as much your daughter as Preston is your son."

"What will it take for you to go away?"

"Everything I've been denied."

"When it comes to you and your actions, I fear it is the bourbon talking."

"You have me confused with Peggy."

"Perhaps you should look to your mother to fill the potholes in your life."

"When you tossed her to the curb, she became a stranger to me."

"Give me the dollar amount and don't cheat on the pennies."

"One hundred grand."

"That's ludicrous."

"Think of it as money well spent. I'll be out of town before sunset. You have my word."

"Why should I trust you?"

"Again, I'm your daughter. Come on, Pops. The way I see it, you really don't have a choice. You should know my mother loved you. She saved every newspaper that mentioned your name or shared your face," she says, dropping her voice. "I understand you had a sister named Molly. I've been told she died in the car accident that put you in that wheelchair."

"Your mother loved everybody. As for my sister, leave her out of this. As for you, give me an hour to draw up a contract."

"I'll sign it, but my signature comes with a price."

"There is one caveat. I never want to see your face or hear your name ever again. Just so you know, it is worth every penny to be rid of you. Should you double-cross me, you can be damn sure there will be hell to pay. To be clear, I do not wish for you a lengthy life. I take some pleasure knowing hell and its fire will be your final resting place."

"Just so you know, I'll accept your hush money and move on, but I'll never erase what I know. As for hearing my name, and given your old age, I'm sure you are aware your days here are numbered."

CHAPTER 83

"Molly left me," Preston shares in a whisper.

"You were warned. It's possible she roped another unsuspecting victim," Duncan says with a smirk on his face.

"What should I do?"

"What you should have done before you tangled with her. Look toward the sky and thank your lucky stars."

Printed in the United States
by Baker & Taylor Publisher Services